Adrienne Chinn was born in Grand Falls, Newfoundland, grew up in Quebec, and eventually made her way to London, England after a career as a journalist. In England she worked as a TV and film researcher before embarking on a career as an interior designer, lecturer, and writer. When not up a ladder or at the computer, she can usually be found rummaging through flea markets or haggling in the Marrakech souk.

www.adrienne-chinn.co.uk

twitter.com/adriennechinn
facebook.com/AdrienneChinnAuthor
instagram.com/adriennechinn

Also by Adrienne Chinn

The Lost Letter from Morocco

The English Wife

LOVE IN A TIME OF WAR

ADRIENNE CHINN

One More Chapter
a division of HarperCollins*Publishers* Ltd
1 London Bridge Street
London SE1 9GF
www.harpercollins.co.uk

HarperCollins*Publishers*
1st Floor, Watermarque Building, Ringsend Road
Dublin 4, Ireland

This paperback edition 2022

1

First published in Great Britain in ebook format by
HarperCollins*Publishers* 2022

A catalogue record of this book is available from the British Library

ISBN: 978-0-00-851783-0

Printed and bound in the UK using 100% Renewable Electricity
by CPI Group (UK) Ltd

For my great-aunts, Marian Jessie Chinn, Ethel Starmer Chinn and Ethel May Fry, and my grandmother, Edith Adelaide Fry Chinn, whose lives as modern women in early 20th-century Britain, Egypt and Canada inspired this story.

'Sisters are different flowers from the same garden.'

– Unknown

Prologue

Christina

Capri, Italy – May 1891

The young woman follows the narrow path, scarcely more than the width of her booted foot, as it winds through the scrub grass that sprouts from the rocky dust-coloured earth. She skirts around the broom bushes that are heavy with tiny flowers the colour of the lemons she'd watched the lemonade seller squeeze for her not a half hour earlier.

Ahead of her in the distance, the three jagged stone triangles of the Faraglioni jut out of the glittering blue sea like the teeth of a giant aquatic dinosaur. There is a haze over the water today which erases the horizon line, so that the world beyond the island's limestone cliffs appears as one large canvas of blue.

She comes to rest on a flat rock under the spreading shade of a parasol pine. She looks around to check that she's alone, and when she's assured that she is, she pulls the pale blue skirt of her dress up to her knees and leans over to unlace her boots. When her white-stockinged feet are free of the suffocating leather, she wiggles her toes in the breeze that drifts up the cliffs from the sea.

The girl has a canvas satchel over her shoulder. She sets it in her lap and unties the leather string. She roots around the lemons inside the bag, and her damp forehead wrinkles in concentration. *Ah, yes! There it is.* Her fingers curl around the metal body of the pen – a new Waterman fountain pen imported from America, a gift from her father *'for your Italian lessons'* – and she pulls it out with a book. This is bound in fine green Moroccan leather pressed with curlicues and stylised leaves. Another gift, this one from her late mother's cousin, Stefania Albertini. Meant, she knows, for her to record her Italian grammar while she is on the island for the summer; but, really, far too pretty to be used for prepositions, conjunctions and interjections.

She opens the book and flips through the pages – only ten or so are covered in neat blue handwriting, as she's only been in Capri a week – until a blank sheet of creamy paper appears. Unscrewing the cap of her pen, she bends over the page and writes.

———

A young man stands at the top of the hill. He has been there for some time. If you were to ask him, he wouldn't be able to say how long. He has been watching the figure in the pale blue dress, has been transfixed by the movement of her hand over the pages of the book. And when she removes her hat, and the sun draws fire from her auburn hair, he is certain of two things: that she is everything, and that he is lost.

Part One

1913

Chapter One

The Frys

Clover Bar, London – February 1913

Nineteen-year-old Cecelia Fry gazes out at the rain as it showers down from the lead-grey sky, dousing the back garden of the family home – christened rather romantically Clover Bar by her mother when the scaffolding on the new house had yet to come down and the garden was nothing more than a quagmire of mud – with an unrelenting drizzle. In the tangled branches of the rowan tree beside the greenhouse, two tiny blue tits, their blue wings flapping as they bounce their round yellow bodies from branch to branch, twitter, seemingly oblivious to the rain.

She scans the long garden, noticing the first pale blossom opening on the winter-flowering cherry tree her sister Jessie and their father had planted the previous year. She frowns at the rivulets of water streaming over the glass panes of the old greenhouse, hoping the putty she'd caulked the seams with in October will solve the leakage, and notes that the Madame Alfred Carrière rose over the arch will need a pruning before the end of the month. A clump of snowdrops has opened under the column of the cedar, and their white bell-like flowers nod like heads as the silvery droplets rain down.

She wonders if it is raining in Heidelberg. She shuts her eyes and waits, with some impatience, as the sparkling blue eyes and the blond hair, the colour of wheat toasted by July sun, slowly materialise. He's laughing at her.

'You haven't finished "The Sorrows of Young Werther", Celie? Professor Obermeyer won't be pleased. You know he's in love with Goethe.'

'I'm finding Goethe rather hard going, Max.'

'Oh, it's Max now, is it? What happened to Herr Fischer, your respected German teacher?'

'You're only four years older than me. It's not like you're Professor Obermeyer, who looks about one hundred.'

Max laughs. 'What is the trouble you're having with Geothe's young Werther?'

'I find Werther's unrequited love for Charlotte terribly upsetting. It's all so … so … emotional.'

'Emotional? This is the very core of "Sturm und Drang" literature. You are a good English girl, Celie Fry. Suspicious of passion. Always with the stiff upper lip.'

'I don't believe I'm like that at all.'

The blue eyes twinkle. 'I think, sometimes, that it's a pity you're a woman.'

'Whatever do you mean?'

'Professor Obermeyer is quite disturbed that an Englishwoman is top of his German literature class. I heard him complaining to Professor Klemm in the Old Crown Pub. Obermeyer says you never say a word in his class, though your papers are exceptional. You need to have more confidence in yourself, Celie. With a mind like yours, you could be anything if you were a man. Become a professor, or a lawyer like I shall.'

'I've tried to speak up in class, Max, but everyone talks over me, as if I'm not even there. Why are young men so confident in their opinions? Anyway, I don't need to run the world. I'm happy enough to be learning German. It brought us together, didn't it?'

'For that I am most grateful.'

'I thought I might teach German at a ladies' college when I'm proficient enough, though I shall have to convince Mama. She thinks me studying German is an awful waste of my time and Papa's money. She says I spend too much time with my nose in books, and says I should be perfecting my piano playing or needlework to become a good wife, "seeing as you have no vocation like Jessie, or artistic talent like Etta". That's what she said. It quite hurt my feelings. If it weren't for Papa… He always supports all of us girls. He says he wants nothing more than for us to be happy.'

'Your father sounds like a good man.'

'He is. Do you know why I wanted to learn German, Max?'

'No. Tell me.'

'We had a German nanny when I was a little girl. Miss Neumann. She was from Hannover and had very pretty blonde hair. She'd sing us German lullabies and she taught me and my sisters some German words. Schnitzel … and strudel, and … and bratwurst. Miss Neumann said apple strudel was her favourite food. Apfelstrudel; I always remembered that. I've wanted to try it ever since.'

'One day, schatzi, we shall visit my family in Heidelberg and we shall eat all the apfelstrudel you wish.'

'Schatzi?'

Max smiles, and it is like the rising sun cresting a hill. 'Sweetheart.'

She smiles at the memory and moves away from the window; she's been reading too many of Etta's romance novels. She picks up her grey felt hat, newly adorned with pale blue rosette ribbons, and sets it on her head, adjusting the pearl-headed hatpin and tucking away a wayward strand of auburn hair. She shrugs into her grey tweed coat and wraps her new lavender mohair scarf – a Christmas present from the twins – around her neck.

Max will be returning from Germany soon, and she will be back to her studies at University College now that her father is on the mend. She's glad she has been able to run his photography studio during his illness, even if it has meant missing the first few weeks of classes, but Jessie certainly couldn't have been expected to interrupt her nursing training, and Etta ... well, that would never have worked. As for her mother ... Celie smiles at the thought of her mother squinting into a camera lens. What a ridiculous notion. No, it had to be her. Everyone can rely on good old Celie.

'Papa's temperature's down. Half a degree off normal.' Jessie Fry shakes out the thermometer and slides it into her leather nursing chatelaine beside the tongue depressor and forceps. 'You'll be right as rain in no time, Papa.'

Gerald Fry struggles to sit up against the stack of fat pillows. 'You're a good girl, Jessie. I'm glad we had you.'

His wife Christina adjusts the pillows behind his head. 'Jessica has been an absolute treasure since you fell ill with this fever, Gerald. She will be a credit to King's College Hospital when she graduates this summer.'

'I have such good daughters. I'm a lucky man.' He points to the pitcher on the bedside table. 'Pour me a glass of water, would you, Tina? My throat is as parched as the Sahara.'

Christina fills a glass and sits on the bed. She watches her husband as he drinks. He looks older, she thinks, all of his vitality drained away, like a grape shrivelled by the sun. What would have happened if he hadn't recovered from the fever? Three unmarried daughters, and she doing all she could to hold the household together on Gerald's modest savings? It doesn't bear thinking about.

Gerald hands her the glass. 'Thank you, my dear. Where's Etta? I miss her sweet face.'

Christina and Jessie exchange a look above Gerald's head. Jessie gathers up the dirty sheets. 'I have to get back to the hospital, Papa. We're observing an appendectomy this afternoon. If there's peritonitis, it's likely to be quite messy.'

Christina shudders, her thick auburn hair threatening to unleash itself from the careful rolls of her pompadour. 'Really, Jessica. Must you be so graphic?'

'I have to learn. I've decided I want to become a surgical nurse.'

'Whyever would you wish to do such a horrid thing?' Christina sweeps her hand behind her ear and taps her hair in an unconscious gesture. 'You should be going out and about to exhibitions and recitals with Etta, and meeting other young people, instead of burying your nose in those textbooks day in and day out. Frankly, I'm rather shocked at the content of some of them.'

'You've looked at my textbooks?'

'A mother needs to know what her daughters are reading.'

'How else am I meant to learn anatomy, Mama? You want me to gad about London like Etta and her art school friends? We may be twins, but we're nothing alike. We don't even look the same. At any rate, I have no intention of marrying anyone. Ever.'

'Don't be ridiculous, Jessica.'

Gerald clears his throat. 'Tina—'

'Mama, this is the twentieth century. There are things a woman can do other than marry.'

'Like what, may I ask?'

'The world is a big place, Mama, and I intend to see it. I have no intention of ending up married to a boring husband with a brood of children in a house in the London suburbs.'

Christina raises a fine arched eyebrow. 'Quite.'

Jessie clamps her lips together. 'I didn't mean it like that. I just meant I want something different. I want an adventurous life.'

Christina rises from the bed and collects the empty pitcher. 'I should be very interested to know how you intend to accomplish that on a nurse's salary.'

The bedroom door slams against the robins and strawberries wallpapering the wall.

'Papa!' Eighteen-year-old Etta May Fry flies into the room, her dress a froth of white lace and cotton lawn. She throws her arms around her father and swallows him into her white cloud. 'I've brought you a present.' She pulls a small red felt bag out of her pocket. 'Give me your hand.'

'Oh, pet, I don't need a present.'

'Your hand, Papa.' She unties the yellow drawstring and shakes out a small grey stone onto his palm.

Jessie huffs. 'A stone? All this palaver for a stone, Etta?'

'It's not just a stone, Jessie. Look at it, Papa.'

Gerald inspects the flat round shape and the ridges that curve along the spiralling spine. 'Hand me my spectacles, pet. Over there on the table.'

Etta sets the spectacles on her father's nose. 'There. Very distinguished.'

Gerald's long, thin face breaks into a smile under his greying moustache. 'An ammonite. Look, Tina.' He points at the spirals and the ridges. 'It's a fossil. Millions of years old. From the time of the dinosaurs. This is just wonderful. Wherever did you get this, Etta?'

'Jenny Bradley's cousin Edith lives in Charmouth and she's always finding fossils on the beaches down there. Jenny gave it to me.'

Christina frowns at Etta's tousled blonde curls. 'Etta, where's your tortoiseshell comb? Your hair's all over the place.'

Etta tucks the escaping strands behind her ears. 'I lost it.'

'I had better not see it in Jenny's hair the next time she's here for tea.'

'You won't, Mama.' Etta smiles sweetly at her mother. 'I shall tell her not to wear it.'

Chapter Two

Jessie

King's College Hospital, London – February 1913

Jessie hastens through the iron gates in front of the handsome red brick and grey stone building, the new home of Denmark Hill's pride and joy – so new the king hadn't even officially opened it yet – King's College Hospital. The caretaker tips his cap and ushers her along with an exaggerated sweep of his arms. "'Urry along there, nursie. You don't want Matron after you.'

Jessie flashes the elderly man a quick smile. 'I most certainly don't, Mr Little. I should make it just in time.'

She dashes under the hospital's impressive Doric portico, across the lobby's gleaming terrazzo floor and up the stairs to the first floor two at a time. She stuffs her navy wool cape into a cupboard and secures her starched cap over her hair with several hair grips.

'Hurry up, Jessie! Matron has her clipboard out.' A plump young nurse with hair the colour of milk chocolate grabs her arm and pulls

Jessie down the corridor. 'It's almost two. It'll be us cleaning the lavatories again if we're even a minute late.'

'I'm coming, Elsie! You're pulling my arm off!'

They push through the heavy swing door into the operating theatre's washing area. The tall, angular figure of the matron stands in the doorway; she taps her clipboard with the rubber end of a pencil. 'What am I meant to tell Mr Goodfellow when my nurses swan into theatre late? That you'd been enjoying a pleasant lunch and lost track of time?'

'No, Matron,' Jessie says. 'We're terribly sorry.'

Elsie nods. 'Yes, terribly sorry, Matron.'

'It will not happen again, am I understood?'

'Yes, Matron. Understood.'

'Find a place at the back of the observation stand.'

'Yes, Matron.'

Inside the theatre, the surgeon, Mr Goodfellow, is having a white cotton mask tied onto his face by an attending nurse. The anaesthetist, already swaddled in a clean white gown, though he has eschewed a cap and mask, sits on a metal stool behind the patient's head, shaking out drops of chloroform onto a gauze mask. The patient lies on the operating table under a sheet, moon-faced and wide-eyed, staring at the ceiling. Jessie hears her mumbling as she rushes past. *Hail Mary, Mother of God, the Lord is with thee...*

Jessie follows Elsie onto the observation platform behind the crowd of nursing students. She jabs her elbow into Elsie's side. 'Shove over, Elsie. I need to be able to see.'

'Fry, one moment. I wish to speak to you.'

'Good luck,' Elsie whispers as she pushes past with the other nursing students.

'Yes, Matron?'

She taps her clipboard with her pen. 'I have the results of the anatomy examination. I was quite astonished by the results. Yours in particular, Fry.'

Jessie gulps, her throat suddenly sucked dry of saliva. *I'm in for it now. I should never have gone to the suffragist meeting with Celie the night before an exam. What was I thinking?*

'I am quite accustomed to disappointment in my position, Fry. So many girls enter into the profession without a clear understanding of the skills and fortitude a nurse requires and I often find myself questioning the motives of some of my charges. I have just heard that Phipps is leaving to marry Dr Jones-Field. You have no such aspirations, I should hope.'

'Oh, no, Matron. I want to be a surgical nurse once I graduate.'

'You feel you're a suitable candidate for such a demanding specialty? You've been tardy twice this month. What am I meant to think about your dedication?'

'I'm – I'm terribly sorry. My father's been ill with a fever. I've been nursing him at home. The tram and bus from Hither Green aren't always on time.'

The matron sniffs.

'He's much better now.'

The senior nurse peers across the top of the document at Jessie. 'You've achieved a perfect grade on the anatomy examination, Fry. This is the first time this has been accomplished.'

'I did?'

The matron narrows her eyes. 'Are you certain you wish to specialise as a surgical nurse? It's extremely demanding. It requires a great deal of stamina.'

'Oh, yes. I have a strong constitution.'

'I nursed for the British Army in South Africa during the Boer War. That required quite a strong constitution. Have you considered joining the Queen Alexandra's Imperial Military Nursing Service? I am involved on its executive committee, and I believe you might be a suitable candidate.'

'Become an army nurse? But we're not at war.'

'Not currently. Consequently, we have only three hundred nurses trained for military nursing, which is woefully inadequate should the situation change. Should you be selected, you would continue with your surgical training here at King's, but as a Queen Alexandra's nurse, until such time as you are required abroad.'

'Abroad?'

'Of course. Wars are generally fought abroad. I should like to put your name forward to the committee.'

Jessie's heart beats a drum in her chest. 'That would be... Yes, yes, please.'

The matron's dark eyebrows draw together. 'Army nursing is a difficult life for a young woman. You are posted wherever the army needs you. Your life isn't your own. You mustn't fraternise with doctors or soldiers. If you marry, you must leave the service.'

'That suits me perfectly. I don't intend to marry any time soon. If ever.'

The nurse nods. 'What will your parents think of this?'

'They'll be fine. They're very supportive.'

The matron eyes Jessie. She scribbles something onto the document. 'I'm recommending you for immediate advancement into the surgical specialty. I suspect we may need trained surgical nurses sooner rather than later. The world is not a peaceful place, Fry. I believe war is inevitable.'

Chapter Three

Christina

Capri, Italy – June 1891

Christina Bishop wanders past the lemonade stand on the Via Matteotti where she'd bought lemons earlier in the day. Its green-tiled counter is laden with baskets of fat yellow lemons and oranges as large as grapefruit. Bunches of fragrant lemons dangle from the woven cane canopy that shades customers from the searing sun. Behind the counter, a sturdy, middle-aged Caprese with a crop of ink black hair shiny with a slick of pomade puts his fingers to his lips and kisses them with a loud, smacking sound. He holds up a glass and a lemon.

'*Buona giornata, signorina! Sei bellissima! Vuoi un bicchiere di limonata?'*

'*Non … no, grazie. Multo grazie.'*

The man laughs. '*Non com quello. "No, grazie mille, Leonardo. Non*

15

voglio un bicchiere di limonata."' He urges her, with a roll of his hand, to repeat.

'He's saying, "No, thank you, Leonardo. I don't want a glass of lemonade."'

Christina looks behind her. A young Englishman in a beige linen suit, which, though impeccably tailored, seems somehow at odds with his sturdy shoulders and solid body, lifts his straw boater and inclines his head. He smiles and waves at the lemonade seller. *'Pronto, Leonardo!'*

Leonardo grunts. Muttering, he saws through a lemon with a large knife.

'Thank you, but I know what he said.' Christina turns and heads down the cobbled lane.

The Englishman falls into step beside her. 'I'm terribly sorry. I shouldn't presume. You simply looked rather confused. I could tell from your accent that you're not Italian.'

'My mother is Italian. She was born here in Capri.'

'Surely your mother must speak Italian to you at home?'

'Mama passed away in February. The Russian flu.'

A shadow falls across the young man's face. 'Oh, I'm terribly sorry.' He stops abruptly in the middle of the lane. 'I've been incredibly rude. You must be wondering who this bloody fellow is.'

'Not particularly.'

'Dash it. And I'd been so hoping to make a good impression. I have to remind myself I'm not with the rowing chaps at Cambridge.' He extends a hand. 'I'm Harry. Harry Grenville.'

'I really must be going.'

He drops his hand. 'Yes, of course. Are you … are you in Capri for long?'

Christina sweeps a cool blue gaze over the young Englishman. 'Good day, Mr Grenville. Thank you for the help with the lemonade, though, as I said, it wasn't required.' She heads down the lane, her pale blue dress swinging around her black-booted feet.

'Are you on the island for the summer?' he shouts after her.

She pauses at the turning into Via Federico Serena, and looks back up past the Via Matteotti's bougainvillea-lined garden walls. 'Until the end of September.'

Harry's heart leaps. 'What's your name?'

A smile tugs at the corners of her mouth. 'Christina.'

He whoops and throws his hat into the air, but it catches on the sprawling branches of an arbutus tree. He turns towards the auburn-haired girl, but she is gone, though the music of her laughter floats up the lane through the rosemary-scented air.

The iron gate into the tiny front garden of Villa Serenissima creaks as Christina pushes it open. She glances up the street but sees no sign of the young Englishman. A judder of disappointment takes her by surprise. *How silly. I'll probably never see him again.*

'Tina? Is that you?'

Christina shuts the gate and climbs the stone steps. The patio is paved with terracotta tiles which are chipped and faded by years of exposure to the Caprese weather. Pots of musky-scented scarlet pelargoniums cluster around the edges of the patio, and a small marble fountain with its water-spilling cupid adds a looping aquatic melody to the shaded spot.

'*Sì, Cugina Stefania.* It's me.'

Stefania Albertini greets her in the loggia outside the villa's arched front door. The woman, no taller than Christina's shoulders, even accounting for her black bouffant pompadour, is dressed in a high-necked white shirt with full sleeves and ruffles across her full bosom, and her long navy linen skirt is cinched – as much as her stout waist will allow – with a wide brown leather belt. 'You have the lemons, Tina? Liliana has been waiting for two hours to make her *Torta Caprese Bianca.*'

'Yes, I have them. Lovely fat ones from Leonardo.' She kisses her mother's cousin lightly on her plump cheeks.

'Leonardo? Who's Leonardo?'

'The lemonade seller.' Christina digs into her satchel and produces a lemon. The skin is waxy and lumpy in her hand.

Stefania ushers Christina across the lobby's glazed floral tiles, decorated with exuberance by some eighteenth-century ceramicist from Vietri sul Mare on the Amalfi Coast in hues of vivid blue and yellow, and into the large white-painted sitting room. Underneath its soaring vaulted ceiling, the room is filled with heavily-carved antique Baroque walnut furniture, waxed by the housekeeper, Liliana, to a high sheen. Two large settees upholstered in mint green silk damask, fraying along the arms where the sunlight persists in eating away the fibres, face each other across a large Persian rug. A light breeze drifts in from the balcony beyond the sitting room and brushes across Christina's damp face like a lover's caress.

'Go sit outside where it's cool, Tina. We'll have some *tisana* and speak Italian.' Stefania reaches out to take the satchel from Christina.

'One minute. I … I need my notebook and pen.'

Stefania checks the gold metal watch pinned to her ruffled blouse with an impatient sigh as Christina roots around inside the satchel. 'You are learning well about Italian time, *cara mia*. The lemons will start growing into trees in that bag.'

'I'm sorry.' Christina retrieves the items and hands her cousin the satchel.

Stefania nods. 'When I come back, you can tell me what you did for the past two hours while we were waiting for the lemons.'

She strides across the Persian carpet toward a doorway at the far end of the vaulted sitting room, her skirt swishing around her ankles. *'Liliana! Liliana! Finalmente ho i limoni!'*

Chapter Four

Celie

Blackheath Halls, London – February 1913

'Etta! Hurry up! Don't forget your pin.'

Celie checks her reflection in the hallway mirror and adjusts the red, white and green National Union of Women's Suffrage Societies pin on the lapel of her tweed coat.

Etta clomps down the carpeted stairs and exhales a dramatic sigh. 'Do I have to come? It's so *boring*. All these women going on and on about the vote. What does it really matter? We've all managed perfectly fine all these years the way it is.'

'The NUWSS ladies have important things to say, Etta,' Celie says as she pins an NUWSS pin onto Etta's coat lapel. 'The least we can do is take one night out of our week to listen to them.'

'I guess.'

Jessie pulls on her gloves. 'Why should we intelligent, capable women give away our autonomy – our feminine voices – to the patriarchal society that holds us in chains, Etta?'

'You sound just like Christabel Pankhurst in *The Suffragette*, Jessie.'

'What do you expect when your own government is jailing and beating women for voicing their opinions? What they're doing to those poor women on hunger strike is outrageous. You do want to be heard, don't you, Etta?'

Etta tugs on her kid gloves. 'I suppose.'

Christina emerges from the sitting room, her grey wool skirt sweeping along the polished encaustic tiles. A wrinkle draws a fine line across her pale forehead. 'You're not going to another one of those suffragist meetings, are you?'

'Yes, Mama,' Celie says as she pushes aside the brocade curtain over the front door. 'We won't be late. It's only over at Blackheath Halls. Why don't you come? Mayor Jackson's wife is always there.'

'Why in the world would I wish to associate myself with mentally unstable women?'

'What do you mean?'

'You know as well as I do that we women have monthly … issues which affect our emotional state.'

Jessie grunts. 'What has that to do with anything?'

'I wouldn't wish to be governed by a woman in an emotional state, would you, Jessica?'

'Queen Victoria managed it for over sixty years.'

'And there was Elizabeth the First,' Etta pipes in.

Christina huffs. 'They were queens. They hardly count.'

'They were women just as you or I, Mama,' Celie says.

'Be that as it may, I think giving women the vote upsets the natural balance of femininity, Cecelia. We have our own natural sphere of influence in our homes and with our families. I don't understand why you can't be satisfied with that. You can wield all the power you wish in the home.'

'We're not married, Mama,' Jessie says. 'Ergo, we're powerless.'

'Once you're married, that will all change.'

'Then we're held hostage by our husband and children. That's why I want to be a nurse. I want to be in control of my life.'

'Honestly, Jessica, that is the most ridiculous thing I've ever heard. Being a wife and a mother is a joy.'

Celie slides an umbrella out of the brass umbrella stand. 'I want that too, Mama. Truly I do. But I feel I have every right to have a say in the running of my own country. Women in New Zealand and Australia have been given the vote. Why not here?'

Christina harrumphs. 'Former penal colonies. They are hardly the best of examples, Cecelia.'

Jessie rolls her eyes. 'As long as the government quashes every suffrage bill that is tabled, I'll be going to these meetings.' She beckons to Etta, who has slumped to a seat on the carpeted stairs. 'Are you coming?'

Etta rises from the step with a yawn. 'I'm coming, but don't expect me to chain myself to any railings.'

'Miss Fry! If I may have a word?'

Celie turns toward the woman's voice. The slender figure of the organisation's revered founder approaches through the crowd.

Millicent Fawcett extends her hand to Celie. 'I'm delighted to make your acquaintance, Miss Fry.' She clasps Celie's hand in a firm grip and points towards a pair of wooden chairs. 'Come, let's sit. I have a proposal which I wish to discuss with you.'

Celie's heart beats so loudly that she's sure the esteemed Mrs Fawcett can hear it. 'Mrs Fawcett, if I may say how much of an honour it is to—'

'Enough of that, Miss Fry.' Mrs Fawcett sits down, her back as straight as a walking stick. Although she is well past sixty, not a strand of grey threads the deep chestnut brown of the woman's neatly pinned-up hair.

'I wanted to say, Miss Fry, how impressed I was by your comments during the meeting this evening. I, too, believe very strongly that something must be done to rehabilitate the image of the suffrage campaign.' She shakes her head, and the fine lines that crease her high forehead deepen. 'Our cause has become stained by the militancy of some of our compatriots in Mrs Pankhurst's society. I believe that our cause will only succeed if people sympathise with it, rather than fight against it.'

Celie's stomach flutters. 'Yes, I couldn't agree more, Mrs Fawcett.'

'I have no doubt whatever that we must support our movement by argument, based on common sense and experience, and not by personal violence or lawbreaking of any kind.'

'Yes, of course.'

Mrs Fawcett exhales a deep sigh. 'I believe that, in order to succeed in our mutual endeavour of securing votes for women, the NUWSS should organise a peaceful, joyful event of solidarity. Mrs Pankhurst's members will be welcome, so long as they understand that this is to be a peaceful event. We're proposing a march, Miss Fry.'

'A suffragist march?'

'Mrs Harley of the Shropshire Society of the NUWSS proposed the idea, and I believe a march of peaceful suffragists, women and men, to London from all corners of Britain, would be just the thing to turn the tide of public opinion in our favour. We shall march to Hyde Park where we shall hold a suffragist rally. And from there, I shall lead a deputation to Prime Minister Asquith himself at Downing Street. He will see that women are people as well as men; that we have the right to be seen as human beings with a voice.'

Celie's breath catches in her throat. 'Yes, absolutely, Mrs Fawcett. This is exactly what is needed. What can I do to help?'

'You, Miss Fry, will help me organise it.'

Celie stretches her arms as the final notes of 'Macushla' fade away. She sits back on the piano stool and stares at the ivory keys. She tinkles two keys, then stops abruptly.

'Mama?'

Christina looks up from the purple iris she is embroidering on a large square of white linen. 'Yes, Cecelia?'

Celie spins around on the stool. 'When you met Papa, how did you know he was the one you would marry? Did you know right away?'

Christina slides the needle through the linen and pulls the purple thread through. 'Your father was a very nice man. And kind. Very kind.'

'Of course. But when did you *know* he was the one who was set on this earth for you? When did you know you would marry Papa?'

Christina glances over at her daughter. 'Love is not always what you might think, Cecelia.' The corners of her mouth twitch. 'It was when he bought me a box of chocolate cannoli from Terroni's.'

'Cannoli? You fell in love with Papa because of cannoli?'

'*Chocolate* cannoli.' Christina snips the thread and pulls a purple strand off a thick skein of wool.

Celie taps at a piano key. 'Do you think love can survive separation?'

Christina sets the embroidery in her lap. 'Whyever are you asking a question like that?'

'I… Well … there's a young man. His name is Maximilian Fischer. He … he teaches the German classes at University College.'

'A German?'

'Yes. He's in Heidelberg at the moment visiting his family. His little stepbrother broke his leg skiing—'

Christina peers at her daughter. 'Who exactly is this Maximilian Fischer?'

'You'd like Max … Mr Fischer, Mama. He's ever so polite. His contract at University College ends next year. Then he's planning to return to Heidelberg to study law.'

'Surely there must be a nice young Englishman in one of your classes who would be more appropriate.'

'Mama, Max and I … we have an understanding.'

Christina's fine eyebrows shoot skyward. 'An understanding? Has he proposed? Without speaking to your father first?'

'No, no. Nothing like that.'

'I see.' Christina yanks the purple thread through the needle. 'He's been a gentleman?'

Celie's eyes widen. 'Of course. He's a perfect gentleman, Mama. The thing is, he's returning to Germany for the summer and Mrs Fawcett of the NUWSS has just asked me to help her organise a suffragist march and a rally in Hyde Park this July. I – I'd been hoping—'

'A march? You won't be chaining yourself to railings?'

'Oh, no. Mrs Fawcett doesn't believe in violent means. She believes we need to cultivate the support of the population and of government, rather than ostracise people. It's a huge honour to be singled out like this by her. The thing is—'

'And you feel capable of taking on such a task? You've never struck me as a leader.'

'The thing is, Mama, I had hoped that I might go to Heidelberg to take an advanced German course this summer—'

Christina drops her needlepoint into her lap. 'You cannot be serious, Cecelia.'

'You've said that I should be braver, like Jessie, or get out more, like Etta, Mama. I –I've found a rooming house for women students. It's not dear at all. Papa thought it might be all right—'

'Your father's agreed to this folly?'

'He said it would be all right … if you agreed. I haven't told Max yet. I wanted to speak to you first. Papa said he'd take the train to Paris with me, then set me on the train to Heidelberg. Max will meet me there. It's all perfectly safe.'

'I absolutely do not agree to this, Cecelia. Travelling across Europe without a chaperone? Into the arms of a … a…' She picks up the needlepoint and stabs the needle into the heart of the iris. 'It sounds to me that this marching project has come along at quite an opportune time, Cecelia. Our Lord is looking out for you.'

'You think I should stay in London and help organise the march?'

'I have no doubt it will be a stretch for you, but I think it is by far the best option.'

Celie ponders the piano keys as an uneasy silence settles over the sitting room.

Chapter Five

The Frys

Hither Green, London – March 1913

Etta ducks under a string hung with drying sepia photographs of new mothers with fat babies dressed in puffy white dresses; serious, moustachioed men in their best suits; and newlyweds looking to their futures with frowns of consternation. The studio's glass-panelled ceiling is hung with white sheets that her mother has sewn together into one large swathe of fabric which can be raised or lowered over the window on a pulley system. A mahogany full-plate camera the size of a coal box – a recent acquisition by her father from Marion & Company in Soho Square – sits, draped with a paisley shawl, astride a wooden wheeled tripod, its brass lens aimed at a painted backdrop of a rural idyll. Scattered around the room, wicker chairs, potted ferns, busts, branch-wood settees, oriental screens, bassinets, parasols and rugs await their selection for the next photography session at Frederick J. Fry and Son Photographers.

She drops her wet umbrella into a Chinese ceramic urn and unbuttons her coat. 'Papa? Celie? Where are you?'

Her father answers from behind a black velvet curtain. 'In here, dove. Cleaning the camera plates.'

Etta hurries across the old Persian rug which Celie has arranged so that the fraying end is well out of view of the camera's lens, and pulls open the curtain. Gerald Fry looks up from the enamel sink where he's scraping excess gelatine emulsion off the back of a glass plate.

'Careful, pet. Don't knock over the developing fluid. Celie, where's the lid?'

Celie reaches into her apron pocket and hands the lid to her sister. 'Etta, put this on the bottle, will you, please?' She pours a splash of bleach into a copper tub full of water. 'The bath's ready, Papa.'

He hands Celie the glass plate, then he glances at Etta, who is shuffling through a stack of recent prints. 'Have you come to help, dove?'

Etta laughs, the sound floating like fairground music over the studio's industrious silence. 'Heavens, no. I'm off to my painting lesson in Camberwell. Mama asked me to stop by and remind you that Mr Jeffries and his son from the auctioneers are coming for dinner tonight. She asked if you can pick up some cheese on your way home. Good cheese. And not to be late. They're coming at six-thirty.'

'I'll wager Mama will sit you beside Mr Jeffries' son, Etta,' Celie says as she hands the clean glass plate to her father. 'How do you fancy being an auctioneer's wife?'

'I don't fancy it at all. I intend to live an artistic life full of interesting, bohemian people.'

Gerald sets the glass plate in a wooden rack to dry. 'I fear young

Mr Jeffries won't be meeting his future Mrs Jeffries this evening. Your mother is destined to be disappointed once again.'

Thomas Jeffries stabs his mahogany cane into the puddle at the omnibus stop on Hither Green Lane and eases his bulk off the bus's step and onto the pavement. He adjusts his black felt derby over his thick head of white hair and draws up the collar of his black wool coat. 'Blasted weather. It's cold enough to freeze Peary's dogs.'

Thomas's eldest son, Frank, steps off the bus and dodges the puddle. 'I expect Commander Peary's dogs would find this to be rather on the balmy side for them, Father, being as they were from the Arctic.'

'This cab strike nonsense is a bloody nuisance. How's anyone meant to get anywhere?'

Frank points at the bus lumbering south, the Oakey's Knife Polish advertisement on the back bouncing with every dip of a tyre into a watery pothole. 'By taking the omnibus, Father. How the other half lives.'

Thomas removes his pince-nez and wipes the steamed lenses on his cashmere scarf. He sets the spectacles back on his nose and runs his hand down his meticulously groomed white beard. 'I'm far too old to be interested in how the other half lives, Frank. Come the new year I shall have my feet up in my study in Nuneaton doing crosswords and reading the papers, and you, my son, will have the joy of running the London office.' He taps his nose. 'Which reminds me, we must stop into Christie's tomorrow morning and see Mr Jamieson about the William III desk we have in storage. No doubt they can sell that to one of the Mayfair lot for a pretty penny. Your mother has her heart set on a new bathroom suite, complete with a red enamel bath, and Mrs Jeffries' aspirations are my directives. When you have a wife, you'll understand this.'

Frank stops in front of a handsome bay-windowed semi-detached house. Three pollarded cherry trees stand sentinel behind the beige London brick wall. He pushes open the black iron gate and ushers his father ahead of him along the black and white tiled path.

Thomas rings the doorbell. 'I'll wager you five shillings they'll serve roast chicken.'

'Five shillings! My wages won't stretch to that. My employer is tight.'

'You have free room and board, and a laundry service, in a very nice house in Pimlico. You have no need for a great deal of money, my boy. Money only causes young men to get into trouble.'

Milly Smith, the Frys' maid of all work, ushers the Jeffries men into the sitting room and disappears down the hallway carrying their hats and coats. Gerald rises from his favourite leather armchair and sets down *The Illustrated London News* as he extends his hand to the senior Mr Jeffries.

'Gentlemen, I'm delighted to welcome you to our home. Come, come. Do have a seat. It's so much nicer to discuss business in this environment than in an office, wouldn't you agree?'

Thomas Jeffries settles into an armchair slipcovered in a cheerful floral chintz, while Frank finds a perch at the end of the chaise longue which sits pride of place in the centre of the room. Thomas points at the newspaper as Gerald sits in his chair.

'What do you think about this airship scare? They're saying the Germans sent one over Sheerness in October. It's just a matter of time before the eastern sky is full of them, I say.'

Gerald opens the newspaper to the double-page spread. 'It says here that there have been reports of airship sightings all over Britain this winter.'

'Figments of people's imagination, I should think,' Frank says.

Thomas raises a thick white eyebrow and throws his cool grey gaze at his son. 'Do you now, Frank? What has made you such an expert on the subject?'

Frank clears his throat. 'The *Spectator* and the *Economist* had articles on this very subject this week. The consensus is that people are panicking and their imaginations are running away with them. They're not even sure that the Sheerness incident wasn't just a lost pilot from the navy's flight training school in Eastchurch.'

Thomas sniffs loudly. 'If Germany wishes to send airships over Britain there's no one to stop her since we're so far behind in the air. One of these days we may wake up, mark my words.'

As Christina sweeps into the room from the hallway, the men rise in unison. 'What's all this about airships, Gerald? We're meant to be discussing the sale of Papa's furniture, aren't we, gentlemen?'

Gerald smiles at his wife. She has dressed in the maroon silk dress he likes so well, and her auburn hair in its pompadour shines with a golden lustre in the gaslight. Two years past forty, and still as beautiful as the day she'd walked into his father's photographic studio over twenty years before. 'Christina, my dear. May I introduce Mr Thomas Jeffries and his son, Mr Frank Jeffries, from Jeffries Auctioneers.'

'Delighted, gentlemen.' She gestures towards the hallway. 'If I may interrupt what sounds like a fascinating discussion, Milly has prepared a delicious dinner for us this evening. Our daughters will be joining us. I do hope you like roast chicken.'

Gerald pulls back the bedcovers and slips into the large brass bed beside Christina. 'That was a success, I should think.'

Christina sets down her novel. 'Do you think so?'

'I do. I managed to talk the old man down to a five per cent commission. We should easily afford the storage fees we've been accumulating on your father's furniture over the past eighteen months.'

'Why did my horrid Aunt Henrietta feel she had any right to contest Papa's will? It's because of Mama, I'm sure of it. The aunts never accepted her.'

'Of course they did.'

'No, they didn't. The Catholic daughter of an Italian plasterer? She was never going to accept me as Papa's heir.'

'You have no worries about that now, my dear. Her claim has been thrown out of the court.'

'But she has the house. That beautiful house in Portman Square *and* the Yorkshire house. What does she need with two houses? She's on her own since Aunt Margaret passed away.'

'The house was in your grandfather's name, not your father's. And we have a house. A very nice house.'

'In Hither Green.' She glares at her husband. '*Below* the Thames.'

Thomas leans across the bed and gives his wife a peck on her cheek. 'Good night, my love.' He settles back against the pillow and, after tugging the covers up to his chin, shuts his eyes.

Christina examines her husband's exhausted face. 'I'm sorry, Gerald. Clover Bar is a very nice house.' She picks up her book, the latest from Mrs Glyn, and closes the cover. 'Poor Etta tried so hard with that young Frank Jeffries.'

Gerald grunts. 'He's duller than a Victorian shilling. His father has him under his thumb.'

'At least she tried. Jessica spent the evening with her nose in a book, and was exceptionally rude when she did say anything. Imagine asking him how he should like to be force-fed through a tube for expressing his convictions! I feel I must apologise to young Mr Jeffries. She's such a strong-willed girl.'

'Just like her mother.'

'I was never like that.'

Gerald rolls his head toward his wife. 'Celie made an effort to smooth things over with Mr Jeffries. She's a safe pair of hands.'

'Gerald, did you tell Cecelia she could study in Germany this summer? I have no intention of permitting my daughter to gallivant across Europe unaccompanied.'

Gerald sits up against the pillows. 'She's told you about her young man, Mr Fischer.'

'I seem to be the last one to hear about him. How could you countenance such an idea? We would be throwing her into the arms of a dubious young German! Is that what you want? Our daughter to end up compromised?'

'Celie is a very sensible young woman. You have nothing to fear on that account.'

'I know that young men cannot be trusted. I shall not have her going to Germany this summer, is that understood, Gerald?'

'Understood, Tina.'

'She's told me she's been asked to help organise some march in London for the suffragists this summer. I told her I thought it was a good idea. She needs to find something she's good at. She doesn't seem to have any particular talents that I've noted.'

'Celie has quite a good eye for photography, Tina.'

'What kind of skill is that for a woman?'

'I thought you didn't approve of the Suffragettes, my dear.'

'They're by far the lesser of two evils.'

Gerald rubs his hand over his eyes. 'You're her mother. You know best.' He settles under the covers and rolls onto his side. 'Good night, my dear.'

Christina stares at the back of her husband's head, at the thinning brown hair threaded with grey. The problem is the past is still alive inside her. She carries it with her every second of every minute of every hour. She will never be free of her past. It stares her in the face every day, every time she looks at Cecelia. She can't let Cecelia make the same mistake with Maximilian Fischer that she'd made herself during that long, hot summer in Capri.

Chapter Six

Max

Heidelberg, Germany – March 1913

'So then the captain handed me a Mannlicher rifle and said, shoot at the dummy!' Friedrich Muenster – Fritz to his friends – spears a slice of sausage with his fork. 'I've never held a rifle in my life and I was meant to shoot it!'

A cherub-faced student in the same grey military uniform as Fritz's sets his stein of beer on the wooden table and pulls up a chair. 'It was funny. Someone drew a moustache on the dummy and put a French beret on its head.'

Max frowns. 'Dieter, that's really not called for.'

Fritz slices through a sausage. 'Everyone knows the French hate us, Max. They're still mad about us taking Alsace and Lorraine from them in the last war. When the next war starts, the English should join us. The French don't like them either.'

'Calm down, Fritz. There isn't going to be a war. Nobody has to take sides here.'

Fritz looks at Max as he chews his sausage. 'Spoken like a true diplomat, professor. You could learn from Max, Dieter. You don't have to hit people over the head with your opinions all the time. Don't the English have a saying? "You catch more flies with honey than vinegar"?'

'Dieter, Max is right. You shouldn't joke about the French like that.'

Max nods at the young blonde woman sitting beside Fritz. 'Thank you, Anneliese. At least somebody's on my side.'

'Of course.' Anneliese takes a sip of her beer. 'Even though nobody likes the French.'

'Anneliese!'

'Well, it's true, Max. Though they do make lovely dresses. Does your girlfriend wear lovely dresses, or does she look like one of the dumpy English girls with their sturdy shoes and their tweed skirts?'

'Celie is a very nice girl in every way, Anneliese.'

Fritz throws a lanky arm around Max's shoulders. 'Max, Max, you've been captured, I can see that. Maybe I should go to England and get myself an English girl. I can speak it a little.' He clears his throat and says in an exaggerated English accent, "Good day, madam. Would you care to join me for a cup of tea?" That's good, isn't it?'

'I don't think that will get you very far, Fritz.'

'Perhaps I need to be more romantic.' Fritz reaches into his pocket and pulls out a thin sheet of paper. He unfolds it and reads: 'My lovely schatzi—'

Max grabs for the letter. 'Give me that, Fritz.'

'Schatzi? Did you hear that?' Dieter says as he chews on a sausage. 'Did you kiss her yet?'

'Oh, do be quiet, Dieter,' Anneliese says.

Fritz holds the letter out of Max's reach. 'My lovely schatzi, You

34

were in my dreams last night. We were walking along the Neckar River by the Old Bridge and your hair shone like fire under the moonbeam—'

Max grabs the letter and shoves it in his breast pocket. 'Where did you get it, Fritz?'

'It was in the pocket of the jacket you lent me the other day when I took Anneliese to the cinema. Of course I read it. Don't be so sensitive.'

Max pushes his empty plate away. 'It's been a long day. I had a meeting at the *Landsturm* office. It looks like I shall be joining all of you next year when I'm finished with my teaching contract in London. They won't let me put off my military training any longer.'

Fritz thumps Max's arm. 'Finally! The professor joins the soldiers!'

Max pushes away from the table. 'I'm going home. I'll see you tomorrow.'

Max crosses a small cobbled courtyard and runs up the brick steps to the Fischers' townhouse on Sandgasse street. The front door is pulled open before he can turn the doorknob.

'Frau Knophler! You surprised me!'

'Come in, Maximilian. I saw you coming across the courtyard. There's a letter for you on the hallway table. Do you want some coffee? I've baked a lovely plum tart.' The housekeeper pinches Max's cheek. 'Your favourite.' As she speaks, her jowls wobble, and the lace ruffles of her voluminous blouse quiver over her generous bosom.

Max hangs his grey wool flat cap on a wall hook. 'You're spoiling me, Frau Knophler. Mama and Papa will be back from the hospital soon with Hans. He will miss his cast. I think he had everyone in Heidelberg sign it. Perhaps we should wait.'

'Shall I cut you a small piece of plum tart for now? It's fresh out of the oven.'

'Only if you have a piece as well. Why don't you make some coffee and I'll be down in a quarter of an hour?'

A wide smile breaks across the housekeeper's broad face. 'You'll want cream, of course, with the tart?'

'What is plum tart without cream?'

He grabs the white envelope off the lace table runner and dashes up the stairs. Once he is safely inside his bedroom, he tosses his leather satchel onto the single bed and tears open the letter.

> *Clover Bar*
> *Hither Green Lane,*
> *Hither Green, London*

February 22nd, 1913

My dearest Max,

I hope you are well and that Frau Knophler is not making you fat with her strudels and dumplings. Papa is so much better now. He has been back working in the studio for the past fortnight, though I ensure he doesn't overtire himself. I have been relegated back to scenery arranger and glass plate cleaner when I'm not back at the college, which is a shame as I quite enjoyed experimenting with Papa's new dry plate camera. Etta was a very willing model. She's quite taken with the American film actress, Miss Lillian Gish, and has begun wearing her hair long and draping herself in silk shawls. Mama does not approve, as you can imagine.

I am so looking forward to your return next month! Professor Obermeyer makes for a very stern German language professor. He disapproves of my accent. He says I sound like an Austrian. Is that a bad thing?

You know I was hoping to study in Heidelberg this summer? My father has agreed, so long as Mama does as well; but Mama is not so easy to convince, though I do not think it's altogether impossible, given time. I've told both of them about you, Max. About us. It's no longer a secret, which is a relief. I can't bear secrets.

The thing of it is, something has happened now which has put my mind in a spin. Women's suffrage is a cause which I feel quite strongly about, as you know. I attended a meeting recently where we were very fortunate to have the society's leader, Mrs Fawcett herself, speaking. I had occasion to comment during the meeting, which brought me to Mrs Fawcett's attention. She asked to speak with me after the meeting. My heart was beating so rapidly, I expected it to leap right out of my body!

Mrs Fawcett has asked me to help her organise a suffragist pilgrimage to London this summer, which shall end with a huge rally in Hyde Park. It is such a great honour, and I am flattered beyond belief. Of course, there is you, my dearest Max. I have been dreaming of walking with you on the Philosopher's Walk – the Philosophenweg I think you called it – and standing on the old stone bridge watching the water of the Neckar River flow beneath our feet. I have imagined meeting your friends Fritz and Dieter, eating schnitzel and strudel in Seppl, and meeting your family, of course, particularly little Hans.

My dearest Max, I have been anguishing for the past week about this. I hope you understand my decision, but I have decided to stay in London this summer to help Mrs Fawcett and to make myself useful in Papa's studio. The fever has taken quite a lot out of him. I've also thought about how you say I should be braver, and get involved with life, rather than watching it from behind my notebooks. The march will be the perfect opportunity for me to do this. The thought of it is making me quite nervous, I must confess!

Let's speak about it when you're back in London. We shall have the spring together, Max. England does spring so very well. We shall both be busy this summer, me with the march and you studying for your law school entrance examination. The months will fly by, you will see! September will arrive before you know it, and we shall have another glorious year together over verbs and declensions.

> *With loving fondness,*
> *Celie*

Max folds the sheets of the letter and slides them back into the envelope. Rising from the bed, he walks over to the small wooden table stacked with papers and textbooks. He sets the envelope on top of the university library's copy of *The Odyssey*, picks up his fountain pen and sits down on the faux bamboo chair.

> *Sandgasse, 10,*
> *Heidelberg, Germany*

March 6th, 1913

Dearest Celie,

Please do not worry about anything. I understand completely. I shall miss you every day this summer, schatzi. I am already counting the seconds until I see you again. One, two, three … there, you see?

I am thinking I shall join the football club here this summer. You are quite right about Frau Knophler and her cakes! She has just baked a quetschekuchen. I can smell it now, and you know how much I love plums. I shall be as large as Herr Obermeyer if I am not careful. Therefore, the football, I think.

Four, five, six … I am still counting. Only one more week and I shall be back in London.

> *Your loving Max*

P.S. Why are you so far away from me?

Chapter Seven

Christina

Capri, Italy – June 1891

In the Piazza Umberto I – or the Piazzetta as Christina has learned to call it – the black iron minute hand of the tiled clock in the Torre dell'Orologio clicks onto twelve. The bronze bells in the belfry chime. Christina counts the rings as she watches her cousin argue with the vegetable seller. Eight, nine, ten. She glances at the tower which stands like a tall, sturdy guard over the cobbled piazza.

The piazza bustles with villagers visiting the weekly market. The sky is a blue which she has never seen in England; pure and clean and uplifting. English blues may aspire to the purity of the blue Italian sky, she thinks, but they expire, greyed and puffing, on the climb to the pinnacle of blueness.

Stefania Albertini is objecting to the price of zucchini. *'No! Sei un ladro! Voglio solo sei zucchini, non venti...'* The vegetable seller argues back in kind, as he does with Stefania Albertini every Wednesday when he and the other traders set up their stalls laden with green zucchini, ropes of garlic, tubs of glistening black olives, tomatoes shaped like pears, aubergines shining like purple lacquer, balls of white mozzarella, wedges of parmesan and wheels of goat's cheese. Twice a month the town's butcher sets up a stall as well, offering tongue and offal, chunky pork sausages, lamb in the spring and mutton later in the year, but he isn't in the Piazzetta today. Today, the fishmongers are doing a good business, selling their stocks of anchovies marinated in vinegar, black-shelled mussels, sea bream, octopus and cuttlefish.

Stefania drops coins into Christina's hand. 'Tina, go to the baker and buy three loaves of bread and half a dozen cannoli. It's in the lane around the back of the church. I'll be at the fish stalls.'

Christina wanders past the church of Santo Stefano with its pilasters and dome, the white paint of the once grand ex-cathedral now faded and peeling from the hot Italian sun. She pauses to pet an orange cat who rubs itself against her hand, purring.

'Well, hello there.'

Christina squints into the sunlight.

Harry Grenville smiles at her from beneath the brim of his straw boater. 'You appear to have found a friend.'

'Oh, hello. Yes, he's very friendly. He reminds me of our cat when I was a little girl. Papa named him Ozymandias, though I called him Ozzy.'

'I'm not sure Mr Shelley would have approved of that for his great king.' Harry Grenville holds out his hand. 'What brings you to this bustling piazza today?'

Christina accepts his hand and rises to her feet. 'I'm here with my Cousin Stefania. She's actually my mother's cousin, so I suppose she's my second cousin, or first cousin once removed. Something like that.' She jingles the coins in her hand. 'I've been instructed to buy some bread and cannoli.' She frowns under the wide brim of her hat. 'Do you know what cannoli are?'

'You haven't had cannoli? You're in for a treat. They're crispy pieces of heaven filled with dollops of sweetened cream as light as angels' clouds.'

Christina laughs. 'You could have been a Romantic poet yourself.'

'Not one Mr Shelley nor Mr Byron would have been too concerned about, I suspect.'

'No, I don't believe either of them ever used the world "dollop" in their poems.'

He offers Christina his arm. 'May I accompany you to the bakery?'

Christina glances back at the fishmongers' stalls under the clock tower. Stefania's black straw hat is just visible above the heads of the villagers crowding the stalls in their scrum for the best fish. She slides her hand into the crook of Harry's arm. 'All right. But I have to meet my cousin back by the fish stalls shortly.'

'I shall be sure to deliver you back in one piece.'

They head through the crowds and down a lane beside the church. At a street lamp on the corner of a cobbled alley, Christina stops and sniffs the fragrant, yeasty scent that beckons them down the alley. 'There,' she points. 'Where the canopy is. I can smell it.'

They stroll down the lane, past white-painted buildings with metal balconies spilling over with red pelargoniums, and stop in front of the large glass window of the bakery with *Pasticceria De Rosa* painted on the glass in black and gold. The scent of baking bread, like a cloud of perfume, wafts through the open door. Harry follows Christina into the tiny shop, which is painted a fresh, bright yellow. Behind a wooden counter, a stout woman of about forty in a black cotton dress adjusts her spectacles as she eyes the two visitors.

'*Sì, signorina?*'

Christina glances at Harry. 'How is your Italian? I'm afraid I'm not a terribly good student.'

'I thought you told me you spoke Italian.'

'Yes, well,' she holds up her thumb and finger in a pinching motion, '*un po.*'

Harry smiles. 'I should be able to buy bread and cannoli.'

'Wonderful. I need three loaves of bread and six cannoli.'

Harry holds up three fingers to the shopkeeper. '*Tre pagnotte di pane e,*' he holds up six fingers, '*sei cannoli, per favore, signorina.*'

The woman giggles and says something to Harry in Italian. He responds, and the woman giggles again. She rolls the bread into brown paper and hands it over the counter. She points at the plates of chocolate and vanilla cannoli. '*Cioccolato o vaniglia?*'

'Oh, chocolate, please,' Christina says. 'I understood that.'

As Harry places the order, Christina bites her lip and fixes her gaze on the terracotta floor tiles, willing her pounding heart to settle.

Harry holds up a paper bag. 'There you go. Cousin Stefania's order filled.'

'Thank you so much.' She frowns at her handful of coins. 'How much is it?'

'No, no. Absolutely not.' He reaches into his pocket and, counting out the *lire*, sets the coins on the wooden counter.

The shopkeeper scoops the money into her hand. '*Grazie, signor, signorina.*'

Outside the shop, Christina turns to Harry. 'That was very kind of you, Mr Grenville, but please, let me repay you.'

'I wouldn't hear of it. You can use the money to buy lemonade at Leonardo's stall. And it's Harry. Just Harry.' He laughs. 'My father would shudder if he heard me say that.'

'Whatever for?'

'It's all very dreary, really. He's an earl and I'm his eldest son, so I'm a viscount. We have an estate up in the Scottish borders. Ancient and very draughty. Officially, I'm the Right Honourable Harold Grenville, Viscount Sherbrooke.'

'Good heavens!'

'Hard to believe, isn't it? I'm travelling the Mediterranean this summer to escape all that, before I attend Sandhurst in January.'

'Aren't I meant to call you "Sir" or "Lord" or something?'

'Just Harry.'

The bells of the clocktower chime, filling the piazza with their echoing clamour. She glances in the direction of the square. 'I should go back by myself … Harry.'

'Are you sure? It's no bother.'

She has no idea what her cousin would think of her springing a young aristocrat on her, but she isn't quite ready to find out. 'Yes, I'm sure. I mustn't keep Cousin Stefania waiting.'

'Of course.' Harry hands Christina the bread and the bag of cannoli. 'Miss Bishop? If I may … I've found a path down to a Roman grotto. It winds all along the southern side of the island.'

'Have you?'

'It has lovely views out to the sea. Apparently, the grotto was a nymphaeum – a shrine to water nymphs. I read about it in my Baedeker guide. There's quite a stunning natural arch to see on the way. I thought perhaps you might like to accompany me there on a walk … well, it's more like a hike. It's quite steep and rather a climb back up the hill afterwards, but, if you're up for it, it brings you all the way to the Faraglioni.'

'Those rocks in the sea? You can get close to them?'

'Yes, very close. It's well worth it. I've been wanting to sketch them.'

'I'm not sure. Cousin Stefania was very cross with me for being out so long the day you helped me buy lemons.'

'Perhaps I should call on your cousin to introduce myself.'

Christina's eyes widen. 'Oh, I'm not sure that's a good idea—'

'It's a very good idea. An absolutely necessary idea. You see, I have no intention of this being our last meeting, Miss Bishop.'

Christina looks at Harry from under the wide brim of her straw hat. In the sun, his eyes are as blue as the Italian sky. The bluest of blue.

'Then, Harry, I shall look forward to it.'

Chapter Eight

Celie

Victoria Train Station, London – March 1913

Celie peers through the crowd of passengers disembarking from the boat train from Dover.

'Celie! *Schatzi!*' A slender young soldier in a rumpled grey uniform, his face the epitome of joy, waves at her.

'Max!'

He pushes through the crowd and, after dropping his carpetbag on the platform, sweeps her into his arms and kisses her on her cheek. *'Schatzi!'* He twirls her around the platform as she laughs, the two of them oblivious to the grumbles of the disembarking passengers.

He sets her down and hugs her against the scratchy wool of his uniform. 'You have no idea how much I have counted the moments until today.'

'Max, what are you wearing?'

He stands back and pats the grey wool jacket. 'Do you like it?' He adjusts the flat beret edged with red. 'It's my uniform for the *Landsturm*. Do you think I look handsome?'

'You look … you look very distinguished. What's the *Landsturm*?'

'In Germany, everyone, well, every young man, I should say, is required to do military service for two years when they turn twenty. When I was at university, I made an arrangement to be a "one-year volunteer" to train as a reserve officer when I graduated, so that I could finish my studies and my teaching contract first. I had to have an interview and everything. It's very strict. I received a letter when I was home, then had my induction and got my uniform. I must join for one year next September.'

'Why are you wearing the uniform now?'

'To impress you, of course! Fritz is quite upset. He wasn't accepted to be a one-year volunteer as his grades weren't good enough. He started his service in January for two years. He will have to finish his studies later.'

'Max, you don't suppose there's going to be a war, do you?'

'Don't be silly! Why do you think that?'

'There's been talk in London. People have said they've seen zeppelins along the coast. It's been in the papers.'

'It's just people's imaginations. I haven't even seen a zeppelin and I live in Germany!' He picks up his carpetbag. 'Come on, *schatzi*. I have been dreaming about the fish and chips from the wonderful old place in Covent Garden. I hope you are hungry.'

They walk hand in hand past the soaring granite obelisk of Cleopatra's Needle on the embankment by the Thames. The turgid grey water of the river slides by like a huge river snake, and the evening sky is heavy with clouds the colour of charcoal.

'I told Mama about you.'

'You said in your letter.'

'She said, why couldn't I find a nice young Englishman.'

Max laughs. 'I suppose I should have expected that.'

'Max, if only she were to meet you, I know she'd change her mind. Everyone likes you. You're the most popular German teacher at the college.'

'That's not hard when the others are Professors Obermeyer and Klemm. What does your father think?'

'Papa is fine. He understands me. We're similar. We're both life's observers rather than life's doers. Papa loves nothing more than to record the world through his cameras. He used to travel around Britain when he and Mama were first married, taking pictures of towns and landscapes for the British historical record. He doesn't do that anymore. It's mainly portraits now.'

'I look forward to meeting your father.'

'You'll like him. He's a kind man.'

'Your mother is not kind?'

'My mother is ... well, she's my mother. She thinks I'm too reticent. That I need to come out of my shell. I feel like I'm a disappointment to her, and I don't know why. Sometimes I catch her looking at me like I've done something awfully wrong, and I have no idea what it is.'

'I'm certain that's not true, *schatzi*. You are the smartest, kindest girl I have ever met. You could never be a disappointment to anyone.'

They walk along the river in silence. Celie shivers and rubs her arm. 'Something's changed, Max. Can't you feel it? On the omnibuses and the trams. I heard a man on the tram just last week tell his wife to stop going to the German butcher because he "wasn't going to eat another German sausage".'

'Maybe he doesn't like German sausages.'

'It's not that. Even you. Look at you in your army uniform, and you're not even in the army yet.'

'You don't like my uniform?'

'I prefer you in your normal clothes. That's the Max I know.'

'I'm still the same Max.'

Celie stops under the brick arch of Waterloo Bridge. 'Are you, Max?' She looks up at him and removes his army cap. A street lamp throws a warm glow on Max's blond head. She brushes his hair with her fingertips. 'There. That's better.'

'*Schatzi.*'

She slides her hand along his smooth cheek. A groan escapes Max's lips. His breath is warm on her fingers. He drops his carpetbag on the pavement and wraps his arms around her body.

'I am your Max, Celie. I shall always be your Max.'

He kisses her, and all the months of longing, of waiting, of dreaming, are in each press of his lips against her skin.

Chapter Nine

Etta

Piccadilly, London – May 1913

E tta huddles under her umbrella, skirting puddles as she hurries down Piccadilly as quickly as the narrow hem of her hobble skirt will permit; mincing past the bowed windows of Hatchards booksellers with its gilded royal warrant on proud display above the door; and the King's grocer, Fortnum & Mason, with its Easter display replaced with windows full of picnic hampers and a selection of teas under faux branches of lilac. The torrent has sent the Friday shoppers and businessmen scurrying for cover, leaving Etta with puddles rather than pedestrians to worry about in her hobbled rush down the street.

In front of a pyramid of 'Teas of the World' in Fortnum's window, she waits for a break in the traffic. She sees her moment and, stepping awkwardly over a puddle collecting above a street drain, she shuffles across the street and under the archway to the

Royal Academy of Art. The granite cobbles of the large courtyard are slippery under her feet, slowing her progress even further. By the time she makes it through the doors into the marbled lobby, the hem of her skirt is soaked through.

The ticket seller behind the front desk, a thin-faced young man with round, black-rimmed spectacles and an expression of anxious irritation, eyes her dripping raincoat as he hands her a ticket to the Summer Exhibition. 'You might wish to leave your wet things in the cloakroom, miss. We can't have anyone slipping on the floor.'

'Oh, no. Of course not.'

He exchanges her money for an exhibition catalogue. 'The Royal Family's picture is in the Oils Room.'

'Oh, I haven't come to see that, though of course I shall.' The words spill out of her mouth in a flood of excitement. 'Mr Rutter in *The Sunday Times* said that this year's Summer Exhibition is evidence of *"triumphant feminism".*' She reaches into her handbag and extracts a much-folded newspaper clipping. She unfolds it and reads: '*"A remarkable success achieved again this year by women exhibitors."* Isn't that exciting?' She fans her face with the catalogue as she catches her breath. 'I'm an artist, you see. One day, my work will be in here too.'

The ticket seller drops the change into Etta's gloved hand and gestures to the person behind her. 'Next.'

Etta stands in front of Annie Swynnerton's *Peter, son of Sir John Grant Lawson, Bt.*, having duly let her eye *'grow accustomed to the glare of bright sunlight'*, as advised by Mr Rutter, in order to best admire the *'blaze of colour'* of the little boy on a pony.

'Do you agree with Mr Rutter?'

Etta looks up at the tall man in a grey tweed suit and a high-collared shirt standing beside her. His black hair is waved by the rain, and his face is the warm tan of sunnier countries. He has a neat black moustache over his full lips. He smiles at her, his dark brown eyes shining warmly under his thick black eyebrows.

'I beg your pardon?'

He removes a newspaper clipping from the pocket of his jacket and shakes it open. 'Do you agree that this is,' he squints at the small print, '"*one of the most powerful and convincing works in the exhibition*"?' An Italian accent rolls off his tongue in loops and swirls.

A dimple forms in her left cheek. 'You've read Mr Rutter, too.'

'Of course. I think he is one of the most, uh ...' he waves his left hand as he searches for the word '... progressive critics of art in London. I am always interested to read what he has to say when I am in London.'

The blue ostrich feather in Etta's wide-brimmed black felt hat flutters as she nods. 'I absolutely agree. I read his column every Sunday when I can pry the paper out of Papa's hands.'

She points to an exuberant painting of spring flowers. 'That must be Miss Browning's *March Flowers*. Those flowers! They're the colours of joy after a long, dreary winter, don't you think?'

'It reminds me of Van Gogh's *Sunflowers*.'

'Does it? I've heard of Mr Van Gogh from my tutor at the art college.'

'Have you not seen any of his *Sunflowers* paintings? One of them was at the Post-Impressionist exhibition here three years ago. A great many incredible paintings were on display – Manet, Cezanne, Gauguin, Picasso. It was ... how do you say ... marvellous!'

'I'm sorry to have missed that.' How could she tell him she'd been fifteen then, far too young to attend the exhibition the newspapers had branded pornographic, degenerate and evil? After she'd read those reviews, she'd made sure to visit the library to read whatever she could about those wild, passionate artists. This is the way she wished to paint, from the very core of herself, though Mr

Lester, her art tutor, frowned at any innovation beyond the Victorian Romantics.

The man leans forward to inspect the painting's brushwork. 'You can feel the artist's energy by the way she has used the brush and the paint so fearlessly. Like a *spadaccina*.'

'A *spadaccina*?'

The man nods his head, unleashing a black curl which strays over his forehead. 'How do you say … swordsman. She is like a swordsman with her paintbrush. *Bellissima*. This is much more beautiful than those horrible nudes in the Watercolour Room that look like they've escaped from a Victorian cartoon.'

Etta feels the heat rise in her cheeks. Did he say *nudes?* Her heart rattles against the confines of her corset. She tucks the newspaper clipping into her handbag. 'Yes, well, it's been a pleasure. If you will excuse me.'

Horror draws itself on the man's expressive face. 'I'm so sorry, *signorina*. Please forgive me, I forget myself. I forget Englishwomen are more modest than we Italians.' He pats the tailored lapels of his suit. 'Permit me to introduce myself. I am Carlo Marinetti. I'm an artist from Napoli. I am in London for business and I thought I would visit the exhibition to see what the English artists are offering.' He shrugs. 'Mostly it's pretty pictures, I think. Nothing which disturbs. It is very …' he waves a hand in the air '… polite.'

Etta sweeps her eyes over the Italian. She should nod, politely, of course, and take her leave. She shifts on her feet; she absolutely should go.

She offers Mr Marinetti her gloved hand. 'I'm Etta Fry.'

Carlo raises her hand to his lips. 'Miss Fry, it is a great honour.'

'My elder sister Cecelia is Miss Fry. I'm just Etta.'

He releases her hand. 'No, no, no. You are not *just* anything. You are … you are … *sei bellissima*.' He smiles, his teeth a flash of white in his tanned face. 'I should very much like to see it.'

'I beg your pardon?'

'Your painting. When you exhibit here.'

She laughs. 'You heard me at the ticket desk.'

'Yes, I heard you. And I saw you.'

'I was just so excited to be here, I blurted it out. I think the poor man thought I was a lunatic.'

'Then he is blind.' Carlo offers Etta his arm. 'May I have the pleasure of escorting you around the exhibition, *Signorina Etta*?' Her name rolls off his tongue like honey dripping from a spoon. 'This is a lovely name. In Italian it means "little".'

Etta slides her hand into the crook of Carlo's arm. 'I should like that very much.'

'*Brava*. We can talk all about the Royal Family and the unfortunate nudes in the Watercolour Room, and then I shall take you to tea.'

Chapter Ten

Jessie

Clover Bar, London – May 1913

The greenhouse in the back garden of Clover Bar sits gently decaying under the branches of a rowan tree laden with blossoms like posies of white lace. Jessie roots through the packets of seeds, rolls of twine, garden gloves and secateurs until she finds what she is looking for. She pulls out a long stick with a metal hook which has slid down the back of the shelves. Hooking the end through a loop on the pane in the glass roof, she levers the window open. She balances the stick on the potting shelf and nods with satisfaction.

The seedlings of salvia, ageratum and zinnia are sprouting nicely. If the warm weather keeps up, she might plant them out in another week, though you never could tell in England. *Ne'er cast a clout till May be out.* Probably best to wait.

She sets out a wooden tray and sprinkles in a layer of potting compost. Shuffling through the seed packets, she selects lettuce. She tears open the packet and tips the seeds into the palm of her hand. One by one she pokes them into the compost.

The wooden door creaks on its hinges and Christina enters, shucking off her leather garden gloves. Her beige gardening smock is streaked with mud where she's been kneeling in the rose bed, and her large-brimmed straw hat, secured on her head with a violet cotton scarf, is askew. She drops the gloves onto the potting shelf and leans over the tray of zinnia seedlings, squinting as she inspects the delicate green shoots. 'Those are coming along well, Jessica. I do so like zinnias. They're so jolly in the garden in late summer.'

'Celie says they're vulgar. She says they're like sweets in the candy shop – all bright pink and orange without any subtlety or refinement.'

Christina hangs her hat on a hook. 'Cecelia is far too particular for her own good. She frustrates me no end. She has neither your drive nor Etta's charm. When she's not frittering away her time in your father's studio, she's burying her nose in German books. What use will that do her when she's married?'

Jessie taps down the compost and shifts the tray to one side. 'The King is German.'

Christina sifts through the seed packets and selects the French beans. 'Be that as it may, the King was born in London, and his grandmother was Queen Victoria. That makes him English.'

'You're more English than the King is, and you're half Italian.'

'And very proud of it, too, Jessica. I have my mother's Innocenti blood in my veins, as do all of you. If Cecelia had had any sense, she would have studied Italian. I still have relatives in Capri.'

'I thought the Innocentis cut us all off after Grandmama ran off with Grandpapa. A Protestant Englishman. Heaven forbid!'

'Not everyone. Mama's cousin Stefania is lovely. She and Mama grew up together in Capri. It's a lovely place.'

'When did you meet her?'

Christina jabs a French bean into the compost. How could she have been so stupid? 'She … uh, she visited London with her husband once when I was a girl. I think his name was Albertini. A very nice man. She told me all about Capri.' She wipes her hands on her smock. 'Has Cecelia told you anything about a young man in Germany?'

Jessie tears open a packet of carrot seeds. 'No.'

'You're absolutely certain?'

Jessie's jaw tightens. It's always about Celie – how she's such a disappointment, or Etta – the apple of Mama's eye. She sets down the seed packet. 'Mama, I've signed up for the Queen Alexandra's Imperial Military Nursing Service.'

'What? Did you say military?'

Jessie thrusts out her chin. 'I was top of my class in the surgical training. Matron put in a word for me with them. She was in South Africa with the Queen Alexandra's during the Boer War.'

'Indeed.'

Jessie swallows down the ball which has formed in her throat. 'The Queen Alexandra's are army nurses, Mama, but we're not at war with anyone. I shouldn't imagine I'll be doing much more than patching up a few bruises and a broken arm or two on one of the army bases in the English countryside or abroad somewhere.'

'You can do that at King's College Hospital, at least until you marry.'

'Mama, I told you I want to travel and see the world. If I'd known you were in touch with relatives in Italy, I would have been very happy to cultivate an interest in Italian.'

'Italy is no place for a young woman on her own.' Christina stabs a label into the potting tray. 'Jessica, I'm not a fool. I've heard about the zeppelin sightings along the coast. It was all the Jeffries could talk about when they were here for dinner. What am I to think? One daughter in thrall to a German, and one bent on gallivanting around the world with the army. I raised you all to have happy, secure lives as good Catholic wives and mothers. It appears Etta is my only hope.'

'Good luck with that.'

'Why can't you simply marry a nice man and have a family, like I did?'

'Married women can't nurse.'

'Nurse here in London until you marry. There's nothing wrong with that. It's a respectable profession. Earn some money for your trousseau. Papa would appreciate that. You know how he worries about money. What about that nice young Mr Jeffries? His family's auctioneering business will be his one day.'

'Frank Jeffries? That was one time I actually felt sorry for Etta, Mama, having to sit beside him all night and listen to him drone on about French polishing and dovetail joints. If I ever marry, it will be to an interesting man, not a dull fellow like Frank Jeffries.'

'Dull fellows have a great deal to recommend them, Jessica. They're solid and reliable, just like your father. He has never caused me a day of worry, other than when he was ill last winter.'

'Papa's not dull. He's artistic.'

'He is a photographer offering a service. Your father is a respected member of the middle classes. He is hardly an *artist*. It's fine for a young woman to dabble in art. Many young men are quite taken by a young woman with a talent for watercolours, but it simply isn't an acceptable profession for a gentleman.'

'Cousin Roger is an artist.'

'Your father's cousin *was* an artist. He has obviously seen the error of his ways and is opening a housewares shop catering to London's upper classes this summer.' Christina waves an empty seed packet in the air. 'This is by the by, Jessica. You are forbidden to become an army nurse.'

Jessie grabs her gardening hat from the hook and slams it on her head. 'It's too late, Mama. I've signed up. As soon as I'm posted abroad, I'm going, and neither you nor Papa can stop me.'

'We certainly can and will stop you, Jessica. You're not yet of age.'

The greenhouse door slams. Christina watches her daughter duck under the rose arch and stomp down the gravel path to the house. She runs her fingers around her ear and surveys the garden. The graceful necks of the foxgloves wave in the light breeze, jostling with the billowing, pink-flowered peonies. On the wrought-iron arch, the Perle d'Azur clematis cloaks the white buds of the Madame Albert Carrière rose with a fall of blue-mauve flowers.

Everything is so perfect just as it is. Why must her daughters test the patience of the angels? Angels can be truculent and spiteful, and no amount of Hail Marys and tearful confessions in the Confessional appeases them when the mark has been overstepped. This she knows, intimately. She will do everything in her power to keep her daughters secure and safe.

Chapter Eleven

Jessie

King's College Hospital, London – June 1913

'That's it, ladies! Straight backs, please.'

Gerald steps away from the class of graduating nurses whom he has arranged under the hospital's Doric portico. So crisp and efficient they look, he thinks, in their grey dresses and starched pinafores and caps.

He scans the nurses to seek out Jessie's heart-shaped face. Her thick dark hair is piled neatly on top of her head, crowned by the starched cap. She's much prettier than she thinks, with her strong features and green eyes so piercing that when she settles her gaze on you, it's like she delves past all the pretensions to the very core of your being. She is so much like his own long-departed mother, though there is no doubt she's Christina's child. They are identical in their wilful stubbornness. He'll have to check the door hinges after all the door slamming that has gone on since Jessie announced her enrolment in the Queen Alexandra nurses. It was all he could do to persuade Christina to attend the graduation today.

He holds up the shutter release cable. 'That's lovely, ladies! One, two, three, smile!'

'Jessie, is that Dr Mitchell?' Elsie checks her cap and brushes a stray strand of fine brown hair off her forehead. 'What do you suppose he's doing here?'

Jessie glances at the tall young medical resident as she sips her elderflower wine. 'I suppose he's on his way to work. It is a hospital, after all, Elsie. Things don't stop simply because of our graduation.'

Elsie watches the young doctor's tall figure as he disappears through the hospital's entrance doors and sighs dramatically.

'Good heavens, Elsie. Don't tell me you've gone through all of this training simply to find yourself a doctor for a husband. I thought Maude Phipps had that area covered.'

Elsie sips the sweet wine. 'There's no harm in looking, is there? I'm only human. Of course I intend to nurse, Jessie, but I'm not like you. I have no intention of patching up soldiers in Timbuktu. I've been assigned to the obstetrics ward here at King's. Expectant ladies and babies suit me just fine.'

'It doesn't look like I'll be off to Timbuktu any time soon. The Queen Alexandra's have assigned me to paediatrics here. So much for exploring the world.'

'Paediatrics? You haven't a motherly bone in your body, Jessie Fry.' She clinks her glass against Jessie's. 'Here's to the King's College Hospital's nursing class of 1913. Destined to stay in Denmark Hill.' She gestures over Jessie's shoulder with her glass. 'It looks like your mother has cornered Matron.'

Jessie spins around, splashing elderflower wine over her white pinafore in her haste. Her mother, resplendent in a new seafoam green hobble dress, has, indeed, cornered Matron in front of the cake table. Although her mother's face is obscured by her large feathered hat, Jessie can easily guess, judging by the senior nurse's tight-lipped expression and the jabbing of her mother's seafoam green parasol into the clipped lawn, the subject of the conversation.

'Oh, crumbs.'

'It's terribly amusing, Jessie. I've never seen Matron on the other end of the stick.'

'Where's my father? He should have known not to leave Mama on her own.'

'I saw him taking portraits in front of the college. I can't wait to see the one he took of me. Will it take long before it's ready?'

'I've no idea.' Jessie shoves her glass into Elsie's free hand. 'Wish me luck.'

'Why do you suppose it was reasonable to put the ridiculous notion of becoming an army nurse into my daughter's head?'

The matron sets her shoulders back and lifts her chin as she prepares for battle. She peers down her angular nose at the agitated woman in the absurd hat. 'Your daughter is a talented nurse, Mrs Fry. She has a rare combination of compassion, organisation and aptitude for some of the more challenging aspects of nursing. Though, it must be said, she must apply herself to her timekeeping.'

'I appreciate that Jessica is a good student; she is extremely competent. However, I must draw the line at army nursing.' Christina stabs her parasol into the lawn. 'I have no intention of allowing my daughter to gad around the world with battalions of men.'

The nurse presses her lips into a thin line. 'Mrs Fry, army nursing is a perfectly honourable career. I nursed for the army in South

Africa during the Boer War. The soldiers were most appreciative and respectful.'

'It's not the soldiers I'm worried about. They're ill, and hardly able to…' Christina takes a breath to compose herself. 'There are doctors and … and foreigners.'

'I have no doubt that your daughter is more than capable of handling herself, Mrs Fry. She will be with other nursing sisters and matrons. You needn't have any fear of improprieties, if that's what's concerning you.'

'Mama! I see you've met Matron.'

The two women turn to stare at Jessie like she's a teacher breaking up a childish spat. Christina nods her head stiffly, the peacock feathers protruding from her hat jerking in the air. 'I have had the pleasure, yes.'

Jessie attempts a smile and gestures to her mother. 'Matron, my mother, Mrs Gerald Fry.'

'Ah, of course.' The matron smiles stiffly at Christina. 'Your husband is the photographer. I hadn't made the connection, Fry being such a common name.'

Christina's right eyebrow arches. 'I suspect the Frys with whom you are acquainted aren't related to the cocoa manufacturers, as we are.'

Jessie loops her arm through her mother's. 'Mama, shall we go find Papa? I hear he's taking portraits. Why don't we have him take one of us together in front of the college?'

'Jessica, your matron and I have been having a very … enlightening conversation.'

'Have you?'

The matron nods. 'I have been assuring your mother that you shan't be kidnapped and sold into slavery when you are nursing our brave soldiers in a remote corner of the world.' She smiles tightly at Christina. 'If you excuse me, Mrs Fry, I have a duty to circulate.'

Jessie watches the matron stride toward a cluster of graduates.

She releases her hold on her mother's arm. 'Mama, I *am* becoming an army nurse, whether you like it or not.'

'But, Jessica—'

'I'm not going to discuss this any further. Now, I'm going to find Papa and have my portrait taken. You may accompany me, or not, as you wish.' She juts out her chin, her body rigid with tension, as they stand in a silent stalemate.

Christina offers her elbow to her daughter. 'I have spent a considerable amount of your father's money on this dress, and it should be commemorated in a photograph with my clever daughter. I shall discuss this with your father later.'

Chapter Twelve

Christina

Capri, Italy – July 1891

'Here it is.' Harry holds up the Baedeker red leather guidebook. '"*The Arco Naturale is a natural limestone arch dating from the Palaeolithic age, and is the remains of a collapsed grotto. The arch spans twelve metres at a height of eighteen metres above ground.*"'

'Isn't that beautiful, *Cugina Stefania*?'

Christina's cousin fans her flushed face with a black silk fan embroidered with vibrant roses as she holds a Chinese paper parasol over her head in the other. 'Yes, yes. Very nice.' She sits down on a large rock beside the dirt path with a groan.

Harry steps off the path. 'Come look through the arch, Miss Bishop.'

'Go, go, Tina.' Stefania presses her hand, protected by the

ravages of the sun by a black lace glove, against her corseted waist. 'Let me catch my breath.'

Stefania watches the two young people pick their way over the scrubby grass toward the arch. Harry draws circles in the air with his arms as he expounds on its history. A handsome boy, in a broad-faced English way. The build of a labourer rather than that of the slender, whey-faced aristocrats she's seen bathing by the marina, or buying bread and cheese for one of their interminable hikes. The English do love their walks; a ridiculous activity in this summer heat, climbing all over the island's donkey paths. She waves the fan more rapidly under her hat.

Christina nods and smiles as she listens to the boy. She is such a lovely girl, Stefania muses. So like Isabella in the daguerreotype her cousin had sent her all those years ago after her marriage to the Englishman – a Protestant no less! She never would have imagined such a thing of her childhood playmate. Isabella had been so timid she'd even refuse to play down in the grotto, so fearful was she of hearing the sirens' song.

Things must have changed after Uncle Umberto emigrated with his family to Britain, though Isabella gave no hint of it in her letters. Every letter, in Italian, with a full copy in English. She has Isabella to thank for her facility with the ugly language now. She dabs at her damp forehead with her gloved finger. To have been cut off by the family must have been a difficult thing for Isabella, but it was understandable. At least this James Bishop had made an honest woman of her before Christina's birth. Stefania shakes her head. Poor Isabella. Only thirty-nine when she and the baby had been called home to God in February.

Harry says something and Christina laughs, the sound floating on the humid air like bells tinkling in a breeze. Flicking the fan closed, Stefania heaves to her feet with a laboured sigh as Harry and Christina trek back through the scrub grass and yellow-flowering broom to the path.

Harry pulls the Baedeker guide out of his jacket pocket. 'Right-o. The Grotta di Matermania is down the path this way.'

'You two go. *Andare al grotta*. I have walked sufficiently today.' Stefania opens the fan with a snap of her wrist and fans her florid face. 'I shall expect you back at the villa no later than three o'clock, Tina.' She settles a stern look on Harry. 'You are invited to tea when you return, *Signor Grenville*. Liliana has made *Torta Caprese* with chocolate and almonds. I expect that you will not be late.'

Christina picks her way down the steep stone steps that hug the cliffside. In places, the only barrier between a false step and a dramatic exit into the churning waves below is a shoulder's width of rocky earth sprouting tuffs of grass and broom.

'Good heavens! No wonder Cousin Stefania turned back.'

'Don't worry, Miss Bishop. There's plenty of room. I wouldn't put you in any danger.'

'Oh, do stop all this Miss Bishop nonsense. It's Christina. And watch where you're going, you nincompoop.'

Harry gallops down the final steps. He holds out his hand to Christina as she descends onto the compacted earth in front of the grotto. Nestled within the arch of a limestone cave, a two-roomed structure of cobbled stone walls inlaid with tiny mosaics of ancient glass opens onto a view of the jagged Amalfi coastline and the turquoise sea.

'*Voilà!* We're here.'

Christina steps up into the grotto and runs her hand over a cobbled wall. 'This is probably the oldest thing I've ever touched.'

Harry scans the guidebook. 'They believe it was where Cybele, the goddess of the earth, was worshipped. It would have been decorated with marble statues and coloured glass mosaics and seashells.'

'It must have been beautiful.'

'The Romans thought that these caves were where the sirens sang their songs to sailors to lure them to their deaths.'

'Really? I've heard of that. The sirens' song – something so beautiful it can't be resisted, but it ends badly for anyone who hears it.'

'Though some say that if a person hears the sirens' song and escapes, the sirens are fated to die.'

'Oh dear.'

'They throw themselves into the sea.'

'How awful.'

Harry steps up into the grotto and removes his straw boater. 'They say the sirens only sing in the middle of the day, when it's calm and quiet, so their song can be heard in its full beauty.'

'It's the middle of the day now.'

He steps towards Christina. 'Close your eyes, Christina. Listen. Can you hear it?'

She shuts her eyes. 'I'm not sure—'

Her sentence is stopped by the press of his lips upon hers. Her eyes fly open and she pushes him away.

'Christina? I'm sorry. I—'

She steps forward and reaches her hands around his neck. Then she opens her lips to his soft, warm kisses.

Chapter Thirteen

Etta

Omega Workshops, London – July 1913

OMEGA WORKSHOPS LTD
33 FITZROY SQ. W

*You are invited to
an Exhibition of
Decorative Art at the
above address; examples
of Interior Decorations for
Bedrooms Nurseries etc,
Furniture, Textiles,
Hand-dyed Dress Materials
Trays Fans and other
Objects suitable for
Christmas presents.*

Etta fans her face with the invitation she'd received so unexpectedly from her cousin – second or third, or possibly something once removed, she wasn't quite sure – the art critic Roger Fry, to the opening of his new design showrooms in Bloomsbury. She has borrowed her mother's seafoam green silk hobble dress, which fits her quite well, though she is concerned the colour is casting an unflattering green shadow on her skin and pale hair. She has foregone a hat for a tumble of curls through which she has woven a mauve silk ribbon in the style of the American film actress Miss Lillian Gish, to whom she has been told she bears a striking resemblance.

She accepts a glass of champagne from a young waiter with tousled brown hair and soulful blue eyes, who is rather disconcertingly dressed in a wrinkled beige linen jacket with a button missing on the left sleeve, though his emerald green silk cravat adds a jaunty note to his bohemian appearance. She hovers in front of a three-panel screen painted with green-skinned bathers in a landscape of thrusting mauve and ochre mountains, and bends over to look for the artist's signature.

'There you are, my dear! I see you've found Vanessa's screen. I'm afraid you won't find her name on it. I have a policy of all our pieces being anonymous. Objects and furniture should be valued for their beauty rather than because of the reputation of the artist.'

Etta looks up into the face of her distant cousin. There is a whisper of a resemblance to her father in the length and sharpness of his features, but the gullies of his bone structure throw a grey cast on his cheeks and shadow the brown eyes behind the wire-rimmed spectacles. A mass of wiry grey hair springs from a centre parting above his high forehead.

'Cousin Roger! Thank you so much for inviting me. It's quite amazing to be here.' She gestures towards a beautiful young woman with a pile of dark golden hair, clad in an exquisite beaded ivory gown. 'Is that Miss Gladys Cooper? Of the stage?'

Roger glances towards the young woman, who has attracted a coterie of admirers. 'It is indeed. I shall have to go and speak to her in a moment. It all helps with the publicity.' He kisses Etta on her cheek. 'I'm delighted you could come, my dear. We artists must support each other, mustn't we?'

'Thank you so much for helping me get a place at the art college in Camberwell. I'm enjoying it no end.'

'You have a lovely talent, my dear. Talent must be nurtured.'

'I'm awfully sorry about what Mama put you through at dinner last week.'

Roger chuckles. 'Don't worry. Your mother's quite right to harbour reservations about us lot. We do enjoy provoking bourgeois sensibilities and anything with the whiff of the status quo. I hope I managed to assuage her concerns, now that I've told her I've become a humble shopkeeper.'

'You're hardly a shopkeeper, Cousin Roger! This place is amazing! It's like an exotic bazaar of wonders.'

'Roger! Darling, Roger! How *are* you, my dearest?' A woman of extreme height capped by a mass of flaming red hair bends to air kiss Roger on either cheek. The ropes of pearls twined around her long neck clatter like beads in a doorway. Swathes of violet silk drape from her statuesque figure, cinched at her waist by a jade green tasselled sash.

'Ottoline, my dear. So glad you could come. Will you be joining us for dinner later? We're heading over to Vanessa's. She's here somewhere. I saw her come in with Duncan and Clive.'

'*Ebsolutely*, darling.' The remarkable woman settles an intense aquamarine gaze on Etta. 'But tell me, *who* is this delightful young sylph?'

'Forgive me, Ottie. This is my cousin, Etta Fry. She's an aspiring artist. Etta, this is Lady Ottoline Morrell, a grand patron of modern art.'

Etta bends her knees in a curtsey. 'Delighted to meet you, Lady Morrell.'

The giantess laughs, a deep, guttural sound which seems to rise up from her feet like water rising in a tide. 'No need for all that, my darling girl. Just call me Ottie.' She reaches a marble-white arm around Etta's shoulders. 'Now, come with me and I shall introduce you to *everyone*. By the end of the evening your name will be on the lips of *tout le monde bohémien*.' She stops abruptly and sweeps her ethereal gaze over Etta. 'You are a good artist, I trust?'

'I – I'm trying to be a good artist.'

'*Excellent*. You *must* come to tea and show me your work. *Clive! Darling!* You must meet this wonderful young artist I've just discovered. Where's Vanessa? I must tell her how much I *love* her screen. I believe I shall have to purchase it for my boudoir.'

Roger stands before a large curtained mural of elongated nymphs cavorting in an ink blue forest and clears his throat.

'Thank you, ladies and gentlemen, for joining me and my co-directors and fellow artists, Mrs Vanessa Bell and Mr Duncan Grant,' he gestures toward a tall, attractive, dark-haired woman, and the handsome waiter with the piercing blue eyes, 'as we open the doors of the Omega Workshops to celebrate the creation of items for the interior which encapsulate forms expressive of the needs of modern life. We believe that it is time that the spirit of fun is introduced into furniture and fabrics. We have suffered too long from the dull and stupidly serious ...'

'I see you have found your way into the *crema* of the art world, *Signorina Etta*.'

Etta jerks her head around to the unmistakeable voice. 'Mr

Marinetti! What are you doing here? Aren't you meant to be in Naples?'

'Obviously not, as I am here.' Carlo takes her hand and brushes it with his lips. 'May I say you are even lovelier than I remember? And in my memory, Botticelli's Venus was a poor second to the beauty of Signorina Etta Fry.'

Etta gifts him with her most winning smile. 'You are very kind, though I think quite possibly blind, Mr Marinetti.'

He offers Etta his arm. 'Come, let us have a promenade. I shall be exhibiting my work here in November. Help me to find the best location to hang my paintings.'

Etta rests her hand on Carlo's arm. 'Only if you promise to send me an invitation to the opening.'

'*Cara mia*, you are the subject of the centrepiece painting. As soon as I heard about the Omega Workshops, I wrote Roger and demanded I be the first artist to hold a solo exhibition here. All so that I could see you again.'

'You did not.'

'I most certainly did. Did you not wonder how it came to be that an invitation to the opening that all London's *beau monde* wished to attend dropped into your letterbox?'

'But I thought Cousin Roger... I don't know, I was just so pleased to receive the invitation, I didn't give it all that much thought. Mama insisted he come to dinner, of course, to ensure everything was right and proper. She gave poor Cousin Roger quite a grilling, but he passed with flying colours.'

'I would have expected nothing less of him. Roger could persuade King George to dance a tango.'

Etta giggles, aware of the attractive dimple that forms in her left cheek. 'I should like to see that!'

'You should like to see what, my dear?'

Etta looks up into the gravely beautiful face of the artist Vanessa

Bell. 'Oh, Mrs Bell! I'm delighted to meet you. I'm Etta Fry, Roger's cousin. I love your screen.'

'I'm delighted. Roger's told me all about you. Another artist in the Fry family. The world cannot have enough artists.' Her voice is as deep and resonant as a tiger's purr. She turns her serious gaze on the Italian, and leans in to kiss his cheeks. 'Carlo, I wasn't sure you would make it in time for the opening. How long have you been travelling?'

'It was nothing, *cara*. I flew like the bird. The trains are so efficient now. I would not have missed this for the world. But I must return to Napoli in a few days. I am painting a mural in the house of a contessa there, and she is ...' he smiles '... very demanding.'

Vanessa Bell raises an eyebrow. 'Well, you must both come to dinner later. All our disreputable friends will be there. Duncan will ensure the aristocrats come, of course. We'll all get drunk and dance and kiss. The aristocrats will feel they are in the thick of things. I expect orders to flow in like a river.'

'Vanessa, with an invitation like that, how can we possibly refuse?'

'Wonderful. The German Ambassador's wife, Princess Lichnowsky, has already bestowed names on all the new fabrics, and she's having *Mechtilde* made into curtains and bed draperies for her bedroom. I am working on persuading her to engage us to redecorate the reception rooms at the German Embassy. What a coup that would be.'

Roger joins the trio. He slips an arm around Vanessa's waist and the two exchange an intimate look. '*Mechtilde* fabrics for Mechtilde Lichnowsky; she's nothing if not modest.'

Vanessa laughs, the sound almost masculine in its depth and resonance. 'I shouldn't complain, Roger. She is exactly the sort of client Omega needs. Have you said hello to Lady Cunard? I saw her arrive with the Bertrand Russells a quarter of an hour ago.'

'Of course. They'll all be stopping by yours for dinner. It will be quite the party.'

Etta glances from the striking Mrs Bell to the two men. She is meant to be home by eight. Mama had been quite adamant about that. But … a party! At Mrs Bell's! Finally, her life is beginning.

'…A work of art must have the power of making the outsider, whose eyes are the least active of his senses, aware of something real and exciting…'

'Oh, Roger, you do run on sometimes.' Vanessa rises from her chair and tosses her napkin onto the table. 'Come, everyone, let us retire to the drawing room for our coffees. Clive, darling, put a record on the gramophone. Something gay.'

'What about the children, pet?'

'They're used to the racket. The boys could sleep through a hurricane.' She beckons to Carlo. 'Carlo, come. Accompany me into the drawing room and tell me all about life in the *Città del Sole*.'

A young woman of about Etta's age, who has spent the dinner engrossed in a conversation with a handsome, dark-haired man with a gaze that Etta thinks conjures the worst kinds of thoughts, leans toward Etta as Carlo makes his apologies and disappears through the doorway with Vanessa. Etta looks at the girl. She is not particularly striking except for her large, expressive brown eyes, and for the fact that she has foregone a corset in favour of a loose-fitting dress printed with an abstraction of multi-coloured lozenges and circles.

The girl extends her hand, which is hung with silver bracelets. 'I'm Violet Hayter. You must be Roger's cousin. I'm studying painting at the Slade. Will you be joining the college in the autumn? It's *the* place to study art, of course.'

'I – I'm hoping so. I shall need to secure some references—'

Violet laughs, the sound light as feathers. 'That shan't be a problem. Just look at who's here! The Bertrand Russells, the Lichnowskys and,' she nods towards her dinner companion as he sidles up to Lady Morrell, 'the artist Mr Wyndham Lewis. His eyes are rather vampiric, don't you think? They suck at one's very soul. Do you see that tall, rather melancholy woman over there in the corner? That's Mrs Bell's sister, Mrs Virginia Woolf. Her husband's here somewhere. An odd fellow, not handsome like Mr Lewis, but a very good conversationalist for a civil servant. She's attempting to be a writer, but,' the young woman shakes her head, which is crowned by a red felt tarbouche, 'she hasn't been well.' She taps her forehead. 'Something wrong up here.'

'It is all very exciting to be here, but I don't know any of these people.'

'Oh, you will! I have a sense of these things.' The throbbing rhythm of a tango drifts out of the drawing room. 'Come on, then. The music calls.' Violet tucks her hand around Etta's elbow and they head towards the drawing room. 'Are you a sensualist, Miss Fry?'

'Oh, I... I...'

'You must be if you're to be an artist. That's my view, at any rate. Artists must be attuned to the vibrations of the earth and all it offers. That why I've joined Omega. It's simply vibrating with energy, don't you think?'

'You've joined the Omega Workshops?'

'Yes, Roger has hired a bunch of us from the Slade as "artist decorators" to design pretty things and scurry around doing whatever needs to be done. It's pin money, really, and we aren't permitted to work more than three and a half days a week so as not to be distracted from our painting, but one never knows who one might meet. I have a dinner engagement with Mr Lewis next Friday. How lucky am I!'

Etta nods. Even she would be circumspect about attending a private dinner with Mr Lewis.

Violet stops abruptly under the drawing room's archway. 'I've just had an idea. Why don't you join Omega? Just ask Roger. No, wait. I'll do it for you.' The young bohemian releases Etta's arm and weaves her way around the gaily slipcovered chairs and tables painted in an explosion of geometrics.

Etta stands in the doorway. The room thrums with conversation and laughter. Lady Morrell and Duncan Grant have commandeered a corner of the Persian carpet and are dancing an energetic tango to the claps and '*Bravos*' of several of the guests. Violet has been waylaid by Mr Lewis, and has, seemingly, forgotten her mission to speak to Roger about a job for her at Omega. The floor vibrates under Etta's feet. She catches Carlo's eye. She watches as he extricates himself from Vanessa Bell and Lady Cunard.

'There you are, *Signorina Etta*. I'm so sorry, but I had to, you know … *conoscere i propri punti di forza…*'

'Know which side of your bread is buttered.' Etta smiles. 'I understand. I know a little Italian from my mother. You're here on business. Artists need buyers.'

'I am afraid this is a reality of life. We must eat.' He takes her hand. 'Come dance with me.'

'I'm afraid I can't.'

Carlo looks at her, his dark eyes wounded. He presses a hand against the breast of his tailored black jacket. 'Forgive me. I am *un pazzo*. A fool. I understand.'

'You understand what?'

'There is somebody else. I am only surprised the room isn't crowded with your admirers. My tragedy is that I live so far away from the most beautiful woman I have ever met.'

Etta feels the blood rise in her cheeks. 'Oh, no. It's simply that I don't know how to dance the tango.'

His eyes flash as they sweep over her. He holds out a hand. 'Come. I shall teach you.'

Etta hesitates for a mere moment. It's well past eight. In fact, she has lost track of the time altogether, and who could blame her? She is amongst the most interesting, most bohemian people of London! She couldn't possibly leave now with the party really starting.

'I should be delighted, Mr Marinetti.'

'I am your most humble servant, *Signorina Etta.*'

Etta glances at the heads turning in their direction as he leads her into the midst of dancers. 'People are looking.'

'Of course they are. We are the talk of the evening, *cara mia.* You have arrived.'

Etta presses her hand against her fluttering stomach and peers through the taxi's dirty window at Clover Bar's shadowy façade. Slivers of yellow light cut into the dark summer night through the slats of the venetian blind in her father's study.

'Papa's still up.' She looks over at Carlo, whose dark eyes glitter in the cab's dull light. 'What time is it?'

He reaches for the chain of his pocket watch and holds it against the window to catch the glow from a streetlight. 'Just after ten o'clock.'

She buries her face in her gloved hands. 'Oh, dear. I shall be in such trouble.'

'*Cara mia,* don't worry.' He waves a hand in the air like he is swatting a fly. 'In Italy, this is nothing.'

'I'm afraid this is London. I was meant to be home by eight.'

'Then I shall accompany you to the door and take all the blame for myself.'

Etta's hazel eyes widen. 'Oh, no, I'd rather you didn't.' But Carlo is already out on the street. She waits as he rounds the taxi and opens her door. Carlo holds out his hand, and, after a moment's hesitation, Etta takes it and steps down onto the pavement. He offers her his arm, but she shakes her head and proceeds up the tiled path ahead of him.

She turns the brass doorknob. Panic rises in her stomach like bile. 'It's locked.'

'You don't have a key?'

'I've never needed one. Someone's always home. I'm never out this late on my own.'

'It is not the end of the world.' He reaches above her shoulder and hammers the brass knocker sharply against the door.

The seconds feel like hours to Etta as she waits for someone to answer. A jangle of keys on the other side of the door. The glow of a gas lamp through the door's leaded glass panes. The door jerks open.

'Mama!'

Christina stands in the doorway, holding a gas lamp, still in her navy linen skirt and white blouse, though she should have been in bed long before.

'Etta, where have you been? Your father was about to leave for the police station.' She sweeps her eyes over the Italian. 'May I enquire as to whom you are?'

Carlo doffs his bowler. 'Permit me, *Signora Fry*. I am Carlo Marinetti. I am a friend of Mr Roger Fry. I wished to ensure your daughter arrived home safely.'

Gerald Fry joins his wife at the door. 'Etta! Thank goodness, dove. Your mother and I have been worried to distraction.' He holds out his hand to Carlo. 'Very kind of you to see her home, Mr Marinetti.' He gestures inside. 'Please, come in and have some tea, or perhaps a brandy?'

'Gerald, it's far too late for socialising.' Christina casts a cool look over the Italian. 'You will excuse us, of course, Mr Marinetti. I'm sure you understand.'

Carlo replaces his hat. 'Of course, *Signora Fry*. It has been my great pleasure to make your acquaintance.'

Christina stands in Etta's bedroom doorway, the glow of the gas lamp casting shadows around the room. 'What on earth made you think you could so blithely ignore your parents' requirements for you to be home by eight o'clock?'

Etta sits on the bed, picking at the white lace bedspread. 'I'm sorry, Mama. I was invited to dinner afterwards, at the home of the artist, Mrs Vanessa Bell. She's a director of the Omega Workshops with Cousin Roger. I'd intended to come home right after the exhibition, but it felt quite rude to decline. I ... I didn't expect the dinner to go on as long as it did.'

'Etta May, you are only eighteen. I can't imagine what Mrs Bell and the other guests must have thought, a young woman of your age gadding about London after hours on her own. It reflects extremely poorly, not only on you, but on myself and your father as well. Had you considered that?'

'I'm sorry, Mama.'

'Your concept of responsibility needs to be reevaluated, Etta. Your father and I had approved of your attending on the stipulation that you would be home by eight o'clock. This you entirely failed to do. As a consequence, there will be no more of these jaunts to London on your own.'

'Mama, please, I'm so sorry. The Omega Workshops are wonderful. I spoke to a student named Violet from the Slade who works there part-time with some of the other art students. She thought I might work there as well. All I need to do is ask Cousin Roger—'

'I'll not have you associating with bohemians. Who was that Italian man at the door?'

'He's an artist from Naples. He's holding an exhibition at Omega in the autumn.'

'You are not to speak to him again, do you understand?'

'But, Mama, he's a perfect gentleman. He insisted upon seeing me home.'

'Perfect gentlemen are the very worst type of men.'

The bedroom door shuts with a jolt. Etta sits on the bed in the shadowy room. She'll speak to her father about working at the Omega Workshops. Not immediately, of course, but in a week or so. She'll get her way. She always does. And Mama can never stay cross with her for long. In the meantime, she'll be the best, most considerate daughter possible.

She lies across the bed, careless of the wrinkles creasing her mother's borrowed dress. She will see Carlo Marinetti again. Of this, she is certain.

Chapter Fourteen

Max

Heidelberg, Germany – August 1913

Clover Bar
Hither Green, London

August 2nd, 1913

My dearest Max,

Oh, Max! I am spinning! I so wish you could have been at the suffragist rally in Hyde Park this past Saturday. Over 50,000 people! It was in The London Illustrated News today. A full page with photographs. I could see Jessie and me in the crowd listening to Mrs Fawcett's speech. I've been in the papers, Max! What do you think of that? Quite a sea of people, women mostly, of course, but not a few supportive men as well. The government can't possibly ignore us now. I bumped into that young auctioneer I told you about, Frank Jeffries, carrying Esther Clothier's banner from the Somerset society. He said he was quite for women's right to vote and managed to escape the auction house for a few hours to attend the rally. I must say, I was rather impressed. You must never judge a book by its cover.

Jessie and I took the train down to Brighton on the 19th to join up with the marchers there. I was quite cross with Etta for not coming with us, but she was off to yet another gallery opening which she insisted she couldn't miss. She has been like a hummingbird flitting in and out of the house for the past few months. She says she is 'educating her artistic eye', whatever that means. She's taken to wrapping her head in a headscarf and sticking an ostrich feather in it for good measure. She is quite the sight. But Mama says nothing, and Papa indulges her no end. She had an escapade last month where she stayed out two hours after she was meant to be home, and arrived back in a taxi accompanied by an Italian! Mama and Papa were very vexed, yet, here we are, a fortnight later, and it is as if nothing happened. Etta has them both twisted around her little finger. Jessie and I shake our heads and simply carry on.

At least I can count on Jessie. She's quite a solid type, and has just graduated top of her nursing class. We are so very proud of her, though she's having quite a time of it with Mama right now, as she is determined to become a nurse for the British Army. Mama has threatened to burn her uniform if she does so. Papa and I spend most of our time in the photography studio, as their arguments and silences are quite a trial to bear. I know Jessie, and Mama hasn't a hope to change her mind. Stubborn as mules, both of them.

The march up from Brighton was quite an adventure. I brought the Brownie camera Papa gave me for my birthday and took loads of photographs. We walked all the way to London, staying in tents on our journey, and held rallies each evening once we'd reached our daily destination. It was all quite jolly, with more and more people joining us along the way, though I did have one lady tip a pot of dried tea leaves over my head from her window in Cuckfield. I expect she thought I would be cross, but they smelled lovely and I waved and thanked her for the 'fragrant shower'!

We reached London on the 26th and assembled in Kennington where more local people joined us. At four o'clock we headed toward Hyde Park. If I were a bird, what a view I would have had! Rivers of women carrying our red, green and white banners through the streets. Whatever must Mr Asquith have thought as he watched us march past his window in the Parliament building?

We had speakers speaking at nineteen platforms, and at 6 o'clock a vote was taken on the motion 'That this meeting demands a Government measure for the enfranchisement of women'. It was passed unanimously. Unanimously, Max! I kissed poor Jessie and jumped about like a banshee! So much for being the quiet girl. I so wish you could have been there.

Mr Asquith has agreed to receive a deputation on August 8th, and Mrs Fawcett has asked me to be a part of the group! I am so very excited. I feel like my life is coming alive. To have purpose, real purpose. I can hear you across the North Sea, 'But you wish to teach German, schatzi, don't you? Isn't that a purpose?' Yes, of course it is, and I still wish that. But Mrs Fawcett has helped me see that there is so much more I can do. We are on the cusp of the government passing a women's suffrage bill, and I've had a role in that.

Oh, my dear Max, I have rabbited on. Please, tell me more about life in Heidelberg. How is your little stepbrother Hans? Still getting up to mischief, I expect. I'm glad to hear he is well-recovered from his skiing mishap last winter.

Are you travelling to the mountains again this summer? I imagine them full of pine trees and goats with air as pure as rainwater. Only four more weeks, Max. Has it really been over two months since we've seen each other? You haven't forgotten me, have you?

Your loving Schatzi

Max folds the pages of the letter and slips them between Acts I and II of *All's Well That Ends Well* in the Heidelberg University's library copy of *The Complete Works of Shakespeare*. He sits down at the small wooden desk in his bedroom and takes a sheet of paper from the drawer. A flash of black and white in the cherry tree outside his window catches his eye. A magpie hops amongst the branches, nudging the ripening cherries with its beak.

'One for sorrow …' Max scans the branches, searching for another flash of black and white in the thick foliage. 'One for sorrow …' A second magpie alights on a branch near the treetop. Max smiles. 'Two for joy.'

He unscrews the cap of his fountain pen, and bends his head over the sheet of white paper.

> *Sandgasse, 10*
> *Heidelberg*
> *Germany*

August 20th, 1913

My dear Schatzi,

You are wondering what happened to me, I am sure. I have just arrived back in Heidelberg from Garmisch-Partenkirchen in the Bavarian mountains with my mother and my stepfather and little Hans.

I have taken a great many photographs with my new Brownie camera. I am very glad you suggested I buy one. My stepfather is a keen hiker, so we were out in the mountains almost every day, and Hans climbed up the hills like a goat in his new lederhosen of which he is so proud. I am quite fit now, though I have been dreaming about Frau Knophler's plum tart. My mouth is watering as I'm thinking of it.

I am so happy your march has been a success. I had no doubt about it.

You are so clever, schatzi. Anything you put your mind to, you will succeed in, I am sure of it.

Enough with all the politeness. I miss you, my schatzi, like the flowers miss the spring rain. You are in my dreams every night; it is the only world in which I am truly happy. It has been so very long. Even though I have kept myself busy, each morning when I wake up and remember that I shall not see your smiling face, my happiness drains away, and I know I must somehow find the courage to meet the day.

I shall be arriving at the train station on the 7th at 4 o'clock. My heart is beating like a drum in my chest as I think about it. I shall be standing on the platform with my hat in my hands watching the crowd for you and your lovely red hair under a big hat. Why do girls wear such big hats, schatzi? I love your hair, have I ever told you that? I think I haven't. It is the colour of the twilight sky as the sun sets over the Neckar River. When I am in Heidelberg, I walk up the Philosophenweg and sit on the stone wall and watch the sun set over the Old Town. I watch as it turns the sky the colour of your hair.

Your loving Max

Chapter Fifteen

Jessie

King's College Hospital, London – August 1913

Jessie plumps the pillow for the boy in Bed 12 in the Paediatrics Ward, whose right leg is buried in a plaster cast which is strung up onto a pulley over his bed.

'Jessie!'

Jessie looks up to see Elsie charging across the polished green linoleum.

'Matron's looking for you. There's been an automobile accident. She wants you in surgery.'

'But I've been assigned paediatrics.'

'Doesn't matter. She wants you there, quick as you like.'

Jessies rushes after Elsie into the hallway. They push through a pair of swing doors and rush down the stairs to the ground floor.

Elsie waves at Jessie in front of the operating theatre doors. 'See you at lunch in the caff, Jessie? You can tell me all about it.'

'Sure. Save me some salmon loaf.'

Inside the operating theatre, the matron gestures to Jessie. 'Scrub up, Sister Fry. We'll be assisting Mr Goodfellow.'

Nurses and orderlies fly about in a frenzy, wheeling in trolleys of equipment and preparing the operating theatre. Jessie grabs the soap and lathers her hands under a tap. 'Sister Webb said there'd been an automobile accident.'

'Yes,' the matron says as she ties on a surgical mask. 'They'll licence any fool to drive one of those abominations. Careering all over the roads at twenty miles an hour. Thoroughfares were never meant to be used by people travelling at the rate of trains. They've only gone and ploughed into a mother and her son stepping off an omnibus on Lewisham High Street.'

The swing doors slam open, and two orderlies wheel in a trolley bearing a woman screeching, 'Simon! Simon!'

The matron points to a space beside a wall. 'Over there.' The doors swing open again; trolley with a young boy this time. The matron gestures to the opposite wall.

Jessie ties the mask over her capped head as she joins the matron. The boy lies still, as if he is sleeping, a seeping bandage tied around his head, his school uniform splattered with blood. The matron lifts the boy's wrist, feeling for a pulse. She opens his left eyelid, then his right, then she rests the boy's hand on his grey uniform jacket. She steps across the polished linoleum floor to the distraught woman, who is clutching a torn sheet, sodden with blood, that someone has tied across her stomach.

The woman grabs the nurse's grey sleeve with a bloody hand. 'Simon! Where's my son?'

'He's here. He's sleeping.'

A groan escapes the woman's pale lips. 'Take care of 'im. 'E's all I 'ave.'

'He's in good hands. The best.'

Jessie sits on a stool by the dead boy.

She has drawn a sheet over his body, but holds his cold hand under the thin white cotton. The matron enters the room and glances at Jessie as she peels off the rubber gloves and tosses them into a bin.

'We didn't even try, Matron.'

The matron turns on the tap. 'We saved his mother.'

'But we didn't even try with him. He's just a boy. With his whole life ahead of him.'

'He was dead, Sister Fry. There was nothing we could do.'

'Maybe … maybe he was in shock. Maybe we made a mistake.'

The matron lathers her hands with the yellow soap. 'You mean maybe *I* made a mistake? It was triage, Sister Fry. You need to assess the casualties and make a decision as to whom to prioritise for treatment. You often don't have more than twenty seconds to do that. Believe me, you hope to God you don't make a mistake.' She turns off the tap and wipes her hands on a towel. 'The boy had no pulse. He wasn't breathing. His pupils were dilated. He was dead. There was nothing we could do for him. But we could save his mother.'

'She said he was all she had.'

'Our job is to mend people. We mended her.'

'But she—'

'When you are on the frontline after a battle, and the casualties lie on stretchers in their hundreds, your job will be to triage and to mend. That is what an army nurse does. It is for Mr Freud and Mr Jung to address patients' psychological states.' The matron rests her hand on Jessie's shoulder. 'Are you quite certain you wish to be an army nurse? I understand you are popular in paediatrics. It's not too late to change your mind.'

Jessie releases the boy's hand.

'I haven't changed my mind. I want to help as many soldiers as I can. I want to be an army nurse. Now, more than ever.'

Chapter Sixteen

Christina

Capri, Italy – August 1891

C hristina tucks her booted feet underneath her, wishing she could untie the laces and release her feet to the summer air and the cool grass in the shade of the parasol pine. If she were on her own, she would. She pops a fat grape into her mouth, savouring the juicy sweetness as she chews. The good-humoured arguments of the housekeeper, Liliana Sabbatini, and her husband, Angelo, waft over to her from the picnic blanket where her cousin sits under a parasol reading a novella. Angelo's donkey flaps its ears at a persistent fly, then bends its head to the grass.

Christina spits the grape seeds into her palm and drops them into the long grass.

'Tina! Use your handkerchief. You are not a fishwife.'

'Sorry, *cugina*.'

Harry chuckles as he dabs his paintbrush at the canvas he has set on an easel under the tree. He frowns. 'This is no good. I need you to take off your hat, Christina.'

'But, Harry, it's so hot. My nose will go red.'

'Please, Christina. If you stay in the shade, you'll be fine. It's such a shame not to see your hair.'

'All right. Not for long, though.' She unpins the straw hat and sets it on the grass beside her.

Harry holds up the paintbrush and gestures like an orchestra conductor. 'Just turn your head that way, facing the sea. Perfect.'

'You're very bossy.'

Christina glances at Harry, who has rolled the sleeves of his white shirt and loosened the knot in his tie. His skin has turned tan from the summer sun, and his somewhat thickset build is slimmer than she remembers from their first meeting.

Had that only been two months ago? It was strange how the days in the sun could feel endless, yet the months could pass so quickly. Was it only a week ago that he had kissed her in the grotto? Her heart flutters as she remembers the warmth of his body against hers, his hands on her shoulders, the kiss, soft like the touch of a butterfly's wings at first, then, hotter and stronger, until she'd been lost in the mindless sensation of his searching mouth. She should feel guilty, but she doesn't.

She catches Harry's eye and he smiles, a beam of sunlight sharpening the blue of his eyes. He waggles the paintbrush at her. 'Turn around.'

'Sorry.'

'You are a very difficult subject.'

'It's just so hard to sit still on such a beautiful day.'

'I'll take you for a walk later. There are some Roman ruins up on Mount Tiberio.'

Her heart skips a beat. They hadn't been alone together since the grotto. 'A mountain?'

'It's more like a tall hill. We'll take our time. There are some lovely views along the way. Oh, and goats.'

'Goats?'

'Mountain goats. They're very friendly.'

She glances sideways at her cousin. 'I'm not sure Cousin Stefania will be up for a long walk up a mountain.'

'Ah, yes, our chaperone.' Harry turns to the Italian woman, who has nodded off under the parasol, a book still in her hand. *'Cugina Stefania!'*

Liliana knocks Stefania's foot with her black shoe. *'Stefania, svegliati!'*

Stefania snorts awake. 'What? What is it?'

'Cugina Stefania,' Harry says. 'We're going for a walk up to the Roman ruins on Mount Tiberio later. Would you like to come?'

Stefania looks around the group, blinking the sleep from her eyes. 'Everyone is going?'

'Well, everyone is invited.'

Stefania's eyebrows draw together over her Roman nose like an arrow. 'It's much too far in this heat. We should go back to the villa and have a rest.'

Christina twists around. 'Oh, please! I'm not in the least tired. We've been sitting here for hours.'

Stefania flaps the book beside her cheek. 'Fine! You English and your walks. Angelo will go with you. Liliana must come back with me to make dinner.'

Angelo secures the easel onto the donkey's back with the panniers, as Harry gives instructions to Liliana for the best way to carry the wet painting back to the villa. They wave Stefania and Liliana on their way with a promise to be back by six o'clock.

When they reach the Piazzetta, Harry takes Angelo aside and, after a whispered consultation, resulting in the exchange of several handfuls of Harry's *lire* for Angelo's water flask and a pat on his back, Harry and Christina are free of their chaperone. Christina watches Angelo depart, and her stomach quivers. Perhaps she should go back to the villa with him. Then Harry slips her hand into the crook of his elbow, and the warmth of his body sends a thrill of joy through her that obliterates any doubt.

They head down the narrow cobbled alley of the Via Longano, past the shoemaker's, the bakery, and the butcher's, where two fresh rabbits hang on a hook outside the door. They turn right onto Via Sopramonte, where the undulating cobbled path takes them past villa walls draped with vibrant bougainvillea. After half an hour, they reach the turn into the even narrower Via Tiberio, where the plastered villa walls become rough stone dwellings, until even these signs of civilisation disappear at the base of the mount.

They stop to drink the last of the water from Angelo's flask, and, after Harry loops the leather strap over his head, he reaches for Christina's hand. 'I know a place with a beautiful view. Let's go there first.'

Christina smiles. She is so happy she feels like her heart is about to burst with joy. 'That sounds lovely.'

They continue up the narrow dirt path, under the wind-whipped pines and columnal cypresses, hand in hand, saying nothing. At the end of the winding path, they break through the shade of the pines out onto a rocky outcrop. Christina gasps. At this height, it is as if she is a bird in the endless blue sky. The fishing boats are nothing but dots on the vast blue sea below, and the wake of the Naples ferry draws a white line in the direction of the mainland.

'Oh, Harry. It's incredible.' Her heart beats a drum in her chest. Then his arms are around her, and she disappears into his endless kisses.

'Come with me, Christina.'

She grasps Harry's hand and follows him past the ancient ruined walls half-buried under scrub grass and vines. He releases her hand as he scrambles over an uneven step and enters through what would have once been a doorway into a small roofless room.

She hesitates for a moment, her foot poised between advancing and fleeing. She knows she should turn back. That it is wrong to be alone here with Harry. But the thundering beat of her heart muffles the warnings. Knowing that something momentous is about to happen.

She steps across the ancient stones into his embrace, and he holds her against his chest until she feels the beating of their hearts unify. He runs the back of his fingers along the skin of her cheek, and attempts to remove her straw hat. She laughs and pushes his hands away, watching him watch her as she draws out the hatpin and sets the hat down on an outcrop of the decaying wall.

She closes her eyes as he traces her face with his fingers. He kisses her; kisses like none she has ever given or received.

'Christina,' he whispers, and it is the sound of a voice in a dream.

He presses his hands against the layers of fabric and lace shielding her body from his touch. She can feel his desire despite the barrier of her corset, but she does nothing to stop him. Gasping, he stumbles away from her and wipes at the sweat beading on his forehead. 'I'm sorry, Christina. I shouldn't. We mustn't—'

She stares at him from the shadows.

It's not too late to stop. They can simply turn around and go back to the villa. Like nothing has happened.

Nothing except that her world has exploded into a million pieces to be replaced by a love for Harry that glows inside her like the sun.

She shuts her eyes and takes several deep breaths. Then she reaches out her hand.

Part Two

1914

Part Two

Chapter Seventeen

Christina

Sussex, England – April 1914

A shaft of sunlight breaks through the branches of the hornbeams and thick-trunked oaks, illuminating the tender new leaves in a phosphorescent glow. At the foot of the trees, blue-violet bluebells spread over the decaying leaves like a lake pushing at the boundaries of its banks. Christina rests her left hand on the moss-coated wood of the fence as she watches her husband adjust the tripod. In a nearby branch a bird trills a pretty song; Christina searches the branches until she spots the red breast of a robin.

'It's a lovely day, Gerald. I'm glad you persuaded me to come down to Sussex. It's so nice to get out of London into the countryside at this time of year.'

Gerald squints into the viewfinder. He twists the lens as he looks at Christina. 'I thought you'd enjoy it, my dear. It's been such a long time since we've had a jaunt out on our own.'

Christina adjusts the new black straw hat that she's had the milliner dress with yellow silk daffodils and a wide white ribbon. 'Yes, well, the girls are all so busy now, Cecelia with her Suffragette activities and her German lessons, Jessica at the hospital all hours, and Etta ...' Christina shakes her head, setting the yellow daffodils quivering. 'Honestly, Gerald, I don't know how she persuaded you to permit her to work at the Omega Workshops. She should be concentrating on her art studies at the Slade. Heaven knows it costs enough to send her there.'

'I thought it would teach her a sense of fiscal responsibility. At least she can pay for her own hair ribbons now.'

Christina runs her hand over her ear. 'I'm not at all happy with the people she's coming into contact with at Omega, Gerald. They're ... they're bohemians. I didn't raise my daughter to become a bohemian. And Cecelia. I am not the least happy with her relationship with this Maximilian Fischer. She has been talking about him for over a year now and we still haven't met him.'

'That's easy enough to resolve, Tina. Have Celie invite him to Sunday lunch. Her birthday's only a few weeks away. Why not then?'

'Cecelia's birthday lunch?'

'Yes, why not? You said you wanted to meet him, didn't you?'

'Yes, though I haven't a clue what to speak to a German about.'

'I've always found the weather useful in most situations.' He smiles at his wife. She can be obstinate, but he knows it comes from a place of love. He simply wishes he could break through the wall she has kept around herself all these years. There are moments when he glimpses a softer Christina, the Christina he'd first met, when her eyes light up at the sound of Celie singing at the piano, or a smile tugs at her lips at his unexpected gift of her favourite chocolate cannoli. He wishes it were more often, but he is happy that it happens at all.

He holds up the shutter release cable and smiles at his stylish wife. How was a simple man like him so lucky to have married her?

'That's perfect, my dear. Don't move.'

Christina packs away the leftover cheese and biscuits into the picnic hamper and looks over at her husband, whose soft snores are already resonating from beneath the straw hat. Twenty-two years married in November. Twenty-two years since he'd rescued her.

Gerald is a good man. He has provided well for her and the girls. She'd done the right thing marrying him. She wishes only that she could … love him a little more. She's tried, of course, but love isn't like water. One could not turn it on like a tap. Still, she has no right to complain. Her life is entirely satisfactory, though it is far from the life she'd imagined that summer in Capri when the world was full of possibilities. When she was young and carefree and happy. The summer that love chose to wrap itself around her like a beautiful cloak. The summer of Harry Grenville.

She lies back on the blanket and watches the clouds puff above her in the soft blue sky. Her heart may not throb with the passion she had felt for Harry, and she may not quake with anticipation at the sound of Gerald's step, but her life is perfectly acceptable. She has no reason to complain and every reason to be thankful. She had prayed to God for her salvation and he had sent her Gerald. She reaches across to her husband and closes her fingers around his sleeping hand. For that she is thankful.

Chapter Eighteen

The Frys

Clover Bar, London – 3 May 1914

'Y ou made it.'

Max removes his bowler hat and sneaks a quick peck on Celie's cheek. 'I did. I confess I am rather nervous, *schatzi*.'

Celie takes Max's umbrella and ushers him into the house. 'Don't worry, we don't bite. Well, I can't vouch for Mama.' She pulls the brocade curtain across the door and drops the umbrella into the brass stand. 'Isn't the weather dreadful? I was hoping we could have my birthday lunch in the garden, but it's as cold as November out there. Another typical English Bank Holiday weekend, I'm afraid.'

Max slides a small box wrapped in blue paper and a white ribbon into her hand. 'Happy Birthday, *schatzi*. Any day I can spend with you is a bright day for me.'

'Oh, Celie, isn't that the most charming thing to say?' Etta flies down the staircase in a swirl of shell pink chiffon. 'You are every bit as handsome as Celie's said, Max Fischer. I have no idea why she's been hiding you all this time.'

'Etta!'

'Well, it's true, Celie.' Etta takes hold of Max's arm. 'Come inside and sit with me, Max, and tell me all about how you met Celie.'

'Etta, please,' Celie protests as she hangs Max's raincoat and hat on the coatstand. 'Let Max catch his breath.'

'Oh, Celie, I'm simply curious. There's nothing wrong with that, is there, Max?'

'Indeed not. I am most happy to oblige, Miss Etta.'

'See, Celie? He's happy to oblige.'

'That's because he's a gentleman.'

Celie follows them into the sitting room and sits in her mother's armchair. She gestures to Etta. 'Max, this is Etta; Etta, Max. Mama says Etta has no sense of propriety, and there are times I would agree.'

Gerald enters the room, his pipe cupped in his left hand. 'Did I hear the doorbell, Celie? Ah, Mr Fischer! You found us.' He extends his hand to Max, who springs to his feet. 'Delighted you could join us for Celie's birthday. Twenty-two already. Where does the time go?'

'Twenty-one, Papa.'

'Twenty-one, is it, pet?' He smiles at Max as they shake hands. 'I've never been very good at keeping track of time.'

'It's a pleasure to meet you, Mr Fry.'

'I hope you're hungry. Milly has cooked up roast lamb, with Christina's Italian cake for pudding.' Gerald sits in his armchair and sucks at his pipe. He frowns as he knocks it against the table. 'Drat. It's gone out again and I've left my matches in the study.'

'I should hope so, Gerald,' Christina says as she enters the room, slender and elegant in her new navy silk day dress. 'A family gathering is no place to smoke your pipe.'

Celie springs out of her mother's chair. 'Mama, may I introduce Max Fischer. Max, this is my mother.'

Max bows his head. 'It is my great honour to meet you, Mrs Fry. Thank you for inviting me here to share Celie's birthday with your family.'

Christina inclines her head, like a queen acknowledging a subject. 'Cecelia was most insistent, which was quite out of character for her. She is not normally one to exhibit such vigour.'

Celie glances at Max, embarrassed, though unsurprised, by her mother's comment. 'Where's Jessie, Mama? She's not usually one to miss *Torta Caprese.*'

Christina takes a seat in her chair. 'She's had to go in to the hospital.'

'On a Sunday?'

'It would seem so, Cecelia.'

'More cake for us, then,' Etta says. 'I'll go see how Milly's getting on. I can't miss my chance at the icing bowl.'

Celie sits beside Max on the chaise longue. 'Max has been teaching German at the college for … how long is it now, Max?'

'Almost two years. It has been most enjoyable and it has given me a good opportunity to improve my English.'

Christina settles a cool gaze on Max. 'Will you be staying in London for long, Mr Fischer?'

'I am afraid I must return to Heidelberg at the end of the summer term. I must do my national army service for the next year.'

'So you will be leaving London shortly?'

Gerald knocks the cold pipe ash into the aspidistra pot. 'Tina, my dear. Don't chase the poor man away.'

'I am certain our guest is quite ready to return to his home, Gerald. London can be quite grey and tedious, is that not so, Mr Fischer?'

Max glances at Celie. 'Heidelberg is a beautiful city, Mrs Fry, but then, so is London in its own way.' He rests his hand over Celie's. 'I

intend to return as soon as I finish my military service. You see, I...
We... Celie and I—'

'Military service?'

'Yes, Mrs Fry. I must do it for a year from September. It's a requirement.'

Etta pokes her head around the sitting room door. 'Hurry up, everyone. Milly has the lamb on the table for carving. The mint sauce smells like heaven. And wait till you see the birthday cake! Jessie will be lucky if there's any left when we're through.'

Celie fingers the delicate coral necklace as she and Max walk down Springback Road toward Hither Green train station.

'Thank you for the lovely gift, Max. I hope it wasn't dear.'

'It is my pleasure, *schatzi*. Please, don't worry about such things. You can't know how excited I was to give it to you. When I saw it, I could not imagine anyone else who would look as well in it.'

'I'm sorry if Mama was... Well, I did say that she can be rather difficult at times.'

'Don't worry, *schatzi*. Your mother is your mother. I must respect her. She is a charming hostess.'

'You haven't been to many social occasions, have you?'

Max chuckles. 'I have been to enough. You mother is only being protective of her daughter. I am a dubious foreigner, after all.'

'Mama's half Italian, so she should know better than to put you on the spot like that. I'm so embarrassed she asked you where your loyalties lie if war were to break out in Europe. Thank goodness for Papa and his cigars. Tell me, Max. What's a cigar like? Is it pleasant? Mama thinks they're horrid and refuses to let Papa smoke them anywhere except in his study. Did you have a nice chat with him in there?'

'I did. He was quite interested in which types of roses grew along the Philosophenweg.'

'Surely you didn't talk only about roses.'

He glances sideways at Celie. 'No, not entirely. I must say, your sister is delightful.'

'Everyone loves Etta. She breezes around like a colourful bird. She doesn't listen to a word Mama says, and is consequently Mama's favourite. I, on the other hand, never seem to please Mama, no matter how hard I try.'

'I am sure that is not the case, *schatzi*.'

'If only that were true.'

'I'm sorry I missed meeting Jessie,' Max says as they skirt around a puddle.

'Just imagine Etta's complete opposite.' Celie stops in front of the modest brick train station. 'We're here.'

'We are indeed.'

Max leans forward to kiss her on the cheek, but Celie turns her head and their lips meet. Then they are in each other's arms, oblivious to the Sunday day trippers streaming in and out of the station. Two lovers engulfed in the endless moment before parting.

'Where is everyone?'

Christina looks up from her needlepoint. 'Your father's in his study and Etta is in her bedroom, no doubt experimenting with another hairstyle.'

Celie sits on the chaise longue. 'So, what did you think of Max, Mama?'

Christina winces as she pricks her finger on the embroidery needle. 'He seemed fine.'

'Fine? Is that all?'

Christina presses her finger against her thumb to stem the

bleeding. 'What do you expect me to say, Cecelia? He was here for a few hours, and was no doubt on his best behaviour. I can scarcely be expected to form a clear picture of his character based on one short meeting.'

Celie hands her mother her handkerchief. 'Papa seemed to like him. They were in his study smoking cigars for an hour.'

'Men and their cigars. I shall never understand it.'

'Etta liked him as well.'

'Etta likes everyone. She has no sense of judgement.'

'Why do you indulge Etta so much, Mama?'

Christina sticks the needle through the canvas and rests the needlepoint on her lap. 'Whatever do you mean, Cecelia?'

'You had Cousin Roger sponsor her place at the Slade, for instance, when you don't even like artists – or Cousin Roger, for that matter. You say artists are self-centred and irresponsible, and yet you did everything you could to secure her place.'

'One can't help one's nature, Cecelia, and Etta has an artistic nature. Besides, an artistic woman is considered by society to be refined, whereas an artistic man is considered suspect. Roger has assured me that the majority of students at the Slade are female, and that he will keep a close eye on Etta at the Omega Workshops to ensure nothing untoward occurs.'

'Why have you been so dismissive of me studying German?'

'I do not object to you studying German, Cecelia, though I can't say I understand your interest in it. I object to you studying German with that man.'

'With Max? Why?'

'Cecelia, the way you looked at him through lunch today, hanging on his every word like a … a lapdog … it was most unseemly. A lady shows restraint and composure at all times.'

'I'm sorry, Mama. I was just so excited to have him finally meet the family.'

Christina tucks Celie's handkerchief in her pocket and picks up the needlepoint. 'My one consolation is that it won't be repeated any time soon.'

'What do you mean?'

Christina frowns at the turquoise wool she is attempting to thread through the needle. 'Isn't Mr Fischer returning to Germany shortly?'

'In September. He's teaching at the college through the summer term. I thought I might take his class in Advanced German and we could all go on a family picnic down on Wimbledon Common. Wouldn't that be nice?'

'Really, Cecelia, you lack sense and foresight. Just like your fa—' Christina stabs the thread through the canvas.

'Just like my father?'

'Just like your family. Your sisters. Dreamers, all of you. Dreams result only in disappointment and unhappiness. You're the eldest, Cecelia. Show some sense and be an example to the twins. Teach German if you must, marry a nice young Englishman and have a family. It is a perfectly reasonable aspiration. Why must I have such wilful daughters?' She pushes the needle through the canvas. 'All of this nonsense has given me a headache. I shall tell Milly to make a pot of camomile tea.'

'Milly's left. It's her half-day.' Celie rises from the chaise longue. 'I'll do it. At least I know how to make a reasonable cup of tea. I am not entirely a lost cause.'

Chapter Nineteen

Etta

Omega Workshops, London – June 1914

Etta teeters on the wooden stepladder as she finishes painting a large pink circle on the showroom's ceiling. 'Oh, do hold on, Violet. The ladder's shaking. I'll drop the brush on your head if you don't hold me steady.'

Violet braces the wooden legs with her feet. 'Do you suppose the King and Queen would have us paint pink circles on the ceilings of Buckingham Palace?'

Etta laughs as she steps down the ladder. 'After their reaction to our sitting room display at the Ideal Home Show last autumn, I hardly think so. What was it the papers said?' Etta puts on a pompous clipped accent, '"*Their Majesties deemed it the perfect example of how not to decorate a sitting room.*"'

'Their Majesties are bourgeois.'

'No publicity is bad publicity, Violet, as Mr Barnum said. And it did draw people into the shop like flies. We did a sterling trade in Mrs Bell's tea cosies for Christmas presents.'

Violet folds up the ladder and sets it against a rack stacked with geometric-patterned fabrics in vibrant yellows, mauves and teal blues. 'We would have sold more of the table runners and napkins if you'd remembered to order the linen in time for us to paint and sew them, Etta. Roger was quite cross about that.'

'I know. It's why he wouldn't let me work on the Chinese Room at Lady Hamilton's London house. I'm afraid it slipped my mind. There was so much happening last autumn with the Idea Home Show and Carlo Marinetti's exhibition.'

'More like you were distracted by a certain Italian artist.'

'Violet, that's not true.'

The bell tinkles in the next room. Etta drops the paintbrush in the large enamel sink. 'I'll go.' She shrugs out of her work smock and hands it to Violet. 'When I get back, we can get started on the wall mural. Mrs Bell says she wants something primeval.'

'Primeval? But it's meant to be a nursery display.'

'We're artists, Violet. Use your imagination.'

She pulls aside a painted curtain to see the back of a tall man in a sharply tailored grey wool suit and a straw boater. He taps a walking stick on the wooden floor as he stands at the window looking out at the lushly planted square across the street.

'Good afternoon, sir. May I help you?'

The man looks over his shoulder. *'Buongiorno, Signorina Etta.'*

'Carlo!' Etta throws open her arms and runs over to the handsome Italian. He takes her into his embrace and hugs her close.

'Cara mia, you've become Italian, I think. Your mother would not approve.'

Etta stands back and brushes a tumbling curl out of her eyes. Her finger catches on the paint-spattered kerchief she's tied over her hair. 'Oh, my word. I must look a fright.' She tugs the offending scrap of fabric off her head.

'This would be an impossibility.'

She tucks the kerchief into her skirt pocket. 'What are you doing here? I thought you were in Italy.'

'I was. But my exhibition here last autumn has finally, how do you say, borne fruit. Lady Cunard has persuaded her husband to meet with me to discuss a mural for the boardroom of the new Cunard Building that's just been commissioned in Liverpool.' He waves his hand in the air. 'It will be years before it is built, of course, but Lady Cunard is most insistant that I be involved in the design of the boardroom from the start. It is certain to give me and the architect many years of interesting arguments.'

Etta claps her hands. 'Oh, that's marvellous, Carlo. Everyone who's anyone travels on a Cunard liner. You will be rich and famous.'

'Artists do not traditionally become rich, *Signorina Etta*. Famous, perhaps.' He rubs his thumb and forefinger together. 'But fame does not pay for spaghetti.'

Etta's face crumples into a frown.

'What is it, *cara mia*? Did you believe that I was a wealthy man? I assure you, this suit has been purchased on credit as any decent artist would do.'

'No, no. Heavens, money doesn't matter to me one jot. No, I thought Lady Cunard was living in London with her daughter, Nancy, while Lord Cunard stays at their estate in Leicestershire.' She lowers her voice to a whisper. 'They say she's stepping out with the novelist Mr George Moore. Some say that Mr Moore is Nancy's real father.'

'Is that so?'

'Oh, yes. You hear *everything* about *everyone* here at Omega.'

Outside the window, a pair of well-dressed women shuffle past the shop in their hobble skirts. They glance up at the window as they pass. Carlo takes hold of Etta's elbow and steers her deeper into the shop.

'I must leave Thursday morning on the train to Liverpool to meet Lord Cunard and the architect. I was hoping you might do me the honour of accompanying me for lunch and a walk around Regent's Park tomorrow while I am in London.' He leans closer. 'I miss you, *Etta mia.*' His eyes sweep over Etta's face. 'You are as lovely as a Botticelli angel.'

A delicious shiver washes up through Etta's body. Her heart jumps and flutters against her ribs like a lost butterfly. She reaches forward, as if mesmerised, and places her hand over Carlo's heart. He breathes in sharply and covers her hand with his own. *'Cara mia.'*

The bell above the entrance door jingles, and Etta and Carlo step apart as quickly as two schoolchildren caught planning a prank. Violet appears from behind the showroom curtain. She glances at Etta, whose cheeks are colouring, and raises an eyebrow. She turns to the smartly dressed woman and her young daughter entering the shop with an effusive 'Hello! May I be of service?'

Etta picks up a folded tablecloth. 'Yes, sir. I shall arrange for the tablecloth to be sent around to your address in the morning.'

'Thank you, miss.' Carlo takes a white card and a fountain pen from his breast pocket. He scribbles on the card and hands it to Etta. 'Here is my address. I shall tell my wife to expect the package tomorrow.'

Etta glances at the card. *12:30 Water Lily House, Botanic Garden, Regent's Park.* 'Certainly, sir. I'm certain she will like it very much.'

Carlo tips his hat and hooks his walking stick over his arm. 'Of this, I am most certain.'

At thirty-five minutes past twelve the following day, Etta enters the vast iron and glass structure that houses the water lily collection in Regent's Park. The humidity sits on the air as heavy as wet feathers, and she presses her hand against the frills of her bodice as she catches her breath. The air smells of damp and earth and moss, and it reaches inside her body, thickening her blood. She steps forward, her footsteps echoing on the damp tiled floor. Before her, hundreds of lily pads, some as large as wheels, with delicate flowers in pink and white and yellow, float in a black pool that shines like liquorice under the glass roof.

'You've come. I was worried you might not.'

Etta resists the urge to spin around and throw herself into Carlo's arms. She swallows and takes a breath to compose herself. 'Of course. I'm very fond of water lilies.'

She feels his warm breath brush against her neck. '*Nympheas.*' He says the word like a caress. 'The flowers of the forest nymphs. Flowers of purity and grace.' He leans closer. 'The flowers of Etta Maria.'

Etta closes her eyes. His hand is on her waist, though she cannot feel its warmth through her corset. A child squeals and Etta jolts back from the daze. Across the pool a father lifts his young daughter over the iron railing and sits her on a large lily pad.

'Heavens, that child! She'll fall into the water. What is her father thinking?'

'Don't worry. She will be fine. It's a Victoria water lily.' Carlo points to a description affixed to the railing. 'It says they can grow as large as ten feet in diameter and support a weight of up to sixty-five pounds.'

Etta looks over at the wailing child, who is slapping at the plant's rubbery green skin. 'Still, I'm sure he's not meant to be setting his child on a lily pad in Regent's Park, Carlo. She's not at all happy about it.'

'You are one to follow all the rules, of course?'

'Well, unless they're silly.'

'Like the time you ignored your parents' instruction to be home by eight o'clock?'

Etta looks sideways at Carlo and smiles prettily. 'Well, it was frightfully early. And I was almost nineteen—' She takes a sharp breath and bites her lower lip.

Carlo laughs, his teeth a flash of white under his dark moustache. 'Almost nineteen is a delightful age for a young woman.'

'You'd think I was still a child if you were to judge by the way my parents treat me. My twin sister is only ten minutes older than me, but they let her work at the hospital at all hours without uttering a word of objection. She could be out dancing the night away for all they know.'

'You have a twin sister? It is beyond imagining that there are two Botticelli angels here in London.'

'Oh, Jessie's nothing like me. She has brown hair and green eyes, and she's taller and, um, rather sturdier than I am. And she's awfully serious. She wants to be an army nurse, but Mama is dead set against it. They've been arguing about it for months. It's awfully tedious. I had to take the job at Omega for my own sanity.'

'So, Jessie would not be out dancing the night away, as you say.'

'Oh, no. Never.' Etta giggles. 'I couldn't imagine it.'

'So, of course, your parents don't worry about her. But, *Signorina Etta*, she loves to dance, does she not?'

'Well, yes. There's nothing wrong with that.'

'And she enjoys the company of artists and bohemians.'

'They are by far the most interesting of people.'

'And, I think, *Signorina Etta* has a romantic heart, rather than a practical one like her sister.'

'An artist must have a romantic heart.'

'If I were your father, I would be most concerned about you as well.' The smile fades from his face. 'You must be careful, my angel. There are people in the world who would take advantage of such beauty. Tragedy doesn't arise from practical people, *cara mia*. It needs beauty and romantic hearts to nourish it.'

Carlo pays the waitress and tucks his wallet inside his grey wool jacket. He is wearing a navy silk tie with flecks of green, which Etta thinks suits him very well, particularly with the jade and silver tie pin. A crisp white handkerchief peaks from the top of his breast pocket and his starched collar sets off the warm tan of his skin. He has slicked his black hair back from a neat side parting, and Etta thinks she is the luckiest young woman in the café, having such a dashing luncheon companion.

She holds her teacup between her hands and looks out from under the shade of the trellised terrace. The flower beds are bursting with ebullient peonies and bearded irises like purple spears, and the borders foam with yellow-green lady's mantle and pink-flowered geraniums. Despite it being a Thursday, the pathways are full of people enjoying the fine summer day: nannies pushing baby carriages; children running on the grass spinning hoops and throwing balls; an elderly gentleman walking a panting bear-like Newfoundland dog; a woman laughing at her companion's comment.

She wouldn't have missed this day for the world. Life isn't all about studies and jobs, though her sisters appear to think so. Someone has to have some fun in life. It may as well be her.

'Shall we go for a walk in the flower gardens, Etta? I have saved some bread to feed the ducks in the boating lake.'

Etta sets down her teacup. 'That sounds lovely.'

They join the promenaders along the twisting gravel paths, stopping from time to time for Etta to sniff the perfume of a rose. Carlo cuts off a yellow bud with his penknife and slips the stem through his buttonhole.

'Very dashing, Carlo.'

'I must be for you.'

They approach a narrow path which veers away from the wider

promenade. A small sign with an arrow directs them to the Fern Dell.

'Shall we go?' Carlo asks.

'Yes. It will be nice to get out from under the sun.'

They follow the path through a copse of birches, past thick banks of waxy-leafed rhododendrons with flowers the colour of blood, into the shade of the dell. A pond constructed of moss-covered rocks sits under the leafy green canopy of the towering plane trees and elms, and the orange scales of goldfish slide against the pond's clear surface. Carlo leads Etta to a stone bench, and they sit for a few moments in silence.

'Carlo, thank you for today. It's been so love—'

Then he is kissing her, his arms wrapped around her; she holds him tight, opening her mouth to his as he whispers her name between kisses.

All she knows, all she has ever known since that first day in the art gallery, is that she loves him with every breath in her body.

They walk along the path beside the boating lake where bright blue rowboats with their happy passengers bob on the rippling water. They stop to throw scraps of bread to the honking Canada geese. When they are done, Carlo takes Etta's hand and holds it between his own.

'I must see you again before I go back to Italy.'

'Yes.'

'Sunday. Can you meet me?'

'Sunday's difficult. Everyone's at home.'

'Monday, then, *cara mia*. Here? In the Fern Dell?'

Etta nods. 'Yes. That's perfect. I have art classes at the Slade on Monday, just nearby.'

'At three o'clock? It doesn't disturb your studies?'

Etta smiles as she looks into Carlo's dark eyes, which shine with a light which sends a thrill through her body. 'I shall be thinking about you all day. How could I possibly study?'

'How am I meant to discuss work with Lord Cunard when the vision of your lovely face will be all that my mind will see?'

Etta feels the heat rise in her cheeks. 'What are we going to do, Carlo? You live in Italy and I'm in London. It's impossible.'

He squeezes her hand. 'It is not impossible. You are in the world and I am in the world, *cara mia*. This is all that matters. We shall find a way.'

Chapter Twenty

The Frys

Clover Bar, London – June 1914

J essie sets the bone china teacup and saucer – her
grandmother's good Royal Worcester set with its delicate
hand-painted flowers and gilding, as tea tastes so much better
in bone china – on the wirework garden table under the trellised
arbour behind the house. She sits in a wicker chair and yawns. She'll
be glad when she is back on day shifts at the hospital in a fortnight.
It's an odd thing to be up while everyone sleeps, and sleeping while
the world goes on its way without her. She lifts her face to the warm
afternoon sun. Still, it's Sunday and she is off; church and lunch are
done, and the afternoon is finally hers before she heads off to an
early night's sleep and the luxury of a morning lie-in.

The door to the greenhouse swings open and Celie steps onto the
gravel path. 'Tea? That's a grand idea, Jessie. Is there any left?'

'The teapot's in the kitchen. Bring out some of Milly's shortbread biscuits too, will you, Celie?'

When Celie returns, she sets the tray on the table, and settles into the wicker chair beside Jessie. She picks up her teacup and sips at the hot tea. 'The Perle d'Azur clematis had some wilt that I had to cut out. I have no idea why that happened. It was perfectly healthy yesterday.'

'You haven't overwatered it, have you?'

'Not unless you've been watering it as well.'

'Ah, there's your answer. Too many gardeners spoil the clematis. Papa's probably been watering it too.'

Celie chuckles. 'We should probably put up a schedule in the greenhouse.' She takes another sip of tea and sits quietly for some minutes.

'Jessie, have you noticed anything odd when you're out in London?'

Jessie licks shortbread crumbs off her lips. 'What do you mean?'

'There's all this talk about zeppelins, and the Germans militarising, and people refusing to buy German sausages. One of the windows of Steiners' haberdashers on the high street had a brick thrown through it the other night.'

'I heard about that. I suppose it's because people are afraid. The Germans are making people nervous.'

Celie surveys the garden in its fulsome June beauty. 'Max has had to join something called the *Landsturm* in Germany. It's like an army reserve. All the German boys have to serve when they reach their twenties. He starts his training in September when he returns to Heidelberg. It will be a year before I'll see him after that.'

'Oh, dear. How do you feel about that?'

'It's his duty, I suppose. I keep hoping all this war talk will blow over. On a beautiful day like today, I can almost believe it will blow over, and everything will return to normal.' She picks at a loose piece of wicker on the arm of the chair. 'I'm going to miss him terribly, Jessie.'

'A year goes by so quickly, Celie. It will be over before you know it.'

'I suppose.' She glances at her sister. 'I expect we shall marry when he's finished his training.'

Jessie sets down her teacup with a clatter. 'Really? He's proposed?'

'No! Please don't say anything. He hasn't asked me yet, but Max and I belong together. I've felt it ever since the first day we met in German class.' She smiles. 'I never expected to fall in love with my teacher.'

'He isn't ancient, is he?'

'He's only twenty-five. I expect we shall live in Heidelberg after we marry. Perhaps I can teach English there. Isn't that a funny thing, after studying German these past two years, to end up teaching English?'

The garden door slams against the wooden fence. 'Jessie! Celie! There you are. I've been looking for you everywhere.' Etta swings through the door and flops into an empty chair. She is wearing billowing peacock blue silk bloomers with a lacy white blouse, her blonde curls tumbling over her shoulders from beneath a red felt *tarbouche* she has set on a jaunty angle.

Jessie peruses her twin. 'Etta, you look a sight.'

'I'll take that as a compliment, Miss Dowdy Drawers.'

'You've not wearing a corset, are you? Whatever will Mama think?'

'Corsets are bourgeois. That's something Violet at Omega says about boring people and things.'

'I guess I'm bourgeois, then.' Celie rises from her chair. 'I have to go. I promised to help Papa rearrange the studio this afternoon. We have several schools coming in all next week for their graduation photographs and we won't have a moment to spare.'

Etta grabs Celie's arm. 'What about Mama's tea for Mr Jeffries tomorrow? You're meant to be there with me.'

'I'm sorry, Etta. I've told Mama I can't as I have to help Papa. I think she was rather glad. She's convinced that Frank Jeffries fancies you. I was simply there to fill out the numbers.'

Etta chews her lip as Celie leaves. She leans across the table and lowers her voice. 'Jessie, I need a favour.'

Jessie reaches for another biscuit. 'Don't you have somewhere to go, Etta? It's a shame to waste your outfit on dowdy old me.'

Etta grabs hold of Jessie's hand, rattling Jessie's teacup. 'I'm sorry. I don't mean it, Jessie. You know me; I speak before I think. I think you're very admirable, being a nurse and all of that. I should really try to be more like you.' She smiles, her cheek dimpling. 'You wouldn't credit that we're twins, would you?'

'What is it this time, Etta?'

'You must promise not to say a word to Mama or Papa.'

'I suddenly seem to have become the keeper of the family secrets. What are you up to?'

'I'm meeting someone in town tomorrow at three o'clock, and I'm meant to be home no later than four for Mama's tea for that tedious Frank Jeffries.'

'Ah, yes, the one who never goes to the cinematograph theatre. Mama didn't tell me a thing about it. Funny, that.'

'I suppose she thought you might be working, but you're doing nights now so you're free. Can you step in for me, especially now that Celie isn't going to be there? I can't leave Mama on her own with Frank Jeffries. I'd never hear the end of it. I'll tell Mama I was delayed at the college when I get home. I shouldn't be later than five … or sixish.'

'Who are you meeting?'

'It's no one. Really.'

'I'll not do it unless you tell me whom you're meeting.'

Etta puffs out a long breath. 'His name is Carlo Marinetti. He's an artist. I met him at Omega's opening party last summer.'

'Where are you meeting him?'

'What does it matter?'

Jessie reaches for the teacup.

'Oh, all right, Jessie. We're meeting in Regent's Park. We're simply going to have some tea and walk around the lake. Whatever's the harm in that?'

'What's the urgency, Etta? You can meet him another time.'

'He's leaving for Naples tomorrow evening. I don't know when I might see him again.'

'You and Celie both.'

'What do you mean?'

'You both have admirers, it appears. And I am left with Mr Jeffries.'

Jessie reaches for another of Milly's scones, choosing to ignore her mother's arched eyebrow. She splits open the golden pastry and scoops a large dollop of clotted cream and a spoonful of strawberry jam onto its warm centre. She takes a bite and dabs at her mouth with a linen napkin. 'So, Mr Jeffries, it seems from what you've said that the auction business is going well.'

Frank sets down his teacup. 'Yes, the younger married couples in London prefer simple Arts & Crafts furniture to heavy Victorian pieces, though outside the city, the taste is still for Victorian style. So we buy up the old pieces here and my father sells them to the country set from our auction house in Nuneaton. He spends most of his time at our house there now with my mother and younger brother, though he does show up unannounced in London with rather alarming regularity to take back the reins if he feels I've made an unwise purchase.'

Christina takes Frank's teacup and, setting the silver tea strainer over its rim to catch the fragrant Earl Grey tea leaves, pours it full of steaming tea. 'It's only natural for your father to keep an eye on the family business.' She lifts off the strainer and scoops two spoonfuls of sugar and pours a touch of milk into the tea. She hands the teacup back to Frank. 'You must trust him to steer you in the right direction so that you can provide sufficiently for your future family.'

'Yes, of course, Mrs Fry.'

Jessie dabs her lips with her napkin and lays it on the table. 'Mama, Mr Jeffries, I'm afraid you must excuse me. I'm working at the hospital at six-thirty, and I must get ready or I'll be late. I'm already in enough trouble with Matron about tardiness as it is.'

'Is it that time already?' Christina glances at her silver wristwatch. 'Quarter past five.' Christina smiles apologetically at Frank as Jessie leaves. 'Etta was meant to join us this afternoon after her studies.'

'And Miss Fry, is she not here?'

'Cecelia? No, she's having to help her father in the photography studio this week. They're run off their feet with graduation portraits.' She rings a small silver bell on the table just as Etta rushes into the sitting room like a gust of blonde wind.

Etta unpins her hat and tosses it onto the chaise longue. 'Mama, I'm so sorry. Mr Tonks wished to see me about my piece for the college's summer exhibition, and I couldn't very well just leave, could I?' She rolls her hazel eyes dramatically. 'He went on and on.' She extends her hand to Frank and flashes him her most winning smile. 'Mr Jeffries, it's an absolute delight to see you again. I'm absolutely fraught that I missed the tea. Milly bakes the best cakes and scones in London.'

Milly enters the sitting room. 'Yes, ma'am?'

Etta turns to the maid, who stands in the sitting room doorway, politely attentive in her neat navy dress and starched white apron.

'Speak of the devil. There's our Milly now. It looks like Mr Jeffries is on his way, Milly. Would you kindly see him to the door?'

Christina gestures to Jessie's empty chair. 'That's not necessary, Milly. Etta, now that you're here, come and join our guest for a cup of tea before he leaves.'

'I would love to, Mama, but I'm frightfully late. I'm meeting Violet at the pictures at seven in Lewisham. I only have time for some toast and a quick bath before I have to be off.' She picks up her hat and waves at Frank. 'It was lovely to see you, Mr Jeffries.'

Milly shifts on her feet. 'Ma'am?'

'I shall be off, Mrs Fry,' Frank says. 'Thank you for a lovely afternoon.'

Christina rises and extends her hand. 'Thank you for being such an attentive guest, Mr Jeffries. Please give my regards to your father. I shall endeavour to have all my daughters here the next time you visit. Milly will see you out.'

When Frank has gone, Christina exhales an exhausted sigh. An entirely fruitless afternoon. Frank Jeffries' prospects as a son-in-law appear to be vanishing by the minute. She runs her fingers over her ear and pats her hair. Yet, hadn't Frank Jeffries enquired about Cecelia? She will file that nugget of information away for the future. Once this Max Fischer is back in Germany, things will be so much easier.

Christina looks at the tiered cake stand and reaches for one of Milly's walnut squares. She pops the entire square into her mouth. Closing her eyes, she savours the sweet nutty cake as she chews, remembering a day when Harry Grenville fed her walnuts in the warm Capri sun. Before everything went wrong.

Chapter Twenty-One

Christina

Capri, Italy – September 1891

Christina watches Harry as he paints. He frowns, deep in concentration, looking at her, yet not seeing her; or, rather, seeing her in the way a scientist might view cells under a microscope. *Look at me!* she wants to shout. I'm more than my red hair and my blue eyes, though I know how these affect you. Do you love me, or do you simply wish to be in love?

Where has her mood come from? She has been out of sorts for a week. But, of course, she knows. The letter from her father arrived a week ago Monday. In a fortnight it will be October; time to return home to London. Her cousin Stefania will accompany her as far as Rome and her father will meet them there. Then, she will leave with her father on the train for Paris, then London. He will ask her questions about Capri, and her cousin, and the food. He'll ask her to speak to him in Italian, and he will be delighted at her new proficiency. He will ask her all these things as the train pulls her further and further away from Harry, and from the warm, hazy days of their love.

'Tina? Tina?'

Christina looks at Harry. 'Yes?'

He smiles, his blue eyes alight with amusement. He tosses her a fat brown walnut from a paper bag. 'Where were you?'

She juggles the nut from hand to hand. 'On the moon.' She throws the nut back at Harry. 'You'll have to crack it for me.'

He sets the nut on a rock and hits it with another rock, sending its shell flying over the long tufts of grass. He scoops up the wrinkled kernel and wades through the grass to Christina.

'Close your eyes and open your mouth.'

Christina laughs. 'What?'

He kneels beside her. 'It'll taste better. Trust me.'

Christina shuts her eyes. He slips the warm nut between her lips, and she chews, savouring its softness and fleeting sweetness. She opens her eyes. 'You're right. It tastes better.'

Harry brushes a loose strand of hair behind her left ear, then pulls her head towards his. He kisses her, and she reaches for his face, holding it closer as they kiss in the hot September sun.

'Tina.'

Harry's voice is edged with roughness as he presses her against the ancient mosaics in the grotto. 'Tina.' He presses his hands onto her neck, her shoulders, her arms. He finds the small mother-of-pearl buttons on her bodice, and unbuttons them, his hands shaking. She shuts her eyes as he frees her breasts from her chemise and buries his head against her soft flesh. He whispers that she is a goddess, a siren, that he is her slave, that he would die for her.

She pushes away the guilt at her weakness, the thought of the atonement she will need to make in church, possibly for the rest of her life. A thought flits through her mind. Is this how the angels fell? If it is, she understands. How could they have resisted? Why would they have resisted?

She kisses Harry's dark hair and pulls his face to hers, pressing kisses onto his lips. He feels for the opening in her drawers, and she pulls him closer, entrapping him with a stockinged leg. She reaches for him and guides him past the barriers of cotton and lace to her hidden place. She gasps as he enters her, and then they rock against the grotto's walls as the gulls cry out over the sea below.

Stefania calls out to Christina from the shadowed balcony. 'Tina! Did you bring the walnuts? What took you so long? Liliana says she could have gone to Naples and back in the time it's taken you.'

Christina hurries across the cool tiles and through the balcony's glazed doors, which Liliana has opened to draw the faint breeze into the sitting room. Stefania sits in a wicker chair, drinking one of her favourite herbal *tisanas* from a delicate china teacup as she holds the saucer in her hand. She sets down the cup and saucer beside a plate of hazelnut biscuits. 'Did you take off your hat? Your face is flushed. You must be more careful, Tina. The sun here is strong, even in September.'

'I took it off for a bit to catch the breeze. I'm sorry I'm late, *Cugina Stefania*.' She hands her cousin the paper bag of walnuts and unpins her hat. 'I met Harry in the Piazzetta and we went for a walk. He … he bought me a lemonade from Leonardo. I'm afraid I lost track of the time.'

Stefania sniffs at the walnuts, then sets the bag on the table. 'I think I must tell your father to buy you a wristwatch. We shall have to wait until tomorrow for Liliana's *Torta Caprese alle noci*.'

Christina reaches for a biscuit. 'That's all right. We can eat her hazelnut biscuits for *dolce* after dinner.'

'Biscuits are for the afternoon. *Torta* is for *dolce*.' Stefania pours tea into an empty teacup and pushes the saucer across the table towards Christina. 'Sit. We must talk about our journey to Roma to meet your father.'

Christina's knees begin to shake and she feels her blood rush to her feet. She drops the biscuit and sits down heavily in a chair as the pillars and rose-laden trellis spin around her.

Stefania is on her feet. 'Tina, put down your head. Breathe, *cara mia*.'

Christina takes a deep breath and looks up into her cousin's worried brown eyes. 'I must have been out in the sun too long.'

'Tina, when did you last bleed?'

'What do you mean?'

Stefania sits back down in her chair. 'When did you last have your monthly time?'

'It was … it was … early July.'

She takes a sip of tea. 'And August?'

Christina shakes her head.

'September?'

'I thought … I thought…' She looks down at her belly and rests a hand over the folds of her dress.

'Tina, have you been intimate with this English boy?'

Her shoulders slump. 'Yes.'

A silence descends over the terrace as Stefania sips her *tisana*. She sets down the teacup. 'I shall write your father to say that you wish to continue your Italian studies through the winter. I shall tell him that you have taken an interest in Italian cookery, and that Liliana will teach you this as well. I shall tell him how proud Isabella would have been of your progress, and of your love for your Italian heritage.' She peers across the table. 'You will stay here until the child is born, and pray to our Heavenly Father to forgive you. Then you must return to London and face the consequences of your actions.' She folds her hands in her lap. 'You are not to see this boy again. Do you understand, Christina? Never again.'

Her cousin's dark eyes, and the red roses on the trellis, and the blue sky, and the teacups and hazelnut biscuits and the paper bag of walnuts spin around Christina like a giant kaleidoscope until the world turns black.

Chapter Twenty-Two

Celie

Clover Bar, London – August 1914

C elie folds a cotton petticoat and lays it on top of the lace-trimmed chemises and knickers in her dresser drawer. She wipes the back of her hand across her damp forehead and sits on the bed. Outside her bedroom window, the blue sky is puffed with clouds and a blackbird sits on a branch of the cherry tree, warbling. A door slams downstairs, and she hears the muffled voice of Milly greeting the visitor.

A sharp rap on her door. 'Miss Fry? There's a young man 'ere to see you.'

Celia opens the door. 'A young man? Who is it, Milly?'

'It's Mr Fischer, miss. 'E says to 'urry. Somefink is 'appening.'

Celie shuts the door and follows Milly down the stairs. Max stands in the hallway in a grey suit, squeezing his flat cap in his hand. He nods at Milly before she disappears down the hallway.

'Max? What is it? Milly said something's happened.'

'Germany is at war with Russia. There are reports that France and Belgium are mobilising at the German borders.'

Celie's heart jumps. 'What about Britain? Are we at war, Max?'

Max runs a hand through his cropped blond hair. 'Not yet, *schatzi*, but it's only a matter of time. I have to go back immediately.'

'But you weren't meant to leave till next month.'

'I've received a telegram. The *Landsturm* is pulling my training forward.' His blue eyes cloud over. 'If Germany and Britain go to war … I don't know what we are going to do, *schatzi*.'

'Oh, Max. What if … what if you can't come back? What if—'

'Don't think about that. Can you come to Victoria Station in the morning? My train leaves at seven o'clock.'

'Yes, yes, of course.'

He sets his cap back on his head, and glances down the hallway. He leans forward and brushes Celie's lips with a kiss.

She presses her lips hard against his. Then he turns and he is gone.

Celie follows Max as he shoulders their way through the flood of travellers on the concourse at Victoria Station. The air snaps with a strange energy, like the atmosphere before it releases an electric storm. The least misstep or accidental thrust of an elbow could lead to sharp words.

'Why is it so busy, Max? I've never seen it like this.'

'Everyone's coming back from their holidays in Belgium and France before the borders are shut.'

'But Germany hasn't declared war on France or Belgium.'

'It will happen. Everyone is lining up behind either Austria–Hungary or Serbia. It was the assassination of the Archduke in June that started all of this. There's no stopping it now.' He points to the Dover train. 'My train is here already.'

When they reach his carriage, Celie turns to Max. 'Promise me you'll come back safe as soon as you can.'

'Of course, *schatzi*.'

'And then...'

'And then we shall marry. A Christmas wedding, what do you think?'

Celie throws her arms around Max and kisses his cheeks. 'Yes, Max. Yes. Yes. Yes.'

'One moment, *schatzi*. We must do this properly.' He tears at a brass button on his uniform sleeve. He drops to his knee and holds up the button. 'Fraulein Cecelia Sirena Maria Fry, will you do me the honour of becoming my wife?'

'Oh, Max, you know I shall.'

He rises to his feet and places the brass button in her palm. He folds her fingers over the button. 'It says *Gott Mit Uns*. God is with us, *schatzi*. You and me. No matter what happens.' Then he hugs her, and they stand on the platform, silently, in each other's arms, as the travellers surge around them.

Chapter Twenty-Three

Jessie

King's College Hospital, London – August 1914

'Jessie! Have you heard the news?'

Jessie looks up from the meal trolley, a tray with a bowl of porridge and a plate of toast and marmalade in her hands. 'What news?'

Elsie dashes down the aisle between the beds waving a newspaper. 'We're at war with Germany! Since midnight. It's all here in the paper. I'm afraid it's wet. It's raining a gale outside.'

'What? Really?' Jessie sets down the tray and takes the damp *Daily Mail* from Elsie. '"*The announcement was issued by the Foreign Office at 12:15 a.m. Britain had sent an ultimatum to Germany which expired at midnight. This was due to Germany's refusal to leave Belgium neutral and her invasion of that country. The German ambassador went to 10 Downing Street at 12:10 a.m. to receive his travel papers. He looked a broken man.*"'

'Didn't you say your sister has a German boyfriend?'

Jessie hands back the newspaper. 'Yes. Max Fischer. They met at University College.'

Elsie tucks the newspaper under her arm and reaches for a tray of food. 'I'd watch what you say around her, if I were you.'

'What do you mean by that?'

Elsie shrugs. 'You never know what might get back to the other side.'

'My sister is not a snitch or a spy, Elsie. She's as honourable as they come. She's a Suffragette, for heaven's sake.'

'Just saying.' Elsie smiles at the small boy in a nearby bed. 'We have some lovely porridge today, Tommy, and marmalade for your toast. We'll have you fit as a fiddle in no time and then you can go fight those nasty Germans.'

———

Jessie knocks on the door to the matron's office and enters the small high-ceilinged room. The rain pelts against the one tall window, distorting the view out to Bessemer Road. 'You wanted to see me, Matron?'

The matron looks up from her desk and nods at a wooden chair. 'Yes, please. Sit.'

Jessie sits on the edge of the chair, straightening her shoulders as her mother has frequently reprimanded her to do. She folds her hands in her lap and crosses her ankles, not in an attempt at decorum, but rather to still the quivering that has taken over her body since the news of war.

The matron caps her fountain pen and lays it on the document she has been reading. 'You have heard the news, I expect? Sister Webb has been broadcasting it throughout the hospital this morning.'

'Yes. It's the most shocking thing.'

'Is it? I've been expecting this for some time.' She sets her elbows on the desk blotter and presses the tips of her fingers together. 'The head office of the Queen Alexandra's has rung me. They will be activating the Reserves with immediate effect.'

She slides the document across the green blotter towards Jessie. 'You're to read this and sign it. King's College Hospital is to become one of four military hospitals in London. It will be called the Fourth London General Hospital for the duration of the war. We are to reorganise the wards in preparation for receiving wounded soldiers. We shall, of course, attend to our current patients in the meantime, but no further civilians will be admitted to this hospital. You, as a Queen Alexandra nurse, will be given charge of one of the new wards, and will be expected to encourage our existing nurses to sign up for service in the Queen Alexandra's as well. Is that all understood?'

'Yes, Matron.'

The matron picks up the pen and hands it to Jessie. 'I expect many nurses will sign up, but no doubt we shall need to recruit entirely untrained young women as well.' She huffs and shakes her head. 'I expect we shall have a run of silly girls with romantic dreams of tending handsome soldiers. They will require strict handling. I expect you to be up to this, Sister Fry. Read the document and, if you are in agreement, sign it, please. Once you've signed, your life will not be your own until the war is over, do you understand?'

'Yes, Matron.'

Jessie bends her head over the document:

I, Jessica Margarita Fry, being a fully trained Nightingale nurse, do offer my services to the Queen Alexandra's Imperial Military Nursing Services Reserve for so long as my services are required during the present emergency.

Signature _____

Date _____

Witness _____

Her mother's irate face flashes into Jessie's mind, but she wills the image away. She uncaps the pen and writes in her name and the date. This is the moment her life changes. There's no going back.

The matron picks up the pen and the document. 'Thank you, Sister Fry. You do understand that you will need to lead by example, of course.'

'Yes, of course.'

'I shall expect your timekeeping to improve. Your regular tardiness of five minutes each morning is a source of profound irritation to me.'

'I'm sorry, Matron. I'll do much better. I'll borrow my sister's bicycle.'

The matron scrawls her signature over the bottom of the document. 'That will be all, Sister Fry. Send in Sister Webb. I must have a word with her about decorum.'

Chapter Twenty-Four

Etta

Asheham House, Sussex – August 1914

Etta scans the platform through the window as the train rolls into the small country train station at Glynde. He's there, as he'd promised. So tall and handsome in his grey suit, though today he is bare-headed and his dark hair curls over the collar of his white shirt. It's grown longer since she last saw him. Wilder. And his skin tanned a dark brown from the hours he's been working in the gardens at the country house rented by Vanessa Bell's sister, Virginia, and her husband Leonard. A thrill rolls up her body like a wave sweeping over sand. She shifts her gaze to her reflection in the train's window and pinches her cheeks. After taking a deep breath, she collects her carpetbag and hurries to the carriage door.

'Etta Maria, my beautiful angel!' Carlo sweeps her into his embrace and kisses her full on her mouth.

'Carlo! People will see.'

Carlo throws back his head and lets out a deep laugh. 'There's no one here, unless you count the station master, who is most likely watching us from his window. Let us wave at him, shall we, *cara mia*?'

She sticks out her lower lip in a pout. 'The people in the train can see us. It's not proper.'

'My darling Etta, I think your ideas of what is proper may change after this weekend.' He takes her bag and points towards the station house. 'I've brought us bicycles from Asheham House.'

She follows him through the station and out onto a paved concourse. 'Bicycles?'

'Oh, *Santa Maria*!' He slaps his head. 'You do know how to ride a bicycle? I never thought to ask.'

'Yes, I used to ride to the art college in Camberwell.' She looks at the white frills of her dress. 'It's just that I'm not exactly dressed for it.'

He holds the second bicycle steady as Etta tucks her skirt and petticoat around her legs and mounts the bicycle. He jumps onto the other bicycle and leads her toward the dirt road.

'You will love Asheham, Etta,' he says over his shoulder. 'It's a very pretty house at the bottom of a green hill with only a shepherd's cottage nearby. Nobody bothers anybody, unless they wish to be bothered. Your cousin Roger arrived yesterday. Vanessa and Duncan are painting a mural for Omega in the living room. It isn't far. We shall be there in fifteen minutes.'

They reach Asheham House down a winding lane flanked by towering oaks and beeches which rustle like paper in the warm breeze. The house's white stucco glistens in the morning light in front of a green mound of the South Downs. Elegant arched French windows along the front façade lend the house and its two side pavilions a romantic air, which is augmented by the array of flowers – roses, of course, and hollyhocks, purple asters, yellow marigolds, and dahlias with blooms as large as hats. By the front door, a woman in a large straw hat kneels over a flower bed, pulling out weeds. She turns and waves at them when she hears the crunch of the bicycles' tyres on the gravel.

The woman rises to her feet and pulls off her gardening gloves. 'Hullo! Do come out to the back and have some tea.' She wears a loose white blouse and a beige canvas skirt, and she has tied a thin navy cardigan around her slender waist. A string of fine pearls encircles her long neck, their cool gleam accentuating the sharpness of her features. Though she is only a couple of inches taller than Etta's five foot four, her bearing is so upright and regal that she appears a giantess.

She regards them with hooded dark eyes, which would be intimidating if it weren't for their glint of humour. She greets Etta with a firm handshake and a kiss on the cheek. 'You must be Roger's cousin, Etta. I saw you at Vanessa's dinner after the Omega Workshops opening. I'm sorry I had to leave early that evening, or I would have introduced myself. I'm Vanessa's sister, Virginia. Aren't you a lovely thing? Quite like a woodland nymph, were England to have nymphs.'

She tucks her arm through Etta's and walks with her to the house. 'Tell me, what were the people like on the train today? Did you see any soldiers? What is it that you're currently reading? Do you cook? I attended some cookery classes in London a few months ago and distinguished myself by cooking my wedding ring into a suet pudding! Consequently, Mrs Funnell, the shepherd's wife, is cooking our luncheon today, for which we all should be thankful.'

They cross the threshold and Virginia calls towards a room off the hallway. 'Vanessa! Duncan! Carlo's back and he's brought a lovely young nymph with him.'

The young artist with the soulful blue eyes from the Omega

party pops his head around the doorframe. He waves at them with a long, thin paintbrush, inadvertently splashing dots of bright yellow paint across his cheek.

'Ah, Roger's cousin! Perfect timing,' he says as he thrusts the paintbrush into Etta's hand. 'Come on, then. I've got a problem with a face and Vanessa's absorbed with dappling the leaves. Have a go at the hay bale, would you?'

Virginia takes the paintbrush from Etta and hands it back to the paint-splattered artist. 'Duncan, there is more to life than art. Come have some tea.'

Etta sits on the edge of the canvas lawn chair on the stone patio behind the house, where the group has clustered on lawn chairs amongst the roses and honeysuckle trailing over trellises. She takes a sip of the fragrant tea. Carlo is in a lawn chair across from her, and her usual grace has abandoned her as she fumbles with her napkin, the scone and the china teacup. She is conscious of his eyes on her, but whenever she darts a glance in his direction, he is in rapt attention to Virginia and her gossip, Roger and his witticisms, or Duncan and his flirtatious quips. She looks over at Virginia's husband, Leonard – a thin, brown-haired man with a long, serious face who says very little – and watches him make notations in a black-covered notebook in his lap.

'Mongoose, whatever are you listing now?' Virginia says to her husband. 'The spoonfuls of sugar we've consumed in our tea?'

'If you must know, my dear mandrill, the cost of John Teasel's cream has gone up by three pence. I must keep abreast of these things or we shall be living in penury before you know it.'

'We already live in penury, Mongoose.'

Virginia's sister, Vanessa, sets down the canvas she is embroidering with roses and playing cards. 'Why on earth are we talking about the cost of cream? War has just broken out. Why is no one talking about that?'

Roger Fry spoons a dollop of strawberry jam onto a scone. 'What is there to say, Vanessa? There will be a few skirmishes over on the Continent, exactly like what happened in the Franco–Prussian War, and everyone will be home for Christmas, which is fortunate as we shall have a fully stocked shop for the holidays.'

Etta sets her teacup down in the saucer in her lap. 'The train station in Brighton was heaving with soldiers leaving on trains for London. I almost missed the train to Glynde because of them. They were all very jolly, like they were going off to a party, singing songs and everything.'

Virginia's long, serious face brightens. 'Really? What were they singing?'

'It was all about Tipperary. Quite a jolly song.'

Leonard slams shut the notebook. 'It's all senseless and useless. It's absolutely ridiculous to solve political disagreements by violent force. Italy has the right idea. Staying neutral.'

Roger brushes a crumb from his lip. 'Hold on. Wasn't Italy signed up with the Austrians and the Germans in the Triple Alliance before the war broke out? Shouldn't you be on the other side, Carlo?' He taps his lips. 'Maybe we ought to watch what we say around you.'

Carlo crosses his legs and leans back in the lawn chair. 'I am in agreement with Leonard. War is senseless and useless. The war in Europe is none of Italy's, or my, affair. If anyone steps onto Italian soil, this, of course, will be another matter.'

Virginia sets down her teacup with a rattle. 'War is just a preposterous masculine fiction. The chief occupations of men are the shedding of blood, the making of money, the giving of orders, and the wearing of uniforms. I have had quite enough of it already.' She turns to Duncan, who is scribbling doodles in a scrapbook. 'Duncan, tell me, who are you sleeping with this month? Anyone here?'

Etta coughs up her tea as the others chuckle. Carlo reaches out his hand to Etta. 'Come, *cara mia*. I think we do not need to hear about Duncan's love affairs. Let us go for a walk. We must work up an appetite for Mrs Funnell's lunch.'

———————

They break through the shade of the forest trees to a small clearing where a wooden shed, no larger than the greenhouse at Clover Bar and faded to a gentle silver from the assaults of the English weather, sits under the spreading green-leafed branches of a beech. A pile of recently cut wood has been stacked to one side of the shed beside the wooden barrel of a water butt, and an axe protrudes from a stump, awaiting a hand to swing it at its next log.

'What is this place?'

Carlo reaches into his pocket and retrieves a large black key, which he uses to unlock the door. He sweeps his hand before him. 'Welcome to the gardener's shed, or, as I prefer, the *Palazzo di Arte*.'

Etta slips past Carlo into the shed where splashes of sunlight dance amongst shadows cast by the leaves of the large beech. Inside, in a corner by the single, four-paned window, a half-finished painting of Asheham House – its whiteness glowing in a landscape of green trees and golden fields – sits on an easel beside half-finished paintings leaning against the faded green paint of the wooden walls. A narrow metal bed, jumbled with sheets and a grey wool blanket, is shoved against the back wall.

'Is this where you're living?'

'Sometimes. When Virginia and Leonard have house guests.' He shrugs. 'And other times, if I wish to be on my own.'

She leans against the table and looks at Carlo. 'Why didn't you stay in Italy? Don't you have a studio there?'

'Yes. In Napoli. But, *cara mia*, it is difficult in Italy. Many people are arguing to … how to say … to intervene in the war, some with the Germans and Austrians and others with the French and British, and others wish to remain neutral. The Italians are not a quiet people. It was not so long ago we were many kingdoms with different dialects and customs fighting amongst ourselves. There are protests and arguments. It is not a time for art or artists. So, I came here, and now I am a gardener.'

Etta nods at the easel. 'And a painter.'

'Yes, always a painter. It is all I have ever wanted to be. To be a painter and to live free. I have no desire to live in a comfortable small house in the suburbs of Napoli with a tired wife and six children running around my feet. That is a life for someone else.'

'What about your family?'

'Family?'

'Your parents? Brothers? Sisters? You've never mentioned them.'

'No.' He clears his throat. 'My mother had a sister living in Messina on the island of Sicily. She had married a Sicilian she'd met in Napoli, a fish merchant from Messina, and had a large family. She and my mother hadn't seen each other for many years, so my parents and my three sisters travelled to visit them over Christmas and New Year. It was ... it was six years ago. I was twenty-five. I was living in Napoli and painting, and ... well, I had no interest to go there.' He picks up a paint brush and flicks his fingers through the bristles.

'My uncle bought everyone tickets to see Giuseppe Verdi's opera *Aida* at the theatre in Messina on December 27th. As far as I know, they went and had a wonderful evening. Very early the next morning when everyone was still sleeping, an earthquake struck the city and they were all ... they were all killed.'

Etta presses her hand against the lace at her throat. 'Oh, Carlo.'

He looks at her. 'Life is ... it is a strange thing.' He sets down the paint brush. 'So, *Etta mia*, how is it that you managed to come here for the weekend? I am surprised your parents agreed.'

'They didn't, not exactly. I said I was invited to the seaside with

Violet and her family for my birthday. I had Violet ring my father on the new studio telephone and issue the invitation formally. She's quite a good actress. She even met me at the house this morning carrying a suitcase.'

'Your birthday?'

'Yes, today's my birthday. Jessie's as well, of course. We're twenty.'

Carlo leans towards her and kisses her softly on her cheek. 'Happy birthday, *il mio angelo*.' He stands back. 'It is not a good thing for you to lie to your family to come see me.'

'I'm not a child, Carlo. I shall be such a good guest and arrive back home exactly when I said, that I shall be invited to Violet's family's cottage quite often this autumn.'

'You are planning to visit me again?'

She runs her fingers along the ridges of the table. 'If I'm invited.'

'Of course you are invited.'

'I must be home by Sunday evening for supper. I shall buy some Brighton rock at the train station as evidence for Mama.'

'I shall ensure you catch the train in good time.'

She wanders over to the paintings and flips through the canvases of ghostly floral still lifes and landscapes devoid of sky. 'Why haven't you finished any of these?'

'Because you are not in them.'

She looks over at him and sees him watching her. The air is heavy, like the air before a storm bursts. The fine hairs on at the nape of her neck prickle.

'We should go, *cara mia*.' His voice is rough, the vowels strangled.

Etta steps away from the easel and stands in front of Carlo. 'Why?'

'*Cara mia*,' he whispers. He buries his hands in her hair.

Etta places her hands on his chest. 'I want to be with you, Carlo.'

He sucks in a deep breath and pushes her hands away. 'I can't. You don't understand—'

'What's wrong?'

'I have nothing to offer you, Etta. No money, no future. With the war—'

'I don't care about the war.'

He turns away from her. 'You should. It will affect us all. Look at me. I am far away from my country, living in a shack in the woods as a penniless artist. I have nothing to offer you.'

'You have everything to offer me, Carlo.'

'What have I to offer you, Etta?'

Etta walks to him, stopping just before their bodies touch. 'You, my darling. This is all I want.'

He looks down at her lovely face, at the golden curls toppling over her shoulders. He clutches her against him, and kisses her with all the passion and anger and frustration that surges through his body.

He pushes her against the table and they tear at each other's clothes. She parts her legs and he thrusts inside her, and they rock together against the table in their act of love.

A movement in the beech tree outside the window catches Carlo's eye. He spies a magpie on a branch of the huge tree. It flies away before he sees another.

Chapter Twenty-Five

Christina

Capri, Italy – October 1891

Christina stands in the shade of the Grotta di Matermania's cobbled wall and stares at the blue haze of the horizon. Out of the shade, the sun beats down on the dry earth and burns the grass yellow where the goats have chewed it down to stubs. The gulls soar and keen over the sea, and, when a fisherman hauls a net laden with fish up into his boat, the birds cluster and bicker above him, waiting for him to toss a silver fish their way.

Her stomach flutters and nausea sweeps over her. Sweat beads her forehead and she wipes it away with her fingers. She looks around for somewhere to perch, but she is hit with another wave of nausea and she sinks to her feet beside the wall.

She presses her face into her hands and breathes deeply until her stomach settles and the dizziness passes. She sits up against the cobbled wall. The smooth, round stones press against her back like eggs. Closing her eyes, she cups her hands over her belly, though there is still no hint of the life she is carrying inside of her.

For the past fortnight, Stefania has not let her out of her sight. *I'm no better than a dog on a leash*, she thinks. Her excursions to the market or the lemon seller have been given back to Liliana, who stamps around the villa, grumbling at the additional demands on her time, the fact that these had been her duties prior to Christina's visit long forgotten.

She'd heard the brass knocker at the door several times, but was always beaten to the door by Liliana or her cousin. She'd strain to hear Harry's voice, and her heart would beat a drum when she'd catch a word, muffled by the barrier of the thick wooden door, before he'd be sent on his way with a curt, *'Lei è malata. Non disturbarla.'*

But today is Sunday, and Christina had pleaded illness with morning sickness as Stefania had readied herself for church. Liliana had left them a lunch of cold ham and cheese, and dishes of fat, oily olives and sun-dried tomatoes, and had departed early with Angelo for Anacapri up in the hills to attend her son's wedding the next day. This was Christina's chance, and she was going to take it.

She'd made a good show of it, retching and groaning on her bed that morning. With the Lord calling from Santo Stefano, and assured of Christina's incapacitation, Stefania had finally left her on her own. As soon as the final chimes of the bells in the clocktower had faded, and she was certain that her cousin was on her knees in prayer in the church, Christina had thrown off the bedcovers and hurried to the front door; but Stefania, not being one to tempt fate, had locked it behind her.

Luckily Liliana wasn't so assiduous, having left the kitchen door not only unlocked but ajar. After leaving a message for Harry with Leonardo, the lemon seller – who had become an accomplice to their assignations based on the softness of his own amorous heart and the *lire* Harry slipped him – Christina had made her way down the path to the grotto.

She hears the distant chime of the clocktower's bells as they ring the half-hour. For the first time she gives thanks for the priest's long-winded sermons. She has another hour and a half before her cousin would be home. *Please, Harry. Please, come.*

She cocks her ear. A pebble rolls down the path. The stamp of feet on the dry earth. Then he is there, panting, hatless. 'Tina!'

'Harry!'

He reaches for her, and they cling to each other. He kisses her face and she melts into the joy of him. A gull screeches nearby, jolting her to her senses. 'Harry, I need to talk to you.'

He brushes his hair from his damp forehead. 'Yes, of course.' He scans her face. 'Are you all right? Stefania said you've been ill. I came to the villa several times, but they wouldn't let me see you.'

'It's true, I have been ill.'

He threads his fingers through hers. 'But you're all right now?'

She takes a deep breath and the words tumble out of her. 'I'm … I'm expecting a baby, Harry.'

Harry's fingers slide away from hers. 'You're what?'

She reaches for him, but he steps back. 'I'm expecting a baby. Our baby.'

'Are you sure?'

She stares at him. 'Yes, I'm sure. I haven't bled since July and I've been ill in the mornings. And I've been ever so tired no matter how much I sleep.'

'I see.'

'We can marry and be a family now, Harry. Perhaps … perhaps we could marry here. Or back in England. I don't mind—'

'Marry? I – I… You're having a baby?' He rubs his forehead. 'How could this be happening to me?'

Christina's mouth drops open. 'How could this happen to *you*?

What do you mean by that?' She reaches out for him, but he backs away further.

'You don't understand, Tina. I'm to start at the Royal Military Academy at Sandhurst in January. It's taken me over a year to secure my place. I can't not go.'

'That's all right, Harry. We can find a little house in Sandhurst—'

'No, Tina. That's not an option. I'll be living at the college with the other cadets.'

'But what about the baby?'

'Well, you haven't had it yet. Something might happen. Women lose babies all the time, or … there are other ways.'

Christina shrinks back against the cobbled wall. 'Harry, it's our baby. Why aren't you happy?'

'It's rather a shock, to be honest. My father...' He brushes his fingers against Christina's flushed cheek. 'You're so lovely, Tina. Why did this have to happen?'

Christina looks into his blue eyes, but it's like he is looking at something other than her, something deep within himself. 'What shall we do, Harry?'

He drops his hand and steps out of the shade into the sharp white sunlight. 'I need to think about this. Let me think about this, Tina. I need some time.' He turns away from her and runs up the path until all that is left is the echo of his feet on the hard earth.

Chapter Twenty-Six

Max and Frank

North Of The Aisne River, France – September 1914

September 15th, 1914

My darling Celie,

I am quite wet through, and my uniform smells like the wet sheep I remember on my grandfather's farm all those years ago when I was a boy in Bavaria. How long ago that seems to me now. It has been raining for the past three days, and the earth, which was so dry just one week ago, is now a sea of mud, with not a blade of grass to be seen. We are all of us destroyers. I do not know how nature will ever forgive us for what we are doing. The birds are gone and the trees are nothing but black skeletons in the greyness. I live like a rat in the trenches we have dug along the forest line north of the Aisne River in France. My greatest weapon in the war so far has been the spade, and my hands are covered in blisters from the hours of digging.

You must have read in the newspapers by now of our defeat at the Marne. Our progress for the past month through Belgium and northern France has been so quick. The French army have been scrambling to keep us at bay, but with little effect. We were in sight of taking Paris, only 15 kilometres away near Claye-Souilly, but General von Kluck decided to have us chase the French army south of the Marne, and...

I'm sorry, schatzi. I do not wish to think about this right now. I am drinking a hot cup of tea. I am safe and they feed us well enough, though I am missing Frau Knophler's quetschekuchen. You know how I love it. I have taken up smoking, as have most of us. It calms the nerves through the relentless thunder of the guns. It is like living in the middle of a storm where everything is black clouds and thunder and cold, cold rain.

I know I mustn't say all these things to you. You are the 'enemy' after all! But, schatzi, how can you ever be my enemy? Our destinies are no longer our own. For now, we must follow the paths that have been placed before us, although I cannot say I understand what this is all about except for countries protecting their own political and economic interests. We are told by the Kaiser that we are protecting the Fatherland from a circle of invaders, but my feet are on the soil of France, so how is this so? And now I hear that we are in France to protect the villagers from the brutal onslaught of the British. I do not listen anymore. I am German and I must fight for my country, as the French fight for theirs and the British for theirs. The old kings and politicians squabble, and the young men fight and die. It has ever been this way.

I don't know if you will ever read this letter, schatzi. Ho—

The ink in the fountain pen runs out. Max swears under his breath as he shakes the pen, but no bead of ink forms on the pointed silver nib. He retrieves a tin box from his canvas bread bag, and, after opening the lid, takes out an eye dropper and a small bottle of ink. He is squirting blue ink into the pen when Fritz throws his lanky body down on a sandbag beside him.

'Another letter to your girlfriend, Professor? I'm surprised you have any ink left.' He jostles Max's arm, and ink splashes over Max's fingers.

'Fritz! Watch it!' Max wipes his hand against the rough hessian of a sandbag. 'Look what you made me do. I can't afford to spill ink. What will I write with if I lose it?'

'Maybe then you will concentrate on being a soldier instead of a lover.'

Max screws the nib back on the pen. 'You're just jealous because Anneliese won't pay you any attention.'

Fritz puffs out a breath. 'I was doing fine with her until Dieter made his move. How was I to know that she liked flowers? They weren't even roses. Did you see them? Carnations! I would have bought her roses.'

'But you didn't, did you? Maybe you'll learn for the next time.' Max picks up his tin mug of tea and glances at Fritz. 'You want something?'

'The commander wants you on the howitzer by that big dead tree. The British are giving us a hard time of it. It's a disaster we didn't take Paris. Now look at how they've pushed us back almost to Belgium. The French and the British shell us and we shell them. We are all stuck here together and nobody goes anywhere.'

Max nods. 'I'll just finish this letter and then I'll go. Tell him I'm in the latrine.'

'All right.' Fritz springs to his feet and stretches. A bullet whizzes by his head. *'Scheisse!'* He crouches down in the trench. 'Why did I have to be so tall, eh, Max?' He salutes his friend. 'See you later. Anneliese sent Dieter a set of cards. We can play Skat after dinner.'

Max watches Fritz weave through the crowded trench until he disappears behind a bend. He sets down the tin mug and rolls the pen between his fingers. He bends over the white sheet.

…How can I post it to you from a muddy trench in France when your countrymen and the French are doing their best to push us back to

Germany? I don't imagine a French postman being very accommodating, do you? I shall save it with all my other letters to you, and when this is over – they are saying by Christmas, so I am hopeful for that – and we are together again, you will have much to read!

I miss your letters, and hearing about serious, hard-working Jessie and gay Etta, who seems to fall in love as often as a bee flies between flowers. And you, of course. How are you in London? Are you still a Suffragette? Are you working with your father in the photography studio? I imagine he is busy taking photographs of handsome young soldiers. I hope your mother hasn't invited any of them to tea. I mustn't think about it or I shall become jealous. I miss you with all my heart, schatzi. Please don't forget about me.

I must go now. My commander is calling me to man one of the howitzers. I have a new helmet to protect my thick head – it has a large spike on top which is quite dashing, I think. At any rate, it helps us know not to shoot each other.

Stay safe, schatzi. I am thinking of you always. One day this will all be over, and you will be in my arms again.

Your loving Max, always

Frank Jeffries sweeps the pile of filthy banknotes and French coins off the top of the sandbag and stuffs them into the pockets of his khaki uniform jacket. 'Sorry, chaps. Better luck next time. I'll try not to spend it all in one place.'

A sturdy, square-faced young private who Frank suspects is still some months off his eighteenth birthday picks up his cards and riffles through his tricks. 'What a load of ol' bollocks. I was just one bloody trick short o' Nap. I'm cleaned out now till payday.'

A slender sergeant readjusts his peaked cap and slings his rifle over his shoulder as he rises from the makeshift card table. 'Don't take it so badly, Davy, old chap. No doubt you'll win it back at some point. Swings and roundabouts and all that.' He turns his head in the direction of the German bombardment. 'Blighters have got themselves rooted in there. They're not budging an inch. Bloody nuisance. Still, we chased them away from Paris.' He taps the brim of his hat as he heads off down the trench. 'Cheerio, chaps. Till payday, then.'

Just beyond the trench, a shell from a German howitzer blows a crater into the dead earth. Frank and the young solider hunch over as black dirt showers them. Davy blinks at Frank and rubs his eyes. 'Bloody Nora. That was close.'

Frank claps his hand on Davy's shoulder. 'Close is as good as a miss.' He pulls a couple of grimy French notes out of his pocket. 'Here. Some seed money for cards tomorrow.'

Davy's grey eyes light up. He stuffs the notes into his pocket as he rises from his perch on a sandbag. 'Cheers, mate. I could use—' He jerks back as the small hole on his forehead turns bright red with blood. Frank reaches out as the boy's legs crumble beneath him, but Private David Pinch – only son of John and Clara Pinch of Limehouse, London – is dead at seventeen.

Chapter Twenty-Seven

The Frys

Clover Bar, London – October 1914

Milly picks up the platter with the roast goose stuffed with apples and pushes open the kitchen door with her elbow.

'Ah, there it is!' Gerald exclaims as Milly enters the dining room. 'I could smell it cooking all the way from church, Milly. I'm surprised we don't have the whole neighbourhood knocking at the door for our Harvest Sunday dinner.'

Milly smiles shyly and sets the platter on the table with the serving bowls of roast potatoes and parsnips, tender green brussels sprouts glistening with butter, and sweet carrots from the vegetable plot beside the greenhouse.

'Thank you, Milly,' Christina says as she takes her place at the table. 'I know you have already taken your half-day this week, but as it's a special day of celebration, once lunch is cleared up, you may have the rest of the day off.'

'Oh, fank you, ma'am.'

When grace is said, Gerald sharpens the carving knife on the sharpening steel with a flourish, and slices into the goose's golden flesh.

Etta takes a third scoop of salt from the salt cellar and shakes it over her food. 'I'm terribly sorry about Max, Celie. It must be awful having him over in Germany. Especially now that you're enga—'

Jessie kicks her sister under the table. 'Etta, isn't that enough salt? You're turning into a plump pickle. Have you been sneaking Milly's walnut squares?'

'I haven't!'

Jessie pushes a roast potato onto her fork with her knife. 'You've been eating for Britain lately. You'll soon be as big as one of those zeppelins.'

Christina shudders. 'Thank heavens there haven't been any zeppelin attacks over here.'

'I'm afraid they may yet come, my dear,' Gerald says as he helps himself to more brussels sprouts. 'This isn't a war being fought just on the battlefields anymore.'

'We've had ambulances arriving at the hospital all week,' Jessie says. 'The military hospital down at Netley is already full of soldiers wounded in France, and they've had to arrange for ambulance trains to bring the casualties up to Waterloo Station.'

Gerald pours more gravy over his goose. 'They must be from the battles at the Marne and Aisne. It's all over the papers. I've heard young Frank Jeffries and his brother have signed up. I was speaking to their father this week.'

Christina tuts. 'I'm glad we have daughters. I would hate to think of my son over there.'

'They're sending nurses out there now, Mama,' Jessie says. 'I expect I may be told to go any day.'

'I shall not countenance you going to France, Jessica.'

'Don't worry about that, my dear,' Gerald says. 'There is still some hope this war will be over by Christmas, or perhaps Easter. I can't imagine it will go on longer than that.'

'I think that is quite enough of war talk, Gerald.'

'Of course, dear.' Gerald dabs at his lips with his linen napkin. 'Here's something I read about yesterday in the paper. Have you heard the news about Lord Sherbrooke?'

Christina looks up from her meal. 'Harold Grenville, the Earl of Sherbrooke?'

'Oh, yes!' Etta exclaims. 'It's in all the papers, Mama. A terrible scandal. He's divorcing his wife and marrying an actress named Pearl Higgins. They say he saw her in *Gipsy Love* at the Daly's Theatre and fell immediately in love with her beautiful auburn hair. I think it's terribly romantic.'

'People don't fall immediately in love, Etta,' Christina says. 'Proper relationships develop over time.'

Celie sets down her wine glass. 'What about the children?'

'He hasn't any,' Gerald says. 'That may have been the problem. He needs an heir, you see.'

'I read that Lady Sherbrooke loves nothing more than fly fishing up at their estate in Scotland,' Etta says. 'Fly fishing, can you imagine it?'

Jessie reaches for a second helping of potatoes. 'Fly fishing sounds quite jolly to me.'

'I think that's quite enough of Lord and Lady Sherbrooke,' Christina says.

'I quite agree.' Gerald clears his throat and stands. He raises his wine glass. 'May I say how happy I am to have all my lovely daughters together on Harvest Sunday. Let us give thanks that we are all together in these most uncertain of times.' He smiles across the table at Christina. 'I'd especially like to toast the beautiful woman who has made me the happiest of men. To my own dear Tina.'

Christina smiles tightly. How she hates it when Gerald calls her

Tina. *Tina*. Harry's name for her. Why is it that the mention of Harry still sends a shiver down her spine? *So, he is divorcing his wife because he doesn't have an heir. But he does have an heir.*

She glances over at her eldest daughter. Cecelia has Harry's blue eyes, a constant reminder of her own weakness all those years ago. Her mortal sin. It is why she can't bring herself to love Cecelia the way she loves the twins. She knows it is wrong, that Cecelia is innocent. But loving Cecelia is like loving Harry, and she can never let herself do that. Never again.

———

Jessie pulls Etta into their bedroom and shuts the door. 'What's going on?'

Etta rubs her arm. 'Whatever do you mean?'

'All the salt on your food. An appetite like King Henry VIII when you've always eaten like a bird. And I've heard you being sick in the chamber pot in the morning when I've been trying to sleep after a night shift.'

'I don't know what you're talking about.'

'Are you expecting a child?'

Etta's eyes widen and she looks down at her belly. Jessie takes hold of her hand and leads her to the chaise longue in front of the bay window. 'Sit down. Tell me honestly, have you been intimate with the Italian artist?'

Etta's bottom lip trembles. 'I know I shouldn't have, Jessie. I know that you're supposed to wait until marriage. I suppose I won't get into Heaven now. But I love him. I love him so much.'

Jessie pulls her into a hug as her sister weeps into her shoulder. 'Of course you do, angel. Does he love you?'

Etta looks into her sister's piercing green eyes. 'Of course. He must.'

'I don't think anyone else suspects anything, Etta. If you keep eating the way you have lately, they'll simply think you've gained some weight.'

Etta rests a hand on her belly. 'I ... I haven't bled since July. I didn't want to think about it. I didn't want to believe it, I suppose. Everything is so perfect with Carlo just as it is.'

'This is what we shall do. I know a midwife who can examine you. Do you still have the birthday money from Papa? You'll need to pay her ... ten shillings, I should think.'

'Ten shillings! But I was saving for a new hat for Christmas.'

'Etta.'

'I'm sorry. Yes, of course. I must see the midwife.'

'I'll organise it as quickly as possible. Then you must tell him.'

'Carlo doesn't have a phone in Sussex, but he's moving to a room above Omega when the Woolfs move to Richmond for the winter next month. I'll tell him then.'

'No, that's too long. You'll need to write him as soon as the midwife confirms it. Then you will have to marry as soon as possible. It's either that or elope, and Mama would never speak to you again if you did that.'

Etta rubs the pink silk over her belly. 'What have I done, Jessie?'

'It wasn't only you, Etta. If Carlo's a decent man, he'll take responsibility, and everything will be fine. Is he a decent man?'

'Yes, of course he is. I mean, he's handsome and exciting and ... and an artist.' She brushes a tear from her cheek. 'Jessie, I don't actually know him all that well.'

'I shouldn't worry about that, Etta. You will have a lifetime to get to know him. You might think twice about being so impulsive in the future. There are often consequences.'

Chapter Twenty-Eight

Carlo

Asheham House, Sussex – October 1914

'Carlo! Where are you? Ah, there you are. There's a letter for you.' Virginia waves the white envelope as she steps down the gravel path to the new flower beds Carlo is planting around the patio.

Carlo sets down the trowel and slaps the soil off his hands on his trousers. 'A letter? From Italy?'

'No, from London. Oh, wonderful! You're planting the Bleu Aimable tulips Roger brought us from Holland. They'll look so jolly next spring when we're back here.' She steps over the mound of tulip bulbs and hands him the letter. 'I believe it's from Etta Fry. It looks like her handwriting. It's been lovely that she's been able to visit so often this summer. Do invite her to dinner in Richmond a week Friday. She's a delight to have around. We shall have a lovely party to christen the new house. It overlooks the green, did I say?

It's almost like living in the country. Such a relief to be out of the city. I just can't bear it there, it's like a boiling cauldron with all the war agitation going on.' She drums her fingers against her grey wool skirt. 'It's quite nerve-wracking, don't you think? All these soldiers and marches, and the drums and singing... I find it all quite a lot to take in.'

'It is a changed world, Virginia.' He looks around at the russet and golden leaves of the beeches and oaks, and the field poppies like drops of blood in the waving grass on the hill behind the house. 'Though it is difficult to imagine those things here, in this place.'

Virginia gazes up at the soft blue sky with its scudding clouds. 'I'm so sad we've let out this place for the winter. Leonard finds it rather bleak here in the winter months. Have you found somewhere in London yet?'

'Roger has given me a room above Omega. It is big enough to paint and to sleep. I am finally an impoverished artist in the garret.'

'I don't imagine you will be impoverished for long, Carlo. Your paintings are lovely. The world simply needs to catch up to your progressiveness. Vanessa and Duncan sing your praises, you know. They are quite taken with how you use vibrant blocks of colour to create form.'

'Thank you, Virginia. One day I hope this will be true, but I think it will not be until this war is over.'

'The papers are still saying they expect it all to be over by Christmas.'

Carlo shrugs. 'I hope so.'

'What will you do if Italy joins the war?'

'I shall return to fight for my country, of course.'

'But what if Italy joins the Germans and the Austrians against us?'

'I am not a political man, Virginia. This war is all about politics and self-interest. I shall fight for my country because I am Italian. Whether it is for the Central Powers or the Allies, it makes no difference to me. I wish only to paint. I shall do what I have to do, and try to come out of it alive.'

'Clive says he and Duncan will become conscientious objectors if the government introduces conscription. Roger's far too old, of course, but Leonard says he'll go, though I very much hope it doesn't come to that. It's an awful business.'

'It is a tragedy.'

Virginia nods. 'I'll put on some tea, shall I? Mrs Funnell has made some butter tarts.'

'*Grazie*, Virginia.'

When Virginia is gone, Carlo strides across the lawn and sits on a weathered stone bench under the muscled branches of an oak. He slits open the envelope with his thumb and slips out the creamy white sheet.

Clover Bar
Hither Green, London

October 9th, 1914

My darling Carlo,

It has only been ten days, I know, but how can I tell you how much I miss you? You are everything to me. I think of your little hut in the woods at Asheham as our own dear house, and all the joy of my life exists within those four green walls. Do you like the red geranium I potted up for you? I think it looks very well on the window ledge.

I am so very glad that you will soon be living above Omega. We shall be able to see each other every day. My heart is beating as I think of it. Did I say how much I missed you?

I am sure Violet will be happy as well – I think the charade of my seaside visits to her family's fictitious cottage has begun to wear on her. I have bought her a new silk scarf from Liberty's as a gift which I hope will make up for it all.

My darling, I have news which cannot wait. I am bursting to tell you. I wish Asheham had a phone and I would be on it now with you, giving you the news and listening to your own dear voice.

We are expecting a baby, my love! Jessie guessed it at Sunday dinner last week. She's helped me find a midwife to examine me. I am almost two months along, my darling. It must have happened on my birthday. Jessie is insisting I tell Mama and Papa, but I can't bear it. Not just yet.

I am in the shop all week. Come to me as soon as you arrive in London. We are both waiting for you, my darling.

Your Etta

A gull, blown inland on the October breeze, wails overhead. He watches as the bird glides against a patch of blue between the dense white clouds. It flaps its wings and comes to rest on the ridge of the house's red-tiled roof. *A child. His child. Their child.* He rolls the word around his mind like a multi-coloured marble, like he is examining every new colour combination.

Another child.

How could he have been so stupid? He had meant for it to be nothing more than a casual flirtation, like all of his others – the art students and models and wealthy, bored women who had so willingly fallen into his bed in Italy and Paris and London. It had been a game to him. A game of sensuality and pleasure. Until he had met Etta. Her beauty, her unworldliness, her adventurous spirit mixed with a certain propriety, her endless curiosity, her talent … all of it spun a web around him that he is helpless to escape. That he doesn't want to escape.

Etta mia. Etta mia. This was not meant to happen.

Chapter Twenty-Nine

Christina

Capri, Italy – October 1891

Liliana pads across the Persian rug and the polished floor tiles of the sitting room in her house slippers, frowning at the impatient rapping of the door knocker. Outside, the iron gate to the lane rattles. She opens the door, but whoever had been knocking so urgently just moments before is gone. A package, rolled in brown paper and tied with string, lies on the loggia's terracotta tiles. Tucked under the string is a letter, sealed with red wax, addressed, 'Tina'.

Christina throws herself on her bed and tears at the package. Inside is Harry's painting of her sitting forever in the sun of a Caprese afternoon. She drops it onto the bed and breaks the seal of the letter. Several British banknotes tumble into her lap.

My lovely Tina,

I am so sorry. You are everything to me, but it is impossible for me to be everything to you. I am certain you will find it difficult to understand, but my situation is such that it is impossible for me to marry you in your condition. My family would never accept it, and my father would be certain to cast me out without a penny. Then, my lovely siren, what sort of husband would that make me? A Sunday painter without a penny to his name?

I don't hail from a normal family. I told you when we met that Father is an earl. Mummy is the daughter of a baronet, and I am to inherit the earldom one day, so I absolutely must stay on my best behaviour. I do, in fact, have an understanding with a young woman who is the daughter of a marquess in Yorkshire to marry her when I've graduated from Sandhurst. It isn't love, of course. Not like us. It's simply the way things work in my world. You do understand, don't you, my darling?

I am leaving for Naples today and then on to Greece and Turkey. I have left you twenty pounds which I hope you will find useful. I wish only that it could be more, but my father has set a limit on my budget and would ask far too many questions were I to ask for an advance.

I shall never forget you, my beautiful Tina, and wish you and the child the very best in the future. But, please, I must ask that you make no effort to contact me, or reveal my identity as the father. I should very much wish not to have to deny such a thing, which I know would be very hurtful to you.

Your affectionate Harry

The letter slips out of her hand. Nausea rises from her stomach into her throat. Soon her whole body is overtaken by violent shaking. She makes an effort to stand, though her legs shake like rubber. '*Stefania!*' she screams. She is halfway to her bedroom door when her legs buckle beneath her.

She feels hands under her arms, and hears Liliana's shrill Italian vowels. Someone holds her head over a chamber pot as she heaves.

Stefania wipes Christina's face with a cool cloth, and she and Liliana help her over to the bed. Liliana shoves aside the painting with an angry curse, knocking the banknotes and letter onto the carpet.

When Christina's weeping finally settles into an exhausted sleep, and Liliana disappears to the kitchen with the chamber pot, Stefania collects the letter and the banknotes from the tiled floor. When she finishes reading, she slips it into her skirt pocket with the money. She looks over at her young cousin, and from within the deepest reaches of her Catholic soul, she curses Harry Grenville and all of his descendants to the bowels of hell.

Chapter Thirty

Etta

Dover Ferry Port, England – November 1914

Dover Ferry Port heaves with khaki-uniformed soldiers, weeping women, and commanders bellowing orders through tin megaphones to the continuous flow of men disembarking from the London trains onto the new Admiralty Pier. Gulls, drawn like magnets to the confusion of activity, add their squawks and cries to the cacophony as they dive and hover over the crowd in search of a carelessly held biscuit or roll. Berthed alongside the pier, a modest two-stacked steamer ferry sits benignly in the cold water of the English Channel, awaiting its next passengers enroute to the Western Front.

Carlo waves at Etta from the direction of the ferry as he pushes through the throng. 'Come, Etta. I've found us some seats. We must hurry.'

Etta picks up her carpetbag and steps out from under the meagre protection of the station's new wooden canopy. She hastens towards Carlo's disappearing figure.

'Watch it, miss! Mind how you go!'

Etta gasps and stops short as a file of stretcher bearers breaks through the crowd, carrying their cargo of men with mangled bodies towards the ambulance train. A station master with a thick grey moustache knocks the tobacco from his pipe on a metal pillar.

'Just look what those bloody Huns have done to our lads. Some place called Wipers. Been like this for weeks. Doesn't look to me like this war'll be over by Christmas.'

Carlo grabs hold of Etta's arm. 'Etta! You must come now. This may be our only chance.'

Etta turns to look back at the soaring white chalk cliffs and the turreted castle sitting high above the town.

'Etta? Etta, look at me. I can support you in Italy. We shall marry as soon as we reach Napoli. We shall be a family there, I promise you this, *Etta mia*. But I won't make you come with me, if you don't wish it.'

Etta looks at Carlo, at his dark eyes flashing with emotion. The past few weeks are a blur of tears and secrets. Jessie will find her note when she is back from the hospital in the morning. She will wake their parents and Celie. There will be a phone call to Omega, worried conversations with Cousin Roger and Violet, who will know nothing about the escape to Italy.

By then she and Carlo will be leaving their hotel in Paris, enroute to the Gare de Lyon to take the train to Rome. She will sit in the taxi, holding Carlo's hand, and watch the buildings and people of Paris pass by the window, on her way to her new life with the man she loves.

'Yes, Carlo. I'm ready.'

Part Three

1915

Chapter Thirty-One

Celie

Hither Green, London – January 1915

C elie clips a soldier's portrait to the string in the darkroom. She looks at the soldier's smooth, young face, at the eager smile he has been unable to contain, and sighs.

Gerald peers over the top of his spectacles from the sink where he is swishing a photograph through a water bath. 'What is it, pet? You've been quiet all day.'

Celie sits on a stool beside the work table. 'I feel so lost, Papa. Everything that I've worked toward for the past few years – it's all disappeared. Mrs Fawcett has suspended the suffragist meetings for the time being, and no one wants to employ a German teacher now. Even the Home Office Translation Bureau has turned me down. I think my name put them off.'

'What? Fry?'

'Cecelia.'

'I see. Perhaps you could help your mother knit socks and scarves for the Red Cross.'

'Me and Mama knitting? How long do you suppose it would take before she stabbed me with a knitting needle?'

Gerald peers at his daughter over the top of his spectacles. 'You do know your mother loves you, Celie. Very much.'

Celie shrugs. 'I guess.'

'My dear sweet girl, you are everything to both of us. You are kind and sensitive. Didn't this Mrs Fawcett pick you out of everyone to help her with the Society? And you are a marvellous photographer. I've seen your photographs of the suffragist march. You have an eye for a story, Celie. You see the things others miss.'

'Thanks, Papa.'

'You can always reapply to the Translation Bureau in a few months. Things change.'

'Like how the war was meant to be over by Christmas, Papa? It's January, and it's still raging. There's nothing but terrible news in the papers every day from the Front. Jessie says the hospital is heaving with wounded soldiers. I feel terrible for them, of course, but I feel terrible about the German boys, too. The whole situation is simply awful. I feel so useless.'

Gerald hands Celie a dripping photograph with a pair of metal tongs. 'You're worried about young Max Fischer.'

Celie glances at her father as she clips up the photograph. 'I expect he's at the Western Front now, if he's … if he's still alive.'

'I'm sure he's clever enough to keep himself from harm.'

'It isn't about being clever, is it, Papa? It's about luck. I don't know what to do. I write him all these letters, but I can't send them anywhere. I can't tell anyone about him, because he's German. Every battle victory for our side I read about in the papers fills me with dread. Is that an awful thing to say?'

'Under the circumstances, it's understandable, dove.' He picks up a photograph with the tongs and submerges it in the water bath. 'There's much to worry about at the moment.'

'You're thinking about Etta, aren't you?'

Gerald rubs his forehead. 'Yes.' The photograph slips out of the tongs and slides to the bottom of the sink. 'Oh, Etta, my darling girl. What have you done?'

'She'll be fine, Papa. Her letter said that she's with Carlo and his family in Naples, and they had a lovely small wedding there before Christmas. She'll be safe there. Mama's written to tell her to go to Cousin Stefania in Capri if she has any problems.'

'Yes, of course. I'm glad she has a relative nearby.'

'Papa?'

'Yes, pet?'

'Before he left for Germany, Max asked me to marry him. I … I said yes.'

Gerald looks at his daughter. He loves all of his daughters, of course, but Celie is far more able and intelligent than many of the men he has encountered in his life. She simply needs to learn to believe in herself and her own strength. She is like the Christina he first met all those years ago when she walked into his father's photography studio in Baker Street.

Christina had changed over the years. The softness and vulnerability that had made him want to protect her and love her had hardened into a shell of practicality and a single-minded desire to keep the girls safe and secure at all costs. He would always love her, no matter what; he simply wished he could find a way to make her look at him with love rather than resigned acceptance. Love is important. If Celie has found love with this young German, who is he to stand in their way?

He reaches out and squeezes Celie's hand. 'Mama and I both know. Etta let it slip on Harvest Sunday. We've been waiting for you to tell us yourself. Max is a very fortunate young man.'

'Thank you, Papa.'

'You know, pet, he asked me for your hand in marriage when he was here for your birthday last year.'

'He did?'

'He said he loved and respected you and wanted to do everything the right way. I told him that if you said yes, then I would have no objection whatsoever.'

Celie throws her hands around her father. 'Thank you, Papa.'

He pats her awkwardly on her back. 'You are my own best girl, Celie. Max is a very lucky young man indeed.'

Celie counts out the last of the coins from the till and slides them into a cloth bag. 'Nine pounds, six shillings and four pence, Papa. Putting the portraits of the soldiers in the front window is certainly drawing them into the studio.'

'Excellent. Put a pound in the box for the Red Cross, would you?'

'Already done.' She ties the string on the bag and slips it into the safe.

Gerald beckons her over to his battered oak desk. 'Come over here, Celie. I want to show you something.' He unties the ribbon from around a large red cardboard portfolio and carefully opens it to the front page.

Celie leans over his shoulder. 'Goodness, is that Jessie, Etta and me at the waterfall near Keld in Yorkshire?'

'That's right. Three years ago, now. That was a lovely holiday, wasn't it?' He flips over the page. Three yellowing photographs of a young woman in a long dark dress and a flowered hat, posing, rather serious-faced, on rustic wooden bridges and in tree-lined country lanes, have been carefully pasted under a scribbled title 'Record of a tandem trip through Kent and Sussex'. 'I took these of your mother the summer after we married. We took a short trip in the countryside. You see here? That's a boatman's house by a small lake near Penshurst, and in this one she's on the wooden footbridge at Ecclesbourne Glen.'

Celie leans over the sepia photographs. 'Where was I? I was born in May the year after you and Mama married. Didn't you bring me with you?'

Gerald flips through the heavy paper pages. 'We left you with my mother for a week.'

'But I must have been only a couple of months old. And I was a few months early. Weren't you worried about me?'

He reaches a large photograph of King Edward VII and Queen Alexandra in full royal dress. He taps the king's pointed grey beard. 'I took this at Buckingham Palace. Queen Alexandra was a beautiful woman. Very kind, though she could barely hear a thing.'

'Buckingham Palace? When did you take that?'

'Back in 1905. There are more.' He flips the page. Another photograph of the monarchs, this time in street clothes in an elegant sitting room. 'I was one of the court photographers, just like your Grandfather Fry had been. Some of his photographs are in here as well, of Victoria and her family.'

'I had no idea, Papa.'

Gerald closes the portfolio and ties the ribbon. 'Celie, I've been thinking a great deal about things since I had the fever. About the business, and what would happen were I to—'

'Don't even think those kinds of thoughts, Papa.'

'I must think these thoughts, my dear. I have responsibilities.'

'You needn't worry about us.'

'Perhaps not, but I'm your father. I do. Celie, sit down and hear me out. I have a proposal for you.'

Celie sits in the wooden chair beside the desk. 'What is it, Papa?'

'I'd like you to work in the studio twice a week taking portraits. Not just as a helper, but as a proper assistant. I've seen how the soldiers relax when you're here in the studio. I know that the portraits you took today will be excellent, very likely better than mine. I shall pay you as I would any assistant and I shall teach you everything I know about photography.' He opens a drawer and takes out the Soho Reflex camera and sets it on the desk beside the portfolio. 'Your Brownie is a fine little camera, but this is much better. I've adapted it with a film roll holder which will be much easier than plates when you're out and about. Consider it yours.'

'Papa!'

'Get out and about in London. Take photographs of whatever you wish. Think about the story you wish to tell, the composition, find out whether you prefer taking photographs of people or flowers or cities or ... whatever. You have a talent, Celie. I saw it in your photographs of the suffragist march. What do you say? Will you be my photography assistant?'

Celie's heart quickens as she picks up the camera. She runs her fingers over the smooth black leather.

'I say yes, Papa.'

Chapter Thirty-Two

Jessie and Celie

King's College Hospital, London – May 1915

Jessie skirts around the orderlies wheeling extra beds into her ward. The beds are so close together that she can only move between them sideways. Some of the soldiers have faces burnt so badly from flame-throwers that their own mothers wouldn't know them; and others, young men barely twenty years old, if that, pat the sheets where a missing limb should have been. By far the majority cough and wheeze and call out for water for their perpetual thirst, victims of the chlorine gas at Ypres.

She steps past the crush of orderlies, nurses and the eager but inexperienced VADs – women in the Volunteer Aid Detachment who joined as trainee nurses, and whom Matron looks upon as a necessary and entirely regrettable evil – and hurries into the hallway in search of clean linen.

'Sister? Water. Please.'

Jessie stops beside a bed which has been left between the wall and a set of swing doors. The soldier attempts to prop himself up on his right elbow, but his arm shakes so badly that he abandons the idea and falls back on the bed. This left side of his face and his hands are bandaged, and the right side of his face is bruised and swollen.

'Whatever are you doing here?' Jessie says. 'I'll see we get you into a ward as soon as we can. I'll bring you water, don't worry.'

'You're Jessie Fry, aren't you? It's me … Frank Jeffries.'

'Frank? Good grief, how are you?'

Frank attempts a smile. 'I've had better days.'

'I'm sorry, that was a silly thing for me to say.'

'Don't worry.' Frank's shoulders shake and his body convulses into a fit of coughing. When it subsides, he runs his tongue over his swollen lips and swallows with some effort. 'The doctor said I should be all right in a few weeks. The burns aren't that bad. Superficial, he said. The Canadians had the worst of it. Poor fellows didn't know what hit them.'

'There are quite a few Canadians here. They said the gas came at them like a strange yellow-green cloud. They'd never seen anything like it.'

'It smelled awful, like burning metal. Fellows were dropping all around me. I don't know how I managed to make it out.' He gasps from the effort of speaking, and presses his hand against his mouth as the coughing takes hold again.

'Let me get you that water, Frank. I'll be right back.'

Jessie grabs a glass from a cupboard in the nurses' kitchenette and fills it with tap water. Elsie looks up from the table where she's sipping a cup of tea. 'You're in a rush.'

'There's a fellow I know in a bed in the middle of the hallway. He was gassed at Ypres.'

'Who is it?'

'Frank Jeffries, from the auction house that sold my

grandfather's furniture. My mother's been trying to marry him off to one of my sisters for years. Why's he been put in the hallway? He'll never get any rest there.'

'Matron's orders. There's no more room in the wards.'

'What about the private rooms upstairs? They're empty.'

'They're for wounded officers, Jessie. We can't put ordinary soldiers up there, you know that.'

'That's simply ridiculous. We can't have our soldiers queued up in the hallways with the lights on all night and people rushing about when there are perfectly good beds up in the private rooms.'

'I agree with you, but those are the rules.'

'The rules are an arse.'

In the corridor Jessie flags down a harried orderly. 'Stanley, you need to move the soldier in the hallway into one of the private rooms upstairs this evening once it's not so busy.'

'But I was told... Who's authorised that?'

'Matron.'

Celie looks up from the wooden table in the kitchen which is covered with sheaves of paper full of scribbles and crossings-out. 'You're home early. I've just put the kettle on.'

Jessie walks over to the hob. 'Good. I could use a cup of tea.' She takes the whistling kettle off the hob and prepares a pot of tea. She sets the teapot and two teacups on the table with a milk jug and a sugar bowl. 'What are you doing?'

'I contacted Millicent Fawcett to see if there was anything I could do. She's proposed that we work on organising another march this summer. She's calling it a "Women's Right to Serve" march. What do you think of this for the lead banner: *Shells Made by a Wife May Save her Husband's Life*"?'

'Sounds good to me.'

Celie shuffles through the papers and picks out a photograph of a young female conductor checking tickets on a tram. She hands it to Jessie. 'If this war goes on, companies won't be able to ignore the necessity of employing women to work as conductors or clerical workers or even munitions workers. When the war is over, the government will have no choice but to give women the vote.'

'Where did you get this?'

'I took it. She was working on one of the trams in Oxford Street. Papa gave me his Reflex camera to use while I'm working as his assistant in the studio.'

'That was awfully trusting of him. He treats his cameras like his children.'

'He's been teaching me all sorts of tricks and techniques.'

'So you're not going to be a German teacher after all, I take it.'

Celie sets down her pen. 'I don't know, Jessie. Who knows anything now? All I know is that when the war's over, I'm going to marry Max.'

Jessie sets down the photograph. 'Celie, if you'd seen those poor soldiers... We've been having ambulances arrive all week from Waterloo with casualties from a place called Wipers in France. Chlorine gas, Celie. The Germans are using chlorine gas on our soldiers.'

'It's pronounced EE-PRA. I've been reading about it in the papers.'

'EE-PRA, then. I saw Frank Jeffries in the hospital today.'

'Our Frank Jeffries?'

Jessie nods.

'What happened to him?'

'He was gassed. He has burns all over his hands and face.'

'Good heavens! That's awful.'

'He's coughing terribly. What sort of monsters would do such a thing?'

'I don't imagine the German soldiers had much of a choice.

They're just pawns in this whole exercise, just as much as our British boys are—'

Jessie slams her hand on the table. 'How can you say that, Celie? My own sister, a German sympathiser!'

'Jessie!'

'Well, it's true, isn't it?'

'I'm not a German sympathiser! I love a German man. How do you think I feel? Don't you think I know what people would say if they knew about Max? I can't talk about him. I can't write to him.' Her voice breaks. 'Jessie, I don't even know if he's still alive.'

Fury boils up through Jessie's body. The anguished moans of her patients, their wracking coughs that stain the pillowcases pink with blood and saliva, the mourning for arms and legs lost to the French mud, the weeping of boys and men who have seen things no person should ever see – all these roil around her mind in a tumultuous whirl. Jessie drops the teaspoon into her teacup and pushes away from the table.

'Maybe it would be better for all of us if he were dead.'

Two days later, Jessie is summoned to Matron's office. The matron looks up from her desk as she arrives and nods at a wooden chair. 'Sit.'

Jessie sits down and tucks her ankles together.

The matron eyes Jessie across the desk. 'Sister Fry, your actions with regards to Corporal Jeffries were the height of both insolence and insubordination. You exhibited a wilfulness and disregard for orders that I find quite astonishing. To lie so blatantly to an orderly using my name! In any other circumstances you would be out without a reference, do you understand?'

'Yes, Matron.'

'However, the circumstances are not normal. It is quite wrong for a hospital to have perfectly good empty beds when sick and injured soldiers are being left in hallways. Your instincts were correct, although your execution was outrageous. Would you agree?'

'Yes, Matron, but I was afraid if I asked permission, I would have been refused.'

'You most certainly would have been refused. However, your action highlighted a flaw in the hospital's protocol, which we have now addressed. In future, the beds in the private rooms will be used by any solider who requires a bed, officer or not.'

'Oh! Thank you, Matron.'

'Let me say one thing, Sister Fry. I would caution you about your extreme wilfulness. Nursing requires compassion and collaboration. We are here to support, not lead, is that clear?'

'Yes, Matron.'

The matron nods. 'Now to another matter. The Queen Alexandra's have been requested to send nurses out to Egypt to nurse on the hospital ships in the Mediterranean. I'm sure you are aware that the Ottoman Empire has joined with the Austrians and Germans against the Allied Forces. Fighting in the region has been extremely severe, with significant casualties. I have written a recommendation for you to join one of our hospital ships out of Alexandria.'

Jessie's heart leaps. 'Me?'

The matron leans forward and steeples her hands on her desk. 'The army requires nurses with a certain quality of stamina, of fortitude and, indeed, of stubbornness in the face of adversity. I believe it may suit your character. You will be far from home for some time, possibly years. You will see things you will wish you had never seen. You will work long hours in conditions which may be,' she shakes her head, 'which *will* be extremely challenging. You will be the face of the mother, the sister, the fiancée or the wife of a man who is dying. You may well be the last face he sees. Do you understand, Sister Fry?'

'Yes, Matron.'

The matron opens up a manila folder. She unscrews the cap of a black fountain pen. 'Sister Fry, do you wish to undertake this assignment? I'm afraid I need your answer immediately owing to the urgency of the situation.'

Jessie looks at the pen poised like a dart in the matron's long fingers. 'Yes. Yes, I'll go.'

The matron nods. She signs the bottom of a document with a quick flourish. 'You have said you wish to travel and see the world, Sister Fry. I hope you won't regret it.' She shuts the folder. 'The ship will be leaving Plymouth a week Monday. You'd best inform your family.'

Jessie hurries up the stairs to the private rooms on the hospital's first floor. She stops abruptly in the doorway to Frank Jeffries's room. Celie sits on a chair beside Frank's bed, and Frank is propped up against his pillow, about to play a card onto the metal dinner tray in his lap.

'Celie? What are you doing here?'

Celie looks over at her sister. 'Hello, Jessie. I decided to pay Mr Jeffries – I'm sorry, *Corporal* Jeffries – a visit. He's trouncing me at Hearts.'

Frank waves a bandaged hand at Jessie. 'I hope you didn't get into too much trouble moving me up here, Jessie. I was getting awfully bashed about with that swing door in the hallway.'

'No, it's fine.' She glances at Celie. 'It's the least I can do for one of *our* brave soldiers.'

'I'm sure *any* soldier would appreciate some pleasant company in their hour of need,' Celie says.

'Absolutely, Miss Fry,' Frank says. 'But, please, I'm Frank.'

'Then you must call me Celie.'

He hunches forward, dropping his cards over the sheets as he is racked with a fit of coughing. Jessie reaches into her chatelaine and removes a small glass vial and a spoon. 'Time for your morphine, Frank.'

She measures out a spoonful of liquid morphine which Frank swallows gratefully. 'Thank you, Jessie. I don't think I'd be able to manage without that.'

'I'll be sure that the doctor provides you with a supply of morphine when you're released. You'd best finish your card game before it takes effect. Celie likes to win.'

'Jessie! Wait!'

Jessie turns around to see Celie hurrying down the hospital hallway toward her. 'What is it?'

'Jessie, we need to stop this.'

'Stop what?'

'You know what I'm talking about.'

Jessie shrugs. 'I think I'm justified in my opinion about your German fiancé. If it were me—'

'But it's not you, is it? It's my life. I love Max. I want to be his wife.'

'Good luck living in Britain with a German husband, Celie. I don't expect it'll be any easier living in Germany, what with you being British. Have you thought about that?'

'We'll find a way. Perhaps we'll emigrate to Australia or Canada.'

'That's a good idea, because you won't be welcome here in London. I'm simply warning you.'

'Fine. Noted.'

'How can you marry him, Celie? A German? You saw Frank, with his burns and that horrible cough. He's not the worst by far.'

'Don't you think I'm torn up about this? You're my sister, Jessie.

Why can't you give me some support? I'm sure Etta would understand—'

'Etta? She's thoughtless and irresponsible. Imagine eloping to Italy in the middle of a war! Has she considered the worry she's caused Mama and Papa? I fail entirely to understand either of you. At least the Italians have finally joined our side. I don't think I could bear having two sisters with—' Jessie clamps her mouth shut.

'With what, Jessie?'

'With enemy husbands.'

Celie pulls on her gloves. 'How are we meant to live together if that's how you feel?'

'I shouldn't worry about it, Celie. I'm being shipped out to Egypt in a fortnight. One of us Fry sisters will be doing her bit for the war.'

'I *am* doing my bit for the war. I'm organising a march—'

'You and your marches. Shy little Celie coming out of her shell. Bully for you.'

'Nursing isn't the only way a woman can contribute to the war effort.'

'I don't care what you do, Celie. It's of no consequence to me.'

'Have you told Mama and Papa that you're going to Egypt? They'll be worried sick. You can be sure Mama will do anything to stop you.'

'It doesn't matter what they think. I'm going and God help anyone who tries to stop me.'

Chapter Thirty-Three

Christina

Capri, Italy – March 1892

The path to the grotto is still slippery from the rain that showered the mountainsides and alleyways of the island through the dreary, cold month of February. Christina steadies herself by clinging to the rocky face of the cliff, slipping only once. The jolt shakes her, and sets the baby turning inside her swollen belly. When she reaches the limestone arch of the Arco Naturale, she sits on a stone and rests for a quarter of an hour. She lifts her face to the warming caress of the sun's rays and shuts her eyes to listen to the waves and the cries of the gulls, until the sickening swoops of anxiety that have plagued her since Harry's abandonment settle.

By the time she descends the final stone step to the grotto, the morning haze has been replaced by an unseasonable midday heat that causes sweat to dampen her armpits and the tender skin under the high collar of the dress. She climbs the steps into the shade of the grotto and sits on the ruins of a cobbled wall. Framed by the cave's arch, the turquoise water of the Tyrrhenian Sea glistens before her. In the distance, the scrub-covered ridges and mountains of the Amalfi Coast rise into the blue March sky.

The darkness that has hovered over her since Harry's departure descends like grey ash. How can she face her father with her shame? She is thankful that her mother hadn't lived to see her ruin.

The baby kicks, and Christina rests her hands on the round bump. *You are a child of love, little one. At least, that's what I thought.* Christina's shoulders slump under the weight of her depression. *I was foolish. I thought your father loved me, but how could he have loved me, if he could abandon us like this? The world is a cruel place for people like us, little one. I won't be a foolish woman with a fatherless child. I shall not bring you into a world where you will be ridiculed because of your mother's folly.*

Christina rises and walks down the grotto's steps into the bright sunlight. For a moment she is dazzled by the abrupt change, and she sways on the path. She reaches out to steady herself against an ancient cobbled wall and looks out at the sunlight sparkling like crystals on the blue sea. She steps off the path onto a strip of scrub grass. Two more steps. Then it will be done. She makes the Sign of the Cross. *Heavenly Father, forgive me for what I am about to do and spare my poor child your wrath.*

A hand closes around her arm. She turns to see Angelo's dark brown eyes shining with compassion in his weathered face. 'No, *signorina*. It is not your time. Today is a day to live.'

Chapter Thirty-Four

Etta

Naples, Italy – May 1915

E tta pegs the last of the washing onto the clothesline which spans the narrow street, along with the hundreds of other clotheslines that form a permanent grid of rope over the streets and alleys of Naples. Today is washing day, and clothes and sheets flap from the lines like colourful flags, throwing shadows onto the hot pavement. After six months in Carlo's one-bedroom flat above a cobblers' shop, she has become accustomed to the weekly routines punctuated by the almost constant ringing of church bells.

She rolls her head and presses her hands into the small of her back. Less than a fortnight now. *Not much time left to get married before you arrive, little one. Don't worry. Your Papa has promised. It surely will be any day now. Then we shall be a proper family.*

The door to the flat slams and she hears the stamp of Carlo's boots on the tiled floor of the main room.

'Etta?'

'Out here. On the balcony.'

She turns to greet Carlo, but freezes at the sight of him standing in the doorway in the high-collared grey-green uniform of the Italian army.

'Carlo? What have you done?'

His eyes shine at her from beneath the brim of his flat-crowned hat. 'I'm so sorry, Etta. I had to.'

Her legs begin to shake, and she clutches at the rusty balcony railing. 'But the baby's coming any time.'

Carlo crosses the threshold and takes her hands in his. Their warmth spreads into hers, which are still icy from the wet laundry. 'I know, *cara mia*. But since Italy declared war against the Central Powers on Sunday, you must have known this was coming. I'm an Italian. I must fight for my country.'

Etta runs a hand over her belly. 'What about the baby? What am I to do? What about the wedding?'

Carlo drops her hands. 'It must wait, *angelo mio*. I must report to my regiment this afternoon. They are sending us to the mountains near the Austro-Hungarian border. I don't know how long I shall be gone. This war, who can know what's happening? Hopefully, I shall be back here soon. Then, we shall marry, I promise, and it will be the happiest day of my life.'

'But the baby won't have a father. It won't have a name, Carlo.'

'Of course it will. I am the father. It is *our* child, *cara mia*.' He takes hold of her arms. 'Etta, I shall never abandon you. You must believe me. I shall come back.'

'Why haven't we already married?'

Carlo turns away. 'I have had to … to organise some things, and I must earn money for a family. You see how I have been living? I am an artist. I had no need for anything more than a bed and a table and a room to paint in. This is not acceptable for you and our child. I want to bring my wife to a proper home on our wedding day.'

'I don't care about any of that. I just want to marry you and be a family.'

'But *I* care, *cara mia*. Come, sit, I shall make a *tisana*.'

Etta sits in one of the two mismatched dining chairs at the small wooden table. She watches Carlo as he moves around the stove and sink as he prepares the tea. As long as he is here, filling the small, musty rooms with his presence, she is able to dampen down the worry that has threatened to grow like a weed in her mind.

She has told no one about the baby in the letters she has sent off to London. She had apologised for her impetuosity, and had blamed the quick-moving developments of the war on her decision to elope to Italy with Carlo. She and Carlo had married, she'd lied, in a beautiful ceremony in the Church of Sant Anna dei Lombardi in Naples, with his loving parents in attendance. She was a married woman now, living in a beautiful home in Naples near his parents' villa. It was everything she'd ever wished for.

If only it were true.

Carlo sets a cup of fragrant fennel and thyme tea in front of Etta. He pulls up the second chair and tosses his hat on the table. 'Etta, here's what you must do. You must send your cousin in Capri a message that you are living in Napoli with your Italian husband, and that he has had to leave with the army. Tell her you are expecting our first child shortly. Ask to go to her.'

'But, Carlo, I don't know her. What if she says no?'

'She will never say no. She is Italian and you are her family. She will welcome you *a braccia aperte* – with the open arms. Go to her and stay with her until I come back for you, *cara mia*. Then, we shall marry and be a family. I promise you this, with all my heart.'

Chapter Thirty-Five

Etta

Villa Serenissima, Capri, Italy – June 1915

Stefania enters the airy interior of the sitting room in Villa Serenissima just as Liliana appears from the kitchen carrying a tray of coffee, milk, freshly baked rolls, pats of cold butter and a dish of grape jam.

'Here, Liliana,' Stefania says. 'Let me take it. I see she's out on the balcony with the baby.'

Liliana releases the tray into Stefania's hands. 'Her milk has come, finally. She seems much happier today.'

'Good. I still don't understand what happened. Everything seemed perfect after the birth. Then, the next day, rejecting her own baby like that ...'

Liliana shrugs. 'It happens sometimes. My daughter-in-law sat in her bedroom and cried for a month after Mario's birth. But it passes.'

'Yes, well, tell Elisabetta we won't be needing her milk any longer. Pay her a little extra for her services. Send Mario to the market to buy some fish for dinner. And some cannoli from the *pasticceria*. Make sure he counts the change.'

Stefania sweeps through the double French doors out into the cool shade of the balcony. The air is heavy with the perfume of climbing roses and jasmine, and early clusters of unripe grapes hang like green pearls from the overhead trellises. Etta sits in a wicker chair by the table, the baby suckling at her breast.

'Good morning, *cara mia*! You look much recovered.'

'I am much better, thank you, Cousin Stefania. Isn't it a lovely day? Oh, ouch! Careful, Adriana. I'm glad you don't have teeth yet.'

'You will both become used to it soon enough, I'm sure.'

Etta watches Stefania pour the milky coffee. The older woman, though not tall, carries herself with an elegance which belies the sturdiness and age of her sixty-eight-year-old body. Her dark hair, almost black, shines with threads of silver and is arranged in an unfashionable pompadour.

'Cousin Stefania, I'm so sorry about everything. I don't know what came over me. I felt so heavy, like an elephant was sitting on my chest. I could barely find the energy to lift my head. Even if I could, it wouldn't have done any good. It felt like it was packed with cotton wool.'

Stefania pushes the coffee cup across the table. 'But you are feeling better today?'

'Oh yes! I wrote Mama and Papa a letter this morning telling them about Adriana. I'll write Carlo after the baby's fed.' She frowns. 'I don't know how to send him the letter. He's in the Second Army, Thirteenth Infantry Division. He wrote it down for me before he left.'

'Give me the letter when you've written it. I shall speak to the mayor. I am sure he will know how to ensure Carlo receives it.' She spreads one of Liliana's fresh rolls with butter and jam and hands it to Etta. 'Now, eat. You have a baby to feed.'

Etta dips the pen into the inkwell and looks at the creamy sheet of Stefania's best stationery. Today, so unlike yesterday and the days before, she feels like all the world's joy throbs inside her body, straining to explode into a shower of jubilation. The energy buzzes into her fingers; she is an angel, a messenger of joy. How has she been blessed with such a gift as Adriana? How is it possible that she has such a wonderful husband as Carlo? Perhaps not a husband on paper yet, but truly a husband in every other sense of the word. Smiling, she bends over the paper:

Villa Serenissima
Capri, Italy

June 9th, 1915

My most darling husband,

Carlo, oh, my dearest, we have a beautiful daughter. I have named her Adriana Christina. She was born on May 30th, just a week after you left. She has hair as golden as the sunrise and eyes as dark as chocolate. Truly, she is a gift of our love. I so wish you could see her; you would surely fall in love with her, as I have.

Cousin Stefania and her housekeeper, Liliana, have been taking excellent care of me, so please don't worry about that. You were right to tell me to come here. On this island it is easy to pretend the war doesn't exist, with the beautiful skies and sea and the scent of roses and jasmine. How I wish you were here, my darling. How I wish to hold you in my arms again.

I shall paint a portrait of Adriana for you and give it to you when you come. When I'm feeling better, I shall go for a walk and find a pretty church for us to marry in. Then, such a happy little family we shall all be. Perhaps we could find a small house here in Capri, with a lemon tree in the garden and roses, of course, and a view of the blue, blue sea. We can start all over here, after the war, you and I and Adriana, and we can paint and drink lemonade and be so very happy, with not a care in the world.

I am sending you all my kisses. We are both waiting for you.

Your loving wife,
Etta

She sits back in the chair and folds the letter. A dull ache has begun to form at the back of her head. She rubs at the ache and blinks. A circle of zigzagging colours forms in her vision, shimmering like the kaleidoscope she'd owned as a child. She closes her eyes and sits as still as a stone as the zigzags strobe against her eyelids. The headache spreads up the back of her head to press against her forehead. She clutches onto the desk until the shimmering zigzags gradually fade away.

Etta opens her eyes. She picks up the pen and dips it into the inkwell. Her hand shakes, and she takes several deep breaths to calm her racing heart. *Sergeant Carlo Marinetti, 2ⁿᵈ Army, 13ᵗʰ Infantry Division, Italy*, she writes. She slides the letter into the envelope and, dipping her finger into her water glass, moistens the gummed edge. She seals it shut as the cotton wool fills her throbbing head.

Chapter Thirty-Six

Jessie

Port Of Alexandria, Egypt – July 1915

T he HMHS *Letitia* sits alongside the dock, dwarfed by the grey-painted hulks of battleships being loaded with sacks of provisions and ammunition from the railway trolleys on the supply line which runs along the Port of Alexandria. Horses stand patiently queuing in the burning sun, flicking at flies with their long tails as they await their turns to embark for the Gallipoli peninsula on the eastern Turkish coast.

Jessie picks up her new leather suitcase – a parting gift from her parents – and, adjusting her straw hat, hastens past the horses and the crowds of raucous Australian and New Zealand soldiers toward the large white hospital ship with green crosses painted along its hull. She steps onto the wooden gangway, and, with one last backward glance at the teeming port, heads up onto the ship.

'Lovely, isn't it? Ya'd nevva know there's a war on, would ya?'

Jessie looks over at the plump young brunette nurse who has joined her at the ship's railing. She has a wide, high-cheeked face and mud brown eyes, and she wears the short scarlet cape and grey cotton dress of the Australian Army Nursing Service.

Jessie nods. 'All these islands with their charming fishing villages, and this turquoise sea … it's all so idyllic.' She smiles and extends her hand. 'I'm Jessie Fry, with the Queen Alexandra's.'

'Ivy Roach, AANS. Yeah, like the cockroach.' The girl brushes her flapping white nurse's veil out of her eyes. 'I'm thinkin' of changin' it to de la Roche. Nice ring to it, don't ya think? Couldn't do it when I lived at home, of course. Pa'd have a fit. Now I'm out here, I reckon I can do what I like. Ivy de la Roche, that's the new me.'

'Were you a nurse in Australia before the war?'

'Yeah. At the Royal Melbourne. Did a bit of everythin' there. Still, when the chance came to head outta Australia, I jumped at it. I've been to Malta and Cairo already. Had a ride on a camel to the pyramids. I highly recommend that, though you'll be battin' off blokes runnin' after ya sellin' tat all the way to the Sphinx.'

'I'd love to see the Sphinx. We had a stopover in Malta for a day on our way down from England. I had an ice-cream in the Barrakka Gardens. It was lovely. I've always wanted to get out of Britain and see the world.'

Ivy looks out at the craggy coastline of yet another sun-drenched island. 'Yeah. Shame it has to be under these circumstances. I met a nurse at the pyramids who'd just been transferred to the hospital at Abbassia, just outside of Cairo. She'd been on the HMHS *Assaye* for four months. Said Gallipoli was an awful place. Said she scratched herself raw from the fleas and crawlers that came ovva from the mainland with the wounded.'

'I brought lye soap, just in case. My matron was a nurse in the Boer War. She warned me about fleas and lice.'

Ivy's face breaks into a toothy grin. 'Why didn't I think of that? You'll be the most popular nurse on the ship. Dibs on bein' your best mate.'

Jessie laughs. 'Sure.'

'I'm gonna head down to the mess for some tea. Do ya wanna come?'

'Not just now, thanks.'

'Sure thing. Catch ya later.'

Jessie watches Ivy march down the deck and disappear through a doorway into the ship's mess. She turns back to the view of the island slipping quickly past the port side of the ship. The blue-green waves ripple and crest in the gentle breeze, and a small bright blue fishing boat comes into view. Jessie waves at the two fishermen and they wave back. She has no idea if they are Greeks or Turks.

She grasps hold of the white metal railing as the ship lurches over a wave. What if they were Turks? The Turks who were even now blowing the British, Australians, New Zealanders and Newfoundlanders to pieces down the Turkish coast at Gallipoli? It wouldn't do to think about it. Life is easier if you keep an eye on the line in the sand. There's our side, and there's the enemy side. Us and them. Celie would do well to understand that. Max is on the enemy side.

Chapter Thirty-Seven

Christina

Clover Bar, London – July 1915

Christina collects the post from the black and white tiled floor under the letterbox and sifts through the stack. She slips a thin white envelope with several Italian postage stamps to the top of the pile. She stops in the doorway of Gerald's study. He is seated in the green leather chair at her father's large mahogany desk, engrossed in *The London Illustrated News*.

She deposits the post on the desk, keeping hold of Etta's letter. 'We've just had a letter from Etta.'

Gerald looks up, his blue-grey eyes almost colourless behind his spectacles. 'That's wonderful. I've been worried about her.'

'It's postmarked the fifteenth of June. The ships from Italy take so long now.'

'I suppose we should be thankful we're receiving them at all. It's not like poor Celie with Max. She hasn't a hope to hear from him until after the war.'

Christina sits in the mahogany chair opposite the desk. 'Celie can expect nothing but grief and obstructions if she marries a German. We can't possibly permit the match, Gerald.'

Gerald removes his spectacles and, after folding them carefully, places them on top of the newspaper. 'I'm afraid I must disagree with you, my dear. Celie is a grown woman and Mr Fischer appears to me to be a fine young man. I'm not going to be one of the obstructions to her happiness.'

'But, Gerald, the neighbours…'

'Will simply have to mind their own business.'

'She will be ostracised.'

'Tina, you can't protect the girls from life. They will have to face challenges, just as we have. You must let go and trust them, or you will lose them, my love. I know that's the last thing you'd wish.'

'I simply don't want the girls to be hurt, Gerald. Is that so wrong?'

'Of course not, Tina. You know, you should tell them you love them from time to time.'

'Of course I love them. I'm their mother.'

'Sometimes it's nice to hear it.' He puts his spectacles back on and picks up the newspaper. 'I've been reading about the Gallipoli campaign. Thinking about Jessie out there.'

'I can't bear this war. Whatever are we doing in Turkey, of all places?'

'Well, the Russian tsar requested our help because of the Ottoman interest in the Caucasus, and we're allied to them, so—'

'I don't want to hear about it, Gerald. It's like a game of *Noughts and Crosses* to me. Politicians and generals playing games with the lives of young men, and now young women like our Jessica, from the safety of their offices.'

'Perhaps Lord Sherbrooke shouldn't have been so vocal in his support of Churchill's plan to send our navy to Turkey to take Constantinople. He said Turkey was the sick man of Europe and it would be a simple thing to knock it out. He's quite the orator, that Sherbrooke. He swung the support in the House of Lords, but it's been an absolute folly. Forty-five thousand casualties on our side, and it's still going on. It's a wonder he and Churchill can sleep at night.'

'I don't want to hear about Lord Sherbrooke or Gallipoli.'

'Of course, Tina. Though, speaking of Sherbrooke, he's divorcing again. It's in the papers today.'

Christina's heart jolts. 'Didn't he divorce his wife just last autumn to marry a dancer, or some such?'

'He does seem to run through women. I expect we'll hear of another marriage before the year's end.'

Had she simply been one of a long string of women Harry had loved and discarded like a used shirt? Had she meant nothing to him at all?

Gerald gestures to the envelope that Christina is still holding. 'What has Etta to say?'

She looks down at the envelope. 'Of course.' She slits through the envelope with Gerald's brass letter opener.

Villa Serenissima
Capri, Italy

June 15th, 1915

My dearest Mama and Papa,

I am so very sorry not to have written sooner, but everything has been so very hectic here these past few months. Carlo joined the army in May. He has been sent to the mountains in the north of Italy where they border Austria-Hungary. It wrenched my heart to see him go, as you can imagine. And me, left behind in Naples with a baby on the way.

I should have told you sooner, I know. I suppose I felt that I'd given you enough of a shock with the elopement. Truthfully, I have been somewhat unwell, although I am feeling much better now. At any rate, you will see from the address above that I am with Cousin Stefania in her lovely villa in Capri. It's a beautiful place, Mama, with a balcony that faces out to the sea. I'm sure you would love it as much as I, if you were ever to visit.

Cousin Stefania is so very kind. She is quite plump and not much taller than my shoulders, and she has a lovely housekeeper named Liliana who must be nearly seventy, though she is here every morning by six baking bread and ordering around her grandson, Mario, who tends the garden since her husband passed two years ago. We are a jolly little group, especially now that we have a new addition…

This is my news. I have had the baby! She is a sweet little thing that I've named Adriana Christina. Adriana after the Adriatic Sea and Christina after you, of course, Mama. You and Papa are grandparents! She was born on Sunday, May 30th. 'The child who is born on the Sabbath Day is bonny and blithe, merry and gay.' Do you remember that rhyme? She is all of these things. She is as sunny as the month of her birth, with a smile that melts your heart, eyes as dark as the night sky, and a head of golden curls.

I shall stay here at the villa until Carlo returns, so please don't worry about me. Adriana and I are in the best of hands. I've drawn you a picture of Adriana so you can see your first grandchild's sweet face.

I shall write again soon.

> *With all our love,*
> *Etta & Adriana*

Christina unfolds the sketch of Adriana. The child's smiling, chubby-cheeked face is crowned with yellow curls, and her dark eyes shine in joyful amusement. A sob rises in Christina's throat as the memories of those first days with Cecelia rush into her mind. She presses her lips together and gives Gerald the drawing.

'Isn't she lovely, Tina! She looks just like Etta did when she was a baby.'

'Etta's eyes are hazel. Hers are brown.'

'They must be her papa's eyes.'

Christina rises abruptly. 'Frame it and put it on your desk.'

'You don't want to put it in the sitting room with the family photographs?'

'I can always come in here if I wish to see it.'

Harry Grenville's painting of Christina lies unrolled on the white crocheted bedcover. Christina sits on the bed beside it, examining the face of the girl in the painting. Forever looking out over the blue sea as her lover paints her picture on a grassy hillside in Capri. Was she ever that happy? That hopeful? *Harold Grenville, Lord Sherbrooke. I'm glad you can't stay married. I'm glad you have no other children.*

The two things Harry had left her: the painting and Cecelia, though Cecelia will never know the truth. No one but Stefania, Liliana, Aunt Henrietta and Harry, of course, knows the truth of that summer in Capri. Not even Gerald.

Now here is Etta, in Villa Serenissima with a baby daughter in her arms and a husband away fighting a hideous war. Christina supposes she should be thankful that Etta and Carlo had married, even if it had been an elopement. She would never wish her situation, in those lonely, anguished days and months after Harry's abandonment, on anyone, least of all one of her daughters. But now, with that drawing of Adriana with her father's eyes, all the memories are flooding back. She can't have that. She can't bear it.

Guilt tweaks her conscience. She should have told Gerald the truth before their marriage. That she wasn't really a widow. That the story of her young Italian husband's drowning was fabricated by her father to hide the shame of her situation when she had returned with Cecelia from Italy. Now, it's simply too late. Gerald must never know about what happened between her and Harry Grenville, Lord Sherbrooke. And Cecelia must never know that Gerald isn't her father. Gerald has kept his word about that. It would never do to have Cecelia dig into a past that is nothing more than a mirage. To find out that she had been a terrible mistake. Maybe the Heavenly Father has sent Max Fischer to take Cecelia away. To relieve Christina of the burden of her guilt whenever she looks at her eldest daughter.

There is still one problem to be resolved; Cecelia's birth certificate, or, rather, the lack of one. There had been an Italian one, of course, with Harry's name on it, but that is with Stefania in Capri. How is she to obtain a British birth certificate for her daughter with Gerald's name on it and the amended birth date? Cecelia must never know she is a year older than she believes. It is best that everything continues just as it has since the day of her marriage to Gerald.

She runs her fingers along the outline of the girl's face in the painting. Thank heaven for Stefania. She will take care of Etta and her baby the way she took care of herself in the bleak days after Cecelia's birth. The days when, in the delirium of the fever that took hold of her, all she had wanted to do was walk into the sea until it closed over her head.

She rolls up the painting and wraps it in the brown paper, securing it with string. She slides it onto the top wardrobe shelf behind her hatboxes, gloves and scarves, and the green leather diary, where she knows Gerald will never find it.

Chapter Thirty-Eight

Celie

London – July 1915

C elie shrugs into her raincoat and adjusts her navy straw hat, which she's adorned with patriotic red, white and blue rosettes, in the mirror. A movement catches her eye; Milly is watching her from the sitting room, a feather duster in her hand.

'Milly? Isn't this your day off?'

"Alf-day, miss. Mrs Fry says I'm needed to 'elp 'er keep the 'ouse right wif the Red Cross ladies coming tomorrow to knit.'

'Mama shouldn't take your half-day away from you. I'll have a word with her.'

'Oh, no, miss, don't bovver 'er. Knittin' for our boys in France is important.'

Celie fastens the tiny pearl buttons of her gloves. 'Milly, have you heard about the "Women's Right to Serve" demonstration?'

A quick bob of her capped head. 'Yes, miss. In *The Suffragette*.'

'You read *The Suffragette*?'

Milly twists the feather duster nervously in her hands. 'I'm sorry, miss. Am I not meant to?'

'Oh, heavens, no. I mean, you may read whatever you wish, Milly. I had no idea you were interested in the suffragist cause.'

'Oh, yes, miss. I've seen you at some of the meetin's at Blackheaf 'Alls.' Her face freezes. 'On my days off. I 'aven't been skivin'.'

'You should have said hello.'

'Didn't fink it was my place, miss.'

Celie frowns at Milly's pale, sharp-chinned face. She pulls a green umbrella out of the stand and holds it out to the girl. 'Put on your raincoat. I have a banner to hold up during the march. Why don't you come and help me?'

'What about Mrs Fry? I wouldn't want 'er to be cross.'

'I shall speak to Mama later. Come on then, Miss Smith. We have work to do.'

Celie stands beside Milly, who is wildly waving their banner in front of a large plywood platform which has been erected beside Landseer's bronze lions in Trafalgar Square. She takes the Soho Reflex camera out of her canvas bag, loads a roll of film and clicks pictures of Milly's excited face, the reporters in bowler hats and raincoats sitting on collapsible stools in front the stage, and the bobbies in their navy uniforms and egg-shaped helmets doing their best to hold back the vocal crowd. The huge square is massed with people – both women and men – who spill out onto the surrounding streets. The red, white and blue rosettes on the women's hats bob like ducks on the Thames.

She focuses the lens on Emmeline Pankhurst as the woman stirs the crowd with her impassioned speech: 'I have been thrilled at the enthusiasm expressed by the thousands of women, some of whom have attended many suffragist rallies, and some who have joined a march for the first time. I have also heard the scoffs of some of our spectators…'

A rumble ripples through the crowd.

'Yes, the scoffs of some of the spectators, who have raised objections to women joining the workforce in our munitions factories. I heard one man say that it was nonsense as the factories would be required to build lavatories for the women!'

The crowd bursts into laughter, and someone whistles.

'How can we say to our grandchildren that we lost the war because the factory owners refused to build women's lavatories? Imagine that, the war lost for want of lavatories? I think this is a surmountable problem, wouldn't you agree?'

The crowd roars like a great awakening beast. Celie scans the faces with the camera, clicking until she comes to the end of the roll of film. She digs into her pocket and changes the film, then focuses the lens once more on the women on the stage. Her heart pounds as she listens to the speech, aware that history is unfolding in front of her eyes. A history that she can catch with her camera.

Emmeline Pankhurst moves across the stage, thrusting her hand into the air to emphasise her words.

'What we women are marching for today is to be given the opportunity to do something meaningful for the war, and to be paid a living wage to do so. We are strong. We are capable. My message to the factory owners – and I know some of you are here today – is to employ us! My message to the women here today is to sign up to the National War Register, so you can be called upon in our country's hour of need! If our men must go to war, we must do our utmost to fill their places in all the existing munitions factories. We must be ready in every city, at every bank till, on every train or tram, behind every desk, as men respond to our country's call. Let us serve!'

The square erupts into thundering shouts and applause. A hand squeezes her arm. She looks into Milly's clear green eyes.

'I should like to do somefink for them poor soldiers, wouldn't you, Miss Fry?' Milly points at Celie's camera. 'You should send your pictures to the papers. A picture's worf a fousand words, that's what me Pa always says.'

Celie looks at the camera. Could she do that? Would anyone be interested in pictures taken by a woman?

'You should do it, miss. I would if I was you.'

Maybe Milly is right. Maybe it's time to put herself out there, to find her life, the way that Jessie and Etta have found theirs. No one wants a German teacher; even the Translation Bureau isn't interested in her – but photography, that's something she could do.

She smiles at Milly. 'What a wonderful idea, Milly. I believe I shall.'

Chapter Thirty-Nine

Max and Frank

Gallipoli, Turkey – August 1915

Max holds the binoculars up to his eyes and scans the swathe of Suvla Beach, which just two days before had been as empty and peaceful as the beaches at De Panne in Belgium he had visited in his childhood. Now the beach is teeming with British and Australian troops unloading crates of supplies and pitching tents. A huge armoured ship is anchored only a few metres from the beach, disgorging yet more soldiers down wide metal ramps that run directly up to the sand.

'Let me see,' Fritz says as he crawls up to join Max at the top of the ridge.

Max hands him the binoculars. 'I hope Lieutenant Colonel Kemal's reinforcements arrive soon. Major Willmer said we have no hope of holding off all these battalions with only fifteen hundred men and no machine guns. They've already taken the two small hills beyond the salt lake. We can't let them get up to the higher ridge.'

Fritz glances over to a high ridge to his left. 'They'll definitely go for the Sari Bair ridge. If they get up there, they'll surround our trenches at Anzac Beach.'

'Exactly.' Max shuffles down the sandy hill to the goat track that winds along the ridge. 'Hurry, Fritz. I need to tell Major Willmer what we've seen.'

'*Jawohl*, Lieutenant Fischer.' Fritz salutes Max, then he digs his heels into the hill and propels himself onto the goat track. 'Why do you suppose they haven't made me a lieutenant yet?'

'That's easy, Fritz,' Max says as he loops the binoculars around his neck. 'Would you want to be commanded by you?'

'Very funny.'

'You know as well as I do that it's because you failed your officer exams.' They head through the marsh grass and wind-swept pines, back to their battalion on the far side of Sari Bair. 'You have to learn to apply yourself. At least there are no girls here to distract you, Fritz.'

'So, that's your secret. No English girlfriend to distract you. You'll be a major before you know it, because you're never going to see her again.'

Max yanks the sleeve of Fritz's uniform. 'What do you mean by that?'

Fritz pulls his arm away from Max's grip. 'Seriously? You're a German officer now. You'd be shot as a traitor or a spy if you ever got in touch with her. She's an enemy.'

'Don't ever speak like that about Celie again, do you understand me?'

'I'm just saying the facts—'

Max steps close to Fritz until he is staring straight into his friend's startled grey gaze. 'Do you understand me, Corporal?'

'Yes. Okay.'

'Good.' Max turns away abruptly and heads down the hill. He glances over his shoulder at Fritz's lanky frame in the too-large uniform. 'Hurry up, Corporal. What are you waiting for?'

Frank looks up from his perch in the sand in the shade of a dune. He is safe here from the snipers and the shrapnel from the sporadic shells being lobbed onto the beach by the Turks. He'd seen more than his share of men cut down by bullets and shrapnel in France. You would have thought you'd get used to it. But you never do.

He hears a shout and watches a horde of bantering men – some of them looking no older than fifteen, if a day – splash in the turquoise water of the bay, their white bodies glistening with a wet sheen as they toss around a cork buoy like a football. Out in the bay, the HMS *Jonquil* sits at anchor, the elderly General Stopford still having not set foot on the beach after having slept through the initial attack on the smaller hills the previous day.

Frank chews his lip as his pencil hovers over the sheet of writing paper. They should be up on the ridge, taking advantage of the sparse opposition. By now, the Turks and the Germans knew they were in the bay. They wouldn't waste any time sending reinforcements. Any idiot could see that. Instead, his sergeant had said they were under Stopford's orders to 'consolidate their position'. He scans the high ridge surrounding the bay like a huge horseshoe. Sitting ducks, that's what they were. They'd lost their chance at an easy run up to the ridge.

He wets his lips with a dribble of water from his canteen. There's another problem; twenty thousand men and barely enough water for half of them. Somebody somewhere had forgotten that August in the Mediterranean is a bloody furnace. He wipes at his dripping forehead and sinks further back into the shade of the dune. He props the sheet on his knee and taps at it with his pencil. He may as well write to her, even though he knows it's a lost cause. She's never given him any reason to hope. Still, he has nothing to lose.

Somewhere in Turkey

August 8th, 1915

Dear Miss Fry,

I am sitting on a beach on a very hot summer day somewhere in Turkey. I can't say where we are, though truthfully, I'm not sure I could find it on a map if I were asked. Still, it's better than sitting in the mud in a French trench, so for that I am thankful.

I also wanted to thank you very much for visiting me when I was laid up in hospital in London this spring. Your visit was like a breath of fresh air, and you were very kind to let me beat you at Hearts. I must insist on a rematch when I am back in London, and I shall expect you not to restrain yourself. I should be quite honoured to be trounced in Hearts by Miss Cecelia Fry.

I hope you and your family are keeping well. Please give my kindest regards to them all, and to your sister Jessie, especially, for her sterling care of me when I was in hospital. I am feeling very much better.

Yours faithfully,
Frank Jeffries

Max shuts his right eye and peers down the barrel of his rifle. Below his battalion on the summit of Scimitar Hill, at the foot of the Sari Bair ridge, mist and smoke rise from the salt lake and scrubby terrain that separates the beach from the ridge. The shrapnel has set the tinder-dry grass burning, and the smoke blends with the salt lake's evaporating water in a dense cloud that sits over Suvla Bay like the steam from a boiling pot. Emerging from the fog like spectres in a bad dream, shadowy shapes of men run blindly toward the foot of the hill.

He aims for one of the dark forms and pulls the trigger. The figure twitches and falls backward into the embrace of the dense cloud.

'Good shot, Max.'

'Pay attention, Fritz.'

'It's like picking off ducks on a pond. There's no sport in this. What's happened to the machine guns?'

'They're sending them down the line. Kemal's brought them in.' Max adjusts his elbows on the rocky ground behind the sandbag barricade and aims for another dark form. 'It's not a sport. It's war.' He shoots, but the figure simply spins around and clutches its arm. Another shot rings out and the figure sinks into the smoking grass.

Fritz pumps the air with his balled fist. 'Bull's-eye! Another stinking Tommy hits the dust.'

Max glances sideways at his friend. 'Don't get cocky.'

'There's no fun in this at all, Max.' Fritz glances behind him. 'I'm going over.'

'What! No, stop, Fritz. Fritz, it's an order!' But Fritz is already over the sandbags and sliding down through the rocks and scrubby earth.

'Stupid idiot.' Max hesitates for an instant. Then he climbs over the top of the sandbags and follows Fritz into the cloud.

Frank Jeffries stumbles up the hill, coughing as the smoke settles in his damaged lungs. He holds his primed rifle at the ready. Every now and then he catches his foot on a rock, or a charred bush, or, worse, the smoking uniform of a dead soldier. He presses on through the fog, the moans and cries of injured men drowned out by the barrage of shells and bullets.

Mother of God. Mother of God. Holy Jesus. Mother of God. Soon he is in a rhythm. *Mother of God. Mother of God. Holy Jesus. Mother of God.*

A figure crashes out of the smoke in front of him. In the next second he sees the spike on the soldier's helmet, the bayonetted rifle. He pulls the trigger. The soldier collapses at his feet. He steps over him and hurries up the hill through the smoke.

Chapter Forty

Jessie

Hmhs Letitia, Gallipoli, Turkey – August 1915

Ivy Roach dips behind a steel strut on the HMHS *Letitia's* deck as a shell explodes in the sea about thirty metres away, sending a spout of water over the prow of a nearby barge of wounded soldiers. 'Blinkin' hell. That was close. Can't they see the crosses on the sides of the ship?'

'They're not aiming at us.' Jessie scours the dark waters of the bay for the long flat shapes of the barges being towed out to the hospital ship by small, sturdy trawlers. 'They're aiming at the barges of wounded. We're lucky there's no moon tonight. It's harder for the Turks to find them.'

'And more likely they'll hit us!' Ivy tuts. 'Those poor blokes. As if they haven't been through enough already.'

'I've managed to count seventeen barges so far.' Jessie nudges

Ivy's arm. 'Come on, let's get downstairs. It looks like we're going to have a busy night.'

Ivy hurries after Jessie down the narrow staircase to the hospital ward. Rows of beds, neatly made up with bleached sheets and pillows, are crammed along the grey metal walls. Nurses and Egyptian orderlies fly in and out of the ward, carrying supplies and bandages in preparation for the first arrivals.

'I'd best get to the operating theatre, Ivy. We'll need to get as many boys patched up for the journey to the hospitals on Lemnos as we can.'

'Right-o. I'll be needin' some of your lye soap later. I can't bear the lice.'

'I think the lice are winning that war.' Jessie pushes aside the curtain over the door to one of the four storerooms which have been converted into operating theatres. A white-masked anaesthetist sits at the head of the operating table, and an orderly stands beside the two equipment trollies. Jessie quickly washes at the sink and pulls on a pair of rubber gloves.

'Hurry up! In here!' A surgeon pulls aside the curtain and two orderlies barge into the room carrying a groaning soldier on a stretcher. 'Get him onto the table. Quickly!'

Jessie looks over at the surgeon, who has the black hair and dark skin of an Egyptian. The surgeon addresses the anaesthetist as he pushes past the orderlies. 'Get him under. Sister, clean him up while I get ready.' His voice carries the rolling accent of the orderlies, though unlike the majority of them, his English is fluent. 'Shrapnel. Pick out what you can with the tweezers.'

Jessie's eyes widen. 'Pick out the shrapnel? But, I've … I've never done th—'

The doctor glares at her as he lathers his hands at the sink. 'Then find me a nurse who can.'

'No, no, I'll do it.'

She turns to the orderly and points to the scissors. 'Cut his jacket off, please.' She leans over the soldier, a young British infantryman with a shock of ginger hair and green eyes glazed with pain and fear, and smiles at him reassuringly. 'Don't worry, we'll have you right as rain before you know it.'

The soldier clutches her hands. 'Please. I don't want to die. I want to see my mum. I don't want to die. I want to go home.'

Jessie eyes the wound that gapes like a mouth spewing blood across the soldier's belly. She swallows. 'You'll be fine. I promise.'

The anaesthetist drips chloroform over the gauze mask he holds over the soldier's face; the soldier's eyes roll back and his grip relaxes. Jessie takes a glass bottle of Dakin's Solution from the trolly and points to the rubber tube that is curled like a snake amongst the bandages. 'Hand me the hose, please.' She twists the cap off the Dakin's Solution and gives the orderly the bottle. She makes a pouring gesture. 'Pour it into the hose slowly while I wash out the wound.'

Jessie holds the end of the hose over the wound and splashes the antiseptic solution into the deepest recesses, exposing black shards of shrapnel that stick out of the shredded pink flesh like broken black eggshells. She hands the tube back to the orderly. 'Continue, please.' She picks up the tweezers and squints at a long black splinter. Grasping it, she carefully pulls it free.

Jessie peels off the rubber gloves and drops them into the sanitary bin for sterilising. She picks up the yellow soap and lathers her hands over the portable sink. Her limbs feel as heavy as lead and a dull ache spreads behind her forehead. She has lost count of the soldiers with their gaping shrapnel wounds, their faces burnt beyond recognition, their arms and legs riddled with bullet wounds. Surely, there has to be an end to it.

The surgeon joins her at the sink. 'Soap, please, Sister. Excuse me, Lieutenant.'

'Sister is fine.' Jessie hands him the soap. 'No one calls us Lieutenant.'

'I shall call you Lieutenant. We are at war and you are an army nurse.'

They stand beside each other in silence as they soap their hands and arms. Jessie feels her cheeks redden. Why does he look at her like he's judging her every action and finding her wanting? She thrusts her hands into the sink at the same moment he does. She pulls away as if she's been burnt, water splashing over his surgical gown.

'I'm terribly sorry, Captain.'

He looks at her with a gaze so intense that it is like being pierced by an arrow. He gestures to the sink. 'After you.'

The curtain flaps open and two orderlies enter with another stretcher.

'*Shazaya?*' the doctor asks in Arabic.

The older orderly shakes his head and says something she doesn't understand.

The surgeon looks at Jessie. 'We may be here for some time. He has a bullet wound near his heart. He is lucky he is still alive.'

Jessie quickly rinses off the soap and dries her hands. She pulls on a fresh pair of rubber gloves and watches the orderly cut away the uniform. A German uniform.

'Lieutenant, irrigate please.'

But she is rooted to the spot, as surely as if she were a tree with roots reaching down through the floor to twine around the engine room's ovens below.

'Quickly!'

'He's … he's German.'

'What is that to us? He is a man and he is wounded. It is our duty to help. Do you understand?'

'Yes, sir. But—'

The surgeon's voice hardens. 'Irrigate the wound, Lieutenant. That is an order.'

'Yes, Captain.'

She lifts off the makeshift bandage which is saturated with the man's blood. Picking up the bottle of Dakin's Solution, she pours it into the wound.

Jessie tugs at the sleeve of Ivy's uniform. 'Where are you going with that pillow? Not that German again?'

Ivy raises her eyebrows. 'He's finding it difficult to breathe, Jessie. Poor fella's not gonna last the night. It's the least I can do.'

'You seem to be going out of your way to help him.'

'Jessie, he's a patient. I wouldn't care if he were the Kaiser himself. Where's your humanity?'

'I save it for our soldiers.'

'Then ya shouldn't be a nurse.'

'I'll have you know I was top of the class in the surgical rotation. And anatomy.'

'Well, bully for ya. When ya find your heart, let me know.'

The soldier coughs and gasps for breath. He reaches to catch hold of Ivy's apron as she slides the pillow under his head. '*Wasser, bitte*. Please, water.'

Ivy pours a glass of water and holds it to his mouth when the coughing subsides. He drinks as if he has been lost in a desert for days. 'Thank you.' He wipes his hand across his streaming forehead. 'I am so hot. Please, can you take off the sheet?'

'Of course.' She folds back the sheet to the foot of the steel-framed bed. She looks up at him to find him staring at her with his clear blue eyes.

'Yes? Is there something else?'

'I had a letter. In my jacket.'

'I'm afraid that will have been burnt. We had to cut it off you to operate.'

'Oh.' He swallows. 'The letter… It's important.' He grasps Ivy's hand. 'Please can you see? Please?' His shoulders heave and the coughing shakes his body.

Ivy squeezes his hand. 'I'll see if I can find it. I promise.'

Ivy steps off the metal ladder into the heat and hissing noise of the ship's boiler room. A man shovels coal into one of the grates under a huge boiler, and she heads past the pipes and coal heaps toward him.

'Excuse me! Sir?'

The stoker stands up and rests his elbow on the handle of his shovel. His pale eyes peer at her through a mask of grime. 'Sir, is it? Do I look like the King of England? What're ya doin' down 'ere, love? Ya want my job, you can 'ave it.'

'Thanks all the same, but I'll stick with what I know. You don't happen ta know where the clothes that need to be burnt are? The ones from the soldiers?'

The man points his thumb at the rear of the boiler room. 'Down there. It's a bloody mountain.' He laughs and slaps his hand on the wooden handle of his shovel. 'Bloody mountain. Ya 'ear that? That's a good one.'

'Thanks.'

She finds the stack of filthy clothes wedged behind the far wall and the second boiler. Pulling on the rubber gloves she's stolen from the supply cupboard, she leans into her task.

'Where is he?'

Jessie looks up from the bed she is making. 'Where's who?'

'The German soldier.'

'You were right, Ivy. He didn't last the night. One less to worry about.'

Ivy stares at Jessie. 'He was a person, Jessie. Caught up in this stupid war like the rest of us.'

Jessie tosses the pillow onto the bed. 'Why are you looking for him?'

Ivy fingers the letter in her uniform pocket. 'Just wanted to see if he needed anything, but it looks like I'm too late.'

Chapter Forty-One

Carlo

The Italian Front – August 1915

Carlo bends over his sketchbook and adds crosshatch shadows to the shaded side of the mountains he is sketching. Below him the Isonzo River slides like a turquoise snake between the craggy, pine-covered mountains separating Italy from Austria-Hungary. But for the clamour of men's voices, the neighing of the supply horses, and the thuds of sandbags being stacked into defensive walls behind him, he could almost imagine a world without machine guns and heavy artillery, of bad food, and thirst, and death.

He'd harboured no romantic illusions about the war when he'd signed up. At thirty-two, he had seen more of the world than most, had loved more women than was his fair share, had earned and spent money without care. Except where Marianna was concerned; he'd always ensured his wife's medical bills were paid, though no amount of money seemed of any use to help bring her back from the dream world she inhabited.

How a youthful indiscretion had changed the course of his life! A forced marriage at nineteen to the wild and unstable Marianna Ludovisi, who had lost her last hold on the realities of this world after the birth of their son thirteen years earlier. Aside from Paolo, God had bestowed one gift upon him. He could draw. And this gift had been his route to a small fame and modest wealth. As long as he could draw and paint, Marianna and Paolo would be well taken care of.

But now, there is another family.

He reaches into his pocket and takes out Etta's letter. His eyes travel across the familiar looping curls of her handwriting. Adriana Christina, born the thirtieth of May. *'"She has hair as golden as the sunrise and eyes as dark as chocolate. Truly, she is a gift of our love."'*

He draws Etta's fine features, her hazel eyes almost as green as olives, and the billowing luxury of her golden hair, in his imagination. His beautiful angel. His heart judders and the exquisite pain of yearning grows within him. She is the true love of his heart; so joyful, with an infectious enthusiasm for life that he'd long thought he'd lost, but, with her, he has found once again. And now, there is the child.

How can he tell Etta he can never marry her while Marianna is alive? Marianna's Catholic family would never permit a divorce. And if he dies somewhere up in these mountains, what then? What of his beloved Etta and his little daughter then?

He folds the cover of his sketchbook over the drawing. There is only one thing for it. He must stay alive.

Chapter Forty-Two

Christina

Capri, Italy – July 1892

The day is fine; another Caprese July day like the previous one and the day before that. Days with skies as blue as her mother's favourite delphiniums, turquoise seas rolling in the summer breeze, the air perfumed with spicy rosemary and lemons. Days that she had held inside of herself and unfurled in her mind's eye when the skies had darkened and life became bleak and hopeless in the dreadful month after Cecelia's birth.

She lifts her face to the sun and shuts her eyes, willing the heat to penetrate through the leaden layers of her skin. The backs of her eyelids glow red and tears prick at her eyes. The tears come, a trickle at first, then a sudden surge, spewing from her eyes and down her sun-reddened cheeks, over her lips to her tongue. Salt. The only thing she can still taste.

'*Cara mia, cara mia*. Don't cry, my darling girl.' Stefania Albertini brushes Christina's auburn hair with her hand as the girl weeps into her shoulder. 'You must be strong, Tina. You are an Innocenti, like your mother and like me. You must bury the pain deep inside yourself. What is done cannot be undone. You must move forward. You are not a girl any longer. You have someone else you must live for. You are a mother now.'

The whitewashed buildings clustered along the shore grow smaller, their inhabitants going about their lives on the island – rolling out the dough for the thick ribbons of scialatielli pasta; arguing over the price of the fat shrimp or octopus in the market; climbing over the hills hunting rabbit to be slow-cooked in a terracotta pot with white wine, rosemary, garlic and herbs for Sunday lunch – as if nothing has changed.

The ferry's wake churns a white V into the blue sea on its passage to Naples, setting the moored blue fishing boats bobbing on the waves, and the gulls dive and glide around the boat, on the lookout for a titbit from a benevolent passenger.

The baby stirs in Christina's arms, and a tiny arm frees itself from the swaddling. The pink hand balls and flexes, and Christina extends a finger. The tiny fingers, with their nails like mother-of-pearl, close around it.

Stefania joins her beside the railing. She looks at the retreating limestone cliffs and green hills of Capri. 'You always have a home here, if you need, *cara mia*.' She clears her throat and holds out her arms.

'Come, let me hold the baby, so I can always remember how she feels in my arms, when you are both so far away in England.'

Part Four

1916

Chapter Forty-Three

Jessie

Egypt – January 1916

No. 15 General Hospital, Alexandria, Egypt

'Jessie! Over here!' Ivy waves at Jessie from her table in the hospital canteen. She wipes scone crumbs from her lips with her fingers. 'Have you heard? Colonel James is organisin' a musical and dramatic society. There's a note posted on the canteen board. What do ya fancy? Wanna give it a go?'

'I'm not much of a performer, Ivy. That's my sister Etta's forte.'

'Oh, c'mon. How else are ya gonna get friendly with the doctors? Captain Delmege and Captain Darling are to be the musical co-ordinators, though I don't imagine that awful Captain Khalid will be joinin' in. I've nevva met a grumpier man. He had a go at me the other day for forgettin' to wash a soldier's feet. Like I don't have a million other things to think about!' She follows Jessie into the hospital's bright, airy staff canteen.

'I have to be back in the ward in half an hour.'

Ivy grabs her plate from the table. 'Hold on. I wanna get another scone.'

Jessie heads toward the lunch queue and collects a metal tray, followed by Ivy.

'So, Jessie, are ya gonna join the dramatic society?'

'I didn't join the Queen Alexandra's to sing and dance, or find a husband, Ivy.'

Ivy shrugs. 'I'm a red-blooded woman, aren't I? I know Matron has all these rules that we mustn't socialise with soldiers, but she hasn't said anythin' about doctors, has she? We're young, Jessie. Work hard, play hard, that's my motto. Look, I'm headin' down to Cairo on Saturday with some Anzac nurses to show them the pyramids. You can be an honorary Aussie for the day. What do ya say? All work and no play make Jessie a dull girl.'

Jessie watches the server scoop spiced mutton stew onto a plate. 'Maybe. I haven't seen anything except the inside of the hospital and the nurses' residence since I arrived here. I could just as well be back in London.' She takes the plate of food and sets it on her tray.

Ivy pokes Jessie on the shoulder. 'Come on. Come to Cairo with us. It'll do ya good.'

'Oh, all right. I'll switch my shift with someone else.'

Ivy grabs a scone from a plate on the serving counter. 'Righty-o, that's settled then. I'll give ya some tips on how ta ride a camel.'

'What kind of tips?'

'Basically, hang on for dear life and don't fall off.'

Jessie climbs the marble staircase up to the second floor, then up the narrow access staircase to the former school's flat concrete roof. She pushes open the wooden door and steps into the brilliant sunshine of the Egyptian winter day. A cool breeze wafts up the hill where the three solid brick buildings of the former Abbasia Secondary School, now hastily converted into the No. 15 General Hospital, squat on the crest of the hill.

She walks to the edge of the roof for the view of Alexandria spread out below the hill. Around the hospital buildings on their plane of dusty earth, Jessie counts twenty-three canvas tents which hold the overspill of wounded from the Gallipoli campaign. At the foot of the hill, the roofs of the ancient city's jigsaw of buildings cluster together between alleyways and roads that wander through Alexandria like dirty streams. In the distance, the blue water of the Mediterranean glitters under the midday sun, the romance of the view marred only by the hulking grey shapes of the naval destroyers steaming east toward the military camps and hospitals of Port Said. She sits on the ledge and bites into an apple.

'You have washed that, I hope.'

She spits the apple into her hand. The tall figure of Captain Khalid stands in a corner shaded by the doorway. 'Excuse me?'

'You have washed the apple, I hope,' he says as he rolls up a small rug. 'You should peel it before you eat it. It may make you ill otherwise.'

'Oh, I didn't know that. I only arrived in Alexandria a week ago.' She looks at the mangled apple. 'I was looking forward to this. I haven't seen an apple since England.'

He tugs a handkerchief out of the pocket of his white medical coat and walks over to her. 'Wrap it in this so you can eat it later.' His lips twitch under his black moustache when she hesitates. 'It is clean, don't worry.'

'Thank you.' She wraps the handkerchief around the apple.

'Don't eat ice either.' He presses a hand against his chest as he inclines his head. 'Permit me to introduce myself. I am Captain Aziz Khalid, senior surgeon for the British Army in Egypt.'

'We've worked together on the *Letitia* at Gallipoli. Several times. I'm Lieutenant Jessica Fry.'

'I know.'

He turns abruptly and heads towards the door.

Shepheard's Hotel, Cairo, Egypt

The nurses dash up the steps to the canopied terrace of Shepheard's Hotel on Ibrahim Pasha Street on the boundary of the European and Arab quarters of Cairo. To one side of the grand glass and wrought-iron terrace, a military band in bright red jackets bangs out a spirited rendition of 'A Little Bit of What You Fancy Does You Good' under the shade of the towering palm trees. Ivy cranes her neck over the heads of the British and Anzac army officers and immaculately dressed European women crowded into the terrace's wicker chairs. 'There! Hurry, girls!'

They shuffle past the crowded tables, apologising and giggling as they bump against the chairs, and flop into the seats. 'There ya go, ladies,' Ivy says as she waves her hand around the terrace. 'The best seats in Cairo. *Everyone* who's *anyone* comes here… Theda Bara … Anna Pavlova … kings and queens …'

'And Anzac nurses!' a young red-haired nurse with a New Zealand accent pipes up to hurrahs from the others.

'Right ya are, Mabel.'

A flush-faced young nurse named Nancy from Adelaide unpins her straw boater and fans her face. 'I could kill a lemonade right now.'

A soldier in the khaki uniform of an Australian Light Horse regiment leans back in his chair at a nearby table. 'Is that an Aussie accent I'm hearin'?'

Nancy giggles. 'It certainly is. I'm Nancy Evans. From Adelaide.'

'Pleased to meet ya, Nancy.' The soldier nods at his three companions who all wear the Light Horse uniform. 'We're from all ovva Oz. Mick here is from – where'd ya say it was, Mick?'

A blond soldier with a broad, sunburnt face answers. 'That'd be Wagga Wagga, mate.'

'Right-o. Mick there is from Wagga Wagga, Tommy-boy is from beautiful Brisbane, and Ralph over there is from Sydney.' He picks up a plumed hat from the table and tips it at the nurses. 'Sergeant Archie Winter from Adelaide at your service.' He winks at Nancy, who bursts into giggles.

Jessie rolls her eyes and picks up a menu. Archie's blue eyes twinkle as he appraises her. 'Where abouts are ya from, Sista? You're a New Zealand girl, aren't ya? I'll wager you're one of those serious types from Wellington.'

'I'm afraid you'd lose your wager. I'm English.'

A white smile flashes in the young soldier's tanned face. 'There's always one bad apple.'

Nancy erupts into another fit of giggles, earning her a sour glare from Jessie. She smiles at the waiter, who stands stiffly beside the table in a smart white jacket and red felt *tarbouche*, a starched white cloth folded neatly over his forearm. 'We'll have four lemonades, please,' Jessie says. 'Very cold, but no ice, if you would.'

The waiter inclines his head and retrieves the menus from the nurses. Archie Winter tosses his hat onto the nurses' table. 'Bring us four beers as well, will ya, mate? Cheers.'

As the waiter retreats through the grand entrance doors into the dark interior of the hotel, the four soldiers push their chairs around the nurses' table. Jessie watches the activity with growing annoyance. All she'd wanted was a nice day out with the other nurses, away from hospitals and war and soldiers. And here they are, swooped upon by a group of insolent Australians.

Archie fixes his gaze on Jessie. 'So, you're a Pommie, then.'

'I suppose I am a "Pommie". I'm from London.'

'Long way from home, then, Miss—'

'Aren't we all?'

Ivy prods Jessie's shoulder. 'Jessie, lighten up. He's not goin' ta bite.'

The soldier grins and holds out his hand. 'Pleased ta meet ya, Jessie.'

Jessie sighs and grasps his hand. The warmth of his skin travels through her fingers and up her arm, and she shivers involuntarily. Releasing his hand, she folds her arms. She glances over at the hotel's entrance doors, willing the waiter to hurry up with the lemonades.

The soldier chuckles. 'That lemonade betta be the best you've evva tasted.'

'What do you mean?'

'Because you seem more interested in lemonade than findin' out all about this handsome young soldier from Adelaide.'

Jessie bites her lip as she struggles to suppress a smile. What is she so worried about? Isn't this exactly what she's always wanted? To experience life in new places? Here she is on the terrace of the famous Shepheard's Hotel in Cairo, Egypt with a group of lively Australians and New Zealanders. She's a long way from Hither Green.

She relaxes against the ridges of the wicker chair. What's the harm in enjoying the attention of a saucy young soldier? She rather likes his forwardness. It's a refreshing change from the few tongue-tied English boys who'd crossed her path in London. They'd mostly been interested in Etta at any rate. Etta, the pretty sister, or Celie, the polite sister. Just like that Frank Jeffries.

What sister is she? Jessie the stubborn, ornery, difficult sister? Celie is Papa's favourite, anyone can see that, and Mama indulges every silly wish of Etta's... Well, at least she did until Etta ran away with the Italian. Knowing Etta, she'll come out of that smelling like roses, too. Whose favourite is she? No one's. She's no one's favourite.

It doesn't matter. Not in Egypt where nobody knows her from Adam. Here she can be whoever she wants to be.

Jessie unpins her straw hat and sets it on the table beside Archie's. She turns to the young soldier. 'So, Sergeant Winter, what do you do when you're back in Adelaide?'

Chapter Forty-Four

Celie

Hither Green, London – February 1916

C elie rubs her forehead and rolls her head from side to side, but a dull throb has taken hold and refuses to dissipate.

We are writing to acknowledge receipt of your letter of reapplication to work as a German translator in the Translation Bureau. We are currently sufficiently staffed. We shall keep your letter on file should the situation change in the future. Thank you for your interest.

She folds the letter from the War Office Translation Bureau and slides it into the folder with the three other rejection letters. She can pass any German test they give her with flying colours. It's ridiculous not to use a woman's skill simply because of her sex. She slams the drawer shut and bites her lower lip, squashing the tears that threaten to erupt. She misses Max so much. If only she could hear from him. Why did this stupid war have to happen?

She picks up the Reflex camera and turns it over in her hands. She misses the suffragist meetings and marches, as well, but understands why Mrs Fawcett and Mrs Pankhurst have turned their attention to funding hospitals and encouraging women to work. But writing and distributing flyers isn't the same as marching for the vote.

Perhaps she'll head uptown on the omnibus. She's had an idea for an article on women in transport for the *Daily Mirror*. They'd loved her photographs of the 'Women's Right to Serve' rally and the speculative piece on 'Spiritualistic Quacks in Wartime' about the mediums and palmists preying on worried wives and mothers. *'Give me anything about women,'* the feature's editor, Mr Grayson, had said when she'd met him in his office. *'Knitting for the soldiers, things like that. The advertisers love that. Royal Vinolia Face Cream signed up for a month of advertisements after that quack piece. They said sales went through the roof. Keep them coming. No one needs to know you're a woman.'*

No one needs to know she's a woman? But they do. Absolutely they do.

She hears her mother's heels click on the wooden floor of the hallway. A knock on her door. 'Cecelia? I want to talk to you.'

Celie opens the door. Her mother holds a note and looks particularly out of sorts this morning. 'Yes, Mama?'

'Do you know anything about Milly's resignation?'

'Milly's resigned?'

'Yes, I found this note by the teapot. She's left to join Royal Woolwich Arsenal as a munitions worker. A munitions worker, Cecelia! I can think of only one place where she's heard of such nonsense. Why would any sensible young girl leave perfectly adequate domestic employment to make ammunition? It's hardly women's work.'

'Mama, everything is women's work now. The war's changed everything.'

'Well, this has certainly inconvenienced me. Where am I meant to find a maid of all work now?'

'No doubt if you go to the Salvation Army, you'll find someone there.'

'If I do, she will hardly be young and capable like Milly. She knows exactly how I like the vegetables cooked.'

'I'm sure we'll manage, Mama. I'll buy some sausages at the butcher's while I'm out and make toad-in-the-hole for supper. Milly taught me. I'll teach you how.'

'Cecelia, I have never cooked a day in my life, and I don't intend to start now.'

'Sacrifices, Mama. We all must learn new things.' She grabs her hat from the top of her chest of drawers. 'I'm going out for a while. I'll stop by the studio and tell Papa we'll be cooking supper tonight. That should excite him.'

Celie finds her father up a stepladder in the photography studio fixing the pulley system for the blackout sheet covering the skylight.

'Heavens, Papa! You should wait to do things like that when I'm here to help you.' She sets down the camera on a bamboo table and hurries over to grab hold of the ladder.

'Hello, pet. I thought it would be a simple fix, but it's proved to be rather more complicated. If you hold me steady, I think I can manage it.' He loops the loose rope over the metal pulley and gives it a tug. 'There, perfect.' He smiles down at his daughter. 'Thank you, my dear.'

He climbs down the ladder and folds it against the wall. 'I've developed your photographs of the damage near St Paul's Cathedral from the last zeppelin attack. They're very powerful, Celie. You have an excellent eye.'

'Those poor people, Papa, killed in their sleep. Children as well. We're not soldiers; why are they attacking us?'

'It seems we are all combatants in this war.'

'The War Office Translation Bureau still won't have me. I received another rejection letter from them today.'

'I'm sorry, my dear. You would be a great asset to them.'

'I'm quite certain they keep rejecting me because I'm a woman. Can't they see that society is changing? Even our Milly has left to become a munitions worker. Mama is beside herself. She blames me for it, but you can hardly blame Milly for wanting to make a real contribution to the war effort.'

'As you say, the world is changing.'

'I promised to teach Mama how to cook toad-in-the-hole for supper.'

Gerald laughs. 'Did you, now?' He pulls aside the curtain to the developing room and Celie steps inside. Her photographs of the bomb damage in the financial district hang from a string like bunting. She unclips a photograph. The entire façade of a building has collapsed into a mound of smashed bricks and charred wood, and three young boys play on the debris like it is a dune on a holiday beach.

'You should bring that into the *Daily Mirror* next time you go, pet.'

'I don't know, Papa. They want articles about women doing domestic things. Apparently, those sell more face cream.'

'There's nothing wrong with articles about women. It makes a refreshing change from all the news from France.'

'Yes, well, my next assignment is about how to curl your hair using torn sheets. I can't face writing it at the moment so I'm off to the West End to take photographs of conductorettes. I'm going to write a piece on women in transport and see if I can sneak it past the editor.'

'I'm glad to see you keeping busy.'

Celie clips the photograph back on the string. 'I have to, Papa. If I'm not busy, I ... I get upset.' She looks over at her father. 'You're not cross that Max is German, are you?'

'It is a complication, Celie, but he seemed like a very nice young man when he came to your birthday dinner. He makes you happy, and that's all a father wants.'

'Jessie doesn't approve. She told me as much before she left for Egypt.'

'Jessie has seen some terrible things in the hospital. No doubt it's difficult for her to be objective.'

'I suppose so, but what she said was very upsetting. Max is the love of my life, Papa, and I don't even know if he's alive. I have to keep busy, or I'll just...' She chokes back a sob.

Gerald encircles Celie in an awkward hug. He pats her back, the wool of her coat damp under his palm from the rain. 'You'll be fine, Celie. You're strong, just like your mother.'

She leans into her father's embrace. If only it were true. She may appear calm and capable, but her heart is sick with longing for her lost Max.

Chapter Forty-Five

Etta

Capri, Italy – February 1916

Etta slides her fingers over the bumps of the grey stones that protrude from the grotto's ruined walls. A film of sandy dust collects on her fingertips and she wipes her hand on her navy skirt. A gust of cold wind whips across the tops of the umbrella pines on the cliff opposite the grotto's entrance, and Etta pulls her coat collar up against her chin. She blows into her hands and silently chastises herself for forgetting her gloves.

She feels better today, which surprises her, given the leaden sky and threat of rain. The mimosa tree outside her bedroom window has begun to bloom, and she'd woken to the honey and violet scent of its feathery yellow flowers. Truthfully, when she closes her eyes to sleep each night, she's never sure which side of her personality she will awaken to these days. There are nights when the noises and images in her head make sleep impossible, and she has to resort to

Liliana's tonic of laudanum, honey and wine to lull her into sleep. In the mornings after those drugged dreams, she awakes with a heavy head and a fuzziness of thought which makes the effort of facing the day almost too much to bear.

Then, there are the days like today when she wakes and the confusion and dullness have melted away. When she stretches her arms, relishing the joy of her body's release from the sluggishness of the previous days. When she jumps out of bed and reaches for Adriana, holding her close against her breast as she burrows her face into the baby's silky golden hair. When behind her closed eyes she sees Carlo's face and hears his promise to come back to them.

She sits on an ancient stone step and tucks her skirt around her legs against the chill. *If only every day could be like today.*

She opens her cloth bag and takes out a sketchbook and a charcoal pencil. It had been good of Stefania to offer to watch Adriana this morning. It had been some time since she'd felt up to a walk. The villa's thick walls were a refuge from all the uncertainty in the world, from the fear that rose inside her when she thought about Carlo freezing and fighting in the snow of the Italian Dolomites. The walk had been Stefania's idea. She'd demurred at first, but after a breakfast of strong milky coffee and Liliana's lemon cake on the balcony, where the fresh winter breeze had sloughed off the last vestiges of lethargy, she'd felt ready to face the world outside the villa's walls once again.

She bends her head over the sketchbook, and is halfway through a sketch of the umbrella pine that stretches over the view across the sea to the Amalfi Coast, when she hears his voice.

'Etta! Cara mia!'

The sketchbook slips from her lap. She leaps to her feet, and Carlo is suddenly in her arms, his body a solid thing, his kisses hot and real, his voice a caress in her ear. *Etta, my angel, my darling. I've missed you so much. You are my life, my breath.*

She looks up into Carlo's dark eyes, which flash with the ardour of his love above the deep shadows that sit under his eyes like blue crescents. 'Carlo, my darling.' She touches his face with her cold hands, afraid that he is a hallucination; but he is there, solid and warm. 'I thought you were in the mountains. I've been so worried about you up there in the snow. I can imagine how cold that must be.'

He takes hold of her hands and blows on them. He rubs them between his own. 'I told you I would come back, *mio angelo*. I managed to take leave for ten days. I've been travelling since Sunday to come to you and Adriana.'

'Have you seen her? Did Cousin Stefania tell you where to find me?'

Carlo pulls her down onto the step to sit beside him. He hugs her against his rough wool army coat. 'I went to the villa straightaway. Adriana is beautiful.'

'She has your dark eyes and your name. Adriana Christina Marinetti. It's on her birth certificate. The priest wanted to see our marriage certificate, but I told him it had been lost in a zeppelin attack in London. He wasn't happy about it, but Cousin Stefania took him to one side, and he had a change of heart. I believe some *lire* may have changed hands.'

'I shall make sure to make it right with her before I leave.'

Etta brushes her hand along his cheek's rough bristles. He kisses her fingers. 'I am sorry, *Etta mia*. I had no time to shave since I left the mountains. Your cousin must think I look like a *vagabondo*.'

'I don't mind. I'm just so glad you're here.'

He unpins her hat and sets it on the ground. He kisses her hair and enfolds her in his arms. 'My darling, there is something I must tell you.'

Etta nestles more deeply into his embrace. 'That you've missed me every moment of every day? That mine is the face you imagine when you wake in the morning, and the one you dream of when you sleep? That's what you are to me, my darling.' She turns in his arms and reaches for his face. 'I love you, Carlo Marinetti.'

He kisses her, and the warmth of her body enfolds him until she is the only world he needs, the only world he wants. Until the urgency to tell her about Marianna and Paolo wafts away like a leaf on the February breeze.

The following days pass in a blur of Liliana's food; walks along the goat paths in the hills where the first wildflowers have begun to peek shyly through the damp grass, with Adriana bundled up like a plump doll in Carlo's arms; and love. Endless nights of love, where Etta and Carlo find their way back to each other through the entwining of limbs and ardent caresses of their love-making. For Carlo, the days are bittersweet, and on the fourth morning, he knows he cannot delay telling Etta about Marianna and Paolo any longer.

After breakfast on the balcony, when Adriana has been whisked off to the kitchen to 'watch me make bread' by a doting Liliana, and Stefania has retired to her room to read, Carlo reaches across the wicker table and takes hold of her hand. '*Etta mia.* I love you with all my heart.'

She smiles, and to him it is like the sun breaking through clouds on a stormy day. 'And I love you, too.'

'Etta, I must leave today.'

She drops the needlepoint she is working on into her lap. 'Today? But you said you had leave for ten days.'

'It will take me three days to return. I have no choice.'

'I thought … I thought we had a few more days.'

'No. Unfortunately.'

'When will you be back?'

'I can't say this. As soon as I am able.'

'I see.'

'Etta, I must tell you something. It is possible you may think differently of me when I tell you this. You may wish never to see me again.'

'Whatever are you talking about? How can you say such a thing?'

He squeezes her hand. 'Etta … Etta, I am married. I have a wife and a son.'

Etta gasps, the pain in her heart worse than any wound a bullet can inflict. 'What?'

Carlo bounds out of his chair and kneels at Etta's feet. 'Please, let me explain the situation.'

'You're married?' The walls of her life crumble around her.

'My wife, Marianna, is not well. She is in an asylum near Napoli. She lives in a world of fantasy. She does not know me anymore. She has not known me for many years, not since the birth of our son, Paolo, thirteen years ago.'

'You have a thirteen-year-old son?'

'I was young, *Etta mia*. I was only nineteen and Marianna eighteen. We were children playing at life. When she found she was expecting a child, her father insisted we marry. I married her gladly. She and the child were my responsibility, and I loved her. We lived with her parents in their villa in Napoli until the birth. It was a difficult birth, and afterwards she lost her … how do you say … she lost her hold on the world. She saw ghosts and spectres around her, and she refused to touch Paolo, saying he was the son of the Devil.'

Etta's heart trips and races inside her chest. She could never believe anything as terrible about Adriana. Even on her worst days.

'The doctor said she would emerge from the psychosis over time. It is true, she did improve, and for a time she recognised me and cherished the child. It seemed like we would have a normal life. We lived together in her parents' villa.' He glances toward the sea. 'There was another child.'

'Another child?'

He takes hold of Etta's hands. 'Yes. Marianna lost the child, a girl. The psychosis returned. She has never recovered.'

Etta pulls her hands away. 'Where's your son?'

'He is at a boarding school in Roma, a very expensive school. It is why I live so poorly. You must have wondered where my money goes. I spend it on Paolo's education and Marianna's place at the asylum. Marianna's father is a rich man, but he refuses to pay one *lira*. It is his punishment to me for ruining her for a wealthy husband.'

Etta shivers, but it is not because of the cool winter air. 'Are Adriana and I another of your mistakes?'

Carlo grips her arms. 'No! No, my darling. You are the precious wife of my heart, and Adriana is my beautiful angel. I love you. You must believe me.'

'What if you die up in the mountains? What happens to us then?'

Carlo rises to his feet and paces the balcony's stone tiles like a caged tiger. 'Don't worry. I shall find a way.'

'But how? I can never be your wife as long as Marianna is alive. If we don't marry, I am nothing more than … than a mistress.'

'No! You must never say that!'

'Why didn't you tell me this before, Carlo?'

'I was going to, *cara mia*. But then, when you told me about the baby, I … I couldn't.'

'What are we going to do?'

Carlo rests his hand on the cool stone of a pillar and stares out at the ink blue sea and the grey clouds sitting over the hills of the mainland. 'I don't know, my love. But I shall find a way.'

Chapter Forty-Six

Christina

Marylebone, London – August 1892

Christina hooks the handle of her parasol over her arm and pushes the baby carriage out the front door of her father's grand Georgian house on Portman Square. The towering plane trees in the square across from the Georgian terrace shimmer in the humidity, and she wipes away a film of dampness under her nose with her hand. She will need to strip down to her shift when she comes back, and sponge herself with cold water. Her aunts will make another fuss, of course. Calling away one of the housemaids to carry a bowl of water and a towel to her. Disrupting the smooth running of her father's household. Heaven forbid.

She has been back in London barely a fortnight, and already she feels that her father's house is no longer her own now that his spinster sisters, Henrietta and Margaret Bishop, have moved down from the country house in Yorkshire 'for the summer'. Why anyone would choose to stay in London through the suffocating August heat is beyond her comprehension when the breezes across the Yorkshire moors make for a refreshing summer. If the country house hadn't been closed up, she would escape there with Cecelia, well away from the aunts and their judgemental whisperings about her 'fall from grace' and 'weak Italian blood'.

Her aunts are only too happy to remind her, at every opportunity, of the scandal it would cause if the circumstances around Cecelia's birth reached the newspapers. The well-brought-up daughter of one of London's pre-eminent architects, the mother of an illegitimate child! Her reputation and Cecelia's future would be ruined, and the family name raked through the mud in the London tabloids. How could she have done this to them. To them! That's all they care about. What people would think of them!

She refuses to reveal Harry's identity, though even her father has pressured her for it. Why would she? Harry has abandoned her and the baby. *Giving me money! Like I'm a loose woman!* It makes her sick to think about it. She will be happy if she never sees his face or hears his name again while she is on this earth.

If only it were that easy. Whenever she looks at her baby, she sees Harry's face. He haunts her dreams, and her betraying heart still quickens at the thought of him. She lives in terror of rounding a street corner to find him there. What would she do? What would he do? Greet her? Walk by as though they had never shared those blissful hours under the blue Italian sky? She would die if that happened, as surely as if he stabbed her in the heart.

James Bishop looks across the dining table at his daughter. How much like his own mother she looks. The same auburn hair and blue eyes, the straight-backed regal posture; it is in ephemeral things that he catches a glimpse of his late wife, Isabella – in the way Christina runs her hand around her ear, the shape of her mouth when she smiles, or the penetrating look when she seems to see all one's hidden thoughts.

Isabella had harboured such hopes for their only child since Christina's coming out two years before. Despite Christina's beauty and accomplishments at drawing, needlepoint, conversation, and her skill at the piano, the scandal of his own marriage to the daughter of an Italian labourer had shadowed his daughter, and the aristocratic suitors Isabella had dreamt of had kept their distance. Still, there may have been the chance of a marriage to a clever young barrister or physician, or even a young military officer, but this would never happen now. He'd heard the quickly stifled whispers of work colleagues and neighbours since Christina's return from Italy with a baby. For once he is in agreement with his sisters. Something has to be done to save Christina's, and the family's, reputation.

His elder sister, Henrietta, looking as severe and humourless as a thin Queen Victoria, dabs at her lips with a napkin. 'James, you can't avoid this unfortunate situation any longer. It is almost more than Margaret and I can bear, to be under the same roof as a woman who ...' she sweeps her colourless eyes over Christina, '... who has sullied our family name in such a base fashion.'

'Indeed, James,' Margaret, a plumper and even dourer version of Henrietta, interjects. 'The audacity of showing up with a fatherless child in her arms! We are not the Salvation Army. Your marriage to that Italian woman, and Christina's birth seven months later, saw our poor parents into an early grave and dragged the Bishop name through the mud once. The family cannot survive another scandal. We shall all be ruined.' She glares at Christina. 'Is that what you wish, Christina? To see us all in the workhouse?'

Henrietta gestures for a footman to refill her wineglass. 'You certainly do have gall, Christina. You should have done the decent thing and stayed in Italy with your kind.'

'That's enough, Henrietta!' James tosses his napkin onto the table and dismisses the footmen with a wave. He looks at his daughter, whose bottom lip trembles, the food on her plate virtually untouched. 'Christina, you know, of course, that your refusal to reveal the name of Cecelia's father is extremely vexing to me. It is simply not right that he should be permitted to abscond, leaving you behind with a child in your arms. Stefania claims ignorance, and I must take her at her word. I'm asking you one last time. Who is this man?'

'I can't, Papa. I don't want anything from him.'

'Oh, for pity's sake!'

James glares at his sister. 'That will do, Margaret.' He reaches for the decanter and pours himself a large glass of wine before turning to his daughter. 'This is what we shall do, Christina. While you were in Italy to study Italian with Stefania, you met, fell in love with, and married a distant Italian cousin. A Roberto Innocenti. A young physician. You had a child with your husband. Unfortunately, he was taken ill with the Russian flu from one of his patients, and died shortly after Cecelia's birth. You are a widow with a child. Your name is now Mrs Christina Innocenti.' He takes the wineglass and pushes away from the table. 'This is the last I wish to hear on this subject, is that clear? I am retiring to my study, and do not wish to be disturbed.'

Christina sits, frozen in her chair. The realities of her year in Capri were to be erased from her life. Her father has killed Harry, as surely as if he had shot him through the heart.

Christina opens the parasol over her flower-bedecked hat, and takes hold of the pram's push bar. Already the heat of another August day causes her to reconsider, for a brief instant, her decision to escape the dour interiors which seem to have absorbed the personalities of her aunts. It had been so different when her mother was alive. Then, it had been a home of cheerfulness and hospitality, with her pretty, exuberant mother, Isabella, the celebrated hostess of her father's household. Now, her father stays in his study when he isn't out at work or at his club, emerging only for sad, silent dinners in the grand dining room, his handsome features carved with furrows of sorrow.

Despite the enticement of the shade promised by the square's plane trees, Christina turns left onto Baker Street, taking advantage of her aunts' afternoon shopping excursion to Selfridges, which she, of course, has not been invited to join. Today, she will introduce Cecelia to the green expanses and gardens of Regent's Park.

She pushes the pram past the offices and shops that cater to the needs of the wealthy middle classes inhabiting the handsome Marylebone terraced houses. The further she walks from her father's house, the lighter her step. She will buy an ice-cream to share with Cecelia and rent a deck chair to listen to the band in the bandstand by the boating lake. They will feed the geese and ducks the bread she's been hiding in her breakfast napkin the past few days. And, possibly, for a brief few hours, she will remember what it feels like to be happy.

She passes under the awning of a photography studio, and rests for a few minutes in its shade. She peeks under the pram's canopy at her baby, whose blue eyes widen as her tiny pink lips form into a smile. 'You're a pretty little thing, aren't you, Cecelia? It won't do you a jot of good, I'll tell you that.'

She takes a delicate handkerchief out of the pocket of her dress and dabs at her face as she gazes through the shop window where gold lettering curves across the glass – *Frederick J. Fry & Son, Photographers.* She catches the eye of a tall, slender man with neatly brilliantined dark hair and a large brown moustache, which she suspects he has grown in order to disguise his youth. He looks away quickly, as if she has caught him with his hand in a biscuit jar. A smile pulls at the corners of her lips.

'Cecelia, how would you like to have your photograph taken? We'll give it to Papa for his birthday next month. Isn't that a lovely idea?'

A bell tinkles over the door as she enters pushing the carriage. The young man hurries from behind the counter and holds open the door.

Christina rewards him with a smile. 'Thank you.'

'You're most welcome, madam.' He moves around the baby carriage as awkwardly as a boy who has grown six inches in a summer, his arms and legs not quite at ease in his tall frame. 'How may I be of assistance?'

'I should like our photograph taken. My daughter is three and a half months old today, and I should like to mark the occasion.'

The young man's blue-grey eyes light up. 'What a momentous occasion, indeed. I shall be delighted to oblige.'

Christina folds down the canopy, and lifts Cecelia into her arms. The baby's lace-capped head bobs as she looks around the room. She settles her blue gaze on the man and reaches out to touch his moustache, giggling with delight as her fingers close around the bristles. Christina grabs hold of Cecelia's hand. 'Oh, I'm terribly sorry! Naughty girl!'

'Oh, no. Don't worry at all.'

'Her grandpapa has a moustache. She's quite fascinated by them.'

The young man brushes his fingers self-consciously over his whiskers. 'I'm quite flattered, then.'

'Her father doesn't … didn't have one. He … he passed away just after she was born. The flu.'

The man's smile fades. 'I'm terribly sorry. The flu has been such an awful thing.' He holds out his hand. 'I'm Gerald Fry.' He points to the gilded lettering on the window. 'I'm the son in Frederick J. Fry & Son.'

Christina slips her gloved hand into his. 'It's a pleasure to meet you, Mr Fry. I'm Mrs Innocenti. Christina Innocenti.' She jiggles her daughter in her arms. 'This is Cecelia.'

Gerald smiles down at the baby. 'Hello, Cecelia. It's very nice to meet you.'

He gestures toward a green velvet curtain which hangs over a doorway. 'The studio is just through there, Mrs Innocenti. I shall do my very best for you and Cecelia. I'll be sure to develop the photograph directly and put it in a nice frame so that you may collect it tomorrow. Please, after you.'

Chapter Forty-Seven

Jessie

Egypt – May 1916

No. 15 General Hospital, Alexandria, Egypt

J essie double-checks the list of supplies that she is to purchase in Cairo. Not for the first time, she wishes that she had made more of an effort perfecting her handwriting skills when she was in school. She simply hadn't had the patience to perfect the loops and flourishes that Etta had mastered with such relish. A hasty scribble on a piece of loo paper was all she'd been able to manage when Matron had dictated the list to her outside the hospital's nurses' loo.

She tucks the list into her skirt pocket and taps the crown of her straw hat to ensure the pin is holding it securely against the gusts of the dust-filled sirocco winds – a lesson learned when Mabel's straw boater had blown off her head at the pyramids and spun across the desert sand, its journey to Timbuktu halted by the Sphinx's right ear.

She dashes down the hospital's stone steps just as the elegant lines of a green automobile appear on the hospital's drive, the car's canvas top folded back behind tufted brown leather seats. The driver pulls to a stop and leans his elbow on the door, the emu plume on his felt hat rippling in the breeze. He toots the horn and grins. 'Well, well. Looks like today's my lucky day.'

'Sergeant Winter?'

He waves his hat with a flourish. 'At your service, Lieutenant Fry.'

'What are you doing here? I thought you were in Cairo.'

'We were moved up to Alexandria a couple of weeks ago.' He opens his hands. 'Lucky you.'

Jessie laughs. 'That's a rather handsome automobile.'

Archie pats the steering wheel. 'A Vauxhall D. Fresh off the boat from Blighty. The Light Horse just took delivery of two o' them. The major asked for someone to take the ol' girl for a whirl around the city and work out any kinks. My hand shot up straightaway. Told him I'd driven a taxi in Adelaide.'

'Did you? Really?'

'Na, but my pa's a taxi driver, so I've been drivin' since I was a kid.' He puts his hand up to his mouth as if revealing a secret. 'I gotta pick the major up some cigars at the Greek tobacconist's while I'm out.'

'Heaven forbid the major goes without his cigars in the middle of a war.' She pats the spare tyre affixed under Archie's window. 'Enjoy your drive. I have to hurry to the station to catch the Cairo train to pick up some supplies there for Matron.'

'Not on your own, surely?'

'No, I'm meeting someone at the station.'

'Well, hop in, why don't ya? I'll swing by the station. Save you some shoe leather. It's too bloody hot to be trekkin' down there today.' He leans over his seat and opens the rear door, gesturing for Jessie to take a seat on the plump leather upholstery.

'That's very kind of you, Sergeant Winter.' She steps onto the running board and into the car. 'I feel like I'm off to the theatre.'

'I like that you think I go ta the theatre. And the name's Archie.'

Jessie laughs, but her smile freezes when she sees a familiar straight-backed figure step out onto the hospital's stoop.

Archie squints at the officer. 'You know that Arab bloke? Shouldn't he be back in the souk?'

'It's Captain Khalid. He's one of the surgeons. I worked with him on the *Letitia* at Gallipoli. I haven't worked with him here yet, thank goodness. He's the rudest man you'll ever meet.'

The doctor walks down the steps and strides around the car. He opens the passenger door and swings up into the seat beside Archie. He turns and inclines his head at Jessie. 'Lieutenant.'

'Captain.'

He looks at Archie. 'Let's go. We have a great deal to do in Cairo.'

The train steams through the vast flat landscape of yellow-grey sand and scrub. Every now and then a cluster of buildings the same dirty yellow, or a tall palm poking at the sky with its fan-like fronds, breaks the monotony of the view. When the train nears the Nile outside the town of Tanta, the flat dry land transforms into vibrant green fields separated by irrigation ditches shining like silver threads under the throbbing blue sky. A farmer in a wide-sleeved white *jellabiya* carves furrows with a wooden plough harnessed to a camel and an ox, as two children run barefoot about the field. He shouts at the children, but they ignore him and continue to leap across the new furrows as carefree as sparrows.

Jessie peels off the cotton gloves that are damp with sweat.

Lowering the dirt-streaked window, she then breathes in the warm air. She glances at Captain Khalid's reflection in the window. He is sitting diagonally across from her, reading, as he has done since they left Alexandria.

The train lurches to a stop at Tanta, and she sees him turn his head to look out the window. He catches her gaze in the reflection, and she flicks her eyes to the station platform, conscious of her reddening cheeks. She watches the men in flowing *jellabiyas* and red felt *tarbouches* embark and disembark the train as street sellers thrust oranges and dates at them.

The train jolts and squeals to a start. Jessie blinks and presses her hand against her left eye. She blinks again and tears well up, wetting her fingers. She fumbles in her skirt pocket for her handkerchief and wipes at her weeping eye.

'What's the matter?'

'Something flew into my eye.'

He sets down the book. 'Let me look at it. If I may.'

Jessie wipes at her nose which is now dripping in sympathy with her eye. 'Please.'

He sits in the seat beside her and presses his finger gently above and below her eye. His breath is warm on her cheek. 'Blink.'

Jessie blinks. Then she blinks again. And again.

'That's enough.'

'I'm sorry, I can't seem to stop. It's scratching my eye.'

'Give me your handkerchief.'

She hands him the damp handkerchief. He presses her lower eyelid open, and she shivers involuntarily at the touch of his fingers. She is engulfed by his warmth and the faint scent of tobacco. He dips the edge of the handkerchief into the corner of her eye. He hands her the handkerchief. 'There. That should be better. It was a piece of grit. You must be more careful.'

She blinks and wipes at her eye. 'Thank you, Captain.'

ADRIENNE CHINN

He sweeps his dark gaze over her. 'I have seen inside your eyes. Please, my name is Aziz.'

Jessie glances at the damp handkerchief she is kneading with her fingers.'Everybody calls me Jessie, except for my mother. She insists on calling me Jessica.'

His lips twitch under his black moustache. He returns to his seat and picks up his book. 'Jessica is a very beautiful name. It suits you well.'

***

Jessie watches the Egyptian apothecary shout orders at two assistants who are loading crates of iodine bottles and Dakin's Solution onto the back of a donkey cart beside sacks of bandages, hand-carved wooden crutches and canisters of nitrous oxide. She stifles a yawn and fans her damp face. The heat of Cairo hangs like a curtain over the bustling alleyways of the souk. At least it's their final stop; she couldn't swallow another cup of sweet gritty coffee as the doctor and the various chemists and shopkeepers exchange prolonged pleasantries and negotiations before the inevitable handover of filthy banknotes.

A tap on her shoulder. She spins around; the doctor holds out a freshly peeled red fruit the size of an egg. 'Try this. It is very delicious. I have just eaten two myself.'

She sniffs the fruit before taking a tentative bite. A delicate sweetness like watermelon springs from the pulpy flesh as she chews. 'It's very nice.'

'It's a prickly pear from a cactus. They're one of my favourite things. My mother used to say I would turn into a cactus when I was a boy because I ate so many.'

Jessie bites into the fruit, and wipes at a trickle of juice on her chin. 'I had no idea cactuses bear fruit.'

'Not all, but some.' He excuses himself and walks over to the

254

apothecary; a handshake, more conversation, and the slipping of banknotes into the man's hand, a slap on the back and an embrace. He returns to Jessie. 'They will take the supplies to the train. Come, you must be hungry. I shall take you to one of my favourite places here for something to eat.'

Jessie glances down at the grey skirt of her uniform and slaps at the coating of fine yellow dust. 'I'm not dressed for dinner, I'm afraid.'

'You are dressed perfectly well. It is here in the souk.'

'In the souk?'

'Yes. Come with me.'

Jessie stumbles through the jostling crowd in the trail of Captain Khalid, who glances back from time to time to ensure she hasn't been waylaid by an overeager shop seller. The call of the devout to prayer filters through the alleys from somewhere deep in the souk. The hawkers shout from their stalls and cubbyholes, offering an endless selection of colourful fabrics, pungent spices, intricately-wrought leather slippers, turtle shells and animal teeth, potions, honey-soaked delicacies and amulets. Blue smoke wafts over the bobbing heads of the shoppers – mostly men in *jellabiyas* and white skullcaps or red *tarbouches*, although an occasional cluster of chattering women in long sequinned face coverings, their colourful dresses draped with black cotton cloth, elbow their way through the human sea. The rich aroma of roasting meat and spices sets Jessie's stomach rumbling.

Aziz Khalid stops abruptly in front of an opening in a clay wall, and gestures for her to enter. She steps into the shadowed interior of what appears to be a small café. A man in a white skullcap and a brown *jellabiya* which strains at his rolls of fat shuffles over. He bows and exclaims in Arabic as he ushers them to a table lit by the glow of a wall-mounted lantern. The doctor pulls out a wooden chair and stands behind it, waiting for Jessie to sit.

'Thank you.' She settles onto the hard chair. 'I'm afraid I haven't a clue what to order.'

'Then you are in for a treat.' He turns to the host and a debate ensues. After some minutes, the owner heads toward a back room, a satisfied smile above his jowls.

'Please excuse me, Jessica. I shall return shortly.'

She watches the doctor duck behind a curtained niche. The owner approaches her with a bowl and a ewer, a cloth draped over his arm. He nods at her hands and she holds them over the bowl as he splashes them with a stream of cool water. She dries her hands on the cloth and thanks him.

He presses his hand, with its sausage-like fingers, against the rolls of his chest. *'Ash-shukru lillah.'*

'Ash-shukru lillah,' Jessie repeats

Aziz hangs his uniform cap on the back of his chair and holds his hands over the ewer. 'You've just said, "You're welcome."'

'How do you say, "Thank you"?'

'Shokran.'

She repeats the word, attempting to emulate his rolling "r". *'Shokran.'*

'If you wish to say, "Thank you very much", you say *"Shokran bezef."'*

'Shokran bezef. Wonderful! Now I know some Arabic.'

'I would be very pleased to teach you more, if you wish. You will find it helpful while you are here in Egypt.'

'I should like that very much.' She folds her hands in her lap and clears her throat. 'What have you ordered?'

'Ah, you will see.'

'You're not going to tell me?'

'That would ruin the surprise.'

'What if it's something … strange?'

'I guarantee you will never have eaten any of the dishes Hassan will bring us this evening. So, I suppose they will all be strange to you. Don't worry. I am sure you will like everything.'

She scans the room as nerves jab at her belly. 'How did you ever find this place? It's quite tucked away.'

'I was brought here by a great friend of mine. A Captain Lawrence, though I have always called him Ned. We met when we were both at Oxford. A very clever fellow, though he keeps much to himself. He is fascinated by all things Arabic, which is unusual for an Englishman.'

'He sounds interesting. I should like to meet him.'

'I'm afraid he's just been sent off to Mesopotamia. I don't imagine I shall see him again until after the war. He was just awarded the *Legion d'Honneur* for his work in the Cairo Intelligence Office. An unassuming fellow, which I suppose is quite useful for intelligence work. You would never look twice at him in a room.'

'You said you attended Oxford?'

'Yes. My father was a member of the Egyptian Government. He believed that a British education would provide me with … opportunities which might otherwise be out of my reach.'

'Why would opportunities not be offered to you?'

'Because I am Egyptian.' He holds up his hands. 'I have brown skin.'

'Oh.'

'My father was right. My Oxford education and medical training from Imperial College have given me the opportunity to work as a surgeon for the British Expeditionary Force. Basically, my education combined with my knowledge of Egypt made it impossible for them to refuse me.'

'I see. So, you know London, then.'

'Yes, very well.' He settles back in his chair and regards Jessie. 'You don't appear to be bothered by the fact that I am Egyptian.'

'Why should I be?'

'A very great many people are extremely bothered by it.'

Jessie nods, remembering Archie's comments that morning. 'Are you a Mohammedan?'

He raises an eyebrow. 'That's very direct.'

'I'm sorry, am I being terribly rude? Mama has always said I speak before I think far too often. She says I lack decorum. I sometimes feel like an ox in a china shop alongside my two sisters. Celie is full of decorum, and Etta is so ... well, everyone loves Etta. I'm sorry, am I rabbiting on?'

'Not at all. In answer to your question, I am a Muslim. I left to pray when we first arrived.'

'Oh.'

'Christians and Muslims, and Jews as well, worship the same God. We simply call Him by a different name. You are Jessica, and you are also Jessie and Lieutenant Fry. It is all the same. We are all People of the Book.'

'People of the Book?'

'The Old Testament. We all share it.'

'I didn't know that. How interesting. Though I'm not sure that my Catholic mother would approve of me dining with a Muslim gentleman.'

'It is not unusual to fear that which one does not know or understand.'

Hassan approaches with a silver teapot and two tea glasses. He sets the glasses on the table and sweeps the teapot into the air with a flourish. Holding it aloft, he pours a stream of tea, fragrant with mint, into the glasses.

Jessie claps her hands together. 'Oh, well done! I would have had that all over the table.'

Aziz picks up his tea glass. 'I believe you are not one to fear that which you do not know, Jessica.'

'What makes you say that?'

'You wouldn't have become an army nurse, or come to Egypt, if that were the case.'

She picks up her tea glass. 'You mustn't paint too romantic a picture of me. I'm rather selfish, actually. I want a life full of adventure and interesting experiences. I couldn't bear to be cooped up in a house like my mother, no matter how nice it is. I became an army nurse in order to travel and see the world. It was a means to an end. There aren't many opportunities for an adventurous life open to a woman. I've subsequently found myself to be rather good at nursing, particularly the surgical work.'

Hassan looms over them with a tray laden with plates and dishes of fragrant food Jessie has never seen the like of. He sets it on the table and spreads his arms wide over the feast. *'Bil hana wish shifa!'*

'He said, *"Bon Appetit"*.'

She looks at the café owner and breaks into a wide smile. *'Shokran! Shokran bezef!'*

The rhythmic rolling of the train through the Egyptian countryside lulls Jessie to sleep. She jolts awake and glances across the aisle. Aziz is nowhere to be seen, although a copy of an Egyptian newspaper lies neatly folded on his seat. She looks out the window. Streaks of orange and yellow colour the vast expanse of sky, lighting the flat plains with a golden glow.

Such a strange day, what with Archie Winter showing up so unexpectedly, then discovering that Captain Khalid – Aziz – was to accompany her to Cairo. She plays with his name in her head. *Aziz Khalid.*

Then, that meal in Hassan's café. It would have been a simple thing to pick up some sandwiches and eat on the train. Why had he brought her there? He had relaxed in there; the line that etches itself across his forehead so frequently had melted away, along with the chilly reserve. He had laughed! What a surprise that had been. And there had been moments when she had caught him looking at her.

Afterward, he had bought them sweet pastries called *basbousa* soaked in sugar syrup from a pastry shop in the souk, and thick Turkish coffee from a man with an urn in the Cairo train station. She had enjoyed herself. It had been a very long time since she'd felt so light-hearted, so carefree.

The door to the carriage swings open and Aziz appears. She smiles at him as he returns to his seat. He picks up the paper. 'You were sleeping.'

'I know. I'm terribly sorry.'

'There is nothing to be sorry about. It has been a long day.'

'Yes. But in a good way.'

He opens the paper, a whisper of a smile on his lips. 'I believe so as well.'

Chapter Forty-Eight

Celie

London – June 1916

A flash of bright green hair catches Celie's eye and she looks up from the *Daily Mirror*, which, to her gratification, has published her article on 'Knitting to Win the War', complete with a pattern for a chequered waistcoat which could double as a chess or draughtsboard – *'What every frontline soldier would love in his comforts package from home!'* Her byline is still simply C. Fry, but she is a published writer and photographer. She must learn to 'count her blessings', as her mother had advised her when she'd complained about being so cavalierly degendered.

'Milly?'

The green-haired girl looks in her direction. Her face and her hands are as yellow as lemons. 'Miss Fry!' She tramps down the aisle and sits beside Celie. 'Where are you off to?'

'Oh, Milly, just call me Celie. We are both working girls now.'

'Isn't life a funny fing? Who would've fought we'd both be out in the world earnin' our way even a year ago? You look well, Miss F—' She clears her throat. 'Celie.'

'Thank you, Milly. You um … um…'

Milly laughs and pats her hair. 'Yeah, I know. I've got green 'air. It's the TNT what does it.'

Celie folds the newspaper in her lap. 'How is your munitions work going? Are you enjoying it?'

'It's all right. The pay's all right. Eighteen shillin's a week, though after payin' for lodgin' at the YMCA 'ostel and lunches in the canteen, it doesn't leave much for aught else. Still, it's better 'an bein' in service.' Milly presses a yellow hand against her lips. 'Oh, I'm sorry, miss. I didn't mean it like 'at. Workin' for your family was very nice.'

Celie smiles. 'I know Mama can be quite demanding, Milly. She has a very clear idea of how things should be. I suppose it was her upbringing. Her father was well-off, and she was the only child. I think she was quite spoiled. I hope she didn't make life too difficult for you.'

'She was strict, but she was fair. When I did somefing well, she always made sure to tell me.'

'I'm pleased to hear that.'

'I've been readin' your articles in the *Mirror*. The other canaries are jealous I know a writer, though they don't believe you're a woman, even though I tell 'em such.'

'Canaries?'

'That's what people call us. You can't blame 'em, can you?' She holds up her bright yellow hands. 'Just look at 'em. The TNT dust stains everyfing yellow. All the tables and chairs in our canteen are yellow. We're quite a sight, but somebody's gotta do it. It's not like we're sittin' in a trench gettin' bombed and shot at, is it?'

'I think you're awfully brave to be doing what you do.'

'I've been feelin' right queer from the work, it's true. I keeled over this mornin' wif stomach ache. The overlooker's sent me to get checked at the 'ospital. It's where I'm off to now.'

'Oh, dear, Milly. I hope you're all right.'

Milly shrugs. "Appens to us all the time. What can you do? Work is work.' Her eyes narrow as she looks at Celie. 'Say, why don't ya write a story about us canaries? It'd be nice for people to treat us wif some respect instead of like we're lepers.'

'That's an interesting idea. Who do I need to contact at the munitions factory if I can get my editor to agree?'

'That'll be Dame Barker. She's the Chief Lady Superintendent. She scares the life outta me. She troops 'round the place like an army general.'

'Dame Barker, then.' She smiles at Milly. 'How do you feel about having your picture in the paper?'

'Wouldn't me mum and pa be proud o' that!' She reaches up and pulls on the bell cord. "Ere's my stop. Nice to see you, Miss – Celie. I'm 'appy to 'elp if you need. I'm at the YMCA on Manton Road or at me mum's in Poplar of a Sunday.'

'Thank you, Milly. I shall definitely be in touch.' She watches Milly stagger down the aisle of the omnibus as it bumps to a halt. Finally, she has something serious to write about. She will do the canary girls proud.

At home, a letter from Etta is waiting for Celie on the hallway table. She picks it up and calls down the hallway. 'Mama? Are you here?'

She listens for her mother's footsteps, but the house is heavy with silence.

Once she is at her desk in her room, she slides her letter opener under the lip of the envelope and slices it open with a quick flick.

Villa Serenissima
Capri, Italy

April 11th, 1916

Dear Celie,

Forgive me for the long delay between letters. I have sent a separate one to Mama and Papa, but there is something I have been holding inside of me since Adriana's birth, and I can contain it no longer. You are the only one I feel I can tell. You are so solid and sensible, Celie. I wish – oh, how I wish! – that I could simply sneak into your room and slide into bed with you like I did when I was a little girl. You always knew how to chase away my nightmares, when all Jessie would do was be cross with me. It has always seemed a strange thing to me to be Jessie's twin. We are so very unlike in every possible way.

I must ask you not to tell any of the following to Mama and Papa. Please. Swear it, Celie. Swear it on the Blessed Virgin.

Where shall I begin?

Carlo and I are not married.

There, I said it. We are not married, nor does it look likely that we shall ever be married. No, he has not abandoned me and the baby. He managed to visit us here in Capri in February. He loves me; I have no doubt of that. The problem is that he is already married. He has a son named Paolo, as well, who is thirteen years old and lives with Carlo's wife's parents in Naples when he is not away at boarding school in Rome.

I can well imagine what you're thinking. What an awful man Carlo is to have put me in this situation. Truly, it's not like that. His wife has been in an asylum for the insane for many years. Carlo pays for this and Paolo's schooling with the income from his paintings. This is why there is so little left for me and Adriana. We never did live in a villa near his parents in Naples. His parents are dead, and his father-in-law refuses to speak to him. It seems that Paolo was the result of a youthful love affair, and the marriage one which Carlo had no option but to agree to when she – her name is Marianna – well, you understand.

He said he would find a way for us to be together after the war. It's all I have to hold onto. I must believe him. The alternative is simply too awful for me to think about. I've been rash and selfish and irresponsible, I know that. I refused to consider that my actions might have consequences. I simply wished to be carefree and bohemian, like the people I met at Omega. But now, I have Adriana and she is my responsibility. I must be responsible, though some days I find it so difficult...

I have not been altogether well since Adriana's birth, though there are days, like today, when I feel quite my normal self. I have days when I feel like a black fog engulfs me, and it is an effort even to open my eyes, and I cannot bear to be near Adriana for fear of doing her some harm. Then other times, I awake with energy like I've never had before; where I paint, and cook, and take Adriana for a long walk in the hills... Those are wonderful days. But then the black fog descends once again, and strange creatures spin around me until I tear at my hair and fall on the floor, weeping.

Please, don't feel sorry for me or worry about me. Cousin Stefania assures me this will pass in time, as Adriana grows older. I do very much hope so, and it's true that the balance has turned in favour of the bright days over the dark days. In the meantime, her housekeeper, Liliana, makes a tonic of laudanum, honey and wine which helps ease my mind so that I can sleep and recover.

Celie, I have entered into this situation willingly, though I must confess that I wish I'd known about Marianna and Paolo when I was back in England. I believe I would have still embarked on this adventure with Carlo. What else could I have done when I was carrying his child? But it would have spared me the shock of him telling me all of this when I am so far away from all of you in London.

Don't be shocked by this letter, Celie. I love Carlo with all my heart. You know what that feels like; I know you do, with your dear Max.

You can see why it is impossible for me to tell Mama and Papa about this. They would never understand how love can sometimes lead one to do foolish things. Least of all Mama! She has had such a straightforward life, marrying a nice man like Papa and living a comfortable life with her family in London. Wherever do we all get our adventurous spirits from?

I am sending you my love, and look forward to the day when we can be sisters all together again, and you can meet your lovely niece.

Your loving sister,
Etta

Celie sits back in the desk chair. *Oh, Etta, what have you done? What has Carlo done to you and Adriana?* And now she is drawn into the tumult of Etta's life. The keeper of a secret she wishes she had never read.

Chapter Forty-Nine

Carlo

The Italian Mountains – September 1916

C arlo pushes open the asylum's tall double doors – elegant with their rococo carvings of seashells and fern fronds and panes of bevelled glass, remnants of the building's earlier incarnation as the home of a long-extinguished aristocratic family – and stands for a moment in the shadowed hall. Large squares of veined black and white marble from the quarries around Mondragone gleam dully under his feet, and the wooden wall panelling, once most likely painted a soft chalky white or pale pastel green, now shines with thick coats of grey gloss paint, so that the carved cornice, with its once elegant dentil moulding, sits like a thick splodge of frosting around the ceiling's perimeter.

He walks down the hallway, passing doorways with their doors open to deep recesses of darkness. No one appears to be around, but this doesn't surprise him. He hasn't told them he would be coming this evening. It would be much better to be alone.

He comes to the door at the end of the hallway. Like the others, the door is open, and he stands for a moment on the threshold as his eyes adjust to the gloom. Shutters obscure any moonlight, though a chink of pale yellow light crawls through the shutters' edges and trails along the wooden floorboards, up the side of the narrow bed and across Marianna's sleeping face. She is like a sleeping statue, her unlined face serene, her tumble of dark hair curling like vines around her head, her veinless hands clasped together over the tumble of sheets, as if in the perpetual repose of the memorial to a dead queen.

'Marianna,' he whispers as he approaches. 'Marianna.'

She opens her eyes, which glisten like glass marbles in the weak light. Her gaze is fixed somewhere beyond his shoulder in a world far from the earthly plane.

'Marianna, it's Carlo.'

Her eyes flicker, and he sees her vision clear as she focuses on his face. The graceful curve of her mouth turns up into the whisper of a smile. She holds out a hand toward him. 'Carlo. Amore mio.' Her fingers close around his hand, cool and smooth as stone. 'I have been waiting for you for such a long time.'

'Yes.'

'Where is my little one?'

'Paolo is not so small any longer, Marianna. He is almost as tall as I am now.'

Her shining eyes cloud over. 'Not Paolo. The little one, Gabriella.'

He shouldn't have come; he can see that now. If only she hadn't awakened. It would have been so easy to just —

He lets her cold fingers slide from his grasp. He reaches into his waistcoat – Waistcoat? Where is his uniform? – and pulls out a long silk tie. He rolls the two ends around his hands until the tie is taut. 'She is with God's angels, Marianna. There was no place for one so pure on this earth. Wouldn't you like to be with her, my love?'

Marianna's eyes flash as he leans over the bed. 'Oh, yes. Oh, yes, so much, Carlo.'

He presses the tie across her neck. 'I can help you, my sweet one. You know you can trust me—'

Carlo's eyes fly open. Under the wool of his uniform, his heart batters his ribs like a butcher hacking at an animal carcass. Above his head, the thick canvas of the tent ripples in the mountain wind. One of the other soldiers sputters and shifts on his pallet until he settles into a soft snore. He hears a bell, like a cow bell, somewhere in the distance, though he distrusts his ears; the thought of something as exquisitely ordinary as a cow bell in the hell in which he has found himself is far beyond his comprehension.

He presses the pads of his thumbs against his eyes. How could he even dream of such a thing? His stomach lurches, sending bile into his throat. He swallows down the bitter fluid and shudders in disgust, not at the sickly bile, nor the nightmare. But in the knowledge that, now, after over a year of death and killing, he is capable of pressing the tie against Marianna's throat.

Chapter Fifty

Etta

Villa Serenissima, Capri, Italy – September 1916

Stefania collects Etta's discarded coloured pencils and sketches from the dining table and hands them to Liliana. 'Will you put these back in Etta's room when you have a moment, Liliana? She scatters these around like a tree shedding leaves.' She holds up one of the sketches and squints at the half-finished view of the sea framed by two of the balcony's vine-wrapped pillars.

She gives the drawing to Liliana. 'She finishes nothing, not even a sentence. It is like her mind turns so quickly that she is running to catch up to her thoughts, forgetting what she is doing in the moment. I found her out in the garden yesterday with only one shoe on, and the baby with no cap! I am not afraid to say that I am worried for her.'

Liliana rolls up the sketches and slips the pencils into her apron pocket. 'She is like her mother.'

'In some ways, yes. Both of them victims of their love for men who are not worthy of them.'

'At least Miss Etta is married.' Liliana's brow crumples into a row of lines, like an accordion deflating. 'Not like that *bastardo* who broke her mother's heart.'

Stefania glances at Liliana. 'If only that were true. I read the letter Etta wrote to Cecelia. They are not married.'

'Not married!'

'Worse than that. He is married to someone else *and* he has a son.'

Liliana crosses herself. *'Dio mio.'*

'It is a disaster. My only hope is that he is killed in the mountains.'

Liliana's mouth drops open. 'No, no. You mustn't say this kind of thing.'

'I know that. I shouldn't even be telling you this, Liliana, but I have kept it inside me since I read the letter. I cannot hold it in any longer, not when I see Etta sliding further away from us every day. I don't know what to do for her. Some days she seems so well, and then...'

'If he dies, she and the baby will stay here, Stefania. I shall feed her well, and she can walk in the hills and make her drawings. I shall light a candle for her recovery in Santo Stefano every Sunday. The Heavenly Father knows I am a good woman. He will not refuse me my request or he will feel the wrath of Liliana Sabbatini when I cross through Heaven's Gate.'

Stefania smiles. 'This is a good plan. I have only one worry.'

'What is that?'

'What if he doesn't die, Liliana? What do we do then?'

Chapter Fifty-One

Celie

Royal Arsenal, Woolwich, London – October 1916

C elie follows the crowd of women off the train and down Plumstead Road toward the sprawling site of the Royal Arsenal in Woolwich. She has been careful not to wear anything metal, as Milly had advised, not even her suspenders, so as not to cause an inadvertent spark around the explosives. She's had to tie string around the tops of her stockings to hold them up. With every step, she feels her left stocking loosen and slide towards her ankle. She stops abruptly to tug at the stocking.

A woman ploughs into her. 'Careful, love. You almost 'ad me on me 'ead.'

'I'm terribly sorry.'

'Should try wearin' puttees, like me. They'll keep your legs warmer.'

'Excuse me, can you tell me which gate I need for the Danger Buildings?'

'New 'ere, are you? Fourth gate, at the end. Try to get 'em ta give you a job in grenades instead of TNT. You don't wanna turn into one of them canaries.'

'Thank you. I … I shall.'

Celie walks alongside the Arsenal's red brick wall, skirting the queues of women, and a few older men and young boys, at the first three gates. She spots Milly outside the fourth gate, her green hair hidden under a hat, though her face is still as yellow as a lemon.

'Celie! 'Urry up! The train's about to leave.'

Celie hastens towards Milly, her loose stocking working itself free of the string and puddling around her ankle. She bends over and pulls at her stocking. 'Hello, Milly. I'm sorry, I've had an accident with my stocking.'

'We've all 'ad that 'appen. Just roll it under your knee for now.'

Celie adjusts her stocking, then takes a letter out of the canvas bag holding her camera paraphernalia. 'I'm to show this to the security guard at the gate. It's from Dame Barker. I'm meeting her at the Shifting House.'

Milly's green eyes widen. 'She's meetin' us? Oh, my word. Best get me nerve up like I did when I 'ad to vouch for ya in 'er office. I told 'er you're Mrs Pankurst's right 'and woman. She was well impressed by 'at.'

'Milly! How am I meant to live up to that?'

'You'll be fine, Miss … I mean, Celie. I 'ad to make sure she couldn't say no, didn't I?'

'It looks like it worked. She's showing me around the Danger Buildings herself. She's very keen about this article for the *Daily Mirror*. She said on the telephone that it was high time that the women munition workers were acknowledged for their services to the war effort.'

'We're all excited about it. Me mum's been tellin' all the

neighbours I'll be in the paper.' Milly grabs Celie's elbow and steers her through the gates. A security guard checks Milly's work card and Celie's letter and waves them through.

Celie follows Milly across one of the wooden boardwalks that connect the sprawling collection of wooden sheds making up the Danger Buildings and into the Shifting House. Inside, sinks line one wall, and a sheet strung across the middle separates the room into two. Posters with *'Keep Mum She's Not Dumb'* and *'Gossip Costs Lives'* plaster the whitewashed walls. Women chatter and laugh as they change out of their street clothes and into their uniforms of belted smocks, mop caps and rubber shoes, while two women Overlookers in brown tunics tied with green belts check for hair clips, suspenders and jewellery.

'Over 'ere, Celie. This side is Dirty. Over there's Clean. Put your clothes into this kit bag, except for your shift. One of the Overlookers'll give you a uniform over in Clean. You'll 'ave ta leave your camera 'ere as well.'

'Oh, Dame Barker is giving me special dispensation to take photographs in some of the safer areas. Then she's going to gather the munitionettes together for photographs outside.'

'Quite right, Miss Fry.'

Celie turns around to see a tall, broad woman in a smart khaki uniform. Her wide-brimmed hat sits on dark hair as short as a man's. The woman's dark eyes appraise her from behind wire-rimmed spectacles, and she holds out her hand. 'Delighted to meet you, Miss Fry. I'm Dame Barker, the Chief Lady Superintendent here.' She nods at Milly. 'Miss Smith, very nice to see you again. I must say it's the first time we've had a woman journalist visit us, Miss Fry. None of the other journalists have shown the least interest in our munitionettes. If everything we read is written by men, we shall never appreciate the minds and thoughts of women.'

Celie nods. 'I agree completely, though my editor believes that women prefer reading about fashion and cookery to news stories about women at work. I had to threaten not to write about the results of the *Daily Mirror*'s contest for the best mock cottage pie for him to agree to this story. I'll do my very best for you and the munitionettes, Lady Barker.'

'It's a changing world, Miss Fry. I'm sure the *Mirror*'s women readers will very much enjoy your article. I shall wait for you in the detonator building next door to the left. We shall commence our tour there.' She gestures to Milly, who is hovering behind Celie. 'Would you like Miss Smith to accompany us?'

Celie smiles at Milly. 'Absolutely. This article was entirely her idea.'

'Is that so? Well done, Miss Smith. Show Miss Fry where to change and meet me outside in five minutes.'

Dame Barker points to a young woman working on a large artillery shell. 'Now, Miss Fry, here you can see this young woman fixing the case over a shell's detonator. The screws are tiny, as you can see, as is the screwdriver. It requires a steady hand and meticulous vision. If she places too much pressure on the detonator, there's a possibility it may explode.'

'Explode? Oh, my word.' Celie clicks the shutter on the Reflex camera. She looks up at the young munitionette. 'Aren't you nervous, doing what you do?'

The young woman shrugs. 'No, miss. I do it all day long. Best not to fink about it too much, though I 'eard of a woman who was expectin' a baby tamp down too 'ard on a detonator. It blinded 'er and she lost her 'ands. Could only feel her baby wif 'er lips when it was born.'

Dame Barker nods curtly. 'That wasn't here, though, was it?' She looks at Celie. 'We have had no major incidents at the Arsenal, Miss Fry. We take great care to train our workers to ensure their safety, isn't that right, Miss Smith?'

'Y-Yes, ma'am.'

Dame Barker taps Celie's elbow. 'I'm sure you would like to see the TNT building. I'm afraid you will have to leave your camera in the Shifting House before we go in there.'

'Yes, of course.' She picks up the camera tripod and follows the woman out of the detonator shed and down a wooden platform with Milly trailing behind. 'Dame Barker, does it concern you that the TNT turns the munitionettes yellow? Is it safe?'

'I'm assured by our doctors that it is quite safe. Once the women stop working, the colour fades. It's simply like staining one's fingers with ink. That doesn't do one any harm, does it?'

'I've read that TNT exposure can cause toxic jaundice.'

'I can't comment on that except to say we have very strict measures in place to limit exposure by providing the workers with protective clothing. They must wash their hands and face whenever they leave the TNT building, and must change into a clean smock before they go to their cafeteria. We ensure their safety at all times.'

'What happens if someone were to fall ill?'

'Our doctors would examine them, of course, and they would be sent to the hospital for the appropriate treatment, isn't that right, Miss Smith?'

'Yes, Ma'am. 'Ad a bit of a rest, now I'm fit as a fiddle.'

'Excellent.' Dame Barker pushes through the door to the TNT building. 'Here we are. I would recommend you not breathe too deeply. Miss Smith, please, give us a demonstration of how you handle TNT.'

Celie shuts the camera case and slides it into her canvas bag with her collapsible tripod. She waves at the crowd of munitionettes clustered on the wooden boardwalks in front of the Danger Buildings. 'Thank you, ladies! I shall let Dame Barker know when the article will appear in the paper. You'll be famous!'

Dame Barker weaves through the munitionettes toward Celie. She extends her hand and gives Celie's a firm shake. 'It's been a pleasure, Miss Fry. The Chief Superintendent and the board are most interested in the article. Several of them remain unconvinced that a woman is up to the task of writing a news story.'

'I won't disappoint you, Dame Barker.'

'I have no doubt you will acquit yourself admirably. I understand you are Mrs Pankhurst's right-hand woman, after all. Is there anything else I can help you with before you go?'

'Yes, there is, actually. I'd like very much to speak to Milly and some of the canary girls before they go back to work. Would that be all right?'

'Is that entirely necessary?'

'I want people to understand what a great service these young women are giving to the war effort, and the sacrifice they're making for all of us. They should be applauded, not ridiculed.'

'I see. I do understand these concerns, which I agree should be addressed. You will, of course, write that the effects from the TNT are temporary and perfectly safe, Miss Fry?'

'Of course, Dame Barker. I mean, the government wouldn't permit it if it weren't safe to handle, would it?'

'Indeed, it would not. Fine. I shall have some of the girls meet you in the Shifting House. If you could keep it to a quarter of an hour, I would be most appreciative. I have enough explaining to do to the paymistress as it is.'

'Thank you, Dame Barker. That would be perfect.'

Celie shoves aside a stack of papers and sets a folder on the desk of her editor. 'It's all done, Mr Grayson. A full insight into the munitionettes at the Royal Arsenal in Woolwich. A canary girl named Milly Smith has given me quite a lot of help. Without her I'd never have been able to get the munitionettes to open up to me the way they did. Please make sure you include her name in the article. I've included quite a few photographs as well.'

Mr Grayson picks up his pipe and puffs. He looks at Celie across the desk as he exhales a plume of blue smoke. 'Your writing has always been competent, Miss Fry, but it's lacked heart. Am I to expect this to be any different?'

'It's rather difficult to get all that excited about knitting, Mr Grayson. The munitionettes are altogether different. These women are risking their lives every day to ensure our army and navy are supplied with the weapons they need to win this war. People need to know that women are capable of so much more than they've been allowed to do in the past. The world is changing. It will never go back to the way it was.'

The editor sets down his pipe and flips through the folder, frowning as he examines the photographs. He picks up a sheet covered in Celie's neat handwriting and scans the text.

'The men will want their jobs back after the war, Miss Fry. Women will have to go back to their houses and raise their families. I'm afraid I don't believe a great deal will change.'

'I do believe you're wrong, Mr Grayson.'

He taps out the tobacco into a brass bowl heaped with grey ash. 'You may be surprised to hear that I agree with you. I was at the Women's Right to Serve march last year.'

'You were?

'I was covering it for the paper. The news pages, not the women's pages. It was very educational. Your photographs helped a great deal. You see, Miss Fry, I'm not the only one uninspired by knitting.' He taps the folder. 'This is entirely different. You've captured a personal angle. A look inside the life of a canary girl. I like that. I'll give it a double-page spread. I may need to tweak the title.'

'That's wonderful! There's just one thing, Mr Grayson. I'd very much appreciate my full name on the byline. Cecelia Fry. How are women to move forward if we are kept hidden?'

'I'll see what I can do. And Miss Fry, you need to learn to touch type.'

'I beg your pardon?'

'If you're to be a proper journalist, you need to know how to touch type. Sooner rather than later, please.'

———

Celie takes a copy of the *Daily Mirror* from the news boy in front of Hither Green Station and drops a coin into his hand. She flips through the pages until she reaches the women's section. *'Canary Girls Fill Arsenal with Song'*. Mr Grayson certainly did tweak the title. What will Dame Barker think about that? She was awfully sensitive about the canary girls. But it's a two-page spread, including four of her photographs. A proper, serious article.

By C. Fry.

Chapter Fifty-Two

Christina

Marylebone, London – October/November 1892

C hristina surveys the table that the parlour maids have set in the sitting room's large bay window along with two Chippendale chairs from the dining room. The maids have draped one of her mother's best Irish linen tablecloths over the mahogany drop-leaf table, and set it with sterling cutlery and her mother's favourite Royal Worcester bone china tea set. The cook has outdone herself with the selection of delicate crustless egg, cucumber and smoked salmon sandwiches. Currant scones, custard tarts and tiny meringues topped with cream and strawberries sit on the tiered curate stand like a display in the window of Fortnum's. She refolds a linen napkin and sets it back on the table.

A rustle of silk and the click of heels on the hallway tiles. Christina glances over her shoulder as her aunt Henrietta sweeps through the French doors into the sitting room like a ship in full sail.

'I see you've made yourself quite comfortable, pilfering our best china and silverware.'

'It was my mother's china, Aunt Henrietta. I'm sure you wouldn't wish Mr Fry to think we are impecunious.'

Her aunt harrumphs. 'We live in Portman Square. I hardly think anyone would consider us impecunious.'

'My father and I live in Portman Square. You and Aunt Margaret are visitors.'

Henrietta Bishop's eyes narrow. 'Margaret and I have as much claim on this house as your father, quite possibly more, as we are his elders. It has been in the Bishop family since the Napoleonic War. I was born in the blue bedroom.'

'As was I.'

'My mother was a Pembroke.'

Christina juts out her chin. 'And my mother was an Innocenti.'

'A plasterer's daughter! And now we're playing host to tradesmen! It shouldn't be permitted.'

The doorbell chimes. The two women stare at each other in seething silence as the maid receives the visitor. Gerald appears in the doorway, nervously clutching a straw boater and a paper bag.

Christina nods. 'Thank you, Ada. Please take Mr Fry's hat and ask Mrs Cromwell to prepare the tea.' She smiles brightly at Gerald. 'Mr Fry, please come in. Let me introduce you to my aunt. Aunt Henrietta, this is Mr Gerald Fry, the photographer who took that lovely photograph of Cecelia and me. Mr Fry, this is my aunt Henrietta Bishop, my father's eldest sister. She and my aunt Margaret are visiting us from Yorkshire.'

Gerald extends his hand, but drops it when he is met with Henrietta's stony countenance. He brushes his moustache nervously with his fingertips. 'I'm very pleased to make your acquaintance, Miss Bishop.'

'Indeed.' The elder woman throws Christina a condescending glance. 'I am going out with Margaret to an exhibition at the

National Portrait Gallery. I expect the house to be returned to normality upon our return.' She swishes towards the hallway, her taffeta skirt crackling like static.

Christina and Gerald stand in awkward silence as Henrietta's footsteps fade. 'I'm terribly sorry about that, Gerald. She is … well, she isn't the easiest woman. Please, come in. Our cook has been busy all day making all these lovely things to eat.'

'It looks very appetising.' He holds out the paper bag. 'I … I've brought you some chocolate cannoli. I found an Italian delicatessen near Farringdon Station. I hope you like chocolate.'

Christina takes the bag. 'I absolutely love chocolate, Gerald. Thank you very much.'

Gerald smiles. 'I've been looking forward to this since our boat ride in Regent's Park last week.'

Christina opens the bag and sets the cannoli on the curate stand with the other delicacies. She takes a seat and lays a napkin in her lap. 'I very much enjoyed that. It's so nice to have a nanny now for Cecelia. It's given me a bit more freedom. They've gone to the zoo today. Cecelia's very fond of the penguins.'

'I'm very fond of them myself.' Gerald spreads his napkin in his lap. 'I'm sorry to miss seeing her.'

'I'm surprised you still have a moustache from all the tugging at it she does. Really, Gerald, you mustn't allow her. It can't be pleasant.'

'I don't mind in the least. I thought we might—'

Ada enters bearing a silver tray. She sets the teapot and jugs and bowls of milk, loose tea, clotted cream, sugar and jam on the table.

'That will be all, Ada.' Christina sets the silver tea strainer on a teacup and pours out the steaming tea.

'Just a small amount of milk for me, if you would, Mrs Innocenti. No sugar.'

'No sugar? You are modern!' She offers him the teacup. 'I've told you time and again that my name's Christina.' She pours herself a cup of tea. 'You were saying something? Before Ada came in with the tea?'

'Yes, I thought we might take a boat ride on the canal from Regent's Park up to Camden Lock next week. It passes the zoo and all the grand houses of Little Venice. You would scarcely believe you're in London.'

'That sounds lovely. I should enjoy that very much indeed.'

'And you must bring Cecelia. We can stop for ice-cream in Camden Town. She'd like that, I'm sure.'

Christina scrutinises the young photographer. He certainly isn't as handsome as Harry, but he is presentable enough. He'd taken great care with his suit today – a fine grey wool which makes him look like one of those industrious young bank clerks on Oxford Street.

He had been nothing but kind and solicitous since that first day when she had begun to stop by the photography studio with Cecelia on her daily walks. They had exhausted the subject of the weather quickly enough, but there had been much to discuss about photography and Queen Victoria's Golden Jubilee celebrations. One day in September, she had invited Gerald to join them to walk around the boating lake in the park and this had become a regular excursion. Their meetings had given her something to look forward to. The world was somehow brighter on the days when they met. He was a good, solid, unexciting man. A decent man. And Cecelia adored him.

She pushes the tiered curate stand toward Gerald. 'Have some of Mrs Cromwell's sandwiches, Gerald. And a scone. She bakes the best scones in London.'

Gerald smiles, the corners of his moustache rising. 'Thank you, Christina. I don't mind if I do.'

2 November 1892

Christina glances across at Gerald as the registrar reads through the marriage vows. Not a Catholic Church, of course, what with Gerald being Protestant. Not even an Anglican church. A room in the town hall with her father and her scowling aunts as witnesses. It is not the wedding she and her mother had once imagined for her.

He looks at her, and the corners of his eyes crinkle as he smiles. She looks down at her bouquet of white roses. Her heart doesn't leap the way it did for Harry. Gerald's face doesn't haunt her dreams the way that Harry's still does. But she could learn to love him. She would certainly try.

That evening, when they are lying in bed after Gerald's awkward fumblings, Christina turns to him.

'Gerald, there's something I need to ask of you.'

'Yes, of course, my dear.'

'I want us to be a family. You, me, Cecelia and any children we may have.'

'Well, of course.'

'Cecelia must not feel like an outsider in our family if we have other children. I want you to be her father.'

'Of course I shall.'

'What I mean is, I want her to think you are her real father. She'll be a Fry, not an Innocenti.'

Gerald props himself up on his elbow. 'But, surely, she should know who her real father was.'

'He died a few days after her birth. You're the only father she'll ever know.'

'But she was born in May, when you were still in Italy. There must be a birth certificate. She'll know I'm not her father.'

Christina looks up at the shadows around the plaster ceiling rose. 'I left the birth certificate with my cousin Stefania. Seeing my husband's name on it … upset me.'

He pats her hand. 'I understand.'

'We'll tell her she was born in May of 1893, rather than 1892. We'll tell her she came early.'

'Three months early?'

'If she ever questions it, I may need to suggest that we ... were eager.'

'Christina! Certainly not.'

'Gerald, I'm certain it won't come to that.'

'But she won't have a British birth certificate, my dear.'

'I shall figure something out, when the time comes.' She looks over at her new husband. 'Promise me, Gerald. Please. It's the only thing I'll ever ask of you.'

He falls back against the pillows and stares into the room's shadowy gloom. 'All right, Tina. I promise.'

Part Five

1917

Chapter Fifty-Three

Jessie

No. 15 General Hospital, Alexandria, Egypt – January 1917

J essie fills another bottle with a mix of warm water and salt and seals it with a stopper. Rain pelts against the tall windows, and she thinks about Clover Bar, and how the sound of the rain against her and Etta's bedroom window had always made her feel secure and protected as it lulled her to sleep. She presses the back of her hand against her mouth as she yawns.

'You should make yourself some tea, Jessie,' Ivy says as she folds a blanket over the foot of a bed. 'It'll help keep ya awake.'

Jessie nods as she stifles another yawn. 'I shall. If it weren't raining so hard, I'd go up on the roof for some fresh air.'

'Is that where you're always escapin' to? Ya wouldn't catch me on the roof for love nor money. Can't deal with heights.'

A rumble of men's voices erupts from the hallway. A stream of sailors in sodden, filthy uniforms, many with burnt faces and singed hair, file barefooted into the ward.

'So much for tea. Here we go, Ivy. It's going to be a busy night.'

Jessie ties on a cotton mask and pushes through the swing door into the operating theatre with her elbow. A sailor lies groaning and muttering in Russian on the operating table, his left trouser leg sodden with blood below a makeshift tourniquet.

Aziz Khalid stands over the sailor cutting away his trousers. He looks up when Jessie enters. 'Put some gloves on then finish cutting these off, Lieutenant.'

He collects a rubber tube, a glass bottle and a small balloon pump from a table as Jessie cuts through the blood-soaked fabric. 'Watch me closely, Lieutenant. We need to do a blood transfusion or he will die. I'll need you to insert the tube into my arm once I've inserted this end into his. I have type O blood, so his body will accept it whatever his blood type is.'

'Y-yes, Captain.'

He looks at her, his dark eyes serious above his mask. 'You can do it, Lieutenant. I have every confidence in you.'

Jessie steps out onto the roof. The sky glows orange and the sun sits on the eastern horizon. The air is fresh after the night's rain, and she breathes it in, filling her lungs with its welcome coolness. She walks over to the ledge and sits down. The muezzin calls out the dawn prayer from a nearby mosque, and she watches the city slowly awaken beneath the hill.

'Thank you, Jessica.'

She looks behind her to see Aziz Khalid by the door to the stairs, his face drawn with fatigue, dark smudges under his eyes.

'I did what any nurse would do.'

He joins her on the ledge. 'Not everyone could have done the blood transfusion. It saved that sailor's life.'

'I've never seen a doctor do what you did.'

'We needed blood, and I have blood which anyone can use.'

'What would you have done if you didn't have type O blood, and your blood didn't match his?'

'I would have asked to test yours.'

'Oh.'

'Well, it wasn't necessary. I have read that the Canadians and Americans are working on a way to preserve and store blood. This would be a wonderful innovation. It would save many lives.'

He gazes out at the city and listens as the last call from the muezzin fades into the awakening morning. 'You are a very good nurse, Jessica. I have been remiss in letting you know this.' He looks at her and Jessie is suddenly aware of his warmth, and of the way his gaze seems to probe into the very recesses of her mind. He takes a breath as if he is about to say something, but he hesitates, and the moment is lost.

Jessie scans the sea shining orange in the distance. She had expected something to happen after their trip to Cairo the previous May. But there had been no repeat of their companionable dinner once they were back in Alexandria. He had been nothing but curtly professional when they had worked together in the operating theatre. It was obvious he thought of her as nothing more than a competent nurse. It was probably just as well. Archie Winter was much better company.

Aziz rises. 'I must go and pray. You should rest, Jessica. There will be much to do tomorrow.'

Chapter Fifty-Four

Christina

Clover Bar, London – January 1917

Gerald carefully wraps the final Christmas bauble in a page from *The London Illustrated News* and tucks it into the cardboard box. He scans the denuded Christmas tree, a generous gift from the Jeffries from a wood near Nuneaton, and ducks under the branches to winch the base out of the metal stand.

'Gerald? Whatever are you doing down there?'

'I'm putting away the decorations, my dear.'

'Gerald, get off the floor. I've asked Hettie to do that when she's finished the laundry. She agreed on the condition we pay her an additional five shillings. She said it was "outside her agreed contract of work". Whatever is the world coming to? If only Milly hadn't absconded to the munitions factory. Why any young woman would wish to work in such a place is beyond me.'

'I enjoy putting the decorations away, Tina. I remember where we bought each and every one of them. And this tree's far too heavy for Hettie. I'll have the rag-and-bone man take it away tomorrow.' Gerald rises to his feet, the liberated tree in his grasp. A shower of needles drops onto the Persian rug.

'Look what you've done now. We'll be picking spruce needles out of the rug until Easter. Honestly, Gerald, your photography studio is quite untidy enough without you wreaking chaos on our house as well.'

Gerald props the tree against the black metal mantelpiece and slaps the needles off his trousers. 'I'll fetch a sheet and drag the tree out to the garden.'

'No, I'll tell Hettie to do that. She's strong as an ox.' She flaps a sheet of paper in the air. 'Cousin Stefania's written from Capri. You'd best sit down.'

'Oh, dear.'

Christina perches on the chaise longue and holds the letter up to her eyes. '"I had thought dear Etta was much recovered from her illness after Adriana's birth, but she continues to suffer from headaches and periods of melancholia which send her to her bed for days, when even her darling child cannot rouse her from the darkness which enfolds her."'

'Stefania will take care of her, Tina, just like she took care of you when Cecelia was born and your husband was so ill. Etta's always been more highly strung than the other girls, but she's stronger than she looks. She'll be fine. Some things take time.'

'There's more, Gerald. "There is something I have discovered, which I feel it my responsibility to tell you. Etta and Carlo are not married. He has a wife and a child. It doesn't matter how I discovered it, only that it is the unfortunate truth. I worry for Etta's immortal soul, and for the child who has yet to be baptised. Etta insists that Carlo must be present, and will hear nothing from me on the subject. I am torn as to what to do, but I am sure you will agree that Adriana must be baptised as soon as possible. She is an innocent in this matter."'

Christina looks away from Gerald's concerned gaze. The difficult month after Cecelia's birth, followed by the months she had suffered in ashamed silence in the house with her aunts after her return to London, filters into her memory: a time when no one but her father would look her in the eye; when, even then, she could sense his disappointment in her. And now, Etta, with a child conceived out of wedlock. History repeating itself again and again, like a curse. Why is it that the Innocenti women must suffer so for the passions that run in their blood?

She drops the letter onto her lap. 'What are we to do, Gerald? Our daughter is living in sin with a married man, and our grandchild is outside of God's Kingdom. Adriana must be baptised immediately.'

'Yes. I see.'

'Do you, Gerald? The whole situation reminds me of when Roberto and I were so ill after Cecelia's birth, and poor Stefania was trying to organise Cecelia's baptism.'

'I know the situation was difficult for you, Tina.'

'Gerald, why did you marry me? A widow with a baby? My aunts felt I was an embarrassment, just as Mama had been. That losing a husband before Roberto and I had been married a year was somehow my fault. It was my Italian blood, they said, and my baby with an Italian father! They found it all quite dramatic and shocking. Gerald, why did you rescue us?'

Gerald sits beside his wife on the chaise longue. He takes her hands in his. 'I used to watch out the window for you to pass by the photography shop with Celie in the baby carriage on your way down Baker Street to Regent's Park. Every Tuesday and Thursday afternoon punctually at three o'clock. I thought you were the most beautiful woman I'd ever seen. The day you came into the shop and asked for your photograph to be taken was one of the happiest days of my life. When you told me you were a widow, I was beyond myself. I decided then and there to do everything in my power to make you want to marry me. I love you, Tina. I've always loved you.'

'But, Gerald—'

'Tina, I don't wish for you to rake up the sad memories surrounding your husband's death. You and our daughters have made me the happiest man I know. I hope I have made you happy. Have I, Tina? Have I made you happy?'

'What a question, Gerald.' She folds Stefania's letter. 'You're right. The past is the past. Etta has always been so impetuous, but she is an adult woman. She and Carlo must sort out their life together after the war is over. All we can do is offer her our support. I don't wish to do anything which causes her to prevent us from seeing our grandchild. It seems we are forever to be pulled back to that wretched island. I wish in all my heart I'd never stepped foot in Capri.'

'Don't say that, Tina. If you hadn't gone to Capri, you would never have had our beautiful Celie. Your husband's death was a tragedy, and it breaks my heart to think of how you must have suffered through his illness.' He shakes his head. 'No, my dear. It was all meant to be. You must never regret that, not for one moment.'

Christina looks at her husband. *If he only knew.* 'What shall we do about Adriana's baptism?'

'I'll write Etta. I'll explain to her the anguish you and Stefania are being put through about the baptism. I'm sure I can convince her to do it. We've always had a very good relationship.'

'No, Gerald, I'll write her. You're not even a Catholic. It's my responsibility.' Christina rises from the chaise longue. 'Gerald, what if something happens to this Carlo Marinetti?'

'Etta and Adriana will always have a home here. We are a family, Tina. This is all I ever wanted, and you have given me such a wonderful family, such a happy life. You didn't answer me before. Have I made you happy, Tina?'

Christina looks at Gerald's kind, familiar face, at the lines that are etched permanently across his forehead and the hollowness of his cheeks. Had she done that to him? Had she sucked away his youth and his vitality because of her inability to love him the way he deserved to be loved?

'Of course, Gerald. Very happy.'

Clover Bar
Hither Green, London

February 7th, 1917

My dearest Etta,

Your papa and I have received a letter from Cousin Stefania which has greatly distressed us. I am sorry that what she has to say came from her pen, rather than yours. Please don't be cross with her. She did the right thing to contact us. You must know that you and Adriana are not alone in the world, no matter how much the world may be testing you at this time.

We know that you and Carlo Marinetti are not married. We also know that he is already married and has a child. I am certain that you would not have embarked on the rash journey to Italy in the midst of a war had you known these things. There is nothing more dangerous to a woman in this world than a self-interested man. I do not know what he has promised you; but your father and I wish you to know that you and Adriana always have a home here at Clover Bar. You are my precious girl, Etta. I know that I do not say these things as often as I should. You remind me so much of myself before I married. I lay the blame for this unfortunate situation squarely at the feet of Mr Marinetti.

Now, to business. You must see that Adriana is baptised without delay. The situation is causing Stefania a great deal of distress, as she feels some responsibility to your child's immortal soul while you are living under her roof. You cannot wait until Carlo Marinetti is back from the war. I shall be writing Stefania after this letter to instruct her to make the arrangements. Please assure her that Papa and I shall cover any expenses.

Remember me to Stefania, and to Liliana, who I remember makes the most delicious Torta Caprese…

Christina hovers the pen over the letter. She could write that Stefania had sent her the recipe. Or, she could tell the truth; or, at least, a partial truth. She is so tired of holding it all inside of her. Perhaps it would help Etta to know that she'd once been in Capri, too. She dips the pen into the inkwell.

You see, I once stayed in the Villa Serenissima with Cousin Stefania when I was a young woman. What I am attempting to say is that I understand more of your situation than you will ever know.

Your papa and I love you very much. Now, aside from the baptism, you must take this time to get well. Walk in those green hills – the wildflowers will be blooming shortly and I remember how lovely it is when the poppies are out and the air is scented with rosemary. Breathe in the air. Watch the gulls swoop over the lovely blue sea. Let the island heal you, and, once this war is over, come home.

Your loving Mama

Chapter Fifty-Five

Etta

Villa Serenissima, Capri – February 1917

Etta sets down her mother's letter on the walnut sideboard in the villa's sitting room. She walks to the window and throws it open, but even the beauty of the sea view does nothing to still the anger that is rising inside her.

How did Cousin Stefania know about Carlo, about his wife and son? Celie had been the only person she had told about it. Celie must have written Cousin Stefania. How could her sister have betrayed her? *How could they both have betrayed her?*

'Ah, there you are, my dear,' Stefania says as she enters the sitting room. 'I am going to town to pick up some things for Liliana. Would you like to come with Adriana? We can buy some cannoli, if you like.'

Etta's eyes narrow. 'How could you, Cousin Stefania?'

'What do you mean? How could I what?'

She holds up her mother's letter. 'You told Mama and Papa that Carlo and I aren't married. You told them about Marianna and Paolo.'

Stefania rests a hand on the sofa to steady herself. 'Please forgive me, Etta. I had to. You are my responsibility while you are here. It would not have been right of me to keep that secret from them once I discovered it. Believe me, I wish I had never discovered it.'

'Celie told you, didn't she?'

'Don't blame your sister. I read the letter you'd written her before I posted it.'

'You what? Am I to have no privacy here?'

'I'm sorry, *cara*, but you've been so unwell. I wanted to check that you had not simply written ramblings.'

'Ramblings?'

'You do not remember, perhaps, what you said and did on your worst days. I … I wished only to protect you, and to save your sister from alarm.'

'How can I possibly trust you after this, Cousin Stefania? I'm nothing more than a prisoner here.' She juts out her chin. 'Like my mother was.'

Stefania's face blanches. 'Whatever do you mean? Your mother loved Capri.'

'So she *was* here.'

'Yes.'

Etta unfolds the letter. 'What did Mama mean by *"I understand more of your situation than you will ever know"*?'

Stefania gestures to a settee. 'Come, Etta. Sit down. I shall tell you something which you must promise never to tell anyone. Especially not Cecelia.'

'Why not Celie?'

'You must promise.'

'All right. I promise.'

They sit on one of the green damask settees. Stefania folds her hands in her lap and takes a deep breath. 'When your mother was a young woman, before she married your father, she came to visit me here for a summer after her mother's death in the flu pandemic. Her father felt it was a good idea for her to be out of London. I was meant to teach her Italian.

'There was a young man that summer. A young Englishman. They fell in love, but I was blind to its intensity. I still regarded Christina as a child, you see. She was only nineteen. She was so sweet and happy, so innocent, so eager to experience life here.'

'That doesn't sound like Mama.'

'Life is difficult. It changes people, some more than others.'

Etta picks at a thread of the green damask upholstery. 'What happened with the Englishman?'

'He left at the end of the summer. I don't know what he had promised her, or what she had imagined would happen, but her heart was broken.'

'Why did you say I shouldn't tell Celie this?'

Stefania sets her lips in a firm line.

Etta's eyes widen. 'You can't be saying ...'

'Your mother was ill after the birth, with a terrible fever. I was worried that she had caught the Russian flu, but it was an infection from the birth. She had nightmares and hallucinations, just like you. It was a very difficult time. When she was better, she went back to England with her baby ... with Cecelia.'

Etta stares at her cousin. 'But Papa?'

'Cecelia is your father's daughter in every way but that one. I am certain your mother told him the truth before they married. Cecelia must never know that Gerald isn't her real father, and that she was born in 1892, not 1893.' Stefania squeezes Etta's hand. 'You are so like your mother was when I met her that summer, *cara*. She has made a good life for herself and her child. I pray the same for you. I want you to know that you can trust me, the way your mother has trusted me with her secret all these years. Now, I am trusting you. You must never tell anyone what you know.'

Etta sits still, the room's silence broken only by the ticking of the grandfather clock. 'What was his name?'

'I cannot tell you.'

Etta nods. She rises abruptly. 'I must go feed Adriana.'

Stefania watches Etta leave. She slips her rosary out of her skirt pocket. She has broken Christina's trust. She will go to confession tomorrow to cleanse her unworthy soul.

Chapter Fifty-Six

Jessie

Alexandria, Egypt – February 1917

Jessie props open her copy of Baedeker's *Egypt & The Sudan* against the pink granite paws of the Roman sphinx at the base of the enormous granite column. 'It says here that the monolithic Pompey's Pillar was erected by the Romans in 297 AD to commemorate the Emperor Diocletian's victory in a revolt here in Alexandria.'

Archie Winter eyes the huge pillar. 'Bet that hacked off the locals. It's bloody tall.'

'Ninety-eight feet high. It's solid granite from Aswan. How do you suppose they got it all the way up the Nile to Alexandria?'

'Floated it, I guess.'

Jessie looks up from the guidebook. 'You're not really all that interested, are you?'

Archie shrugs. 'It's a pillar. Now, Ayers Rock, that's talkin'. If ya play your cards right, I'll show it to ya sometime.'

'I'd have to travel to Australia for that.'

Archie pokes his feathered hat back off his forehead with a finger. 'Never say never.'

Jessie smiles. 'Here, you'll like this, Archie. In 1803, a British ship commander named John Shortland flew a kite over the pillar and dropped a rope ladder at the top. He climbed up with one of his crewmen, waved the Union Flag and drank a toast to King George III.'

Archie grunts. 'They sound like Aussies.'

'Four days later they climbed the pillar again, fixed a weather vane, ate a steak and toasted the King once more.' Jessie shuts the guidebook. 'So concludes our history lesson. I'm afraid I shall have to give you a D minus. You're a most inattentive student, Sergeant Winter.'

'History was never my strong point.'

'What exactly is your strong point?'

Archie glances around the deserted hill. He steps over a fragment of a marble column and grabs Jessie by the waist. He pushes her against the base of the granite sphinx and thrusts his tongue in her mouth.

Jessie twists her head and pushes against him. 'Archie! What are you doing? Stop it!'

He grasps her head in his hands and plunders her mouth with his tongue. Her mind spins as she fights to breathe. She balls up her fists and beats at him until he finally releases his grip.

'Don't tell me ya didn't like that? Never had any complaints before.'

'Get away from me. Don't touch me.' She elbows past him and runs toward the road.

'Your friend Ivy didn't mind!' he shouts after her.

Jessie looks back to see Archie leaning against the pink granite sphinx, juggling her discarded Baedeker in his hands. 'You are reprehensible!'

'You're nothin' special, Jessie Fry! There's plenty more fish in the sea!'

———

'Good heavens, Jessie! You'll have the door right off its hinges the way you're slammin' about.'

Jessie flops onto her small, metal-framed bed, and bends over to untie her bootlaces. She throws her left boot onto the linoleum floor. 'Why is it so difficult for women to go outside and not be harassed?'

Ivy sticks a hair grip through her neat brown bun and pats her efforts as she regards herself in her hand mirror. 'Isn't it awful in the market? All those shop sellers grabbin' at ya? I daren't go there anymore unless one of the Light Horse boys comes along.' She rubs her lips in the mirror. 'Who was that I saw you sneakin' off with after lunch? Matron would skin ya alive if she heard ya'd been out with a soldier.'

Jessie kicks off her second boot. 'I'd rather not talk about it.'

Ivy tosses the mirror onto her bed and flops down beside it. 'It was that Archie Winter, wasn't it?'

'I have no interest in Sergeant Winter.'

'Ooh, *Sergeant* Winter now, is it? I thought ya were sweet on him.'

'I am most definitively not.'

'In that case, ya wouldn't mind if I got ta know him betta?'

Jessie narrows her eyes. 'Don't you think you know him well enough already, Ivy?'

'What do ya mean?'

'Never mind. You'd best forget about him. He's not a gentleman.'

'Who needs a gentleman? I like a fella with some gumption.' Ivy hops off the bed. 'Look, Jessie, are ya interested in Archie Winter or not?'

'Absolutely not.'

Ivy adjusts her nurse's veil. 'Then, Archie Winter had best watch out, 'cause Ivy de la Roche is comin'. I'm off ta practice for the musical revue. I'm singin' *"Pretty Baby"*. Ya really should join up, Jessie. Ya might even find yourself a mister.'

'Thanks, but no thanks, Ivy.'

'Suit yourself. Oh, message came for ya. I put it on the desk.'

The door slams behind Ivy. Jessie pads across the floor to the desk in her stockinged feet. She picks up the note and breaks the red wax seal. The blue ink handwriting is thick-lined and impatient, more of a scribble than an attempt at clear communication.

Dear Miss Fry,

I would be honoured if you would accompany me for an excursion to the souk on your next free afternoon. Please advise.

Yours,
Aziz Khalid

She rereads the note. Terse, but polite. She opens the desk drawer and takes out a sheet of writing paper and a trench pen.

Dear Captain Khalid,

I should be delighted to join you for an excursion to the souk. I am available Thursday next. I shall meet you at the hospital's entrance gate at 2 o'clock.

Yours,
Jessie Fry

Aziz Khalid drops a coin into the sweet vendor's palm and hands Jessie a paper cup of ice-cream dotted with green pistachios and a small flat wooden stick.

'It is a special ice-cream from the Lebanon called *booza*. It tastes of rose water.' He prods his ice-cream with his stick and scoops an elastic mouthful into his mouth.

Jessie scoops up the ice-cream, which stretches like glue from the cup.

He laughs. 'Twist it around the stick.'

Her eyes widen as the *booza*'s cold stickiness slides around her mouth. 'It's delicious!'

'I am very happy you like it. The sweet seller is not always here. He must wait until he can buy ice from the British.'

Jessie licks the ice-cream from her lips as they head down another of the souk's winding alleyways. 'What will you do when the war is over, Aziz? Stay in the army?'

'Finally! You have said my name.'

'You make such a fuss whenever I call you Captain, I had no choice.'

Aziz chuckles. 'After the war, I shall join a hospital in Cairo, where my family lives. I may teach at the university as well.' He shrugs. 'The path will open.'

'Tell me about your family.'

'I live with my mother and sister. My father died before the war.'

'Oh, I'm sorry.'

'Thank you. That is kind of you.'

They walk on in silence for several minutes.

'You never married?'

Aziz glances at her sideways, his eyes lit with amusement. 'I was engaged to a very beautiful girl named Fatima Zahra when I was twenty-one. Our parents arranged the marriage, but it was hopeless from the start. I was studying for my medical degree and working all hours in the hospital. My fiancée was unhappy at my inattention and broke off the engagement. I decided that were I ever to marry, it would be for love, much to the frustration of my mother who threatens me regularly with her imminent demise as a grandchildless woman, caused by my own selfish stubbornness.' He tosses the empty ice-cream cups and sticks onto a smouldering brazier. 'Tell me about your family, Jessica. You said you had a sister.'

'I have two sisters. Celie is the eldest; she's the clever, studious one. She was studying German before the war broke out. She became engaged to her German teacher before he went back to Germany to join the army. They haven't been able to contact each other since.'

'That's a terrible pity.'

'Maybe it's for the best. Anyway, she's now working part-time in our father's photography studio, writing for the women's page for the *Daily Mirror* and doing some work for the suffragists. Encouraging women to become tram drivers and munitions workers, that kind of thing. She's a busy bee, our Celie.'

'She sounds like you. Strong and capable.'

Jessie skirts around a man who thrusts a large chameleon at her. 'Then there's my twin, Etta.' She picks an ember from a barbecue grill off her sleeve. 'She's petite and blonde. Entirely my opposite in every way. She's the artistic one in the family. She was training to be a painter in London, then she married an Italian artist and now has a baby girl named Adriana. She's living in Italy with relatives while her husband is off fighting in the Italian army.'

'She is adventurous, like you.'

'We have that in common, I suppose.'

'And your parents?'

'My father has a small photography studio in London. My mother has the local ladies over to knit or sew for the soldiers once a week at our house. Other than that, I'm not quite sure what she does. Plays the piano, does needlepoint, orders our maid about, attempts to matchmake her daughters. I've never really thought about it.'

'It sounds like a lovely family. You're very fortunate.'

'We're quite average, really.'

Aziz stops in front of a carpet shop and turns to Jessie. 'You are not average, Jessica. In fact, I think you are quite remarkable.' He takes hold of Jessie's elbow and steers her into the carpet shop.

'Where are we going?'

'Don't you know that everyone who visits Egypt must buy a carpet?'

They enter a vast room stacked to the ceiling with rolled carpets of every size and colour. 'What am I to do with a carpet in the nurse's residence?'

'We are in the land of Scheherazade and the *One Thousand and One Nights*. What else does one do with a carpet but fly away to magic lands on it?'

Jessie laughs. 'When you put it like that, I'll at least have to take a look.'

'Good. Then, afterwards, I shall teach you to smoke a *shisha*.'

'Goodness, Aziz, whatever is that?'

'You wished for a life of adventure, did you not, Jessica? I am your humble servant, or, perhaps I should say, your *djinni*.'

'You are full of surprises, Dr Khalid. I had you pegged for a humourless surgeon obsessed with his work.'

'A humourless surgeon? What an unfortunate impression.'

'I'm having a very nice afternoon.'

'I am as well. I hope that we might do this again, Jessica. Would that be agreeable to you?'

'If you can get me a good price on a flying carpet, I may consider it.'

'Like I said, I am your *djinni*. Your wish is my command.'

Chapter Fifty-Seven

Gerald

Clover Bar, London – March 1917

Gerald shuts the bedroom door quietly behind him and crosses the Persian carpet to Christina's wardrobe. It is a territory he has never explored, and he feels a mix of guilt and naughtiness, as if he is a schoolboy about to engage in mischief. All he wishes is to borrow a pair of her gloves to check the size for the new kid gloves with pearl buttons he plans to buy her for her birthday. She is out at Ellen Jackson's packing gift boxes for the troops in France, and Hettie has left for the market, so this is his window of opportunity.

He turns the key and swings open the doors of the large mahogany wardrobe. A crush of dresses bounces toward him as if exhaling a breath. On the upper shelf a jumble of silk scarves and clutch purses sits amongst several large cardboard hat boxes. He glances nervously at the door, and, although he knows he is safely alone in the house, his heart quickens.

He reaches for the hat boxes and sets them on the carpet. Stretching his arm, he then runs his hand blindly along the shelf until his fingers slide against a paper-wrapped roll. He grasps the roll and pulls it down from the shelf.

The package is not one he recognises. He can think of nothing that Christina owns that would be such a shape. Likely some memento from her father to which she has a sentimental attachment. He lays the package on the bed and continues his search for gloves. This time, his hand finds the tooled leather cover of a book. He takes it down. The green cover is finely wrought with designs of curling leaves. He sits on the bed and opens the cover.

The diary of Christina Maria Innocenti Bishop
Capri, Italy, 1891-2

The diary is like a stone in his hands. He sets it down on the white crocheted bedcover and unties the string on the package. Released of its restraint, the roll unfurls. A young, auburn-haired woman in a pale blue dress sits amongst wildflowers on a hill, staring out at a turquoise sea sparkling in the sun. He recognises the face of the girl immediately: Christina. On the bottom right-hand corner, a signature: *H. Grenville.*

He turns the painting over. *Christina, Capri 1891.*

He sits and stares at the painting and the diary. He knows he should put them back, that whatever they reveal may be something he is better off not knowing. He runs his fingers over the bumps and recesses of the leather leaves. Turning the page, he proceeds to read.

Chapter Fifty-Eight

Celie

Hither Green, London – March 1917

Celie braces her knees against the top of the stepladder and reaches up to clip up the corner of a painted backdrop with a clothes peg. She hears the bell ring over the studio door, and calls out over her shoulder: 'Just a moment! I'll be right with you!' She releases the clothes peg, but it hasn't quite grasped the canvas, which curls forward like a faulty curtain. 'Oh, crumbs.'

'Careful, Miss Fry. Let me help you.'

Celie turns her head. For a moment she doesn't recognise the handsome, dark-haired army officer standing beside the bust of Caesar. 'Frank? Frank Jeffries? Is that you?'

'It is.' He sets his hat on Caesar's head. 'Let me do that for you.'

'That's very kind of you.' She climbs down the ladder and hands him the clothes peg. 'I've been struggling with it for the past twenty minutes. I'm just a tad too short.'

Frank climbs the ladder and clips up the flapping canvas. 'There. Is it straight?'

'Perfect. I thought a country scene would make a nice change for the soldiers.' She points over to a bench that has been painted to look like stone. 'If you grab the other end, we can set it here in front of the backdrop.'

'At your service, Miss Fry. I can be the guinea pig. I need a new portrait for my parents.'

'I'm afraid Papa's out at the moment, Frank, but I can take your portrait if you're not worried about having a woman photographer. And it's Celie, remember?'

'That suits me just fine, Celie.'

They drag the bench across the studio's wooden floor. Frank sits down while Celie retrieves his hat.

'So, Frank, tell me all about where you've been since I last saw you in the hospital. How long ago was that?'

Frank fixes his hat at a jaunty angle. 'Two years in May.'

'Is it really? It seems like this war will never end.' She pulls out a glass plate from a wooden box and slides it into the large Marion camera. 'Sit sideways slightly and look into the camera. I want to be sure to show your insignia on your epaulette. I see you're an officer now.'

'Second lieutenant. They promoted me after the Gallipoli campaign. The Germans and the Turks were a misery there. They're a bloodthirsty lot.'

Celie's jaw tightens. 'Yes, well, it can't be easy for anyone on either side.'

'Well, we gave as good as we got. There were far fewer Germans after the battle, and that's a good thing.' He clears his throat and coughs into his hand. He takes out a handkerchief and wipes at his mouth. 'Sorry. Still rather wheezy from the mustard gas.'

'You're looking rather better than the last time I saw you.'

Frank runs his fingers along his cheek. 'Almost as good as new. Jessie is a good nurse.'

'She is that. She was on a hospital ship at Gallipoli before being posted to Egypt. She said in her letters it was awful.'

'It was. I'm back in France now. At least I can get back home on leave once in a while.' A shadow chases across Frank's face. 'France is awful in a different way. This whole war is a crime.' His eyes clear and he smiles at Celie. 'My mother's been sending me the *Mirror* with her comfort packages. I've been reading your pieces. I particularly liked the one about the munitionettes. Did you know that some of munitionettes send romantic notes to us in the artillery cases?'

'Really?'

'There's always a scrum to open the cases. Some of the fellows have begun writing back. I expect a few weddings from it after the war.'

'That's not a bad idea for a story, Frank,' Celie says as she picks up the paisley shawl. '*"Matches Made in Munitions Heaven"*.'

'Your editor would be a fool to turn it down. What about you, Celie? Do you have a sweetheart in the war?'

Celie laughs as she picks up the paisley shawl.

It is like a knife pierces through her breast straight into her heart. She shuts her eyes and sees Max's face, his blue eyes crinkled with laughter, his hair the colour of summer wheat. Two and a half years since she's seen or heard from him, and he still haunts her thoughts and her dreams.

'Yes. I was engaged just before the war. I ... I haven't heard from him for some time.'

'I'm terribly sorry. I'm sure he's fine.'

She looks at Frank. 'His name is Max Fischer. He's German.'

'German? Seriously?'

'Yes. Seriously.' She drapes the shawl over her head and leans over the camera. 'Hold still, please. I shall be done in a moment, and you can go on your way.'

Gerald looks up from his desk in the photography studio. Celie is sitting on the bench, lost in thought, the soldiers' portraits she has been sorting through abandoned beside her.

'What is it, pet? You've been quiet all afternoon.'

She sighs and collects the photographs. 'I told you Frank Jeffries was in this morning.'

'Yes, I'm sorry to have missed him.'

'I can't help but think about him, and Max, both fighting…' Her shoulders slump. 'I hate this war. I try to put Max out of my mind and get on with things, then Frank asks if I have a sweetheart, and it's like Max is here with me.'

Gerald shifts in his chair, wishing to go to his daughter to offer her comfort, but his ingrained reserve restrains him. His heart, already battered from his discovery that morning, aches for her. 'I'm not sure anyone knows what this war is about anymore, if anyone ever did.'

'I think Frank was mortified when I told him Max was German. I don't imagine I shall ever see him again.'

'I'm sure he understands, Celie. You have to set Max aside for now though and move on with your life, pet.'

'I can't, Papa.'

'You must give yourself a chance to live, Celie, or happiness will pass you by. If I were Max, that's what I would want for you.'

'Do you really think so, Papa?'

Gerald smiles at his eldest daughter. 'I do, dove. Now let's see those photographs.'

Chapter Fifty-Nine

Etta

Villa Serenissima, Capri, Italy – April 1917

'There now,' Stefania Albertini says as she watches Liliana and Mario head down the steps in front of the church of Santo Stefano, hand in hand with Adriana, who toddles between them in her lacy white baptismal dress. 'Adriana is a Catholic under the eyes of God, and I can sleep at night.'

Etta slips Adriana's baptismal certificate into her handbag and checks that her wide-brimmed hat is secured with the hat pin. 'Mama will be happy. Another Catholic in the family.'

Stefania raises her parasol against the beating sun as she and Etta walk down the steps into the Piazzetta. Etta tucks her hand in the crook of Stefania's arm. 'It was good of Father Izzo to let Mario be the godfather. I hope Liliana isn't too upset about not being the godmother, but it had to be you.'

'She is already the godmother of all of her sister's children. She

315

needs to give the rest of us a chance at it, and I quite intend to spoil Adriana as a good godmother should.' She places a gloved hand on Etta's arm. 'Wait a moment, *cara mia*. I have a small gift for my goddaughter.' She opens the pearl clasp on her blue velvet reticule and removes a small red satin jewellery box. 'It was my grandmother's, Margarita Innocenti. She would have been your great-grandmother, and Adriana's great-great-grandmother.' She opens the box and holds up a delicate gold crucifix.

'It's beautiful.'

'I take my role as a godmother very seriously, Etta.' She replaces the crucifix in the box and gives it to Etta. 'What is it, *cara*?'

'I wish Carlo could have been here, Cousin Stefania. Adriana will be two years old next month, and he's only seen her for a few days when he was here last spring.' Her smooth forehead creases. 'I've been trying to sketch Carlo's face, but something's never quite right. Why can't I remember his face?'

'It is not necessary to remember every detail, *cara mia*. You simply need to feel your love for him, and his for you. This is how I remember my dear Federico.'

'I suppose so.' They walk across the bustling Piazzetta in companionable silence, where men are sweeping up the dying flowers from the Easter processions. The clocktower bells strike the half-hour, filling the square with resonant echoes. 'I haven't received a letter from him in months.'

'You cannot rely on the post while we are in a war, Etta. No doubt a letter will come soon.'

'I suppose you're right.' She smiles. 'I should be finished with Adriana's portrait this week. I'd like to have it framed.'

'Of course. There is a woodworker in town who can do that. You have colour in your cheeks this morning, *cara mia*. You're sleeping better?'

'Yes, I'm feeling much better.'

'Good. Now, we must hurry back to the villa for Adriana's celebration or Mario will eat all the *Torta Caprese Bianca*.'

––––––––

Etta sits at the desk in her bedroom, half-finished sketches of Carlo littered around her. On an easel, which Mario has made for her, Adriana's portrait regards her, the child's round face framed with gold curls. Etta looks around the large whitewashed room. The white-painted metal bed with its elaborate brass swirls throws looping shadows over the east wall, and a soft breeze stirs the blue floral curtains. Adriana lies still in her wicker cot beside the bed, her curls a cap on her sleeping head.

She lied to Stefania. She is not all right. Certainly, her body has recovered, and at night she sleeps like the dead, the dancing monsters of her earlier nightmares no longer visiting her dreams. She can't remember the last time she dreamt at all. She is empty, like a beehive robbed of its honey. Each morning she sits in front of her vanity mirror and recreates herself, pinning her hair into soft upswept waves, and pinching her cheeks and biting her lips until they redden into a healthy glow. She has practised her smile until it has become second nature, and chooses her dresses with care. When she is done, not even Liliana, with her knowing perceptiveness, can see that she is anything but a happy young mother. No one needs to see that she is nothing but a shell from which all of life's joy has fled.

Carlo, my darling, where are you? Are you still alive? Why don't you write me, my darling? I miss you so very much. I am dying here without you. I am so very lost.

She rises from the chair and walks over to the window. She spies Mario, long-limbed and graceless in his fifteen-year-old body, sitting on a tree stump in the garden, eating a pear while he bends over a sketchbook. She watches him look out over the sea to the Italian coast as his hand sweeps over the paper.

An idea sprouts in her mind like a spring flower pushing through mud. She has Adriana and she has her art, and one day, when this wretched war is over, she will have Carlo again. What she has lacked in the long, languid days on the island is a purpose.

She collects her drawing pencils and her sketchbook from her desk, and heads out of the room. She has a student and she will teach.

———

Stefania shuts her bedroom door and turns the key in the lock. A ray of sunlight streaks through the window, throwing a white bar across the chest of drawers. She hurries across the Moroccan rug and unlocks the bottom drawer. Kneeling on the floor, she removes a stack of fine silk scarves and sets them on the rug. She reaches into the back of the drawer and her hand closes on the wooden box.

She sets the ornately carved box on her lap and contemplates it. It sits amongst the black fabric of her skirt like a reproach, her treachery made manifest. She opens the lid. The letters nestle inside, a neat stack of dirt-stained envelopes addressed in Carlo's impatient handwriting to Etta. She slides a letter out of her skirt pocket and adds it to the others.

Chapter Sixty

Jessie

Cairo, Egypt – May 1917

The taxi driver opens his door and shuffles from his seat with a grumble. He lifts the latch and pushes open the ornate metal gates. Beyond them, a white gravel drive curves through a green lawn and disappears around a hedge of clipped cedars where a fiery trumpet vine has been allowed to run rampant through the dense green branches.

'You live *here*, Aziz?'

'Yes. My father had it built when I was a child. He called it Altumanina. It means tranquillity. It's a good name, you will see. You would never know the city is outside these walls.'

The driver climbs into his seat and shifts the cab into gear. The tyres crunch over the white gravel. Around the final bend, a handsome Victorian mansion comes into view. The building's solidity is softened into an unexpected elegance by a coral-pink render and the white marble balconies which hang under the tall first-floor windows. Slender cypresses thrust into the blue sky behind the mansion, as if placed there by the hand of a discerning artist as the perfect background for the house.

The taxi grinds to a halt. Jessie steps out and waits on the gravel, which, at closer look, she sees is made up of chips of white marble, and waits as the driver unloads her suitcase. Aziz pays him, and the driver's sour expression transforms into a bright smile and effusive thank yous.

A woman opens one of the pair of tall green-painted front doors. She is young, perhaps a few years older than herself, Jessie thinks, and very beautiful, with delicate, high cheekbones and large amber eyes framed by thick black eyelashes. She wears a long, loose *jellabiya* over loose trousers, but rather than the ubiquitous cotton, her clothing is fine blue silk embroidered with silver thread at the cuffs and neck. A golden silk headscarf is wrapped over her hair in an elegant turban. The young woman's full pink lips turn up into a smile and her teeth flash like pearls in her warm complexion. 'You have brought her, finally, Aziz. We have been waiting all morning.'

'I'm sorry, Zara. The train was delayed at Tanta.'

'No matter. You are here now.' The young woman reaches out her arms to Jessie and takes hold of her hands. 'You are Jessica, of course. Aziz has spoken of nothing but you for months.'

A pained expression crosses Aziz's face. 'Zara, please.'

'Well, it's true, Aziz. I know how taciturn you can be. If you do not tell her yourself, I am more than happy to do it.' She smiles again at Jessie and squeezes her hands. 'I am Zara Khalid,' she says, her r's fluttering like butterflies, 'Aziz's long-suffering younger sister.'

Jessie smiles awkwardly, feeling plain and ungainly in her grey cotton uniform with its ugly white collar, and her functional straw boater. 'It's lovely to meet you. What a beautiful house.'

Zara waves her hand languidly. 'Oh, this. Yes, it is very nice but it's my mother's domain. I cannot take any credit for it in the least. Come in from that sun. I shall have Marta set out some tea on the terrace under the awning. There's a lovely breeze off the river there.'

Jessie follows Zara across the marble floor of the airy entrance hall, past the sweep of a staircase which curves around a huge chandelier dripping with rock crystals. They pass through a grand sitting room with panelled walls painted a cool blue. A large Persian rug in rich blue and gold covers the marble floor under a delicate gold Venetian glass chandelier, and elegant French settees and armchairs upholstered in blue silk damask cluster in conversational groupings around the room.

Out on the shaded terrace, Zara indicates a cluster of wicker chairs with fat chintz cushions surrounding a low brass table. 'Please, make yourself comfortable. We have a lovely view of the garden and the river here through the trees. I shall see about the tea, then you can tell me all about how you met my brother.'

When Zara has left, Jessie looks over at Aziz. 'I must confess, I'm rather overwhelmed. I would have been quite happy staying at the nurses' residence.'

'Nonsense. We have much work to do running around buying supplies over the next two days. We have many comfortable rooms here. It is ridiculous to have them lie empty.'

'It is a breathtaking house.'

Jessie sits down and scrutinises the vast, lush garden with its rose bushes and garden walls swallowed by explosions of purple and magenta bougainvillea. 'You said your father worked in the government. You didn't think about a political career?'

Aziz sits in a chair beside Jessie. 'My father had an ability to understand and work with the British, which the Khedive Tewfik, and then his son, Khedive Abbas II, found useful. Unfortunately, my father was killed in an assassination attempt on Khedive Abbas in Constantinople a few years ago.'

'Oh, that's awful, Aziz. I had no idea. I'm terribly sorry.'

'It was a shock. My father was only fifty-eight.' Aziz shakes his head. 'Perhaps it was the kindest thing. His political career would likely not have lasted much longer.'

'Why is that?'

'The British deposed Khedive Abbas when he was found to be encouraging Egyptians and the Sudanese to support the Central Powers against the British in the war. My father would have been found guilty by association.' He slaps his hands on the knees of his uniform. 'So, now we have a British protectorate and a new Sultan who has several impressive palaces and a comfortable life so long as he agrees with whatever the British wish, whether or not it is to the advantage of Egyptians.' He looks over at Jessie. 'I'm sorry, Jessica. You're English. I don't mean to—'

'No. I understand.'

'Once this war is over, it makes every kind of sense for Egyptians to rule themselves, but I am afraid it won't be easy. At any rate, I had no interest in going into a puppet government. I saw what politics did to my father. Besides, I wished to become a doctor from an early age.' He opens his hands. 'And here I am.'

'But you're working for the British Army.'

'When the war started, I knew that it would spread down to the Mediterranean because of the Turkish involvement. I felt I would be most useful doing what I could for the soldiers who are nothing more than pawns in this whole terrible situation. Death does not respect nationalities.'

'What if Egypt were to become independent of the British protectorate?'

'That is the golden question, isn't it?'

An elegant older woman sweeps through the French doors onto the terrace. There is no mistaking her relationship to Zara, with the same elegant, high cheekbones and pale golden eyes, though she has rimmed hers heavily in black kohl, heightening their ethereal quality. She wears a loose black silk *jellabiya*, a rich red silk turban and scarf, and a long double strand of pearls swings around her neck with every movement.

Aziz leaps to his feet and gestures to his chair. 'Mama, please sit here beside Jessica.'

The older woman glances at Jessie and waves a long-fingered hand in the air, setting her gold bracelets jangling. 'Certainly not, Aziz. You are sitting there already. I prefer the settee, in any case.' Her eyes sweep over Jessie, pausing a moment too long on the plain grey cotton uniform and ugly black laced shoes. 'So, you are the English nurse Aziz has been speaking about. I trust your journey today was not too arduous?'

'No, not at all.'

'You are so fortunate to be in Alexandria. I have always preferred it there by the sea. It feels so much more intellectual with its proximity to Turkey, Greece and Italy and their admirable Classicism than this dusty desert backwater.'

'Cairo is hardly a backwater, Mama,' Aziz says. He turns to Jessie. 'Let me introduce Jessica to you properly. Mama, this is Lieutenant Jessica Fry of London, England, a nurse with the British Expeditionary Force; Jessica, permit me to introduce my mother, Madame Layla Khalid.'

Layla Khalid arches a delicate eyebrow. 'Lieutenant? How very impressive.'

Jessie smiles nervously. 'It's because I'm an army nurse. We're all given that designation, though we call ourselves "Sister" in the hospital.' Jessie swallows, her mouth suddenly dry. 'Thank you very much for allowing me to stay here while we're in Cairo. You have ... you have a lovely home.'

'You are too kind.'

Zara enters the terrace accompanied by a sturdy woman in a black skirt and full-sleeved white cotton blouse, her dark brown hair covered in a floral scarf tied behind her neck. She carries a large silver tray which she sets down on the low brass table. She glances over at Jessica and smiles, her pale blue eyes wrinkling at the corners.

Layla flicks her eyes between the housekeeper and Jessie. 'That will be all, Marta.'

'Yes, madame. Will you need—'

'I said that is all, Marta.'

Jessie glances at Aziz whose face is set into a mask of forced composure. 'There's no need to speak to Marta like that, Mama.'

Zara pours out a cup of fragrant black tea through a tea strainer and hands it to her mother. 'Aziz is right, Mama. Marta has the patience of one of her Coptic saints. If I were her, I would poison the flowers and change the sugar for salt and leave you on the day of one of your grand dinner parties.'

Aziz's cheek twitches. 'I have no doubt, Zara.'

Layla rises, as graceful as an unfolding leaf. 'I am afraid I have taken with a headache. If you excuse me, I shall take my tea up to my room and rest.' She bestows a polite smile on Jessie. 'It was a pleasure to meet you, Miss … I am sorry, *Lieutenant* Fry. I trust you will find your stay at Altumanina comfortable.'

Jessie watches Madame Layla Khalid exit the terrace, her loose silk clothing fluttering around her slender figure in the thin summer breeze. She once saw a moth in a butterfly exhibition at the Natural History Museum, black and red, with wings that shone like oil when they caught the light. A cinnabar moth. Prone to cannibalism as a caterpillar and toxic to predators when it finally emerged from its pupa in all its adult glory. Why had she thought of that now?

Aziz reaches down from his perch on one of the large beige limestone blocks of the Great Pyramid and takes hold of Jessie's hand. 'Not far now. We are almost there.'

Jessie rubs the back of her free hand across her damp forehead. 'I feel like I'm back in Miss Love's PE class in Lewisham.'

Aziz chuckles. 'You'll thank me when we're at the top. The view is spectacular.'

Jessie glances behind her. 'Good heavens. I can see clear across to Cairo. The Sphinx looks like a cat from up here.'

He tugs at her hand. 'Come on, Jessica. Only a few more feet. It is flat at the top. We can rest there.'

Jessie follows him up the final stones. 'You've been up here before?'

'Yes.'

'With a woman?'

He pulls her up to the flat stones at the summit. 'Always by myself. I have never met a woman who would climb up here with me, until you.'

Jessie steps onto the summit, clutching at her hat as the breeze pulls at its brim. 'Oh, my word, Aziz. This really is quite spectacular.' She points over to the next pyramid. 'What's the white stone at the top of that one?'

'That's the Pyramid of Khafre. It still has some of the white limestone casing that covered all of the pyramids at one time. Can you imagine, Jessica? They would have glistened like great white monuments in the middle of the desert.' He points toward the Sphinx at the base of the pyramid. 'Have you heard the story of the riddle of the Sphinx?'

Jessie takes her new Brownie camera out of her shoulder-bag and aims it at Aziz. 'No, but I have a feeling you're going to tell me. Just like the way you told me about the mummies and the statues and everything else in the Egyptian Museum. If you ever decide not to be a doctor anymore, you can definitely become a guide.'

'Are you suggesting I am a know-it-all, Lieutenant Fry?'

Jessie clicks the shutter. 'You? Never.'

'I spent many, many hours in the museum in my youth. I was particularly fascinated by the mummified monkey.'

She turns her camera onto the view of the white-topped pyramid. 'I thought we were meant to be buying hospital supplies. I wasn't expecting a personal tour of Cairo.'

'I have taken care of that. My man Mustapha is arranging for everything to be put on the train for us tomorrow.'

She sets down the camera and looks at Aziz. 'So, I've been brought to Cairo on false pretences.'

'Not in the least. We shall return with the medical supplies and all will be well.'

'Like I said before, you are full of surprises, Captain Khalid.'

'Are you disappointed?'

'Not at all.' Jessie stares down at the small black box of her camera. 'May I ask you something, Aziz?'

'Of course.'

'Why did you wait so long to ask me out after our first visit to Cairo? I had thought you might … follow up. But you didn't.'

'I am sorry. I believed it was for the best. Please don't misunderstand me. I wanted to very much. But you are an English Christian and I am an Egyptian Muslim. I told myself that you would return to England once the war is over, and I would stay here in Cairo. I told myself it would be unwise to encourage anything more than a professional relationship. I let my head dictate my heart, because I believed it was the kindest thing I could do for you.'

'What changed?'

'Ah, that is the thing of it. Nothing changed for me. I had let the *djinni* out of the bottle. I couldn't stop thinking of you. I insisted to Matron Miller that you always assist me in the operating theatre. I refused any other nurse; did you know that? It was the only way I could spend time with you. Then, when I saw you sitting up on the hospital roof after the blood transfusion, I knew beyond any doubt that I couldn't go on like I had any longer. I knew then that I loved you, Jessica.'

He reaches out and brushes her cheek with his finger. A shock like electricity runs through her body. She picks up the camera and focuses on the Sphinx far below. 'You were saying, about the Sphinx?'

Aziz drops his hand and looks down at the half-buried body of the Sphinx. 'Ah, yes. A sphinx was a mythical creature with the head of a woman, the body of a lion, the tail of a serpent and the wings of an eagle. Quite a ferocious, merciless creature who would guard the entrance to temples and cities. She would kill and eat anyone who could not answer her riddle.'

'I rather like the sound of her,' Jessie says. She clicks an image of the Great Pyramid's triangular shadow thrusting over the desert earth and scattered buildings as she tries to quieten her rattling heart.

'There was a sphinx who guarded the entrance to the city of Thebes. The Greek, Oedipus, travelled to Thebes and when he arrived the sphinx posed him the question: "What goes on fours in the morning, on twos in the afternoon and on threes at night?"'

Jessie clicks another picture. 'And? What's the answer?'

'You are impatient, Jessica. I fear the sphinx would have devoured you.'

'I think I might have been able to talk her down. I have a lot of experience with my mother.'

Aziz chuckles. 'Oedipus thought very carefully about the riddle. In the end, he gave her the correct answer. The poor sphinx felt that she had no choice but to end her life, as she felt her value was bound up in having an unsolvable riddle.'

Jessie sits on an ancient stone. 'And the answer?'

Aziz reaches into the breast pocket of his uniform and takes out a small black velvet bag tied with a red silk drawstring and sets it in Jessie's hand. 'The answer is in here.'

'In here?'

'Yes.'

Jessie pulls at the drawstring and takes out a small box wrapped in white paper tied with string.

'Unwrap it carefully, Jessica. The answer is on the other side of the paper.'

Jessie unties the string and unfolds the paper to reveal a small red box. On the paper something has been written in black ink. *Will you marry me?* Her breath catches. She looks at Aziz.

He takes the red box from her and kneels on the summit of the Great Pyramid as the sun flares orange in the western sky. He opens the box and removes a gold ring set with a central diamond and two small blue sapphires.

'Aziz—'

'Jessica Fry, you are a very special woman. I have never met anyone quite like you. I would be honoured if you would take this humourless, know-it-all Egyptian doctor for your devoted husband.'

'Aziz—'

'I know it will not be easy, my darling, but we shall manage. I know it in my heart. There is no one else I wish to live my life with.'

'Aziz—'

'Jessica, *habibti*. I love you. Will you marry me?'

'Aziz, you fool. Of course I shall.'

Chapter Sixty-One

Celie

Clover Bar, London – June 1917

Gerald enters the dining room, sifting through the post as he makes his way to the table where Hettie has laid out breakfast. He picks an envelope out of the stack. 'Letter for you, Celie.'

'Jessie or Etta? I do hope it's Etta. I haven't had a letter from her in ages.'

'It's postmarked France. No return address.'

Her heart jumps. 'France?'

Christina sets down the teapot. 'Who do you know in France?'

Celie tears open the envelope and takes out the letter. 'Oh, it's from Frank Jeffries.'

'Frank Jeffries? Really?'

'Don't sound so hopeful, Mama.'

Christina butters a slice of cold toast and spoons on a dollop of marmalade. 'Well? What does Mr Jeffries have to say?'

'Tina, let Celie be. The letter is addressed to her, not to us.'

Celie pushes away from the table. 'If you excuse me, I'm going to read this in my room. I'll be at the studio in an hour, Papa.'

56th (London) Infantry Div.
Nr. Arras, France

May 16th, 1917

Dear Miss Fry,

First, please let me apologise once again for my terrible fumble when we last met. I certainly hadn't meant to upset you when I spoke about Gallipoli. I have seen quite enough of this war, and I have no doubt the chaps on the other side feel much the same. I often think that, having made it through Gallipoli, the Somme and Arras with a gassing and a few minor burns, my luck may have run its course. If I make it through to the end of this, I want nothing more to do with Britain, or France, or Germany, or any of it, though I don't have any idea, as yet, of how this will come to pass.

I have just come back to this letter from a rather cutthroat game of Nap, and am a few coins richer for it. I have reread what I've written, and it's really quite morose, so let me tell you a little about how we've been entertaining ourselves for the past few weeks while everything has been quiet here. Cards are top of the list – Brag, Pontoon and Nap – with a bit of money changing hands. The other day, when I was playing Nap with a group of fellows, this Canadian chap came around and started watching us. We had quite a pile of French notes and coins collected on the sandbag we were using as a table. Then we noticed he had a Mills bomb in his hands and he was playing with the pin. That made us quite nervous! If the pin comes out, you have only a few seconds before the grenade goes off. Wouldn't you know, the lever flew off! We scrambled like squirrels, some going over the top, some diving behind sandbags. But that chap, he just scooped up all the money and went on his way. He'd already taken the detonator out!

Yesterday we played a football game. The captain has a football named Corporal which he keeps under lock and key in his tent. Morale would plummet were it to go missing! The pitch was a serious drawback. I think it was a cabbage patch once. The weather on the whole has been good, so we didn't have to contend with rain or mud, and we only had to break the game once when the Germans lobbed a few shells our way. We waited till things quietened down, and got back at it. We got a good game in, and, more importantly, won. The captain was very pleased about that and has promoted the football to the rank of sergeant.

Leaves are coming onto the trees here, though No Man's Land is as forbidding as the news reels at the cinemas show, all brown mud and trees like black skeletons. It's best to look backward, where you can see fields turning green in the distance, and wildflowers pushing so bravely through the ground.

We were all happy to hear that the Americans are finally joining us in the war. It will be some months before they get over here, but it has boosted our morale no end. I believe it will turn the tide in our favour. Better late than never, I say.

I hope you and your sisters and parents are well, and that you are keeping safe from the zeppelins which I have heard are making quite a mess of the East End.

If you feel that you might be inclined to answer this letter, I would be very pleased indeed. If not, please know that I am very happy to have made your acquaintance.

Yours sincerely,
Frank (Jeffries)

P.S. I shall look forward in anticipation to reading your next article in the newspaper.

Celie sits at her desk and ponders the letter. It would be a simple thing to put it away and not respond, though this doesn't sit well with her. His letter is friendly enough, and he is putting himself in danger's way for Britain and the Allies over in France. It would very bad manners not to write a polite letter back, like she had when he had written her two years before from Gallipoli. And, really, he hadn't known about Max when he'd said the things he had about the Germans. Max would have forgiven him. He saw the good in everyone.

She opens a drawer and takes out a sheet of stationery and her fountain pen.

Clover Bar
Hither Green, London

June 2nd, 1917

Dear Frank,

Thank you for your letter. I am glad that you are well and that you are managing to keep yourself occupied with such intellectual pastimes. I haven't had the pleasure of learning Nap, although I am a dab hand at Whist, Hearts and Bridge, which I played regularly with my sisters and my parents growing up. While money didn't change hands, lollipops and wine gums most assuredly did.

I'm sorry I missed you when you stopped by the shop to collect your portrait. Papa said that you were very concerned that you had upset me. He said that he had assured you that that wasn't the case. I am sorry if I gave you that impression.

You were not to know that I have a German fiancé fighting on the other side. No one but my family knows. His name is Max Fischer. He taught me

German at University College before the war. I had hoped the War Office Translation Bureau might be interested in my German skills, but it appears they are put off by the fact that my name is Cecelia rather than Cecil.

Max proposed to me at Victoria Station the day he left for Germany. That was the last time I saw him. We can't exchange letters, so I have no idea if he is even still alive. I must simply live in hope.

Celie sits back in the chair. Why is she telling Frank all of this? She'd meant only to give him her good wishes. Is it because he might have seen and experienced what Max has? There is something about Frank, about his quiet-spoken politeness, his good humour and his very decency, that make her want to tell him everything.

You said you read my article about the munitionettes. Our maid, Milly Smith, is now a canary girl at Woolwich Arsenal – she's the one in the photograph in the TNT building. She was ever so helpful, introducing me to the other munitionettes and canary girls. She has invited me to lunch with her family in Poplar in a fortnight, and I'm very much looking forward to that, though Mama is quite concerned that I'm venturing so deep into the East End.

Something happened when I was in the factory which I haven't told anyone. I thought, what if one of these women is making the artillery shell or bullet that kills Max? What if they'd signed up as a munitions worker because of the 'Women's Right to Serve' demonstration I helped organise? I felt sick, Frank, and I had to keep on going like nothing had happened.

I am now writing pieces for the news pages as well as the women's pages, though I am still known as C. Fry. My editor says the management is not convinced news articles will be taken seriously if it is known that they are written by a woman. I beg to differ, of course, but have not yet succeeded in winning this ongoing battle. I used to be so shy; I wouldn't say boo to a goose. Jessie ribbed me about it all the time. It seems the war has brought out my inner Boudicca!

I shall finish off here. I shall remember you to my parents. You are most welcome to visit when you are back in London. Mama has learned to make scones, though (please don't ever tell her this) they are not a patch on Milly's.

Yours sincerely,
Cecelia Fry

Chapter Sixty-Two

Jessie

No. 15 General Hospital, Alexandria, Egypt – June 1917

Jessie knocks on the matron's office door. She smooths the white nurse's veil, wishing she'd had time to press it more thoroughly that morning.

'Come in.'

She enters the small room where Matron Miller sits in a stream of slatted sunlight behind a pile of papers and files at her desk. 'You wished to see me, Sister Fry?'

'Yes, Matron. Something has come up that I need to speak to you about.'

The matron gestures to a wooden chair in front of her desk. 'I can give you five minutes, then I have a meeting with Captain Khalid.'

'Yes. Of course.' Jessie sits down. 'Matron ...' She clears her throat. 'Matron, I'm the recipient of a marriage proposal which I have been very happy to accept.'

The matron's eyebrows shoot upward. 'I see.'

'I ... I felt you needed to know, as stipulated in my contract.'

'Quite right. You will be waiting to marry until after the war is over, I trust?'

'Uh, no, actually. We expect to marry in Cairo after Ramadan ends next month.'

The matron shifts in her chair, the sunlight turning her pale brown eyes a piercing amber. 'Frankly, Sister Fry, I'm surprised that a nurse of your abilities feels that leaving the nursing service in the middle of a war is appropriate.'

'I don't wish to leave, Matron. I have every intention of staying on, as does he.'

The matron rests her elbows on a pile of papers. 'Who is this impatient young man, if I may ask?'

'Captain Khalid.'

The matron's eyebrows shoot skywards. 'Captain Khalid? Whyever would you do something as rash as marrying an Egyptian? Do your parents know about this?'

'I've yet to write them, but I shall ... tonight. It happened when I was in Cairo last weekend. I wanted to speak to you first.'

'Good. It's not too late to reconsider, then, which I strongly suggest you do. Aside from some rather obvious challenges, I'm afraid you would have to tender your resignation as a Queen Alexandra's nurse. We do not have married women in our service.'

'I thought, considering, as you said, my nursing abilities and how busy we are with the malaria outbreak, that I might ... you might ... see fit to keep me on.'

'That's quite impossible, Sister Fry. I am not about to break well-established directives because of the impetuousness of a nurse.' She slides her fingers together and fixes Jessie with a golden stare. 'Sister Fry, I would caution you to consider this proposal very carefully as you will have to forfeit your nursing career should you accept it.'

She stands up abruptly, knocking her chair against the white wall. 'If you excuse me, that is all, Sister Fry. I must go see Captain Khalid, though it is now with some trepidation.'

———————

Jessie sits on the hospital's rooftop ledge and watches the activity of the city's population in the tangled alleyways below the hill. She'd truly thought that she'd be able to continue nursing after her marriage to Aziz, considering they were in the middle of a war and short of trained nurses. There's no question that Aziz will continue his work at the hospital after their marriage; why is it any different for her? She has the training, the experience and the aptitude for the work. *They're cutting off their nose to spite their face.*

She looks up at a pair of swifts sweeping through the sky, sliding and breaking and turning in graceful arcs as they hunt invisible insects. What she wouldn't give to be as free as one of those birds. To be able to fly wherever her heart leads, without worry or consequence.

She loves her work. She is good at it. She feels useful and challenged, despite the long hours and the shortages of supplies and the awful parade of wounded men that seems never-ending. How can she possibly leave it behind? Can she leave it behind?

'I thought I would find you here.'

Jessie looks over at Aziz's white-coated figure as he approaches across the concrete roof. 'I had some bad news from Matron.'

He leans over to kiss Jessie. 'I know. I have just been speaking to her.' He sits beside her on the ledge. 'I am so sorry for that, Jessica.'

'I thought they'd let me stay, but I've been given an ultimatum. You or the Queen Alexandra's.'

He squeezes her hand. 'Haven't you already made your decision?'

She looks at Aziz who is regarding her with eyes lit with love and concern. 'Yes, absolutely.'

'I love you, *habibti*. I shall do everything to make you happy.'

'My happiness is not your responsibility, Aziz. It's quite enough that you love me. The thing is, if I can't nurse, what am I going to do? I'm not one to stay at home and cook and sew. I couldn't bear that.'

He threads his fingers through hers. 'I shall not hold you back from anything you wish to do, *habibti*. I shall do whatever I can to help you. I never want you to think that you have made a mistake in marrying me.'

Jessie frowns. 'There's something else.'

'What is it?'

'You still haven't told me the answer to the riddle of the sphinx.'

He lets out a loud laugh and kisses her fingers. 'You simply must marry me to find it out.'

A movement in the sky catches her eye and she glances up at the pair of swifts, swooping in a graceful aerial ballet in the blue Egyptian sky. They are free and they are a pair. Why can't she and Aziz be just like them?

'Aziz, my darling. Let's get married as soon as we can.'

Chapter Sixty-Three

Celie

Poplar, East London – June 1917

Celie hops off the omnibus on Upper North Street, deep in the heart of London's working-class East End, in front of a school whose Victorian bricks, once the soft yellow of London clay, are covered with decades of black coal soot. In the small paved yard, enclosed by a wrought-iron fence, two teams of boys shout as they pile onto each other in a game of Pie Crust Coming, while the girls play Hopscotch or skip Double Dutch, and one of the teachers leads the infant class in a game of Ring Around the Rosie.

She stops to take a quick photograph of the laughing children for a 'London at War' article she's working on for Mr Grayson. Heading down the cobbled street, she then rounds the corner onto Grundy Street, where even the recently planted plane trees and bright summer sky do little to beautify the uninspiring terraces of brick two-up two-downs that crowd against the cobbled pedestrian pavements. Though the East End had been hit by several devastating zeppelin attacks in the past few years, Celie is relieved to see that Milly's neighbourhood is unscathed.

Two houses down from a shop with a large Woodbine Cigarettes sign over the door, she locates the Smiths' modest house. She checks her watch: twenty past eleven, half an hour early for Milly's lunch. She is in the middle of debating with herself whether to go for a meander down the road – though the prospect rather alarms her – when the door is flung open. For a moment Celie is taken aback by the gauntness and sharp angles of Milly's yellow-stained face and the thinness of her green hair, but she smiles quickly as she recovers herself.

'Milly! Hello! I'm terribly sorry, I'm awfully early. I wasn't sure how long it would take to get here from Hither Green, but it was quicker than I'd thought.'

'Don't worry, Celie. Come in. I saw you from the window.' Milly beckons Celie inside and shuts the door. 'We don't stand on formalities 'ere. Come meet me mum.' She yells down the small hallway. 'Mum! Celie Fry's 'ere!'

A small stout middle-aged woman wearing a stained blue apron over a floral dress appears in the narrow hallway, wiping her hands on a tea towel. She brushes a stand of greying brown hair out of her eyes, leaving a smudge of flour on her cheek.

'So pleased to 'ave you 'ere, Miss Fry,' she says, smiling widely. 'A real lady journalist in our own 'ouse. I see you brought your camera.'

'Very pleased to meet you, Mrs Smith. Please, it's just Celie.' Celie glances down at the Reflex camera. 'I thought I'd take some photographs around Poplar after lunch. People at work and just out and about. I'm writing an article about life in London.'

'Least it's not rainin'. Fank 'eaven for small mercies, I say.' Milly's mother flaps the tea towel toward the open door to the sitting room. ''Ave yourself a sit. 'Fraid it's not posh like what you're used to, though Milly sewed up some nice curtains from your mum's old ones. Too posh for the likes of us, I told 'er, but she wouldn't 'ear a word of it. Even 'ad some material left over for a slipcover for 'er pa's chair, though it 'asn't seen much use since 'e's been away in France. You know what it's like. I'll get us a cuppa. I just put the dumplings in the mutton stew. Shouldn't be too long. I told the little ones to 'urry 'ome from school as soon as the dinner bell rings, as we're 'avin' a guest. Joey 'as a present for you. 'E could barely contain 'imself this morning, 'e was that excited.'

Milly ushers Celie into the tiny front room. 'Have a seat in Pa's chair. It's the most comfortable.'

Celie sits in the chair and sets the camera and her handbag on the floral carpet. She looks around the room as she pulls off her gloves. Barely a surface of the green wallpaper with its diamond trellis pattern is left free of framed prints of country gardens and bucolic landscapes. Her mother's old blue chintz curtains have indeed been cut down and remade to fit the modest front window and slipcover the large Victorian armchair she's sitting in. She smiles at Milly, who has perched self-consciously on the edge of a small crimson velvet settee covered with lace antimacassars.

'Thank you very much for inviting me to lunch today, Milly. It's lovely to meet your mother and see where you live.'

'We're pleased to 'ave you, Celie.' Milly draws her thin face into a frown. 'It still feels odd to call you that. I always want to say "Miss Fry".'

'You'll simply have to get used to it. You have a lovely home.'

'Fank you. It's not a patch on yours, but it's comfortable. Better 'n the YMCA. I like coming 'ome when I can to spend time wif me mum and the little ones.'

'How old are they?'

'Alice is eight and Joey's six. They're as sweet as can be. Alice likes to try on my clothes and pretend she's a grand lady, and Joey can't get enough of marbles. I buy 'im a new one for 'is collection every month when I get my wages.'

'They're quite a lot younger than you.'

'I 'ad another brovver an' sister between us, but they passed o' measles when they was little. I 'ad it, too, but I made it through.'

'I'm sorry, Milly.'

Milly shrugs. 'It 'appens.'

Celie scans Milly's drawn face with patches like purple thumbprints under her eyes. 'How are you feeling, Milly? You said in your letter that you've been off on sick leave for the past month.'

Milly nods. 'I've 'ad to come 'ome as me wages were stopped and I couldn't afford the room at the YMCA. I keeled over in the cafeteria right into the cottage pie. I came over all dizzy and sick. Doctor said it was jaundice and signed me off. I'm not to go back until I feel better, though I can't keep anyfing down just yet but for dry toast an' tea.'

Beryl Smith enters the room carrying a tray of teacups and a plate of lumpy brown biscuits. She sets the tray down and passes Milly and Celie teacups full of milky tea. 'Milk an' two sugars. Everyone likes it that way, don't they?' She sits beside Milly and offers Celie the plate of biscuits. 'Try me carrot biscuits. Alice an' Joey love 'em. Barely a tablespoon of sugar which is a good fing. Sugar's as rare as gold these days. It's getting 'arder to find anyfing in the shops. You can't live on bread alone, I always say, though I suppose we may 'ave to till Milly gets back to work. Money doesn't grow on trees, does it?'

Celie bites down tentatively on a biscuit. She rolls the unusual ingredients around on her tongue. A wave of guilt floods over her. She never should have accepted Milly's invitation to lunch. They'd probably used up a week of food to host her visit today. She coughs as a sliver of raw carrot catches in her throat.

Milly reaches into the pocket of her dress and takes out a small glass marble. She holds it up so that Celie can see the swirls of vibrant blue and yellow. 'Joey gave this to me to keep until 'e got 'ome for dinner. It's 'is favourite. It's 'is surprise for you.'

Celie takes it between her fingers. 'It's so pretty, Milly, but I can't take his favourite marble, though it's awfully sweet of him.'

'Joey's a stubborn little man,' Beryl Smith says as she reaches for another carrot biscuit. ''E'll insist on it.'

'Then I shall act surprised and I shall treasure it always.'

A low buzz filters into the house through the open window, gradually growing louder until it rolls like thunder. The house rattles as something passes overhead.

Milly looks at Celie. 'What do you fink that is?'

Beryl Smith drops her biscuit onto the plate and hurries to the window. She pushes the sash window up and sticks her head outside. 'Oh, my word. They're aeroplanes. The sky's full of 'em. They must be our boys 'eaded off to France. Come look. It's a sight to see.'

Celie and Milly join her at the window. High above in the blue sky, fourteen biplanes soar over London's East End like giant stiff-winged birds. A small black dot falls from one aeroplane, then another, and another, growing larger as they drop like stones through the sky. An explosion rips up a nearby street, knocking several pictures off the sitting room walls.

'It's the Germans!' Milly gasps.

Celie pushes Milly and her mother away from the window and slams it shut. 'Quick, under the table.'

They duck under the small table as the thrum rumbles above them and explosions pound the surrounding streets. They hold each other's hands, scarcely daring to breathe, until the hum of the throbbing engines slowly fades into an ominous silence.

Beryl Smith sucks in her breath. 'The school.'

The three women hurry down the street as the neighbourhood women dash out of the houses. They round the corner onto Upper North Street. The dirty cobbles glitter with smashed glass and crushed bricks. The black railings that had fenced in the schoolyard where, not twenty minutes before, children had played beside the sturdy brick school, sprawl like twisted black skeletons across the road. Part of the school's roof and front wall have been blown away from the force of the bomb's explosion, leaving a gaping yawn through three floors of classrooms. Children's cries pierce the settling dust.

'Oh, my Lord.' The words escape Celie's mouth so quickly that she is shocked, not at the blasphemy, but at her callous disregard of the blasphemy.

'Joey! Alice! My babies!' Beryl Smith clutches at her daughter's arm. 'Where are my babies?'

Milly hugs her mother. 'I'll find them, Mum. Don't worry.'

The teacher Celie had seen earlier in the schoolyard emerges from the building coated in grey dust, an injured girl of no more than five years old in her arms. Another teacher staggers out into the debris strewn across the schoolyard, holding the hands of two tiny weeping children as she coughs. Celie unlatches the lid of her camera and holds it up to her eye.

Milly pulls at Celie's arm. 'What are you doing? We need to 'elp 'em.'

Celie stares into Milly's disbelieving eyes. She glances at the women swarming over the school's debris, screaming for their children. This is a news story. People need to know what's happened here. The paper will print this on the front page. With her name. She'll insist on it. It's what she's wanted since she started writing for the paper. All she needs to do is hold the camera up to her eye and click the shutter.

'Celie!'

She looks over at Beryl Smith, who is sitting amongst the dirt and glass on the kerb, her body wracked with sobs as she cries out her children's names.

She thrusts the camera into Milly's hands. 'Stay with your mother. You're too ill to go in there. I'll do whatever I can.'

Celie leans her head against the omnibus's window, not caring that she is crushing the brim of her summer hat, which is now soiled beyond repair along with her summer dress. She stares absently across the aisle at the panorama of shops and terraced houses that passes by the vehicle's dirty windows as it lumbers towards Hither Green.

The school's caretaker, Mr Batt, found Joey beside his son Alfie under the piles of splintered desks and masonry in the infant's classroom on the ground floor. Mrs Middleton, the schoolteacher from the schoolyard, found Alice on the second floor, in the remains of the girls' classroom, a slate with arithmetic subtractions still in her hands. The bomb had been dropped by one of the fourteen new Gotha GI.V bombers that attacked London that day, killing 162 people and injuring 432. Eighteen children, including Alice and Joseph Smith, died in the school, with another thirty-seven injured. Celie doesn't know the details yet. She will read about it on the front page of the *Daily Mirror* in the morning. Someone else's story; someone else's byline. No photographs.

She shifts in her seat. A hard lump presses into her thigh. She reaches into her pocket and takes out the small blue and yellow glass marble. She clutches it in her hand as the tears that she has been holding inside finally fall.

Chapter Sixty-Four

Jessie

Cairo, Egypt – July 1917

Jessie sneezes and blows into her handkerchief. 'Would you ask the driver to roll up the window please, Aziz?' Coughing, she rubs her streaming eyes. 'The dust is terrible today.'

'Of course, *habibti*, although I'm not sure it will do a great deal of good. The sand gets everywhere when the wind is up.' Aziz says something to the taxi driver, but the request doesn't go down well. Jessie sits back against the hot leather seat, batting at the dust sweeping in through the driver's window as the argument rumbles on.

'He says the window is broken. It only stays open.'

Jessie sniffs as she swallows down mucus. The thin silk crepe of her new white blouse sticks to the sweat in her armpits, and her white linen skirt is crumpled and damp. She pulls at the blouse and flaps the fine silk in the dusty air. Under her straw hat, tendrils of hair cling to her forehead like wet thread; she rubs at the beading sweat with her fingers, her cotton gloves long abandoned.

Aziz tugs his starched white handkerchief out of his breast pocket and hands it to Jessie. 'It is not long now. We are almost there.'

Aziz instructs the driver to pull up in front of a butcher's shop just off Cairo's bustling Qasr El Nil Street. Jessie climbs out of the taxi, and ducks to avoid a sheep carcass swinging from a hook.

'In here, Jessica.' Aziz points with a manila folder to a green metal door next to the butcher's shop. He is dressed, with considerable care, in a black suit and high-collared white shirt, and his grey silk tie is held in place by a tie pin inlayed with bright blue lapis lazuli.

'I thought we were going to the city hall.'

'I have been there already to get the documents in order.' He looks up at the shuttered windows on the first floor. 'The judge for the marriage licence is upstairs here while they renovate the city hall.'

Jessie follows Aziz through the green door and up the dim terrazzo stairwell, which deposits them into a large office on the first floor. The walls are a drab yellow, and the mottled grey and pink terrazzo floor is grimy with dirt. Two wooden desks face each other across the room. At the nearest desk, a male clerk in a white skullcap and a striped *jellabiya* questions an old man in a dusty brown cloak. Yellow leather *babouche* slippers poke out from beneath the old man's cloak; and, in his right hand, he holds the lead to a goat. The animal's yellow eyes regard Jessie and Aziz as they enter.

A man beckons from the larger desk at the far end of the room. He is wearing a starched white shirt with no tie and loose grey flannel trousers. A red *tarbouche* perches on his thick black hair and his heavy square face is embellished by a black moustache. The end of a cigar sticks out of his breast pocket. The man points to a pair of battered grey metal chairs in front of the desk and says something to Aziz in Arabic.

Aziz opens up the folder and hands over a sheaf of documents covered with seals and stamps.

The man peers at Jessie. *'Ingleezi?'*

'Uh, yes, I'm English.'

She watches the two men talk, the judge nodding frequently in her direction. She is conscious of the moisture collecting under her arms, and presses the handkerchief against her top lip to stifle a sneeze. On the wall behind the judge, the new sultan, Fuad I, looking earnest and regal in his gold-embroidered uniform, stares down from a large framed photograph.

'Jessica, the judge has asked what you require me to pay you.'

'Pay me? What for?'

'It is called the *mahr*. I must agree to pay you this as part of the marriage.'

A smile tugs at the corner of her mouth. 'I'm worth a few thousand pounds, don't you think?'

Aziz smiles. 'You are worth everything I own.'

'I don't want your money, Aziz. I just want us to be happy.'

'We shall be happy.' He turns back to the judge and their negotiations resume.

Jessie gazes down at the white linen skirt, crumpled like discarded paper. Her patent leather shoes, which she had polished for over an hour the previous night with vinegar and petroleum jelly to coax them to a high shine, are coated with a film of dirty yellow dust. Sweat trickles off the tip of her nose and drops onto her loose sleeve. The goat bleats, its hooves clicking on the hard floor.

The judge calls over to the clerk, who protests, thrusting his hand at the old man and the goat. The clerk yells at the old man, who begins to berate Aziz. The goat becomes agitated, rattling out a string of *beehhhs*.

The clerk approaches the judge's desk and lays down a handwritten document. The judge sets a pair of spectacles on his nose and scans the document. Nodding, he slides it across the desk to Aziz, who signs it. The judge stamps the document with a large ink stamp and slides it across to Jessie.

She stares at the looping Arabic script. Her father's name is there, misspelled in Roman letters – *GEARLD MATIN FRY* – above her own – *JESSCA MARGRITA FRY*. She wonders if she should point this out, but the goat chooses that moment to relieve itself on the floor, provoking a barrage of angry shouts from the judge and the clerk.

The judge shakes his head, the *tarbouche* teetering precariously, and hands Jessie his fountain pen. She glances at Aziz; there are fine lines across his forehead and threads of grey in the black hair at his temples which she has never noticed before. A jolt of love runs through her body. It won't be easy, she knows that, just as she knows she has been a coward for not writing to her family about the engagement. She had simply not wanted to deal with the flood of warnings she would have received. Once she is married, there is little they can do but accept it. It is her life to live, and she will live it the way she wishes. Whatever the future holds for her and Aziz, she will do everything she can to make a happy life with him here in Cairo.

She rests her hand on Aziz's and he rubs his thumb against hers. 'Are you all right, Jessica?'

'Yes, my love.'

She signs the document and pushes the paper across the desk to the judge. Behind her the goat bleats.

Jessie stands on the balcony of Aziz's bedroom and looks up at the moon, hanging like a golden orb in the glittering night sky. The hum of cicadas fills the warm air and the flap of the wings of some large bird stirs up the languid water of the river. Despite the heat, Jessie shivers and rubs her arms, the thin satin of her dressing gown smooth and cool under her fingers.

The reception his mother had put on for them in the villa's grand dining room had gone well, Layla Khalid the perfect hostess, slipping amongst the glamorous guests in their silks and diamonds and dress uniforms – none of whom Jessie knew but for Ivy and a few other nurses – with the practised charm of a woman confident of her status and beauty. Jessie was thankful for Zara, who, when Layla had secured Aziz as her escort for the evening, had stayed close by her side, making introductions and acting as her translator when Jessie had found herself smiling and nodding at yet another incomprehensible conversation.

There had been a moment, when she had caught Layla's heavily kohled eye, that she had been sure she had seen her mother-in-law smirk before she had clutched her son's arm and beckoned him closer to whisper into his ear. All evening, there had been something about Layla Khalid's cold smile and austere politeness that had wrong-footed Jessie. Like she was an intruder at Altumanina.

She hears Aziz enter the bedroom and move around the room behind her. After some minutes, she feels his hands brush against her arms.

'You are so beautiful out here in the moonlight, *habibti*. I am sorry it took me so long. I practically had to throw the last of Mama's guests out the door.'

Jessie turns into his embrace. 'You're here now, that's all that matters.' She looks up at his handsome face, with its shining dark eyes, thick black moustache and black hair carefully groomed and gleaming in the moonlight; and his smile, which, in the brief moments when it appeared, transformed the serious physician into a man without a care in the world.

'Hello, husband.'

'Hello, wife.' He bends to kiss her, but she moves her head away. 'What is it, Jessica?'

'You promised.'

'I promised?'

'The answer to the riddle of the sphinx. *What goes on fours in the morning, on twos in the afternoon and on threes at night?*'

He chuckles. 'Mankind, who crawls on all fours as a baby, walks on two feet as an adult, and uses a walking stick in old age.'

'Now, Aziz Khalid, my husband, you may kiss me.'

Chapter Sixty-Five

Christina and Gerald

Clover Bar, London – August 1917

Clover Bar
Hither Green, London

August 10th, 1917

Dear Jessica,

What is it I am expected to say upon receiving your letter today about your marriage to an Egyptian? I can only hope it hasn't come about owing to unfortunate circumstances. It is quite enough that we have had to deal with Etta's folly. If this is the case, we shall, of course, do what we can to support your decision to marry, although I can only believe that, had you stayed in London, you would never have found yourself in such a compromising position.

If your father and I are not to expect a grandchild in some months' time, I can only surmise that you have quite lost your senses, Jessica. Hadn't I warned you about the perils of nursing abroad with soldiers and doctors on the prowl for innocent young women such as yourself? You say your husband is a doctor, which would have been acceptable had he been an Englishman, but an Egyptian! Please tell me he is not a Mohammedan. Your father has told me they are permitted to have four wives! That is quite unimaginable. What have you got yourself into, Jessica? It is quite beyond belief.

My only hope is that the marriage may not stand up to legal scrutiny here in Britain. Please consider returning home at the earliest possibility, so that we can all put this unfortunate episode behind us. It would be best not to mention it at all upon your return, and move forward as if the marriage had never taken place. I have no doubt you would be welcomed back at King's College Hospital if you still wish to pursue a career in nursing until such time as you marry a proper English husband. I urge you to reconsider the consequences of your action with urgency before the situation is complicated by the arrival of a child.

Yours,
Mama

Clover Bar
Hither Green, London

August 10th, 1917

Dear Pet,

First, let me congratulate you and your new husband, Dr Khalid, on your marriage. I know he must be a very good man for you to have chosen him. He is a very fortunate man indeed.

No doubt you will hear a great deal from your mother about all the *reasons that this marriage is a mistake. I have no doubt at all that you've considered the difficulties you both will likely face, being that he is Egyptian and you are English, so I won't insult your intelligence by going over things that I'm sure you will have discussed at length.*

If I have one regret it is that you will be living so far away from us. I miss you, my dear. I hope you both will come home to visit us once this war is over. Your mother simply needs some time to digest the news. You and your husband are both part of the family and will always be welcome here at Clover Bar so long as I am still breathing.

Please extend my welcome to Aziz to the Fry family.

Your loving Papa

P.S. I shall go to Terroni's now to buy your mother some chocolate cannoli. I'm sure it will help.

Chapter Sixty-Six

Carlo

The Italian Front – October 1917

C arlo sits on a rock and rests his rifle against his legs. He glances around the quiet hills above the trenches, the sharp crags black against the charcoal sky. A veil of mist hangs in the cold air, though he is relieved the rain of the past week has finally abated. The Italian Front near Caporetto has been quiet for the past month, bar a few cursory skirmishes. He is relieved to be in this backwater. He will do his duty, of course, but he has no desire to be a war hero. All he wants is to get out alive.

He unfastens two of his jacket buttons and slips out an envelope. He slides out a drawing and smiles as he scrutinises the sketch of Etta and Adriana. His two golden-haired angels. How has he been so fortunate to be blessed with them in his life?

A figure emerges from the mist and Carlo grabs his rifle and springs to his feet, the sketch and envelope dropping into the mud. 'Stop! Who's there?' he shouts in Italian.

The soldier raises his rifle in the air over his head. 'Hold on, mate. I'm from the Warwickshires. Just doing my rounds.'

'Okay. Okay. No problem.'

The soldier lowers his arms and trudges through the thick mud. He offers his hand to Carlo. 'Sergeant John Jeffries, First Birmingham Pals, Royal Warwickshire Regiment. You speak English.'

Carlo grasps the soldier's hand. 'Yes. Corporal Carlo Marinetti. I have spent time in London. My wife is English.'

The Englishman shakes Carlo's hand. 'We're just down the road outside of Caporetto. Arrived a few days ago.' He bends down and picks up the drawing and the envelope. He glances at the sketch as he hands them to Carlo. 'Your family?'

'Yes. Etta and Adriana,' he says as he tucks them inside his jacket. He gestures to the large rock. 'Have a sit. It is quiet tonight.'

'Don't mind if I do. How long have you been on the Front?'

'I don't even remember anymore. One day blends into the next.'

'I know what you mean. My brother and I have been in France since the beginning of the show. He was injured at Ypres then sent off to Gallipoli after he recovered. Last I heard he was back in France. I haven't seen him since 1915.'

Carlo looks across at the soldier. He is young, not more than twenty-one or so, and his fair-skinned cheeks look barely able to nurture a beard. 'You have both been lucky.'

'Don't I know it. Frank's a few years older. Before the war he ran the London office of our father's auction business. I'm meant to go into the business once all this is over. Run the Nuneaton office.'

'Frank Jeffries? I think my wife's family knows him. She has mentioned the name.'

'Is that right? Small world, isn't it?' The words are barely out of his mouth when the hills explode with a volley of bursting canisters.

They leap to their feet as a dense yellow-green cloud descends over the valley.

'*Cazzo!*' Carlo shouts. 'It's gas! Put your mask on!'

But the English soldier is already on his feet and running into the mist.

––––––––––

Carlo staggers through the scrub alongside the road to Caporetto with the other Italian soldiers who have survived the night's bombardment. A grenade explodes a few feet to his right, throwing bodies into the air like dolls. He shuts his mind to the screams until they blend together with the rattle of gunfire and explosions into a mind-numbing din.

He gathers his breath and charges forward. If he can make it to Caporetto, he will survive. Only another kilometre or so. *Please God, let me live. Let me see Etta and Adriana again.*

A whistle blows across the valley. The road to Caporetto explodes as mines detonate, spewing shrapnel, mud and stones over the retreating Italians.

––––––––––

'Carlo! Carlo!'

The voice prods into Carlo's brain, stirring it back to sense. He breathes in a smell of chemical smoke and burning flesh. His eyes fly open as he gasps.

The young English soldier leans over him, tying a piece of cloth tightly around Carlo's arm. 'Don't worry. I have the stretcher bearers coming for you. You'll be fine.'

Carlo tries to raise his arm, but Jeffries holds it down. 'Best not, mate. Let the hospital take care of it.'

'You don't understand—'

The grey sky bounces above him as he is grasped under his arms and legs and levered onto a stretcher. Jeffries' face appears above him. 'You're in good hands, Corporal Marinetti. Maybe we can catch up in London when this is over.'

The young soldier watches as Carlo is hurried across the field to an ambulance. It is the last thing he ever sees.

Chapter Sixty-Seven

Gerald and Christina

Hither Green, London – October 1917

'Gerald! You startled me. What are you doing sitting there in the dark? I thought you'd gone to your study to read.' Christina walks over to the large four-poster bed and switches on the table lamp.

Gerald looks at his wife from the bed as she bustles around the room. The green leather diary presses against his thigh where he has tucked it beside him, out of Christina's sight. He had been holding her secret since he'd found her diary back in the spring, but it had been eating away at him like a suppurating wound.

At first, he had been angry; not at the circumstances of Celie's birth – how can one be angry at a young woman abandoned, with child, by a feckless man? – but at the years of Christina's deception. She had lied to him from the very first day of their meeting when she had told him of her non-existent dead Italian husband; then, again, on their wedding night, persuading him of the need to have Celie believe that he was her real father, which had been nothing but a ruse to conceal Celie's illegitimate birth.

He had vowed to himself that, once he'd found the woman he wished to spend his life with, he would be a faithful and diligent husband and father. He would give his wife every reason to trust him, and he, in turn, would trust her. Christina had broken that trust.

Christina appears from behind the Chinese screen in her sea-green satin dressing grown and sits down at her vanity table. She catches him watching her in the mirror. 'Gerald? Whatever are you doing? You look like a cat about to pounce on a mouse.'

He rises from the bed and sets the diary down on her vanity table.

She stares at the book. 'Gerald… I … I…'

'You should have told me, Tina. You should have trusted me.'

Christina swallows down the lump that has formed in her throat. 'I was afraid to, Gerald. I was afraid you would treat me with revulsion. I felt so ashamed of myself, and so worried about Cecelia. I thought my life was over when I came back to London.'

'Then you met me and you thought, here's a nice young man who can solve all my problems, just so long as he never finds out the truth. You never loved me, did you, Tina?'

Christina looks at Gerald's hurt expression, at his eyes veiled with sadness and disappointment, and she feels a jab of conscience. It's true; that is exactly what she had thought. Gerald had been a convenient solution to what she had believed was an unsolvable problem. But then she'd grown fond of him, and he has made her as happy as she could have expected under the circumstances.

The girl who had stepped off the ferry onto Capri with so much excitement and anticipation that long-ago spring day was gone forever, killed the day Harry left her. She'd had to protect herself and her baby any way she could. To do that, she'd had to lock the naïve young Christina Bishop away forever, and become the steely, competent matriarch of the Fry family.

She hadn't expected to love Gerald, but as she watches him shake his head and walk toward the door, she realises that in their long, companionable years together she has come to love him more than she'd ever loved Harry.

'Gerald? Where are you going? It wasn't like that. Please, believe me.'

Gerald rests his hand on the doorknob. 'I'm going to the studio, Tina. I need some time to myself. We can discuss it in the morning.'

Captain Lieutenant Waldemar Kölle holds the binoculars up to a window in the zeppelin's front gondola. The gigantic L 45 airship ploughs southeastward above the thick night cloud, buffeted by a pugilistic gale whipping down from Scotland. A thick mist hangs heavily in the night sky, making it impossible to identify any landmarks far below. They had already missed their target city of Sheffield, dropping half their payload over a city further south, which may have been Northampton, or perhaps Coventry, according to the map. The wireless connection to the zeppelin base in the Danish town of Tønder had been lost early in the flight, and he was flying blind, knowing only, according to the airship's compass, that they were being forced south by the gale.

He sets the binoculars down and removes his leather gloves to pull his watch from the pocket of his woollen greatcoat. The brass watch is like ice, though his hands are only marginally warmer. He blows on them for a moment, then looks at the time: 11:22. They have been 20,000 feet in the air for over seven hours, and the gondola stinks of vomit from the air sickness overtaking the freezing crew.

'Captain Lieutenant!'

Kölle looks over at his navigator. The airman is swaddled in a greatcoat and a fur-lined flight cap with long flaps covering his ears, and he points at the window. 'What is it, Lieutenant?'

'Searchlights. There must be twenty of them. I am sure we're over London.'

The commanding officer picks up the binoculars and surveys the misty night sky. 'See if you can reach the base on the wireless for confirmation.'

'Yes, sir.'

The commander peers through the binoculars. The low clouds are cutting off the yellow beams of the searchlights, and even if the zeppelin is spotted, it is well out of range of the anti-aircraft guns. 'Any luck, Lieutenant?'

'No, sir. Still no connection.'

'We can't wait. The storm is pushing us too quickly. We shall unload the remaining bombs and steer east to France. Cut the engines so they don't hear us coming.'

Lieutenant Maximilian Fischer glances out the window at the beams of the searchlights. Celie is down there somewhere. Celie and her family. 'But ... we don't have clearance to bomb London, sir. Perhaps we should head back to Denmark and await further instructions. We ... we can't afford to lose another zeppelin.'

Kölle turns his back on the young lieutenant. 'I said cut the engines, Lieutenant. We are at war and everyone below us is a target. Cut the engines immediately. We shall drop the bombs.'

Gerald finishes sticking a photograph of Christina and Celie into his father's portfolio. He sits back in his desk chair and rubs his eyes under his spectacles.

It is best that it is out in the open, though he knows he would have been happier not to know about Christina's lies. The truth is not always kind, but a life built on a foundation of lies is like a house built on sand. At some point it is bound to collapse. Better to expose the weaknesses and then work to repair and rebuild. Which, of course, he fully intends to do.

He brushes his finger along the lines of his wife's cheek in the photograph. He is not Harry Grenville, Lord Sherbrooke. He is a better man. He will never abandon Christina nor any of his daughters. Perhaps Christina is right about keeping Celie's identity a secret from her. What good would that truth possibly do her? It would only cause Celie pain, and he can't bear the thought of that.

And, of course, there's the fact he loves Christina. He loves her with all of his heart. For better or for worse.

He picks up his pen. He will finish this and go home. In the morning, they will talk. It will be all right. He bends over the photograph and writes: *Christina and Celie, Hither Green, Lond—*

Celie jolts awake, the crash reverberating in her ears. She sits up in her bed and stares into the black room.

'Cecelia!'

Celie jumps out of bed. 'I'm coming, Mama!' She flings her bedroom door open to see her mother standing in the hallway holding a gas lamp. The pale light throws shadows over Christina's face. 'Did you hear that? It shook the house. The electricity is off.'

'Where's Papa?'

'He's at the studio. He hasn't come home yet and it's past midnight.'

'I'll go. I'm sure he's fine. He's probably on his way home now.'

'I'm coming with you.'

'No, Mama.'

'He's my husband, Cecelia. I'm coming with you.'

Two policemen are already there. The bomb has blasted through the ceiling windows and blown out the shop front. The Marion & Co. mahogany camera, Gerald's pride and joy, lies splintered almost beyond recognition on the pavement. A policeman grabs Celie's arm as she crunches over the glass and smoking rubble.

'No, miss. I wouldn't go in there.'

Christina steps forward. 'My husband is in there. He was working late—'

The second policeman, a sturdy man of about Gerald's age, looks over at Christina. 'Your husband?'

'Yes, Gerald Fry. This is his photography studio.'

'Just a moment.' The policeman staggers over the smouldering rubble and disappears into the smoking ruins of the studio.

The other policeman shakes his head. 'It's best you don't go in, Mrs Fry. I'm afraid there doesn't look to be any survivors. I'm … I'm very sorry.'

His colleague emerges from the rubble. There is something in his arms. He holds it out to Christina. 'I found this with … with your husband.'

Christina stares at the red cardboard portfolio. The front cover hangs off and the ribbon trails over the policeman's hands. 'I don't want it.'

Celie takes it from the policeman. 'Mama?'

Christina stands amidst the devastation of Gerald's photography studio, pressing her lips together until the sobs which threaten to erupt are squashed under the force of her will.

Chapter Sixty-Eight

Christina

Hither Green Cemetery, London – October 1917

The vicar's voice rumbles low and deep at the edges of Christina's thoughts. 'For as much as it hath pleased Almighty God of his great mercy to take unto himself the soul of our dear brother here departed...'

The lowering grey sky, heavy with cloud, rolls like a beaten drum over the heads of the mourners. A cold raindrop splashes onto Christina's cheek. She moves her black-gloved hand to wipe it away, then thinks better of it. They will think it is a tear, that the grief she has held inside of herself since Gerald's death is finally finding a welcome release.

'...earth to earth, ashes to ashes, dust to dust; in sure and certain hope of the Resurrection to eternal life...'

She had thought, at first, once the shock had subsided, that mourning would rise to the surface; that one night she would awaken from her fitful dreams and find herself suddenly overcome by tears and violent grief. But the days and nights had continued their relentless ebbing and flowing, with all the funeral arrangements to be made, the memorial reception at the house to organise, the stream of well-wishers to welcome and thank. She had been glad of the busyness, and of Cecelia's calm efficiency, though she had heard her daughter's soft weeping through her bedroom door, and found herself wishing she could open the door and offer her comfort.

Whether it had been from an ingrained reserve and respect for the private emotions of others, or a coldness within herself that had iced over her heart in the years after Harry's abandonment, she hadn't.

'Mama?'

Christina looks at Celie, who stands beside her, pale in her black hat and coat, her face glistening with tears. 'Yes?'

'The flowers, Mama. It's time.'

Christina looks down at the cluster of vibrant dahlias and purple asters they have collected from the garden.

Such loud, strident colours.

She wonders at the wisdom of their selection for such a solemn occasion; but these had been Gerald's favourites, and she feels he would be happy with the choice.

She steps to the grave's edge and drops the bouquet onto the wooden casket. She looks down at the plain oak coffin with its spray of red and orange and yellow and purple flowers, flowers that Gerald would never see again, and the reality of his death finally takes hold.

Hot tears well up in her eyes and a sob slides through her clenched lips.

She feels a hand on her elbow and turns to see Celie looking at her with concern.

'Mama?'

Her shoulders shake and the tears finally erupt. 'I loved him, Cecelia. I loved him so very much, and I never told him.'

Part Six

1918

Chapter Sixty-Nine

Christina

Lewisham, London – January 1918

C hristina steps off the tram in front of the imposing Victorian red brick edifice of the Lewisham Registry Office. The last time she had mounted these steps had been in October to register Gerald's death and collect his death certificate, which now lay, neatly folded, with their marriage certificate, inside the Fry family bible.

She had always imagined that she and Gerald would live out a long life in the comfort of Clover Bar until their years on this earth finally came to a gentle, inevitable close. Instead, their life together had ended on an ordinary day; she hadn't even looked up when he had kissed her cheek at the breakfast table that morning on his way out to the studio. She brushes her cheek with the soft kid of her glove; she can almost feel the prickles of his moustache on her skin. And then for it to end with that horrible argument.

If only he hadn't found the diary. If only she had said she loved him.

She straightens her shoulders. Today is not about Gerald. For quite some time, she has had a problem whose answer had eluded her. The circumstances of Gerald's death have finally provided her with the solution. She strides across the pavement and up the concrete steps to the Registry Office.

'Will that be all, Mrs Fry?'

Christina reads through the document. 'Thank you very much, Mr Eddison. You can imagine that the past few months since my husband's death have been very distressing. The fact that my daughter's birth certificate had been lost in the bombing seems a minor thing, but I felt it was important to obtain a replacement as soon as possible. Her father would have wished that.'

The young clerk nods his head in sympathy. He pushes his spectacles up his nose. 'Of course. I simply found it odd that I couldn't locate a copy in the files; but, then, it was over twenty years ago. It's likely been misfiled somewhere. We're so much more efficient now.'

'I understand. I appreciate your taking the matter in hand, Mr Eddison. You will make a very decisive supervisor one day.'

The young man's colour rises in his cheeks. 'Thank you very much, Mrs Fry. I'm very happy I could be of service.'

When she is sitting on the tram, Christina takes out the document and scans the clerk's precise black handwriting.

When and Where Born: Third May 1893, The Firs, Hither Green
Name: Cecelia Sirena Maria Fry
Sex: Girl
Name and Surname of Father: Gerald Martin Fry

Name, Surname and Maiden Name of Mother: Christina Maria
Innocenti Fry, formerly Bishop
Occupation of Father: Photographer
Signature, Description and Residence of Informant: Christina Fry,
Mother, Clover Bar, Hither Green Lane, Hither Green
When Registered: Ninth January 1918
Signature of Registrar: A.H. Eddison

She folds the birth certificate and puts it back in her handbag. It's done. As far as anyone will ever know, Gerald was Cecelia's father. Her cousin Stefania, Liliana Sabbatini, Harry Grenville and her Aunt Henrietta are the only other people still alive who know the truth about Cecelia's birth, and none of them will ever reveal it, of that she is certain.

One thing still niggles her. Cecelia must have wondered about her birth date only six months after her parents' marriage, though she has never said anything. Christina runs her hand over her ear. There can only be one answer. If her own morals must be called into question, so be it. She practises the answer in her head. *Your father and I were young, Cecelia. We were ... impatient. You understand what I'm saying, Cecelia? You were conceived before the wedding. I am not proud of it. You will understand if I don't wish to discuss it any further...*

Yes. That will do. She has finally wiped her past clean.

Chapter Seventy

Celie

Clover Bar, London – February 1918

Clover Bar
Hither Green, London

February 6th, 1918

Dearest, Darling Max,

It has happened! Parliament has passed the Representation of the
People Act. Women have been given the vote! Not all women, not yet, only
women over thirty who live in a house, but it's a start. They have given the
vote to all men over the age of 21 as well, no matter whether they own
property or not. The Government simply couldn't justify denying us all the
vote after our contributions in this war.

There is still much to be done, Max, to push for universal suffrage for
all adult women. So many young women have given so much of themselves

nursing, working in the munitions factories, farming, and keeping the country running all these years. I shall be meeting with Mrs Fawcett next week about our next steps, but I had to share this with you as soon as I heard it!

You are in my thoughts day and night, Max. Come back to me as soon as you can.

Your schatzi

C elie blots the letter on her desk blotter and folds it carefully. She opens her desk drawer and adds it to the other letters. She shuts the drawer and picks up Max's brass button from a glass dish on her desk. *Gott Mit Uns.* God is with us.

I hope so, Max. I hope so.

Chapter Seventy-One

Max

Northern Russia – March 1918

Max falls into a snowbank and throws his arm over his eyes against the glare of the midday sun. His body sinks into the melting snow, and for a moment he imagines himself back in his boyhood bed, safe from the horrors that even he, with a boy's vivid imagination, could not have conjured up, but which he now, after the long years of the war, has come to accept with exhausted resignation. The life he had once known as a student in Heidelberg and teaching in London seems like a long-lost dream. The only thing that keeps him alive is Celie.

When he thinks of her now, she is a flash of auburn hair, a quick smile and eyes the colour of the Russian winter sky. And the scent of lilacs. Always the scent of lilacs. She comes to him in his dreams, but slides away before he can touch her. *Were you a dream, too, Celie?*

Someone flops into the snow beside him and pokes him in his

shoulder. Max turns his head toward the broad, flat-cheeked face of the German soldier. 'What, Lukas? The break is over already?'

The soldier holds out a burning rolled-up cigarette. 'I got it from the guard.'

Max sits up and takes the cigarette. 'Sasha?'

'Yeah. I had to trade my wedding ring for it. Burns like shit, but beggars can't be choosers, right?'

Max takes a long draught of the cigarette and exhales a stream of blue smoke. He hands the cigarette back and looks over at the other POWs hammering in the new railway line. 'Rumour has it the Bolsheviks want out of the war.'

Lukas sucks at the cigarette and blows out a smoke ring. 'They've got the czar and his family under house arrest; did you hear that?'

'Yah. Not good.' Max stretches his arms and pats the snow off the sleeves of his army coat. 'Snow's melting. Spring is coming.'

'Like it makes a difference to us.'

Max looks across the snowy landscape. 'It's only two hundred kilometres to the Finnish border. The worst of the winter is over. All we need is a chance, Lukas.'

Lukas sinks the cigarette stub into the snow. 'Like that will ever happen.'

A roar erupts further down the rail line which ripples through the Russian guards like a surging wave. Max and Lukas rise from the snowbank and watch as the guards run at each other, shouting and embracing.

'You're good at languages, Max. What are they shouting?'

'Peace. Land. Bread.'

'Peace, land, bread? That's it?'

'No, there's something else.' He looks at the German. 'Russia has left the war. We're free, Lukas.'

Lukas whoops and throws his arms around Max. 'We're free, Max! We're free! Finally, this shitty war is finished!'

'It's only finished in Russia. We'll be shipped back to France to fight the Americans.'

Lukas spits into the snow. 'Shit.'

Max turns to the soldier and slaps him on his back. He slaps the German on his arm. 'Good luck, Lukas. It's been good to know you.' He turns and heads through the snow toward the western horizon.

'Max! Where are you going?'

'Home. I'm going home.'

Chapter Seventy-Two

Celie

Clover Bar, London – March 1918

Christina sifts through the post as she enters the dining room. She pulls out a letter, dirty and torn around the edges, its black ink smudged. 'Another letter from Frank Jeffries, Cecelia. It appears you have an admirer.'

Celie scrapes a thin layer of butter onto a slice of the dense brown war loaf with studied disinterest. She gouges out a sliver of potato skin from the cold toast with the knife. 'I have a fiancé, Mama. I'm simply corresponding to keep Frank's spirits up.'

'You won't mind, then, if I open it and read it out?'

Celie reaches across the table and plucks the letter from her mother's hand. 'I would rather you didn't, if you don't mind. If you excuse me, I have an article to write.'

56th (London) Infantry Division
Near Arras, France

March 19th, 1918

Dear Celie,

Thank you for your recent letter and all your news from London. You must be over the moon about women over thirty obtaining the vote after all your hard work. I am so pleased about that. And thank you for the socks! My feet thank you enormously. We (soldiers, not feet) have been stuck in these trenches for the past six weeks now, wedged together like sardines. There's nothing but a string of barbed wire between us and the Germans, but at least we know those fellows are as tired as we are, though they're being joined by reinforcements from the Eastern Front now that Russia is out of the war. It's all mud and cold and fog, and everything is dull grey and brown, as if the war has leached all the colour out of the world. The battlefields of the Somme are nearby, and we can't help but feel dread weighing down on us. But now I'm the proud wearer of green socks, and I am the envy of the fellows here. You have no idea how a small thing like that makes such a great difference.

The Germans are up to something, we can all feel it. They're sure to be nervous about the Americans joining up with us. I've met a few of these so-called Doughboys already. Big fellows all brash and full of bravado with names like Karpenko and O'Gallagher. Hopeless at cards, except for Poker which they're all mad for. I've heard a black unit from Harlem in New York has just arrived down the line and is being trained by the French Army, though I haven't seen any of them yet. Over 300,000 more Doughboys are coming over next month. Not a moment too soon, if you ask me.

Celie, I've had some bad news. My brother John has died from the wounds he suffered in Italy in the autumn. He was in a hospital in Vicenza. I received a letter from my father yesterday. John was only twenty-one. I remember climbing the neighbour's apple tree with John when we were boys, egging each other on to see who could find the fattest, juiciest apple without being seen by old Mr Frampton. Somehow, John always managed it. He was like a squirrel.

Your poor father, and now my brother. When will this all stop? This war is an abomination.

I'm so sorry. I'm cold and everything is damp and I can't even imagine what it feels like to be warm and dry anymore. We are all tired and fed up. We know there is fighting ahead and it's nothing but luck which will see who makes it to the end. I don't know what my destiny is.

Whatever happens, I want you to know that your letters have sustained me through this last long year. I shall do everything I can to be one of the fellows who makes it out of here, so that I can see you again in London and thank you with all my heart.

Yours affectionately,
Frank

Celie blinks at the last sentence. What does he mean by *'thank you with all my heart'*? He knows she has a fiancé. She mustn't read too much into it. He's simply grateful, as any poor soldier at the Front would be for some kind letters and warm socks.

She picks up the framed photograph of Max that she'd taken of him at her birthday party. Sadness and yearning rise inside her, and she blinks away the tears that spring into her eyes.

You'd understand me writing to Frank, wouldn't you, Max? When I write him, it's like I'm writing to you. Both of you, out there, fighting this awful, endless war. Come back to me, Max. Please, just come back to me.

Chapter Seventy-Three

Jessie

Cairo, Egypt – April 1918

'Jessie! What are ya doin' here?' Ivy Roach nods at the covered bedpan she is carrying. 'Ya can't be missin' this, even if the hospital is in a palace.'

Jessie hovers in the doorway of the former palace's ballroom on Citadel hill – now, despite its soaring ceiling and painted rococo panels and pilasters, a vast ward in Cairo's Citadel Hospital. She looks past Ivy at the beds of soldiers and the bustling orderlies and nurses. 'I actually do miss all this, Ivy. Can you spare a few minutes?'

'Sure. It's time for my break, anyway. Let me get rid of this. I'll meet ya outside by the fountain. It's my favourite place. An oasis of calm.' She chuckles. 'That's clevva, isn't it? An oasis in Egypt. I've gotta remember that one.'

Jessie sits on the fountain's wide marble base and smiles at Ivy as she pats the head of one of the four diminutive stone lions that spout water into the pool. 'I can see why you like it here.'

'Ya'd think more people would come out here. Usually it's just me and the boys.' She nods at the lions. 'Fred, Stanley, Howard and Walter.'

'They're not very fierce names.'

'They're not very fierce lions.'

Jessie laughs. 'You're right about that.'

Ivy takes a pear out of her pocket. 'Ya don't mind if I eat this, do ya? I'm famished. Didn't have time for lunch.'

'Go ahead. You should peel it first.'

'I like to live dangerously.' Ivy takes a bite of the juicy pear. 'So, what brings ya to my neck of the woods?' She scrutinises the palace's colonnade with its graceful Romanesque arches. 'Gotta say, it's a sight betta than the hospital in Alexandria.'

Jessie trails her hand in the cool water. 'I'm at a loose end, Ivy. There's only so much gardening and cooking lessons and bandage rolling I can take. Don't get me started on the British black satin and pearls set at the Gezira Sporting Club.'

'So, you're slummin' it here with me 'cause ya've had enough of those spoiled bitches.'

'Ivy!'

Ivy shrugs. 'It's true, isn't it?'

'You have a crystal chandelier the size of a Christmas tree in your ward. I wouldn't call this slumming it.'

'Suppose not.' Ivy licks the sticky pear juice off her thumb. 'So, what's up?'

'Oh, Ivy, Aziz is so busy with his new position at the Anglo-American Hospital, I'm lucky if I'm still awake when he gets home at night.'

'Sounds like the perfect marriage ta me.'

'Ivy, I'm bored.'

'What are ya gonna do about it?'

'I want to feel useful. It's one of the reasons I liked nursing. I hated having to give it up when I married. Living in Cairo isn't what I imagined.'

Ivy tosses the pear core into a clump of blue plumbago. 'So, ya wanna feel useful?'

'Yes, I do.' Jessie wipes at the film of sweat collecting on her forehead under the brim of her straw hat.

'Spit it out, Jessie. I can see somethin' percolatin' in that head of yours.'

'The house is so big. We have four reception rooms, Ivy. Who needs four reception rooms? So, I've been thinking… What if I were to open a health clinic in one of the reception rooms?'

'Don't all those posh expats go to the Anglo-American Hospital?'

'Not for the expats, Ivy. For Egyptians. The hospitals are bursting with soldiers. I have no idea where the locals go when they're sick. I don't mean the rich, of course. They can pay for whatever they need. I mean everyone else.'

'Sounds like a good idea ta me. You can patch people up pretty well, and you worked in obstetrics and paediatrics in London, didn't ya? That'll come in handy.'

'The thing is, I'm British and I don't speak Arabic. Do you suppose anyone would come?'

'Maybe get your sister-in-law to be your translator, and help spread the word. I'm happy to do whatever I can on my days off. I've sworn off blokes for the time being. You wanna know something I've discovered?'

'What's that?'

'They're all just after one thing, and it's not a weddin' ring.'

'Don't tell me: Archie Winter?'

'Too right.'

Jessie looks at the four stone lions, at their gaping mouths spewing water. The clinic's a mad idea, of course. She'll need Aziz's help, but he's sure to support her if he thinks it will make her happy. And Zara ... yes, that's a good idea. Zara would be a perfect administrator. What Layla Khalid will think of her British daughter-in-law turning one of the villa's grand reception rooms into a walk-in clinic for Cairo's underclass is another matter entirely.

Chapter Seventy-Four

Jessie

Altumanina, Cairo, Egypt – April 1918

'Aziz. A word, please.'

'Yes, Mama. What is it?'

She nods towards the library. 'In here.'

Aziz follows her through the double doors. His mother stands in front of the bow window in her black silk clothing, as elegant as a black swan.

'Yes? What is it, Mama? I am late. I am sure Jessica is wondering where I am.'

'I wouldn't worry about her. She has been out at the Sporting Club all day with her kind. Why you saw fit to marry an Englishwoman...' She spits out the word like a sour pill. 'Your poor father would spin in his grave.'

Aziz's jaw clenches. 'You are speaking about my wife. Do not disrespect her. If you are unhappy about this living arrangement, I have no doubt one of your Turkish or Albanian relatives will be happy to have you. Don't pretend you love Egyptians. You have not one drop of Egyptian blood in your body. You were only too happy to make that point with my Egyptian father. He was only with the Khedive in Constantinople on that fool's errand to curry favour with the Turks to please you. If it hadn't been for your greed—'

'I have no idea what you're talking about.'

'I am not a fool, Mama. I saw how you harried my father until he gave in to your greed for status and wealth.' Aziz sweeps his hand around the room with its gleaming mahogany bookcases and leather-topped reading table. 'He gave you everything you ever wanted.'

'Don't be a hypocrite, Aziz. I don't see you living in a shack in the Muqattam Hills ministering to the poor.'

'I am quite busy enough ministering to the war wounded currently, if you haven't noticed.'

'For the British!' Layla spits out the words like poison darts. 'I shall never forgive them for deposing my uncle Abbas after your father's death. I have had to work very hard to regain everything my family lost after that. I shall not have that Englishwoman undo all my work.'

'Jessica has no interest in your intrigues. It is one of the many reasons I love her. She is an honest woman. It is no surprise to me that you dislike her. She is nothing like you.'

Layla Khalid waves her jewelled hand dismissively in the air. 'I don't wish to speak about this. There's something more pressing I wish to discuss. It has to do with your wife.'

'What are you talking about?'

'I overheard her speaking to Zara this afternoon about a project she wishes to undertake here at Altumanina.'

'What is wrong with that? It's her home.'

'She is proposing a health clinic for Cairo's poor and unwashed, here, in one of our reception rooms.'

'I'm sure you misunderstood.'

'I did not misunderstand anything. She said it was a shame that so much of the house sits empty when there are people raising families in nothing more than shacks in the city. Wherever has she been, Aziz? You should keep a closer eye on her.'

Aziz expels an exhausted breath. 'I'll speak to her.'

'I should hope so. The executive council of the Anglo-American Hospital would not look kindly on such a venture on their doorstep. I have no doubt they would be pleased to find an excuse to retire the one Egyptian who has slipped onto their staff.'

A nerve in Aziz's face twitches. 'I said I shall speak to her.'

Jessie hears the tread of footsteps in the hallway outside the old nursery, now transformed into her study, which is tucked under the eaves on the second floor of the mansion. She turns in her desk chair just as the door bursts open.

'Jessica, there you are. I have been looking all over for you.'

She shuts her notebook. 'Aziz? What is it?'

Aziz sits in the leather armchair beside the desk. 'I have just been speaking to my mother. What is this I hear about you opening a health clinic in the house?'

'How did she know about that?'

'She overheard you speaking to Zara. Were you going to tell me about this grand plan?'

'Of course I was, Aziz. It's just a thought at the moment. The truth is I'm bored witless. I'm used to being so busy. I've never been one for tea parties and gossip with the expat crowd.'

'I understand, but, Jessica, a health clinic in Altumanina?'

'I had a horrid time with the women at the Sporting Club today so I went to see Ivy at the Citadel. She thought it was a great idea. She suggested I get Zara involved to help with translation and administration. Ivy said she'd help, too, when she could. I thought we could encourage the local population to come. I'd be useful again. I *need* to be useful, Aziz.'

Aziz rises from the chair and walks over to a dormer window. He stares out the window for a long moment.

'Aziz?'

'I am sorry, Jessica. I have left you on your own too much, I can see that.' He smiles at her ruefully. 'I have not been a very attentive husband, but it has been so busy at the hospital. There is no end to the wounded coming in.'

'I know. I remember what it's like.'

He sits in the chair and takes hold of her hands. 'I promise to make it up to you, *habibti*. Why don't we arrange a trip down to Luxor? We can visit the Temple of Karnak and the Valley of the Kings. You can bring your camera and take photographs to send to your family, and tell them all about your Egyptian adventures.'

'What about your work?'

'I have leave accumulated. It can be our proper honeymoon.'

Jessie throws her arms around Aziz's neck and kisses him. 'That would be wonderful, Aziz!'

He looks around the modest room. 'I remember growing up here with Zara when we were small children.' He rubs his cheek against hers. 'Maybe it won't be too long before it will be a nursery again.'

'What about the health clinic, Aziz?'

'Why don't you set that idea aside until after our honeymoon, *habibti*? I shall buy you Baedeker's *Guide to Egypt* and you can plan our grand tour. I'll hire a felucca and we shall sail down the Nile like Cleopatra and Antony.' He glances at his watch. 'I must go. I have a meeting at the hospital.' He gives her a quick kiss. 'Don't hold dinner for me. I shall find something in the kitchen when I am back.'

Jessie listens until Aziz's footsteps fade into Altumanina's early evening silence. She sits down and flips open the notebook. She picks up her pen, and adds to her 'To Do' list: *Find room in the city for clinic ASAP.*

Chapter Seventy-Five

Celie

Clover Bar, London – May 1918

Celie leans back on her heels and brushes a strand of hair out of her eyes. She sets down the garden trowel and raises her face to the warm spring sun. Closing her eyes, she listens to the birds twittering amongst the fading white flowers of the rowan tree. Behind her the kitchen door slams and she hears steps on the gravel path.

'It's a lovely day, isn't it, Celie Fry?'

'Frank?' She springs to her feet and slaps at the dirt on her blue skirt. 'How lovely to see you! What are you doing here?'

'I have a few days' leave. I'm going up to Nuneaton on the train later to see my parents, but I wanted to stop by here first.'

'I'm delighted, but look at the state of me!'

'You're a sight for sore eyes, Celie.'

'Thank you, Frank.' Her heart thumps in her chest, and

every intelligent thought flies out of her mind. 'I've been sowing seeds in our vegetable patch. Cabbage, cauliflower, runner beans and sprouts. It's the only way to guarantee having them, what with the rationing and shortages. I've had to dig up the hydrangeas to make more room, but needs must. I'm thinking of writing an article about it for the *Mirror*. I'm trying to convince Mama of having chickens, but, well, you can imagine. She says we're not a farm and that I'd want goats next.' She glances towards the kitchen, conscious she is rambling. 'Would you like some tea? I'll ask Hettie to put some on, shall I?'

'She's ahead of you. She said there was some trench cake in the pantry, too.'

'She and Mama made several cakes to send to the boys at the Front. She must have kept one back for us.' Celie gestures to the garden bench under the cherry tree. 'Shall we have a seat? It's too nice to go inside today.'

'Yes, that sounds good.'

She perches on the bench and tucks her skirt under her knees. Frank sits beside her and sets his army cap on his knees. 'I was so sorry to hear about your father, Celie. It seems none of us is safe in this war.'

'Thank you, Frank. It was awful. Poor Mama. She was in pieces after the funeral. I'd never seen her like that before. She's always been so stoic. There were times growing up when I wondered if she had any feelings at all. Especially for me.'

'I'm sure that's not true.'

'Well, perhaps not.'

'Forgive me for asking, Celie, but are you … are you managing all right? Your father provided for you? Because, if he hasn't—'

'Oh, Frank! No, we're fine, really. Mama had her inheritance from Grandpapa which Papa had invested wisely, it seems, along with some savings.' She wipes at the dirt drying in splotches on her hands. 'Frank, I'm sorry about your brother. So many young men… Will there ever be an end to it?'

Frank runs his fingers along the peak of his army cap. 'It was a terrible shock for all of us. John was a wonderful fellow. We were meant to run the business together once the war was over. He was engaged to be married. A lovely girl he'd met at school. Olive Henderson. They were childhood sweethearts.'

'I'm sorry, Frank.'

Frank nods. 'Celie, I've often thought about your fiancé, Max Fischer.'

'You have?'

'It was the first battle I was involved in at Gallipoli. I'll never forget that day. It was steaming hot. The whole bay under the Sari Bair ridge was covered in a fog of smoke from grass fires and the steam from the salt lake. You could barely make out the fellow next to you as you ran up the ridge.'

'You don't have to tell me this, Frank.'

'No, I need to, Celie.' Frank shifts on the bench. 'If there is a Hell, it can't be worse than Suvla Beach that day. If they'd had machine guns we would have been goners. It's like you become a machine, Celie. One step and then another step and another. A figure comes at you through the fog and you shoot, hoping it's not one of your own. Then you step forward again until the next figure comes at you.' He looks at Celie, his brown eyes glistening. 'What if Max was one of those figures, Celie? What if I—'

'Stop, Frank. You can't think that.'

'But—'

'No, Frank. Please.' Celie glances towards the kitchen. 'Wherever is Hettie with our tea? I'll go and see where she is.'

Frank grabs her hand. 'There's something else I came here for.'

'Yes?'

'Celie, the past few years in France and Gallipoli, the only thing that's kept me going is the memory of your face and your letters.

You're always there, with me, in my mind. When I wake up and when I sleep.'

'Frank—'

'I don't know what I can offer you. I only know that I intend to leave Britain behind, and make a new life somewhere else after the war.' He fumbles in his uniform pocket and takes out a gold ring set with a sparkling square-cut diamond. He slides down to his knee.

Celie's heart jumps. 'Oh, Frank—'

'I admire you, Celie. I admire you so very deeply. It's been four years since you've heard from Max. You can't wait for him forever. I know … I know you don't love me. I understand that. But I hope with all my heart that you will marry me and we could … fall in love. I know I can love you, Celie. I would be honoured if you would choose to share your life with me. Cecelia Fry, will you marry me?'

Celie stares down at Frank, at his lean, handsome face that now holds the shadow of sadness. He is a good man; she knows that with every molecule of her being. But, deep inside her, Max still fills the space reserved for love.

'I'm sorry, Frank. I already have a fiancé, and that's Max Fischer.'

Chapter Seventy-Six

Etta

Italy – June/July 1918

Villa Serenissima
Capri, Italy

May 24th, 1918

My dearest Carlo,

Please come as soon as you are able, even if it is for a short visit. Our darling angel Adriana has been taken ill with a flu such as I've never seen, not even when poor Papa was so sick that winter five years ago. Liliana has been with her night and day, but has had to leave today with Mario as his mother and two sisters in Anacapri have taken ill as well. Cousin Stefania and I are doing everything we can, but I am in despair. The doctor is too busy to come. People are falling ill everywhere. He has told me simply to 'do my best'!

I'm afraid, Carlo.

My darling, why are you not writing me? I wait every day for your letters, but they never come. Please God, let you be alive. If I were to lose you both...

Etta

The nurse sets the envelope, tattered and dirty from its circuitous journey to the hospital, on the table beside the soldier's bed, on top of the stack of unopened letters forwarded to the hospital from the Italian Front over the long months of the soldier's hospitalisation. All in the same blue ink, postmarked Capri, in the delicate, looping handwriting of a woman. She glances at the patient, his handsome face gaunt from the months of his escape into the realm of unconsciousness. But for his injured right hand, which will never hold a pen again owing to the severed tendons, his body is recovered; but his mind has resisted every attempt at reawakening.

She looks at the letters, and her heart goes out to the unknown woman who persists in writing despite the answering silence. She hesitates for a moment, then she picks up the letter and slips it into her pinafore pocket, knowing that what she is about to do is quite wrong, but certain that God will forgive her.

Loyola Unit
Base Hospital ***102
Vincenza, Italy

June 21st, 1918

Dear Mrs Marinetti,

Please forgive me for opening your letter to Captain Marinetti, but I felt compelled to contact you. I'm Lieutenant Judy Reynolds, an American nurse at a base hospital near the Italian Front. Captain Marinetti was brought into the hospital at the end of October, a casualty of the Battle of Caporetto. He'd sustained several injuries and was progressing well until he fell ill with pneumonia. In his weakened state the illness took hold, and, unfortunately, he fell into a coma. While his injuries have now healed, he hasn't emerged from the coma yet. Someone at the Front has been forwarding your letters to the hospital here, and I've kept them all for him to read when he wakes up.

I'm very sorry to hear that your daughter is sick with the flu. Please don't worry. The flu happens every year, though normally in the winter rather than the spring. Keep her in bed, give her plenty of fluids and wash your hands regularly with soap and water. Your most recent letter is dated over a month ago, so hopefully she has recovered by now.

If you'd like to write to Captain Marinetti here at the hospital, I'd be happy to give the letters to him as soon as he's better. Send them c/o me at the hospital address on this letter.

Yours faithfully,
Lt. Judith A. Reynolds

———

Etta hears the iron gate creak and looks up from the pots of pelargoniums she is deadheading. 'Oh, hello, Barnardo,' she says to the postman in Italian. 'You can give the post to me. I'll bring it inside.'

The postman tips his hat and hands Etta a stack of letters. *'Bene, bene, signora.'*

Etta sifts through the envelopes as she enters the villa. One is addressed to her, postmarked Vincenza. She drops the rest of the post onto the hallway table and settles into a sitting room armchair. She tears open the envelope and reads. She scans the letter a second time, then a third, as her hand begins to shake.

Carlo's in a coma? What if he—

No. She can't think that way. He will be fine. He is alive and he is out of this war. He is safe now. Soon he will walk through the door of Villa Serenissima, and they will be a family again. She folds the letter and slips it into her pocket. She looks out the window at the sky as blue as cornflowers. She will go to Santo Stefano this afternoon and light a candle for Carlo's swift recovery, just as she'd done every day during Adriana's illness. Then, she will work in the vegetable garden and help Liliana make supper and finally finish one of her paintings. When Carlo returns, he will see how strong she has become, how capable. She sees now that she has been a child all of her life, wheedling and charming her way out of responsibility, looking for other people to smooth her path in the world, to solve her problems. She will do everything she can to hold her family together. It's time for her to become a woman.

'There you are, *cara*,' Stefania says as she enters the sitting room with the stack of letters. 'You brought in the post, I see. Any word from … from your soldier?'

Etta glances at Stefania. 'You mean my husband?'

'Tina, he has a wife. You know it is impossible.'

'*I* am his real wife, Cousin Stefania. But, no, nothing from him.'

'No doubt you will hear from him soon. Are you ready to go to the market? Liliana is looking for calamari for supper, and you know she is not to be disappointed.'

Chapter Seventy-Seven

Jessie

Cairo, Egypt – June 1918

The landlord flips through the iron keys on his large key ring, muttering to himself as he rejects one after another. Zara Khalid huffs under her face veil and scolds him in agitated Arabic. He waves his gnarled hand and mumbles irritably as he slots a key into the keyhole. The key turns and a bolt drops; the old door creaks as he pushes it open.

Zara darts her kohled amber eyes along the narrow dusty street heaving with donkey carts and food sellers shooing away cats and shouting out enticements to the shuffling crowds. 'Go in quickly, Jessica. This is not a good area. There are many thieves around here.'

Ivy pokes Jessie's back. 'Go on. I don't fancy the way that fish seller is lookin' at me.'

The landlord, who, with his stooped shoulders and face as lined as old leather, looks eighty but could be thirty years younger, shuffles around the room throwing open the shutters. Shards of sunlight slice into the darkness through the small filthy windows, though Jessie can't help but think that the illumination does the room no favours.

Ivy coughs and flaps at the dust hanging in the stale air. 'What a tip! It's the worst one yet.'

Zara nods. 'Yes, I am sorry to waste your time. I shall tell him it is not acceptable.'

Jessie scans the large room. 'No, wait. It's really not all that bad.'

'Not all that bad?' Ivy kicks at a broken pot on the dirty tiled floor. 'Are we in the same room?'

'No, really, Ivy. It's much larger than the other places we've seen. There's even a tap in the wall over there, so we can have water.' Jessie points to two light bulbs dangling from wires in the ceiling. 'There's electricity, and it's in the type of neighbourhood that can benefit from a clinic. It just needs some titivating. Use your imagination.'

'My imagination isn't that good.'

Jessie looks at Zara, who is peeking under a tattered sheet tossed over a piece of furniture. 'What do you think, Zara? Do you think we can make this into a clinic?'

'It would give me great pleasure to make this into your clinic. I have imagination.'

Jessie runs her finger along an empty shelf and wrinkles her nose at her grimy fingertip. 'Has Aziz asked you anything about the clinic, Zara?'

'He did, but I told him to mind his own business.'

Ivy laughs. 'Bet he took that well.'

'My brother knows better than to argue with me, Ivy. This is a skill I share with my mother. That and obstinacy.'

Jessie rubs her hands together. 'It's settled, then. We'll take it.'

Ivy holds up a finger. 'Hold on just one minute, Jessie. I just wanna make one hundred per cent sure ya know what you're doin'.'

'Ivy, we've already talked about this. I want to open the clinic more than anything. I can finally be useful again.'

'You'll nevva be able to show your face at the Gezira Sporting Club again. All those officers' wives are gonna have a field day gossipin' about us.'

'I don't give a fig about them.'

'What about Aziz? Aren't ya supposed to be plannin' your honeymoon?'

'He'll come around to the idea. I'll make sure of that.'

Zara laughs under her veil. 'You are becoming a Khalid, Jessica.'

'Can you see if you can negotiate a good rental price with the landlord, Zara?'

'Of course. I shall tell him it is entirely unacceptable and work up to a reluctant agreement.'

A shape moves in the chair by the bedroom window.

'Aziz!' Jessie says as she sets her hat on her dressing table. 'I didn't see you. You gave me a fright.'

'I am sorry, Jessica. I didn't mean to.'

'I wasn't expecting you until this evening.'

'It was such a lovely day and it wasn't busy at the hospital, so I thought I would come and spend it with my wife. But, alas, she wasn't to be found. And neither was Zara.'

Jessie sits on the vanity stool. 'I'm sorry, Aziz. I wish I'd known. Zara wanted to show me some of her favourite shops in the souk.'

'Why, then, did Marta pack you a lunch? You could easily have bought food in the souk.'

Jessie pats her belly. 'My tummy's a bit delicate. I didn't want to risk it.'

'You're not …?'

'No. Nothing like that.'

He smiles. 'All the more reason for us to take our honeymoon. How are the arrangements coming along? It will have to be in the autumn. It is Ramadan shortly and then it will be too hot the rest of the summer.'

Jessie runs her brush through her hair. 'It's all fine.'

'Jessica.'

'What?'

'I know where you have been. Marta told me.'

Jessie sets down the brush and turns to face her husband. 'I'm sorry Aziz. I should have told you myself, but you didn't seem too keen on the idea of the health clinic.'

'What made you think that?'

'Well, when I told you about it, you changed the subject to the honeymoon and didn't seem to want to talk about it.'

'Jessica, I don't think the health clinic is a bad idea at all. Just not in Altumanina.'

'Oh. I see.'

'Marta said you have been looking for a place in the city for the clinic. I wish you had told me. There are many areas that are not safe. I would have sent Mustapha with you. Zara should have known better.'

'Don't blame Zara, Aziz. It's my fault. My mother always said I'm too bloody stubborn for my own good.'

'Your mother is right, *habibti*.' Aziz rises and walks over to the vanity table. He rests his hands on Jessie's shoulders and looks at their reflection in the mirror. 'I am happy that you have found something that excites you, Jessica. I shall help you however I can.'

'Even if it means postponing our honeymoon?'

'Luxor is not going anywhere, and neither am I.'

Chapter Seventy-Eight

Celie

London – November 1918

C elie steps down from the omnibus and stands on the pavement in front of the school. In the paved yard outside, children run around, screeching and laughing. A group of boys shouts as they swing stringed conkers at each other, and girls skip and play Hopscotch. New yellow brick patches the walls where the bomb blast had torn away parts of the building, and the new windows gleam in the midday light. Like it had always been this way. Like nothing had ever happened.

She heads around the corner and walks past the shop with its Woodbine Cigarettes sign. She stops at the Smiths' dark blue door and knocks.

The door swings open; Mrs Smith stands there in a floral dress and carpet slippers, her hair greyer than Celie remembers. 'Miss Fry! This is a surprise.'

'Hello, Mrs Smith.' Celie holds out a paper bag. 'I brought some pastries from Terroni's for you and Milly. I thought you might like them for your victory tea. I … I'm sorry I haven't been in touch. Things have been so busy at the newspaper, and I've been meeting with Mrs Fawcett about pursuing the vote for all women—'

'You 'aven't 'eard.'

'Heard? Heard what?'

Mrs Smith takes hold of Celie's arm and ushers her into the narrow hallway. 'It's my Milly, Miss Fry.'

'How is she, Mrs Smith? I can't believe it's been… My goodness, was it Christmas when I was last here? Where is she? I haven't missed her, have I?'

'Miss Fry, our Milly's passed. Toxic jaundice, they called it. They won't say it, but it's the TNT what did it. Destroyed 'er liver.'

Celie's sucks in a breath. 'Milly's died? When?'

'June. Just like little Alice and Joey. June's a cruel month. Their pa's gone, too. Somewhere in France. It's just me now. Doesn't seem right, does it?'

'Where is she?'

'In the East End Cemetery wif 'er brovvers 'n sisters. 'Least they got each ovver.'

Celie kneels down in the damp grass beside the headstone.

SMITH

JOHN GEORGE | AUGUST 14, 1896 – JUNE 16, 1899
NANCY ANNE | JULY 7, 1898 – JUNE 18, 1899
ALICE MARY | MARCH 11, 1908 – JUNE 13, 1916
JOSEPH PETER | FEBRUARY 17, 1910 – JUNE 13, 1916
MILLICENT JANE | SEPTEMBER 8, 1894 – JUNE 20, 1918

She runs her fingers over Milly's name. She takes the Reflex camera out of her handbag and, focusing on the headstone, presses the shutter. *No, Mrs Smith. It's not right at all.*

Chapter Seventy-Nine

Etta

Villa Serenissima, Capri, Italy – November 1918

'Cousin Stefania! Carlo's coming home!'

Stefania sets down the novel she is reading. 'Carlo's written?'

Etta runs into the sitting room flapping a letter. 'He's in a hospital in Vincenza. A nurse there has been writing me since June. He'd been terribly ill in a coma, but he's woken up. She's sent me this letter that he's dictated to her. He says that someone forwarded all my letters to him from the Italian Front and he's been reading them over and over. Isn't it wonderful?'

Stefania removes her spectacles and sets them on top of her novel. She hadn't recognised the nurse's handwriting; that's how the letters had slipped through. 'I'm so pleased for you, *cara*, but why didn't you tell me about this before?'

'I suppose I didn't want to say anything in case … in case… Well, he's awake now. He says he loves me and Adriana, and will come back as soon as he's fit to travel. My darling Carlo is coming home!'

Stefania coughs and dabs at her forehead with a handkerchief. 'Is it hot in here? Has Mario laid a fire?'

'Hot? It's blowing a gale outside. In fact, I should ask Mario to lay the fire when he gets back from Anacapri, now that you mention it.'

Stefania fans her face with the handkerchief and shivers. 'I think I shall go and have a rest, Tina. I must have caught a chill.' She rises and sways unsteadily before she sinks to the ground.

'Cousin Stefania!'

'*Signora*, what has happened?' Mario drops the basket of fresh bread he is carrying and rushes over.

Etta falls to her knees and cradles her cousin's head in her arms. 'Mario, thank God. Where's Adriana?'

'She wanted to stay with my grandmother. *Nonna* will bring her back on Wednesday.'

She wipes her cousin's feverish face with the sodden handkerchief. 'It's best she stay there for now. Help me get Cousin Stefania to her room. This came on so suddenly. She was fine at breakfast this morning.'

Mario's face blanches. 'The Spanish Lady?'

Etta nods. 'I think so.'

Etta leans over Stefania and wipes at the old woman's brow with a cold cloth. Each breath her cousin takes rasps like a rusty hinge. Etta dips the cloth into a bowl of cold water and, folding it in half, lays it across Stefania's burning forehead.

Stefania opens her eyes, blinking as she focuses on Etta's face. She sucks in a laboured breath and pushes out the words. 'You're wearing a mask.'

'Yes. I tore up a sheet to make one for me and Mario. Adriana's in Anacapri with Liliana.'

Stefania runs her tongue over her lips. 'I have it, don't I? The Spanish Lady?'

Etta fills a water glass from a pitcher and, sliding her arms under Stefania's shoulders to prop her up, holds it to her cousin's lips. 'Don't worry. Mario and I shall take good care of you.'

'I must have caught it at the victory celebrations. Everyone was there.' Stefania convulses in violent shivers. 'You must leave me, Etta. Adriana needs you. Liliana and Mario's parents need him, especially since his poor sisters passed in May. No one needs me.'

'I need you, Cousin Stefania. Adriana and I love you. Mario and I shall be fine. We've disinfected everything with Creolina, we're boiling all the dishes and utensils, and wearing these masks.'

'You would not love me if you knew what I have done.'

'Whatever do you mean?'

'Get my keyring. On top of the chest of drawers. Please.'

Etta finds Stefania's keys beside the silver vanity set. 'I have them.'

'Open the bottom drawer. The smallest key.'

'Why?'

'Please, *cara*.'

Etta kneels on the rug and, after unlocking the drawer, yanks it open with a tug.

'There's a box at the back.'

Etta reaches behind the scarves and finds the wooden box.

'Open it, *cara*.'

Etta lifts up the lid. She picks up the top letter on the stack and stares at the handwriting. Then she picks up the next, and the next. She turns to face her cousin as her heart races. 'You had Carlo's letters?'

'Yes, *cara*.'

'All those months when I thought he might be dead ... all that time, you had them?'

'Yes.'

'Why did you hide them from me?'

'Because I love you, *cara mia*. You are my family, just as your mother is. I saw how Christina was destroyed by the man who had claimed to love her, how he'd abandoned her with a baby. When I discovered that Carlo was married and had a son, I ... I couldn't let him do the same to you.'

'Carlo would never abandon us.'

'I hated him, Etta. I hated him for what he did to you, what he's done to Adriana.'

'He's done nothing to Adriana!'

Stefania struggles onto her elbows. Her dark eyes flash in her flushed face. 'He has made Adriana a bastard. Our precious angel has no name!' She collapses back onto the pillow, perspiration rolling down her cheeks like tears.

'Adriana has a name! She is a Marinetti *and* she is a Fry. Her father and I shall raise her to be a proud, strong woman. My daughter has a name and no one can take it from her.'

———

Mario looks up from his perch on the chair beside Stefania's bed as Etta enters the bedroom three days later.

'How is she, Mario?'

'She had another nosebleed, but she's sleeping now. She is not shivering like she was.'

'Good. Go have supper. I've made *spaghetti alla Nerano* with the leftover zucchini. Then go have some rest. I'll take over tonight.'

'No, *Signora Etta*. I can sleep for a few hours and come back at midnight.'

'You've done enough today, Mario. Get a good rest and come at six o'clock in the morning. I need you to help me set up one of the spare rooms for Adriana when she comes back. She's big enough for her own room now.'

When he has left, Etta approaches her sleeping cousin. The laudanum has settled Stefania into a peaceful slumber, though drops of perspiration collect on her forehead. Etta wets a cloth in the bowl of water and wipes her cousin's face.

She watches Stefania's chest rise and fall under the blankets. *You are quite the keeper of secrets, Cousin Stefania. About my mother's affair, about Celie's birth, about Carlo's letters ... so many secrets. What am I to do with all this information? This burden of secrets?*

She rubs her temples and sits in the bedroom chair. She's so tired. She can't think about that now. She unties her mask and takes the bottle of laudanum and a spoon from her skirt pocket. Twisting off the cap, she then carefully pours out a spoonful and drips the brown liquid into her mouth. She grimaces as the bitter narcotic passes over her tongue and down her throat. Then she closes her eyes and waits for sleep to come.

Part Seven

1919

Chapter Eighty

Etta

Villa Serenissima, Capri, Italy – January 1919

Etta looks over from her canvas at Mario, who is diligently copying the shape of one of the lemons in the bowl she has arranged on a table in the sitting room, while Stefania naps in her favourite chair by the window.

'Can I make a suggestion, Mario?'

'Yes, of course, *Signora Etta*.'

'Loosen your shoulders. Roll them around in a circle, like this.' She rolls her shoulders and twists her head from side to side. 'Your hand is very tense. Here, take one of my new brushes from Giosi in Naples. They're the best quality. Hold your brush lightly and don't worry so much about copying the lemon exactly. Try to paint the essence of the lemon.'

Mario's dark eyebrows draw together. 'I don't understand.'

'Of course, you can paint the lemon exactly as it looks. The great

Dutch and Flemish painters of the seventeenth century prided themselves on the realism of their still lifes. An artist named Adriaen Coorte painted twelve paintings of asparagus in order to perfect it. Can you imagine that? But there is another way to paint, Mario. A more modern way. The painter Picasso once told my husband that a circle doesn't have to be round. That is a good lesson.'

Mario looks over at Adriana who is sitting at a small table he has set up for her, covering sheaves of paper with yellow lemons with Etta's yellow drawing pencil. 'Did you hear that, Adriana? A circle that isn't round and a painter who paints nothing but asparagus! Isn't that silly?'

Adriana looks up at Mario, her cheeks dimpling as she giggles. 'It's very silly, Maro. You eat 'spargras. You don't paint 'spargras.'

'But we're painting lemons and we eat lemons, don't we?'

Adriana's dark eyes flash. 'We only eat lemons in Lili's cake so it's okay.'

'Did I hear someone say cake?'

Etta spins around, cadmium yellow paint flying off her brush across Carlo's uniform. 'Carlo!'

Stefania jolts awake. 'What? What is it?'

Etta rushes over to Carlo, but he stops her before she throws herself into his embrace. He touches a finger against his lips and, reaching inside his jacket, carefully extracts a tiny ball of ginger fur. The kitten blinks its green eyes and mews.

'Do you remember me, Adriana, *il mio piccolo angelo?* I'm your Papa.'

Adriana stares at Carlo. 'Mama drew me your picture, Papa.'

'Did she? Do I look like the picture?'

Adriana tilts her head and inspects Carlo's face. 'Yes.' She reaches out to pet the kitten, giggling when it rubs its head against her fingers.

'Do you like the kitten?'

Adriana nods, her golden curls bouncing on her shoulders.

'I have to give him to his owner.'

'Oh.'

He sets the kitten on Adriana's lap. 'He's your kitten, *angelo mio*. He's a little boy. You need to be his mother and give him a name.'

Adriana takes the kitten carefully into her arms, cradling it like a baby. She beams at Carlo. 'Thank you, Papa. I shall love him forever and ever. I shall call him Alice.'

'Alice is a girl's name, sweetie,' Etta says.

Adriana sticks out her lower lip in a pout. 'I like Alice. It's like Alice in the story you read me.'

Carlo runs his hand over Adriana's soft curls. 'I think Alice is a splendid name for the cat.'

'You're spoiling her, Carlo,' Stefania says as she rises from her chair. 'I'll tell Liliana to prepare *tisana*.'

'She's already doing that, Stefania.' Carlo reaches an arm around Etta. 'She met me at the door and hurried off as fast as a runaway train to the kitchen.'

'Then I shall see about some *biscotti*. Mario, come help me.'

'But, *Signora Albertini*—'

'Mario. Now.'

Carlo watches the two disappear through the doors into the sitting room. He shakes his head. 'I don't believe she likes me.'

'I don't care what she thinks, my darling.' Etta reaches up and traces the lines of his face with her fingers. 'I can't believe you're here, Carlo.'

'*Cara mia*, I have dreamt about this day.' He leans forward and kisses her.

'Papa!' Adriana exclaims. 'What are you doing?'

'I'm kissing your mama. Is that all right, *patatina*?'

Adriana kisses the cat on its soft head. 'Like I'm kissing Alice?'

'Exactly. And why are you kissing Alice?'

Adriana buries her face in the cat's ginger fur. 'Because I love him.'

'And I'm kissing Mama because I love her and we can all now be a family together.' He leans toward Etta and whispers in her ear. 'Etta, Marianna has passed away.'

Etta gasps.

'It happened suddenly. In her sleep. Perhaps it was the kindest thing. She is with little Gabriella now.'

'Do you know what this means? We're free, Carlo! Finally!'

———————

Carlo runs the gloved fingers of his left hand down the sleeve of Etta's dress. He sweeps his eyes over her, as if she is an apparition, as if she might dissolve into the quiet darkness of the bedroom. Outside, a gentle rain has begun to fall, and raindrops splash like tears onto the glass panes of the window.

He brushes his lips along her neck. Her shoulders shake with a shiver of pleasure. His mouth finds hers, and the world is her mouth and her searching tongue. She reaches for his hands, but he pulls away.

'What is it, Carlo? What's the matter?'

'Etta, I must tell you something.'

'About Marianna? You don't need to say anything. I am sorry she has died, of course, but—'

'No, my darling.' He holds up his left hand. 'Take off my gloves. This one first.'

Etta takes hold of the soft brown leather and pulls the glove off his hand. He reaches for her face and caresses it with his fingers. 'Now the other one.'

She pulls at the leather and gasps as the mangled hand is exposed. 'Carlo! What happened?'

'A mine. I was lucky. Many men were killed.'

She slides her fingers into his damaged hand. 'Does it hurt?'

'No. The tendons and nerves have been cut. I feel nothing.'

'But you paint with your right hand.'

'I must learn to paint with my left.'

She raises his hand to her lips and kisses the scarred fingers. 'I'll help you, Carlo. We'll manage.'

'There were times I thought you were a dream, Etta. But then one of your letters would come, and I would read your words over and over until they were such a part of my mind that I knew I would never forget them. You and Adriana were all that kept me alive.'

She slides her hands over the rough wool of his uniform and caresses the soft skin of his throat where his pulse throbs under her fingers. 'I'm no dream, my darling. I always believed you would find your way back to us. I spoke to Adriana all the time about you, drew pictures of you, of all of us together. I prayed and I pleaded and I bargained with God for you to come back to us. I would have sold my soul just to have you back safely.'

'Don't say such a thing, *cara mia*. You must never think like that.'

'Oh, my darling man, I am simply happy you are back with me. So much has happened to both of us, I know that. We're together, that's all that matters. And we can marry now. We shall be a proper family. This is the best gift of all.'

Carlo pulls Etta into his embrace and kisses her. 'I love you, Etta. I love you so much.' They stand in the shadows of the room, entwined in each other's arms, as the rain taps softly against the window.

Chapter Eighty-One

Jessie

Cairo, Egypt – March 1919

Zara pushes through the throng of patients and leans out the clinic's window. The shouts and clanging of metal on metal grow louder as the crowd pushes down the street, the brays of donkeys and ding of bicycle bells adding to the cacophony.

'What's happening, Zara? It's a racket out there,' Jessie shouts from behind the curtains separating the two examination rooms from the waiting patients. She ties up the bandage over a boy's hand and pats him on the head.

'Sounds worse than a bunch of Aussies after a football match!' Ivy shouts from the other examination room.

The door flies open and Aziz strides into the clinic, his face streaming with sweat.

'Aziz!' Zara exclaims. 'What are you doing here?'

'Where's Jessica?'

Jessie pulls back the curtain and ushers the boy into the arms of his mother. 'I'm here. What's going on?'

'Saad Zaghloul and two of the other leaders of the independence movement have been arrested and deported to Malta. The city has gone crazy. The British are setting up machine gun posts at the major junctions. You have to get out of here.'

Ivy pokes her head out from around the curtain. 'Bloody hell. I don't wanna get caught in the middle of that, Jessie. We'd best scarper.'

'What about our patients?'

Aziz claps his hands and shouts at the crowd of patients in Arabic. Zara opens the door and waves for them to hurry out of the clinic.

'Good,' Aziz says as Zara locks the door. 'Collect everything you need. We must leave now. Mustapha's waiting in the car.'

———

Mustapha squeezes the horn, but the harsh squeal does little to part the crowd. The car inches forward through the baying protestors. At the bottom of the Citadel, they drop Ivy off.

'Are you sure you'll be all right, Ivy?'

'Right as rain, Jessie. Safest place to be in a riot is a fortified palace, don't ya think?' She kisses Zara and Jessie on their cheeks. 'Get home safe. I'll ring ya tomorrow.'

The car heads back into the streets, turning down alleyways to avoid the crowds on the main streets.

'Jessica, you can't go back to the clinic. It's not safe.'

'Surely this will calm down in a few days, Aziz.'

'Not this time.'

'It's true, Jessica.' Zara reaches into her bag, and, taking out a leaflet, hands it to Jessie. 'It calls for the women of Egypt to support the nationalists.'

'You're part of this?'

Aziz rests a hand on Jessie's knee. 'We both are. That is why we both know how much danger you are in as an Englishwoman. The clinic must stay closed. It may be some time before it can reopen, if ever.'

'*I* set up the clinic, Aziz, and *I'm* the only one who can say if it opens or closes.'

Aziz glances at his sister, who turns to look out the window. 'Jessica, we shall discuss this later. Your safety and the safety of my sister are paramount. The clinic will remain closed.'

Jessie folds her arms and stares out the window as the anger rises inside her. She twists her wedding ring around her finger. There is nothing she wants to do more in that moment than pull it off and throw it in the Nile.

Layla Khalid waves away Mustapha's attempt to refill her tea glass, and fixes her amber gaze on her son.

'Mohammed has been nowhere to be seen today, and his son has left the gatehouse unattended. It's simply unacceptable, Aziz. Any of that riff-raff could have stormed in here today. You must let them go. There are many others who can do their gardening work, more cheaply as well.'

Aziz looks up from his meal of Marta's lemon-roasted chicken. 'My father hired Mohammed thirty years ago, Mama. I am not about to fire him or his son for missing a day of work.'

Layla's beautiful mouth twists into a sour pout. 'They cannot be permitted to leave Altumanina at the mercy of the protestors. Do you wish your mother to be kidnapped, raped and murdered by these … these Egyptians?'

Zara drops her fork onto her plate. 'Mama! I know that you carry the Turkish and Albanian blood of the old Khedive, as you are forever reminding us, but Papa was Egyptian. Aziz and I carry Egyptian blood in our veins. Do not insult the Egyptian people like this.'

Layla raises a fine arched eyebrow at her daughter. 'Don't tell me you are one of these *nationalists*.' She spits the word out like a poison. 'You will be out on the street waving a flag with the students and labourers before long.' She glares at Aziz. 'Is that what you want, Aziz? Your sister out on the streets with these hoodlums?'

'Zara is free to do as she wishes.'

Layla shifts her gaze to Jessie. 'This is all her fault.'

Jessie looks across the table at her mother-in-law. 'My fault? How is that?'

Zara glances at Jessie. 'You cannot blame Jessica for the riots, Mama.'

Layla throws out her arms, her bracelets jangling. 'She has led my daughter into the filthiest part of Cairo to work in that hideous clinic. If people cannot pay for medical care, they should stay home.'

Jessie clears her throat. 'Madame Khalid, if the country's poorly paid labourers, farmers and factory workers – many of whom are women – fall ill and become incapacitated or die, this country will quickly fall apart.'

'Is that so? But you're British, and the British are our so-called protectors. Are you such a disaffected Englishwoman to be speaking treason?'

Jessie tosses her napkin onto the table. 'I am quite a proud Englishwoman. However, I do not agree with all the British government's decisions and directives.'

Layla waves her hand dismissively. 'Unfortunately, the British are a necessary evil in Egypt. They have built factories and cotton farms so everyone can find work unless they are lazy. If it wasn't the British, it would be some other country running Egypt. I only wish it were the Turks again. That was Egypt's golden age.'

'There are children working in these factories, Madame Khalid!

These factories are dirty and unsafe. We have people streaming into the clinic every day with injuries from the faulty equipment. They're all so worried because if they can't work, they aren't paid, even though it's a pittance. If they're not paid, they don't eat. I won't even begin to tell you the condition of the hovels they're crowded into, with no sewage or water. It's shameful. I'm ashamed that my government has a hand in all this! The clinic must stay open. The people need us.'

Zara claps her hands. 'Bravo, Jessica.'

Layla glares at her daughter. 'Aziz, tell your sister she is forbidden to have anything more to do with that place.'

'I shall do no such thing.' He throws down his napkin and pushes away from the table. 'If you excuse me, I have had quite enough of this.'

'Penny for your thoughts.'

Aziz turns away from the view of the river at the back of the garden. 'I am sorry, Jessica. My mother can be a difficult woman.'

'And you can be a difficult man.' She walks across the lawn to join Aziz under the purple-blossomed branches of a jacaranda tree. She slides her wedding ring off her finger and holds it up to Aziz. 'I wanted to throw this in the Nile this afternoon. I was that angry with you about the clinic.'

'I am sorry, Jessica, but it is not safe.'

'I understand, but I don't take kindly to being bossed about, Aziz.'

'I was simply thinking of your safety.' He looks out at the sluggish brown water of the Nile. 'The students are calling for a general strike. There are reports that the British forces have shot and killed demonstrators in Tanta. It is going to get much worse, Jessica.'

'But the people will need us more than ever—'

'Not if you are kidnapped. Or worse.'

'What am I supposed to do? Just give up?'

He takes her ring and slides it back on her finger. 'Just for now, until the situation calms down.'

'I'm meant to stay here in the house with your mother? How do you think that will work out?'

'Jessica, why don't we leave Cairo? Go visit your family in London? It can be the honeymoon we never managed to take in Luxor.' He rests a hand on her belly. 'Maybe we can work on another project together.'

Jessie places her hand over his. 'My mother isn't happy about our marriage, Aziz. She considers you a heathen. You've read her letters.'

'Yes, I'm very sorry about that.'

'Don't be. I have no regrets. I never wanted an ordinary life. Every day I wake up not knowing what the day will bring, and I love that. I love working at the clinic, feeling useful. Don't ever be sorry. I love you, Aziz, even if you are a difficult man.'

He leans his forehead against hers. 'I love you, too, my difficult wife. More than you will ever know.'

Chapter Eighty-Two

Celie

Clover Bar, London – March 1919

Celie flops onto the sitting room's chaise longue and riffles through the stack of letters. Christina looks up from her chair where she is working on an embroidery. 'Anything interesting in the post today?'

'Well, what do you know? A letter from the prodigal daughter.'

'Which one?'

'Jessie.'

'What does she have to say?'

Celie tears open the envelope and scans the letter. 'Oh! They're coming here. Jessie and her husband.'

'Here? To Clover Bar?'

'They're arriving the middle of April for a month. It appears there are problems in Cairo.'

'What kind of problems? With their marriage?'

'No, Mama. Riots. Political problems. It appears the Egyptians want independence from the British.'

'Whyever would they wish that? Doesn't everyone wish to be British?'

'Not everyone, Mama. We've just come through a war. The Germans, Austrians and Turks most certainly did not wish to be British.'

'And look what happened to them. That attitude didn't do them any good, did it?' Christina sets the embroidery aside. 'I shall go speak to Hettie about changing the menu for Easter lunch. I believe Dr Khalid will not appreciate ham.'

Celie waits until her mother leaves the room, then she opens up the envelope Jessie has enclosed, addressed to her.

Dear Celie,

Please sit down. There is something I have to tell you.

You have heard me mention my friend Ivy Roach in my letters before. I met her when we were nursing on the Letitia at Gallipoli. One night a young German was brought on board, very badly wounded with a bullet wound to his chest. Aziz did his very best in the operating theatre, and the soldier managed to make it through the operation. I'm not proud of this, but I'm afraid I refused to nurse him. You know what I was like. I've changed, Celie. I am not the same person I was before the war. I'm so sorry about everything I said before I left.

Ivy, being a much kinder, better person than me, nursed the German soldier. I wouldn't have thought any more of it, except that Ivy found a letter in his uniform after he died. She gave it to me yesterday. She's decided to go back to Australia. I don't blame her in the least. Things have got quite bad here in Cairo. Anyway, she asked me if I might try to find the girl in the letter. He'd written to an English girl, you see. I told her it was like looking for a needle in a haystack. Then I read the letter.

Celie, it was meant for you.

Your loving sister,
Jessie

December 25th, 1914

My darling Schatzi,

It is Christmas Day, and my heart is happy. Why is this? I have just met with some British and French soldiers on No Man's Land. What is this, you may well ask? Have you lost leave of your senses, Max? No, the most wonderful thing has happened. The Front has been quiet for several weeks with not much to do, so Fritz and I found a small fir tree in the woods and we stuck it up on top of the trench. Soon, several more trees sprung up, some of them hung with bottle caps and buttons, feathers... It was quite a jolly forest!

We were given extra rations of beer for Christmas and had a Christmas sing-a-long last night. You can imagine it got rather lively! A few of the Tommies started singing along to 'Oh, Tannenbaum!' – but in English, of course. They were quite terrible singers, and we let them know it!

This morning, Fritz did a crazy thing. He jumped up onto No Man's Land and waved over at the Tommies, shouting 'Merrry Christmas! Merry Christmas!' I think he was still drunk. I tried to pull him back but he wasn't having any of it. Before I knew it some of the Tommies had jumped out of their trenches holding up bars of chocolate and knitted scarves. We all started crawling out of the trenches taking anything we could think of to exchange as souvenirs. I exchanged my Landsturm cap with a Tommy from London. Fritz and my friend Dieter rolled out a barrel of German beer and some of the French fellows had champagne. We exchanged cigarettes and uniform buttons, jam, anything we could think of. It was quite something to see. Schatzi, if the soldiers had anything to do with the war, it would be over tomorrow.

I hope you are having a good Christmas with your family. Please give my best wishes to your parents and your two sisters.

Please, don't worry about me. I think about you every day, and dream of the day we shall be together again. As long as I know you are in the world, I am happy.

I must go now. One of the Tommies has a football they call 'Corporal' and we are going to play football on No Man's Land.

All my love always,
Your Max

Celie's hand shakes, and the letter slips from her fingers, floating like a white leaf to rest on the sitting room's Persian carpet.

'Cecelia, have you seen my knitting bag? I was sure I left it by my chair, but I haven't been able to find it anyw—' Christina stops short beside the chaise longue. 'Cecelia? What's happened?'

Celie wipes at her eyes and looks at her mother through a wet blur. 'Max is dead, Mama. He's dead.'

Chapter Eighty-Three

The Frys

Clover Bar, London – April 1919

Jessie places her hand on her husband's as he is about to ring the doorbell of Clover Bar.

'Aziz, this may not be easy. You know how my mother feels about our marriage. I apologise in advance for any offence she may cause.'

The corners of Aziz's eyes crinkle as he smiles. 'You do not need to worry on my account, Jessica. What she said was said out of love and concern for you, and from fear and misunderstanding of me as an Egyptian Muslim.' He holds up an exuberant bouquet of white lilies. 'I intend to assault her with such a charm offensive that she will be compelled to accept me into the family, even if she feels it is against her better judgement.'

'It won't be easy.'

'You capitulated, didn't you?'

'Quite right. Mama won't stand a chance.' She presses the bell. 'Here goes nothing.'

———

Christina pours out a steaming cup of Earl Grey tea. 'Milk, Dr Khalid? Sugar?'

'Thank you, Mrs Fry. Just black, please.'

'Black? Indeed.' She offers him the teacup. 'I must thank you for the flowers, though in England lilies are generally understood to be funeral flowers.'

Jessie glares at her mother over her teacup. 'Mama.'

'Forgive me, Mrs Fry. I was not aware of this custom. I have always found lilies quite elegant, and, as Jessica has often spoken to me about her mother's elegance, I felt that they were the only flowers which would do you justice.'

Celie's mouth twitches. 'Jessie, pass Dr Khalid the cucumber sandwiches, would you? You have no issue with eating cucumbers, Dr Khalid?'

Aziz takes a crustless sandwich from the tiered curate stand. 'I am quite fond of cucumbers, Miss Fry. Our gardener grows them in our garden in Cairo.'

'We grow a variety of vegetables in Cairo,' Jessie says as she helps herself to an egg sandwich. 'Tomatoes, radishes, lettuce, peas... The soil is quite rich beside the Nile. Papa would be proud.'

'I did wonder what you ate there, Jessica,' Christina says.

'The food in Egypt is delicious, Mama. So full of spice and flavour. We have a wonderful cook named Marta who's been teaching me.'

Celie coughs on her tea. 'You? Cook? That's something I'd like to see.'

Christina looks across the table at Celie. 'Cecelia, why don't you share your news?'

Jessie looks at her sister. 'What news?'

Celie sets down the walnut square. 'I'm getting married to Frank Jeffries.'

Jessie's teaspoon clatters onto her saucer. 'Frank Jeffries? Seriously?'

'Yes. We've been corresponding through the war. He proposed to me last May, but I said no because of Max. But, then, when you wrote me…' She sucks in a breath. 'I've grown fond of Frank. We're emigrating to Canada. It's a chance for a fresh start.'

'You're *fond* of him? Do you love him, Celie?'

Aziz rests his hand on Jessie's arm. 'I'm sure she loves him very much, Jessica.'

'When I received your letter about Max, I was in pieces, Jessie. Max was such a part of me. I couldn't think about any other life but one with him. I showed Frank Max's letter. Frank said he'd been there that Christmas, on the Front. He'd played football with the Germans. He may even have met Max, isn't that incredible? He's been so kind.'

'Still—'

'I have to move on with my life, Jessie. We're getting married at the end of May. You'll stay for that, won't you? I really wish you would.'

Jessie glances at Aziz who nods. 'Uh … of course we shall. Like you say, it's a fresh start. I'm all for fresh starts.'

Chapter Eighty-Four

Christina and Celie

Clover Bar, London – May 1919

Christina stands in the doorway of her eldest daughter's bedroom and watches Celie pin the white veil over her auburn hair. Her heart leaps at the sight of her daughter in her white wedding gown, knowing how much Gerald would have wanted to be here on Celie's special day. *How can it be that this is Cecelia's wedding day? Wasn't it just yesterday that I held her in my arms on the ferry from Capri?* She catches Celie's gaze in the mirror's reflection.

'Mama! You startled me.' Celie turns around on the cushioned stool. 'What do you think?'

'Stand up so I can get a proper look.'

Celie stands and twirls in front of her mother, the fine lace veil fluttering around her.

'You look lovely, Cecelia. Frank is a very lucky young man. But something's missing.'

Celie looks down at the white silk and lace dress with its fashionable dropped waist. 'Something's missing?'

Christina holds up a long string of creamy pearls. 'These were your grandmother Isabella's pearls. I wore them on my wedding day. They were her mother's. Now they're yours to give to your daughter one day.'

Celie runs her fingers over the cool round pearls as her mother fastens the clasp behind her neck. 'They're lovely, Mama. Are you sure?'

'They're for the eldest daughter of the eldest daughter.' Christina turns Celie around and stands back to appraise her. 'You are a lovely young woman, Cecelia. Your grandmother would be proud of you.'

'I'm sorry I never met her.'

'She was a woman with a very strong will. She insisted on living the life she wanted even if it meant alienating her family.'

'She sounds like the twins.'

Christina runs her hand along Celie's cheek. 'Cecelia, I know I haven't always been as supportive of you as I might have been. You've always been so self-sufficient. I felt the twins needed more guidance. Jessica's stubbornness and Etta's irresponsibility caused me no end of worry. Anyway, you were always your father's favourite. You didn't need me.'

'Mama, there were times I felt … I felt you didn't love me as much as the twins. That somehow I was a disappointment to you.'

Christina feels tears prick at her eyes. 'I'm sorry, Cecelia.'

Celie kisses her mother's cheek. 'It's all right, Mama. There's nothing to be sorry for. You're my mother. I love you.'

The image of Harry Grenville's youthful face flashes into Christina's mind. *You should have been here, Harry. Your daughter is getting married. Our daughter is getting married. I shall never forgive you for what you did, but I've been wrong to take it out on Cecelia. It's not her fault that you're her father. The fault is all ours.*

She dabs at her eyes with her handkerchief and smooths the veil over Celie's shoulders. 'At least one of my daughters is marrying a nice young Englishman, even if he is Church of England.' She squeezes Celie's hand. 'Are you ready, my dear?'

'Yes, Mama, I'm ready.'

Frank turns to watch Celie walk up the long aisle of St. Mary the Virgin Roman Catholic Church arm in arm with her mother. His nerves, which have only been heightened by his first foray into a Catholic church, settle at the sight of Celie in her white dress and veil smiling at him like a beautiful, auburn-haired angel. The sonorous organ music soars through the nave. The memories of the long years of war and all the death he has seen momentarily fade, and his heart quivers with happiness.

Celie slips her hand into his and squeezes his fingers lightly. 'Hello, Frank.'

'Hello, Celie.'

It will all be all right.

Chapter Eighty-Five

The Frys

Clover Bar, London – May 1919

A pounding on the bedroom door. 'Aziz! Please, come quickly! Aziz!'

Jessie sits up in the bed. 'It's Celie.'

Aziz pulls on his dressing gown and opens the bedroom door. Celie and Frank stand in the hallway in their dressing gowns. Jessie joins Aziz by the door.

'It's Mama, Jessie. She's been sick all night. There's something terribly wrong. I thought it might have been something she ate at dinner, but she has a nosebleed now which won't stop.'

'Oh, Celie, you don't think it's—'

Frank gives Celie's shoulders a comforting squeeze. 'I'm sure she'll be fine in the morning. We just thought it was best if you would take a look.'

'Yes, of course,' Aziz says. 'I shall meet you in her room.'

'Mrs Fry? Can you sit up?'

Aziz checks Christina's pulse as Jessie holds a handkerchief against Christina's streaming nose.

'There's a thermometer in my nurse's chatelaine, Celie. Give it to Aziz, then you'd best leave us. Go wash yourselves; use as much soap as you can, and wear the masks Aziz gave you.'

'Jessie, I want to help.'

'Celie, please. I'm a nurse. I've seen the flu in Cairo. I know what to do. It's best if you leave, and close the door behind you.'

Celie looks at Aziz. 'It is the Spanish Flu, then.'

Aziz slips the thermometer under Christina's tongue. 'Yes. Do you have aspirin?'

'I don't believe so.'

'Ring the chemist in the morning and order some. Ask for salt of quinine and morphine as well, and more disinfectant. Tell them to leave the package by the door. Tell them we're in quarantine.'

Jessie looks over at Frank. 'Go wake Hettie, Frank. Tell her what's happened, and that we'll need boiled water, as well as a pitcher of cold water and some clean cloths. Ask her to boil some milk with cinnamon for now. Tell her to wash and disinfect all the dishes and cutlery. Give her a mask to wear and tell her to stay downstairs.'

Christina grasps Aziz's hand as he removes the thermometer. Her body shakes as she is overcome by a fit of coughing. Red spittle stains the white sheets like dots of paint. She looks up at her son-in-law, and he sees the fear in her blue eyes.

'Help me, Aziz.'

'I shall, Mrs Fry. I shall do everything in my power, *inshallah*.'

'It's il polpo.'

Christina looks behind her. 'Harry! What are you doing at the market?'

He shrugs. 'Just soaking up the atmosphere.' He holds up his sketchbook. 'Making some sketches. Doing what a tourist does.'

The fishmonger dangles an octopus, its rubbery tentacles flapping, over his offerings of fresh shellfish and glistening fish. 'Signorina, per favore, lo vuoi?'

'Si, si. Octopus. Il polpo.'

Then they are walking along the cliff. She can feel the warmth of the summer sun on her face. She stumbles on a stone and he reaches for her hand. Her heart drums in her chest. He is speaking of his visit to Pompeii, but she hears nothing but the low lull of his voice. The world is the touch of his hand.

They are in the grotto. He presses her against the stone cobbles. When she opens her eyes, she sees nothing but the blue sky and a lone gull hovering high above them. Then the notes of a song float toward her over the air. A song of such exquisite beauty that she weeps.

'Mrs Fry? Mrs Fry, can you hear me?'

Christina blinks as her eyes focus on the stranger's masked face.

'It's Aziz Khalid. Your son-in-law.'

'Mama?' Another face appears.

'Jessica.'

Jessie brushes her mother's forehead with her gloved hand. 'I'm here, Mama.'

'I'm so sorry, Jessica.'

'It's all right, Mama.'

Christina rolls her head from side to side, dampening the pillow with her perspiration. 'It was wrong of me to judge you. You must love whom you must love.' She looks at her son-in-law. 'Please forgive me, Aziz. I was wrong. So wrong.'

'Mama?' Celie enters the room, stifling a gasp when she sees her mother's blue-tinged face. 'Mama, Etta's on the telephone with Adriana. She's calling from the post office in Capri. She received my telegram. I told her I'd give her a message from you. Frank's speaking to her now.'

'No, I want to speak to Etta. I want to speak to my daughter and my granddaughter.'

'Mama, you're too ill.'

Aziz pulls back the sheets and lifts Christina into his arms. 'This is important. Let's go.'

He carries Christina down the stairs followed by Jessie as Celie races ahead. She takes the telephone receiver from Frank. 'Etta? Mama's coming.'

Aziz settles Christina into the hall chair and Jessie holds the telephone receiver against her ear.

'Etta? Etta May, are you there? It's Mama.'

The line clicks and buzzes. 'Mama? It's so good to hear your voice! How are you feeling?'

'I'm fine, my dove.'

'Adriana wants to speak to you, Mama. Adriana, *Nonna* is on the telephone. Say hello in Italian for her.'

A pause. *'Nonna?'*

'Si, il mio angelo?'

A giggle down the phone line. *'Ciao, Nonna. Io sono Adriana.'*

Christina clutches the receiver. *'Ciao, il mio piccolo angelo. Nonna* loves you very much.'

'I love you, too, *Nonna.*'

The line clicks and falls silent.

'Adriana? Etta?' Christina presses the receiver against her chest. 'I'm so sorry. I'm so very sorry for everything.'

Frank takes the package from the chemist's boy and drops an extra coin into his hand with his payment. He reenters the house and stands for a moment in the hallway. The faint murmur of voices wafts down from Christina's bedroom on the floor above, and dishes clatter in the kitchen where Hettie is washing up after breakfast. He opens the door to the study and shuts it softly behind him.

Setting the parcel on Gerald's desk, he then pulls at the knotted string with his fingernails until it slowly unties. He spreads open the brown paper and sees what he is looking for amongst the medicine bottles. Morphine. Six glass vials of his salvation.

He slides four of the vials into his jacket pocket and carefully rewraps and ties the parcel. No one will ever know about the over-orders of morphine so long as he collects the chemist's deliveries. It's best that way. They wouldn't understand that the morphine is one of the only things that makes his life tolerable. The morphine and Celie.

'Jessie!' Celie knocks on Jessie's bedroom door four days later. 'Jessie! Frank and I have just seen Mama. She's sitting up. The fever's broken.'

Jessie drops her pen on the desk. 'Hold on, Celie! I'll be right there.' She ties on her mask and hurries down the hall with Celie.

She throws open the door to her mother's bedroom. 'Mama! You're sitting up! How are you feeling?'

Christina smiles weakly. 'What a question, Jessica. How do you imagine I'm feeling?'

Jessie pushes past Frank and Celie and sits on the bed. She takes hold of her mother's hands. 'You look so much better, Mama.'

Celie joins Jessie on the bed. 'We owe a great debt to Aziz, Mama. He's barely left your side since you became ill. He's a hero.'

Aziz offers a glass of quinine-laced water to Christina. 'Celie has a great imagination, Mrs Fry. I was simply doing my job.'

Christina swallows down the liquid with a grimace. 'I do hope I don't have to drink much more of this, Aziz.'

Jessie takes the glass from her mother. 'Aziz, Mama? Not "that Egyptian"?'

'Whatever are you talking about, Jessica? This young man is my son-in-law, and I intend to call him by his name.'

Downstairs, the front doorbell rings. 'That must be the chemist's boy,' Jessie says as she rises from the bed. 'I'll be back in a moment.'

'I'll see to it,' Frank says as he heads to the door. 'Stay with your mother.'

'Thank you, Frank,' Celie says. 'Mama, Frank and I have been talking. Once we leave for Canada, you'll be by yourself here at Clover Bar.'

'Nonsense, Cecelia. Hettie will be here.'

'It's not the same as family. Frank and I want you to come out to Canada once we've settled. We'll build a farm on our plot of land and make a fresh start.' She takes hold of her mother's hand. 'It's all being paid for by the Soldiers' Land Settlement Scheme, Mama, and Frank's share of the auctioneering business, now that his father has retired. And I still have the money Papa left me. We'll have chickens and pigs and I'll have a vegetable patch. Flowers too, of course. Please, say you'll come.'

'Chickens, did you say?'

'And pigs, Mama,' Jessie says. 'Won't that be fun?'

'Most likely a few cows as well,' Celie says. 'For milk.'

'Cows and pigs?' Christina settles back against the pillows. 'Let me think about it, dear.'

'But, Mama—'

Frank enters the room. 'Celie? There's someone here for you.'

'For me? Who—'

The young man steps into the room. His face is sharper, thinner; the face of a man rather than a youth. But his eyes are the same sparkling blue, his hair the colour of wheat in August.

'Max.'

Chapter Eighty-Six

Celie

Clover Bar, London – May 1919

C elie shuts the sitting room door and gestures to Gerald's favourite chair.

'Have a seat, Max.' Her heart beats a drum in her chest as she turns to the door. 'Would you like some tea? I'll ask Hettie, shall I? Tea would be good, don't you think?'

'Celie. *Schatzi*. Stop, please. Look at me.'

Celie turns to Max, and all the years of longing, of wanting nothing more than to be with him, to feel him against her, flood back. 'Oh, Max.'

Then they are in each other's arms, mouths seeking mouths, hands pulling at each other, in a world where no one exists but themselves.

A soft knock at the door and they pull apart. Celie clears her throat. 'Yes?'

The door opens and Hettie looks into the room, failing to hide her curiosity as she glances at the young German. 'Made some tea, miss. Shall I bring it in?'

'Yes, certainly, Hettie. Just put it on the table.'

Max and Celie stand awkwardly as Hettie sets down the tray.

She watches Hettie shut the door behind her, and turns to Max. He steps toward her and she holds out an arm. 'Max, I'm sorry. We can't.' She shakes her head. 'We can't.'

'Why not? Nothing has changed for me, *schatzi*. There wasn't one day in the past four and a half years that I didn't think about you. You were with me every minute of every day. I wrote you so many letters, Celie. I've brought them for you. All of them. Here in my bag. I love you, Celie. I love you so much. Now we can be together, can't you see? Finally, we can marry and nothing will ever separate us again.'

'Oh, Max. I can't.' Her voice breaks. 'I'm married.'

'Married? But we were engaged—'

Celie sits down on the chaise longue. 'I wrote you, too, Max. I imagined you reading my letters, wherever you were. I imagined finding your letters in the post and running up to my room to read them and reread them. Over and over. I thought about no one but you, Max. But in March, Jessie sent me one of your letters. She was a nurse on a hospital ship at Gallipoli, and a German soldier had been brought aboard. He was very severely wounded and he … he died. He had a letter on him for an Englishwoman that one of the nurses found. She gave Jessie the letter when she left for Australia. When Jessie read it, she thought the German soldier must have been you.'

Max sits beside her and takes hold of her hand. 'But it wasn't me, *schatzi*.'

'When I read the letter, I knew it was you.' A tear runs down her cheek. 'I thought you were dead.'

'It was my friend Fritz. He'd stolen the letter to tease me. He was always playing jokes like that on me.' He brushes the tear away with his finger. 'What are we to do, *schatzi*?'

'I'm married, Max. I have a husband. He's upstairs and I'm sure he's wondering what on earth is going on.'

'I love you, *schatzi*. I love you. I don't care.' He grasps hold of her hands. 'Come with me. We can just go. Come to Germany. We can start over there. No one will know you are married. You didn't know, Celie, you didn't know I was alive. We were meant to be together. Nothing has changed for me, *schatzi*.'

Celie slides her hands from Max's grasp. 'It's too late, Max. Everything has changed for me. I'm married to Frank Jeffries. I'm going to Canada with my husband. It's over, Max.'

Max rises and takes a stack of letters tied with string out of his canvas bag. He sets it on the chaise longue beside Celie.

At the door, he turns to her. 'It will never be over, *schatzi*.'

Chapter Eighty-Seven

Celie and Jessie

Clover Bar, London – July 1919

Celie unties the black ribbon from around Gerald's portfolio and opens the red cardboard cover. 'Did Papa ever show you this, Jessie?'

Jessie looks up from the bed where she is packing her suitcase. 'What is it?'

Celie slowly flips through the pages of photographs. '*Record of a tandem trip through Kent and Sussex,*' she reads.

Jessie looks over Celie's shoulder. 'Is that Mama? On the bridge?'

'Yes, in Ecclestone Glen. And here we are, all three of us by the waterfall in Yorkshire that summer before the war. Etta fell into the water, do you remember?'

Jessie laughs. 'Yes. She was so cross. She'd spent half the morning arranging her hair to look like Mary Pickford's.'

Celie flips to the back of the portfolio and removes a photograph. She hands it to Jessie. 'I've made a copy for you. I've sent a copy to Etta as well. No matter where we are in this world, we'll always be together, Jessie. You, me and Etta. The three Fry Sisters.'

Chapter Eighty-Eight

Jessie

Cairo, Egypt – July 1919

Jessie pays the taxi driver and steps out into the dust of the Cairo street. The sun beats down over the city, the heat bouncing off the buildings until they are almost drained of colour. The riots and upheaval of the previous months have only recently quietened, with the British government's promise to consider an autonomous Egyptian government under British protection, though discontent and suspicion simmer under the oppressive heat like a pot about to boil over.

Clasping the rusty key in her hand, Jessie skirts the donkey carts and heads for the clinic's modest wooden door. She thrusts the key into the keyhole, twisting it one way and another until the lock releases with a thunk.

Inside, the clinic is dark, the smell musty. The shutters have been closed over the small windows and sheets thrown over the furniture. Sharp beams of white sunlight cut through the gloom like knives, illuminating the desert dust that has found its way through the building's crevices to coat every surface. She hangs her straw hat on a hook and, taking a deep breath, she turns to the task at hand.

Jessie folds the final sheet and stacks it on the examination table. She wipes at the sweat crawling down her forehead with the back of her hand, and unbuttons the cuffs of her sleeves, rolling them up to her elbows. She fills the old enamel sink that Ivy had rescued from the Citadel Hospital's rubbish heap for what seems like the hundredth time, and starts to attack the filthy tiled floor.

'What are you doing down there?'

Jessie looks up at the sound of Aziz's voice. 'Cleaning. I think half the desert sand got in here when we were away.'

Aziz shuts the door. 'I'll arrange for some women to come and clean. You shouldn't have come here on your own. It's still not safe.'

'The demonstrations ended months ago, Aziz.'

'It is a bandage on a gaping wound, Jessica. The situation is not resolved, whatever the women at the Sporting Club may say.'

Jessie gets to her feet. 'Those old bats? They're all a bunch of self-important snobs with no interest whatsoever in Egypt or Egyptians. I have no intention of going back there.'

'You can see why we Egyptians are so determined to throw off the British protectorate and govern ourselves.'

'Yes, I can. I feel ashamed to be an Englishwoman here, at times.'

Aziz takes the dirty sponge out of Jessie's hand, and drops it into the sink. 'There is no point feeling like that. You can't help the circumstances of your birth any more than I can. You can only be the admirable woman I love.'

Jessie stretches and rubs her back. 'Aziz, you and Zara aren't still involved in any of that, are you? The British government won't stand for it. Egypt and the Suez are important to them. It's the British route to trade with India.'

'Don't worry, *habibti*. We are both very careful.' He pats the examination table. 'Come. Sit with me. I want to talk to you away from my mother and my sister.'

'If it's about me not running the clinic now that Ivy's gone—'

'It is about the clinic. You know that I have never liked you setting up here in this part of the city.'

She sits on the table beside Aziz. 'I know, but—'

He reaches for her hand and threads his fingers through hers. 'It's not safe for you, *habibti*. It would be a simple thing for you to be taken on the streets out there.'

'But I need to be useful, Aziz. I can't sit about twiddling my thumbs. I can't.'

'I know this very well, Jessica. So, I have a proposition for you. The gatekeeper's house is empty since Mohammed's son has taken on that duty and prefers to live with his father in town. Its rooms are large enough for a clinic, and it is by the road so it is accessible for people, and possibly less intimidating than coming through the garden to the house. It is much safer for you and Zara; and, if you are amenable, I shall join the clinic as the practising physician.'

'What about your job at the hospital?'

'The war is over. The soldiers have been sent home. Egypt is changing and I am an Egyptian. I have been privileged, and my family has prospered under the Ottomans and the British. But my privilege has never sat well with me when I see the poverty in the cities and countryside. I must join the struggle for an Egypt run by Egyptians. I've buried my head in the sand long enough.'

'Are you sure? I thought you weren't all that happy about the clinic.'

'No, I admire your passion and your stubbornness. I was simply worried.'

'I can be awfully stubborn.'

'Stubborn and wilful and uncompromising and opinionated—'

'Fine. All right.'

He laughs. 'And compassionate and tolerant and kind.'

'I always felt I was lacking in those qualities.'

'Not the Jessica Khalid I know. I am proud to be your husband.'

Jessie smiles. 'The gatehouse would be perfect, Aziz. Perhaps we could use part of the garden for people to sit in and rest. There's such a beautiful view of the Nile. I've always thought it was such a pity that no one but us could see it.'

'Whatever you wish, *habibti*. I shall ask Mohammed to help you.'

'What about your mother?'

'Mama will simply have to adjust to the new situation.'

'She won't like it.'

'No, she won't.' Aziz kisses her palm. 'I love you, Jessica. You have my heart as long as you wish it. You have made me a better man.'

Joy bubbles up inside of Jessie. 'I love you, too, you impossible man.'

Laughing, Aziz hugs her close. 'Welcome home, *habibti*.'

Chapter Eighty-Nine

Etta

Villa Serenissima, Capri, Italy – July 1919

Etta adjusts the crown of summer flowers on Adriana's head and gives her a kiss on her plump cheek. 'There you are, darling. You look like a pretty fairy, just like in the stories.'

Adriana grabs the hem of her white dress and twirls around in front of her mother, the long blue satin ribbon at her waist swirling around her. 'I'm a bride like you, Mama.'

'One day you'll be the most beautiful bride, sweetheart. Today, you're mama's special flower girl.'

Stefania hands Adriana a straw basket of rose petals. 'You remember what Cousin Steffi told you, Adriana? When we arrive at the church, you'll walk up the aisle in front of your mama and sprinkle the petals all around. Not till then. It's a very important job you have, *il mio piccolo angelo*.'

Adriana nods, her dark eyes serious. She steps gingerly across the tiled floor toward the hallway, holding the basket out in front of her.

'Where are you going, Adriana?'

'To show Lili, Mama.'

'All right, but no *biscotti*. We'll have cake after the wedding.'

'She's growing up so quickly, Etta,' Stefania says as she watches Adriana skip out of the room. 'Four years old and she has Liliana and Mario wrapped around her finger.'

Etta adjusts her own floral tiara over her long lace veil in the mirror. 'They're not the only ones, Cousin Stefania. I wish my sisters and Mama could be here. And Papa.'

'I know, *cara mia*. Your papa is watching from Heaven. I am sure he is very proud.'

Etta frowns at her reflection. 'I'm sorry I missed Celie's wedding. Don't you think she should know about what happened when Mama was in Capri now that Papa is gone?'

'That is for your mother to tell her, Etta. You must promise me never to reveal to her that your papa was not her father. Some secrets are best left buried.'

'I suppose so.'

Stefania brushes her fingers along Etta's cheek. It is out of her hands now. The Lord has seen fit to join her beautiful cousin in marriage to Carlo Marinetti. If only she could still the doubts about him that niggle her like a pesky fly. Ah well, what can she do but pray that everything turns out well for Etta and little Adriana?

She pulls a daisy out of Etta's tiara and stuffs it into her elaborate grey-streaked pompadour.

'Cousin Stefania, whatever will Father Izzo say?'

'Our Heavenly Father cannot possibly object to a flower in a woman's hair at a wedding. I shall tell Father Izzo as much. Now, I'm sure poor Carlo is wondering if you've run away with the Sirens. It's time to go, *cara mia*.'

Etta slips her hand into Carlo's and looks at him through the filmy lace of the veil. He rubs his thumb against her palm and smiles at her, his dark eyes glistening with emotion.

'You are so beautiful, my darling,' he whispers.

'You can't see me.'

'I can see you in my mind, my beautiful angel. Everything will be all right now. We shall be a family.'

Father Izzo clears his throat. *'Andiamo.'*

Carlo glances at the priest. 'I am sorry, father. You are right. We should start. We have been waiting for this day for a very long time.'

Carlo weaves through the crowd of well-wishers congregated in front of Santo Stefano. He lifts Adriana into his arms and grasps Etta's hand. 'Come with me.'

'Where are you taking them?' Stefania objects. 'We have the reception at the villa. Half the town will be there.'

'Don't worry, Stefania. We shall be there soon.'

He walks past the flower vendors and vegetable stalls on the Piazzetta as Adriana tosses the last of her rose petals over the square. Vendors and customers call out *Congratulazioni!* and *Bella sposa!* as they pass, in awe of the golden-haired bride's beauty and the pretty little flower girl. When he reaches the colonnade of Doric pillars which edge the terrace and frame the view over the marina, he gives Adriana a kiss on her cheek and sets her down.

'Can I kiss Mama now, Adriana *mia*?'

'Yes.' The little girl frowns. 'I don't have flowers to throw at you.'

Carlo takes a shiny coin out of his pocket. 'Go to the flower seller over there. Tell her you need petals for the bride and a pretty flower for the flower girl.'

Adriana peels off toward the flower seller with a delighted squeal.

'You spoil her, Carlo.'

'I have every intention of spoiling both of you for the rest of my life.'

Etta brushes her hand against his cheek. 'My husband. You have no idea how much I've wanted to say that, and for it to be true.'

'My wife. My darling Etta. My beautiful siren. I love you so much. Nothing will ever take me from you again.'

Chapter Ninety

Celie

HMS *Melita*, Atlantic Ocean – July 1919

Celie rests her elbows on the side of the old gunboat and lifts her face to the cool Atlantic wind. Behind her, the sails on the towering masts flap like wings as they catch the breeze, and the single funnel puffs out a plume of black smoke. On the horizon a white spot appears, growing larger as the ship clips through the grey waves. Overhead, the sky is clear blue, the colour of the spring forget-me-nots in the flower beds at Clover Bar, and transparent clouds hang in the sky like veils.

She glances over her shoulder; then, seeing no one there, she reaches into her handbag and takes out a letter. The thin paper is torn and dirty; and, in places, the black ink has dried into illegible puddles where her tears have fallen. She knows it almost by heart, as well as all the others.

'There you are, Celie! I've been looking all over for you.'

Celie quickly folds the letter. 'Frank! You startled me.' She points at the iceberg which has grown to a gleaming blue-white tower just off the starboard side of the ship. 'Isn't that something? It must be very like the one the poor *Titanic* hit just before the war. I must get my camera. There's another iceberg on the horizon.'

Frank glances at the letter. 'What are you reading?'

Celie stuffs the letter into her handbag. 'Just a letter from an old friend.'

'Max?'

'What?'

'It's from Max Fischer, isn't it? I've seen the stack of letters at the bottom of our trunk. I … I read some of them.'

'Frank!'

'I know. I'm sorry, Celie. I shouldn't have, I know that.' He peers out at the horizon. 'Do you remember I told you I'd played football with the Germans during the Christmas Day truce in 1914?'

Celie looks at Frank; his face is thinner now after the long years of the war, though still handsome in its unassuming way. 'Yes, I remember.'

'I exchanged my hat with a friendly German chap. I offered to trade a uniform button for one of his, but he was already missing one. He said he'd given it to his fiancée the last time they'd seen each other because he didn't have an engagement ring. He didn't want to give any other buttons away. He said it was special. He spoke excellent English.' He looks at Celie. 'It was Max.'

Celie's face blanches. She opens her handbag and retrieves a small kidskin purse. She opens up the clasp and takes out Max's brass button. She hands it to Frank.

'*Gott Mit Uns,*' he reads.

'God is with us. It was the last thing he gave me before he left for Germany.'

'Celie, do you regret marrying me? Now that … now that you

know Max is alive? I don't want you to feel that you're trapped with me. I would never want that.'

Celie takes the brass button from Frank and holds her arm out over the churning waves.

Frank grabs her hand. 'Don't.'

'Why not?'

'I know you loved Max and you would have married him if things had been different. I think … I think you still love him.'

Celie looks at Frank, at the pain and uncertainty in his brown eyes. She does still love Max. A part of her will always belong to him. But Frank is a good man, and he is her husband. She will come to love him; she has no doubt. In a different way. Maybe in a better way.

'Frank, I'm here. I'm with you. I've made my decision.'

'I love you, Celie. I hope you might love me, too, some day.'

'You're a good man, Frank. I know you'll be a wonderful husband and father to our child.' She rests her hand, with Max's button still in her palm, on her belly. 'We'll have a Canadian baby, fancy that.'

'A baby? You're having a baby?'

'We are, Frank. We'll start over in Canada. The war is behind us. Europe and Britain are behind us. It's a fresh, new chapter. The story of Celie and Frank.'

Epilogue

Christina

September 1919

'Cioccolato, Signora Fry?'

'Grazie, Giulia. You know chocolate cannoli is my favourite.'

'Si, sempre il tuo preferito, signora.'

Christina pays out the coins and collects the paper bag of cannoli. She packs it into her straw shopping basket with the parmesan and waves at the shop assistant. 'Grazie. Ciao, Giulia.'

'Prego, Signora Fry.'

Christina opens the door of Terroni's delicatessen and steps out onto Clerkenwell Road. The last of the summer's sun has been swallowed up in a steady drizzle of rain, and she pauses under the shop's canopy to unfurl her umbrella. She heads left toward Farringdon Road and the train station, dodging the puddles and the office workers heading homeward.

At the junction with Farringdon Road, Christina waits for a break in the stream of automobiles and horse carts, then, shielding herself from the rain with her umbrella, dashes across the road. She rounds the corner, and, intent on avoiding a large puddle, ploughs directly into a man hurrying from the station.

'Oh, I'm awfully sor—'

'Tina?'

There's no mistaking the blue eyes.

'Harry.'

Acknowledgments

Sitting on my desk at home is a sepia Edwardian photograph of my English grandmother, Edith Adelaide Fry Chinn, as a young woman of about twenty. Her light brown hair (unruly and wavy like mine) is pulled away from her round face in a low pompadour, and she wears a very pretty white lace loose-sleeved blouse. She looks out at the viewer with a direct gaze, serious with just a touch of challenge. She exudes poise and self-confidence, which would come to stand her in good stead in her marriage to a young British infantry soldier and their life on a farm in Alberta, Canada during the dust bowl years of the Great Depression.

The women on my grandfather's side were no less intrepid. One, Jessie Chinn, became a self-employed milliner, photographer and Suffragette, and her sister, Ettie Chinn, became a nurse and served during World War I on a hospital boat off Gallipoli and in hospitals in Egypt. Neither married, having had their fiancés (Ettie had been engaged to a German student) killed during the war.

Their images from old photographs, and wisps of memories from my father and aunt, have played a large role in rooting me, and making me proud to come from a stock of independent, self-reliant women. So, this book, and the two that follow in this series, are my way of acknowledging their spirit and the spirit of all the women who found themselves forging new lives during and after World War I.

Love in a Time of War was written during the pandemic months of 2020, and I must thank the Society of Authors for extending me a Work in Progress grant to help see this project through. I am very grateful!

Thanks, as well, to Jenny and Will Gibbs of KLC School of Design, who have also been a great support, and to my own wonderful sisters, Judy and Carolyn Chinn, for listening to my sometimes incoherent thoughts on the book, and helping me find a path through the three Fry sisters' stories.

I am very fortunate to have good friends who cheer me along through thick and thin (and there were quite a few thin days in 2020!). Thank you Rita Pohoomal, Claire Delisle, Vicky Seton, Cate Creede, Margot Savitskaya, Melvyn Fickling, Hamid Azelmad, Chrissi Miles, the Canadian/American contingent and the Chinn and Edwards clans.

Finally, thank you to my wonderful editor, Charlotte Ledger of One More Chapter; Laura Burge for her eagle-eyed copyediting; Lucy Bennett for designing such an evocative cover; my agent, Joanna Swainson, for her unending support; and to you, my readers, who are in my mind every day I sit down to write.

ONE MORE CHAPTER

One More Chapter is an
award-winning global
division of HarperCollins.

Sign up to our newsletter to get our
latest eBook deals and stay up to date
with our weekly Book Club!
<u>Subscribe here.</u>

Meet the team at
<u>www.onemorechapter.com</u>

Follow us!
@OneMoreChapter_
@OneMoreChapter
@onemorechapterhc

Do you write unputdownable fiction?
We love to hear from new voices.
Find out how to submit your novel at
<u>www.onemorechapter.com/submissions</u>